RUTHLESS QUEEN

BOOK #1 IN THE MOONLIT PROPHECY SERIES

LAUREN MOON

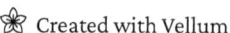 Created with Vellum

To my dog, Bosco, I miss you beyond words. This way you can live on forever in my stories... I will never stop telling our story. Thank you for everything.

Author's Note

Before you dig into Ruthless Queen I just wanted to give you a little helpful information.

This book is written in the main female's point of view. If you would like to read from her mates point of view, please look for the other version of Ruthless Queen, titled The Queen's Flame.

When you see italics, it's the characters speaking in the others mind.

Please be mindful of the triggers, and if you have any questions, please feel free to reach out.

Trigger Warnings for Ruthless Queen:

Violence, Torture/allusions to torture, sexually explicit thoughts, blood/bloody violence, child abuse, death, emotional abuse, Gore.

PROLOGUE

I couldn't help but roll my shoulders as I stared out of the window in the meeting room I was in. Being only fifteen, I was decades younger than all of the other Alphas in the room. I couldn't sit still, listening to them babble on about useless things didn't help matters.

Trading goods... Peace treaties. Boring stuff that I don't want to really hear about. My pack sticks to themselves, I liked keeping it this way.

"They're pathetic and weak anyway." Xena growled, rolling her eyes in the back of my mind.

The woods around the pack house were extensive. I sighed, longing to let her free to let go of this energy I have.

"Scarlett." An older male.

I think he's the Alpha to Spain? Or maybe it was Austraila. I honestly didn't care to pay attention to their names. They all look down on me anyway, for being young and a woman.

I turned around, glaring at him. "It's Alpha Winters. Not Scarlett. What were you babbling on about? A marriage you seem to think you can pressure me in to? You all seem to think

1

that just because I am not a male. I can't rule my pack." I scoffed, rolling my eyes as I strolled back to the large table.

Everyone stayed silent, looking at me as I walked by them. I guess I wanted to be superior, look down on them instead of vice versa. No one spoke up, you could hear a pin drop.

"They think we're weak. But still won't talk to us. Pathetic." Xena rolled her eyes again.

Goddess, all these males are pathetic.

I cracked my neck as I came to stand behind the male that thought he could force me to marry someone I don't want. My first and my only person I will be with is my mate. I grip his shoulders tightly, allowing my nails to extend into his shirt. Barely grazing his skin. I wanted to taunt them, not start a full war.

I felt his body tense under my touch. "Is anyone else going to look me in the face and tell me what to do? Ya see... The last time someone tried to tell me what to do. I ripped their throat out in front of their whole pack." I grinned evilly, licking my teeth slowly. "And me being a shadow wolf in all... I can easily transport us to your territory. To do exactly that."

I smelled fear, anger, and excitement in the room. Oops. That excitement is probably mine. I haven't been able to really sink my teeth into something in a very long time.

"It's been a year. It's been a year since the last time someone in our pack tried to test our power. I haven't been able to make someone submit to me in too long. It would be a lot of fun." Xena growled, and I allowed her to take some of the control.

I felt my body strength as my power soaked the air around us.

"Save... me..." A weak fragile voice spoke in my mind.

I flinched as that voice caused my entire body to tense. What the heck was that? Who was that? I looked around the room, letting go of the male underneath my hands. Who said that?

I felt everyone's eyes on me as they slowly stood up from their chairs. I stood my ground, raising my head as I eyed everyone in turn. I need to find that voice.

"*I... Need you... Please... Save me...*" The males voice cracked inside of my mind.

I growled, baring my fangs. My control over Xena was slipping even more. I can't black out, not here. Not in front of them all. My body felt like it was vibrating as I refused to show weakness in front of them.

"What are you all looking at?" I snapped at them, my voice was harsh as I looked at the ringleader.

And it finally clicked on his name.

Alpha Mario Woods. Alpha to Spain. Oh how I can't wait to sink my teeth into his neck.

"*If he continues to show us disrespect. I'm going to do it.*" Xena growled, she was on edge.

I was on edge, and I was close to falling over the side.

"And you wonder why we know you aren't a good fit to lead your pack. At least if you married my son. He wouldn't be losing control in this meeting. He would have the sense to wait until we dismissed ourselves and handled his freak out when he was alone." Mario rolled his eyes, crossing his arms over his skinny chest.

I have more muscle than him, and that's saying something.

I stalked towards him slowly, my eyes darkening as I looked at him. "So you're saying. Because of my power. It makes you feel less masculine." I said, and Xena agreed with me.

I was right, that's what it comes down to. Their masculinity is tested, and they are trying to stomp me down into nothing to make themselves feel better.

"Oh of course that's what you have to say. A *feminist* would say that." Mario told me condescendingly.

"He's going to kill me!" A whimper echoed through my mind and I flinched.

I lost it, in the blink of an eye. My claws extended, and I had a hold on Mario's neck. His eyes were wide with fear before I grinned at him.

"This is for disrespecting me continuously in front of my peers." I snarled, before he could fight back I ripped his throat out.

His blood sprayed across my face as I let his body drop to the ground. Everyone stared at me in shock.

"Anyone else want to test me? Anyone else want to see how far they could push me? Here you have it folks. I'm the first wolf in the entire world to be the Alpha of not just one pack. But two." I crossed my arms.

They didn't say anything, a few started to bow their heads in submission to me.

"Goddess, who knew a fifteen year old would be such a Ruthless Queen." Another male grinned.

Now that is the Alpha of Australia.

"Now if no one else has anything to say. This meeting is over. Someone get someone to clean up this pathetic excuse for an Alpha. While I go and speak to my new pack." I growled, storming out of the large meeting room.

The hallway was well lit, but I felt like the walls were closing in on me.

My vision started to darken as I looked for the nearest exit. I would jump out of a window at this point. Anything to get me away from people. Xena was fighting for control, she wanted to go and kill someone. Find the male, begging for me to save him.

"Find me... Save me... Please my love..." That same fragile, soft, beautiful voice said. I felt my arm break and I growled.

When I felt a soft hand on my shoulder, I reacted without

thinking. I grabbed whoever's hand and threw them against the wall.

"Don't touch me!" I yelled, there was too much going on.

I felt everything in waves. But most importantly, I felt fear. Anxiety. Pain. And it wasn't mine. It was my mates, I felt it in my bones. I needed to find him. To save him, to free him from whatever is happening to him.

"I'm sorry Ma'am Alpha. Miss. Winters!" The frightened boy said, cowering underneath me.

I immediately let him go. He couldn't be any older than I was. He's probably younger. I frowned, helping him to his feet.

"I apologize... I'm Scarlett Winters." I told him, smiling softly as I looked at his face.

His right side of his face was bruised, I noticed it before he immediately tried to hide it from me. This is probably the male that Mario wanted me to marry.

"I'm Lincoln Woods." His voice was soft, he refused to look me in the eye.

I guess he's the new Alpha.

"Alpha Lincoln Woods. I killed your dad." I stated bluntly, heading towards the exit.

I needed to get away from everyone and everything. I killed one today. I don't need to kill anymore to stake my claim as Alpha. It's my right, I don't need to prove myself.

But there is one thing that I do need to do.

I need to find my mate.

CHAPTER
ONE

Nine years. It's been nine years since I first heard the words of my mate. I've looked and searched for my mate. And I haven't been able to find him, or his scent.

It was slowly killing me, hearing his pleads. I can't take it much longer. I know he's giving up and that worries me.

"We'll find him. We have to find him." Xena said, frowning as she laid down.

I knew she was worried, but having her worry on top of mine. It's not the best idea. I'll panic and probably kill someone.

I looked down at the maps in front of me. Maps of the countries that surrounded my territory were sprawled out on my massive dark oak desk. I rubbed the side of my face as I looked down, dark bags of exhaustion were evident. I refuse to give up, I just didn't know where else to look.

"Please..." I begged quietly, closing my eyes as I gripped the desk. "Please... Give me something. Anything... Tell me where he is... I can't go on without him."

I exhaled shakily as I opened my eyes. The Moon Goddess

has blessed me beyond measure. But if she takes my mate away from me... I won't be able to live past that.

"Give me a sign baby... Give me a sign..." I said softly, my eyes landing on the map of Ireland.

Something drew me to that map before a growl escaped me. I snatched the map, eyeing it.

"Never doubt." Xena smiled softly, her gentle confidence flooded me.

"This is where you are..." My eyes narrowed on the packhouse.

In my heart, I knew this is where my mysterious mate was being held. Memories of the times he called to me in my dreams surfaced. It haunts me, every day and night. I can't get over it.

A pained whimper, begging for me to save him. *"Please... Help..."* Two simple words that made my heart nearly stop from the need to save him. I took the map of Ireland and walked out to leave my office.

If I have to die to save him. I would. I won't let him live in pain anymore, especially not now when I know where he is.

Almost immediately I was confronted by my Beta and my Delta. "Grayson... Madoc..." I spoke with a slight growl, their stances showed everything.

They were nervous and didn't want to tell me about what was happening. "Speak before I have to dig through your mind."

I swear I'm not as crazy as people seem to think I am. I would never hurt my brother or sister. Everyone else was fair game.

My brother, my twin, Grayson spoke first. *"All of the parties you have sent out in search of the male of your description came back. They didn't find anything."* He informed before Madoc summed up the courage to continue.

And I am waiting for my little Madoc to summon the courage to speak.

"They heard rumors... Rumors of the lost heir to The Bloody

Rose Pack... It is said that Pete is holding his heir captive because of destiny..." Madoc explained, looking down at his feet.

My gaze was intense, my normally deep brown eyes were turning a bright fierce purple.

"My turn to have my fun!" Xena grinned in the back of my mind.

I will let her have her fun, but not before I get my answers.

"Ready the warriors. We are heading to meet with Alpha Pete. If this male is there, we will be getting him out of there today. I don't care if I have to burn down Ireland to do it." I explained, shoving the map of Ireland in Grayson's hands. "You will stay here while Madoc comes with me. If someone as much as mentions my not being capable of leading this pack. You chain them in the dungeons, I will deal with them properly when I get back."

I left no room for discussion, and Madoc rushed off instantly to listen to my orders. I cracked my neck as I walked out of the packhouse. They've been taunting me with the fact that I couldn't handle myself. I'm sick and tired of it. The world will fear me, I don't care what I have to do. I'm getting my male.

"I want our army to be prepared to go to war with Ireland if I give the signal." I ordered the guards around me."If they do not give me what I want, I will burn Ireland to the ground."

I growled out as I went to my purple Bugatti Veyron. My prized possession. My favorite thing. The one thing that doesn't stress me out.

"Would you like me to accompany you?" Madoc asks quietly as he followed after me.

An annoyed growl escaped me. If he rides with me, I just might strangle him. His anxiety reeks and I don't want to smell it in the small cabin of my car.

"Just let him come. He'll be sad." Xena told me, and I groaned quietly.

9

You know for a Ruthless Queen, she had a real soft side.

"Don't make me bite you." Xena growled, but she knew I had a point.

"I don't want to hear anything out of your mouth about how this could send us into a war we're not prepared for. I am doing this, and I'm not afraid to snap your neck." I growled out as I got into my car, starting it before revving the engine; showing my annoyance.

He moves too slow for my liking. Madoc quickly got into the passenger side before I sped off. Two large black SUVs followed quickly after me.

My grip on the steering wheel was tight, and the roar of my engine made a slight evil smirk cross my face. "They won't get away with hurting my mate." I told Madoc as he sat there quietly.

He needs to realize, things are going to get bad fast and it's not something he needs to worry about.

"You will make them pay Alpha... If your mate is there and they will not give him to you. You will make them pay and it will be rightfully done." Madoc said with a nervous smile.

He fidgeted in his seat causing me to roll my eyes. He is a butt kisser, and a terrible one. His nervousness makes my anger rise.

"I can smell your scent. You're nervous. For no reason. Pete is too scared to actually come for me. He knows that he wouldn't be able to actually fight me, I would win and his pack would be mine. He'd rather bow to me than give me his pack. You know he doesn't want any female to lead any pack and hates that I have been leading my pack for the last decade." I told, trying to calm my Delta down.

He smiled softly at me as he watched me drive.

This is your fault I have to calm him down Xena. I was planning on keeping the spot open because I knew I didn't need it.

"You got a point. I thought the kid had potential. If he would just get out of his anxiety." Xena groaned slightly.

"You're right Alpha," Madoc said with a nod. "He will give you what you want. You are strong enough to get what you want and so much more. I believe in your power Alpha Winters. I believe in you."

I couldn't help but laugh slightly, the way he goes from terrified to butt-kissing is ridiculously funny.

"You went from absolutely terrified to butt-kissing a second later. Flattering me won't get you anywhere. I want you to believe in the position I gave you. I picked you to be my Delta because I have faith in you. I wouldn't have picked you if I didn't think you could handle this. My pack is strong. The people I have hand-picked for high-ranking positions in my pack are strong." I sighed softly, looking at the road in front of us.

It's awful to say it to the kid, but he has no choice in this matter. I have to have powerful backup. I can't seem weak in any way shape or form.

This is just how things have to be until the world is less sexist. I rolled my shoulders as we sat in silence for the rest of our trip.

TWO

With my fast driving, we arrived at the border of Ireland in no time. I revved my engine, causing the guards at the territory line to move aside for me and my guards to pass through without issue.

"Why can't someone just not be scared of us so I can have my fun." Xena whined to me.

And honestly I don't blame her. I am itching for a fight, the burn for violence ran through my core. It's been engraved in my DNA. Constantly needing to show my dominance.

Maybe this is why no male in my pack will speak to me, and when they do they just stare at their feet.

"Gotta admit. It's funny." Xena snickered.

And she did have a point.

"I am sorry for not having more faith in you Alpha... Alpha Knight has a reputation for being ruthless..." Madoc started, his statement trailing off.

I rolled my eyes as I pulled into a parking spot and turned my car off.

If Madoc is so scared of Pete and how ruthless he is. What

does Madoc think of me? People refer to me as the Ruthless Queen. Have since I was like fifteen. I must be a psychopath to him then.

"Do you actually care if he thinks you're a psychopath?" Xena asked me, and honestly.

No I don't. I would rather be crazy than anything else.

"He has nothing on me. Ruthless or not, if he doesn't surrender what I want. I will rip his throat out like he's nothing." I growled, getting out of my car and slamming the door shut.

If I wasn't boiling with rage, I would've cringed at the way I treated my car. My body tensed as I rolled my shoulders, I walked up the wooden steps to the packhouse.

I faintly heard my guards cars park as they quickly hurried to come stand around me. I understand why I make them angry, I don't exactly wait for them. They jogged to me, their footsteps soft but I felt overly sensitive to everything. Like I could hear a pin drop.

I'm not here to kill anyone. But if they lie to me. Or won't give me what I want, I will kill anyone and everything. Show the world just how ruthless I can be.

"You go girl!" Xena cheered me on.

An eerie sense of anxiousness settled over me. But it isn't mine...

"Save... Me..." A fragile little voice spoke through my mind.

If I wasn't angry before, if I wasn't stiff. I would be now. My body feels like I could cut stone, Goddess I'm ready to rip this place apart. I feel him, but it's a faint little emotion. I feel his fear, and I would do anything to help him get free.

As if someone sensed my arrival, the front door opened.

Alpha Pete Knight was standing there with a wicked smile on his face. Just looking at his face makes me wanna reach out and deck him.

"Scarlett! What a pleasure it is to have you come to visit unannounced!" He licked his bottom lip as I rolled my eyes.

I pushed past him, heading to his office so we could talk privately.

"Or. We could strangle him in front of everyone! That seems like a really good idea." Xena growled, shaking with the restraint I felt.

I didn't want to give up my control, because I didn't want to black out. But I honestly might.

Once we were in Pete's office, I growled at him. My brown eyes were slowly turning purple as Xena needed to show her presence. I balled my fists up before I swung and cracked him in the jaw. That was for his disrespect.

"It is Alpha Winters to you. We are not friends Pete. We are barely allies. I know you know why I am here, skip the crap and let's get straight to it." I told him, leaning against his desk as I refused to take my eyes off of him.

Taking your eyes off of your enemy is never a good idea. And I knew by now, after years of never being good enough for anyone. That they will take cheap shots when you aren't prepared. I came back several times pretty beat up. Ya live ya learn I guess.

Pete rubbed his jaw where I hit him, a red spot was already forming. I like it, I wish I hit him harder.

"Alpha Winters, if I knew why you were here. I would have whatever you want prepared for you." He said, keeping his voice calm.

"I smell the lies." Xena growled, I felt her silent plea to take control.

But not yet...

"Too bad." Xena seized enough control to show her dominance.

I narrowed my eyes at him, my power started to radiate off of me in waves. The office started to shake as my body tensed, I slammed my hands on the desk causing it to splinter as the wood cracked.

"Do you think I'm stupid Pete! You're lying to me!" I yelled, the house started to rumble as various small items started to fall off his desk.

People were heard outside of the office, shouting in fear.

"Earthquake!!" People screamed.

Why does their fear make me happy?

"I am Alpha Scarlett Winters! The first Alpha Female in hundreds of years! And you think you can lie to me!? I want to see the heir to The Bloody Rose Pack." I growled out, my eyes were glowing brightly.

I felt the need to shift.

The large need to rip out his throat for even trying to lie to me. I want him to pay for still thinking I'm a child. I haven't been a child since I was fourteen years old. I may be decades younger than him. But I am a better Alpha.

Pete loosened his stance as he nodded slightly. "My son died years ago, Alpha Winters. I'm sorry but I can show you where he is buried." He informed me.

That is what made me lose it. I heard his voice. I know he's alive!

The office started to darken as I stalked over to him slowly. "I could kill you here... Right now. Or I could take what I want and leave you to watch me burn Ireland to the ground. But I would so enjoy watching the life drain from your eyes." I growled out, my voice was dark.

I stood in front of him before stopping. A faint weak howl caused me to shutter, my eyes brightened.

"He's alive! Let me out! Let me out!" Xena screamed at me, and it took everything in me to keep myself from shifting.

"What will you decide Pete? Will you give me those I want? Or shall I call war and take Ireland for myself? I do enjoy the blood of my enemies. I would have complete justice to do so since you are lying straight to my face while you torture my mate." A shadow wrapped around his throat, slowly squeezing the life from him.

I want to see him pay for the torture I know my mate is feeling. I want to see him bleed.

Pete nodded quickly, gasping as he struggled to breathe. I waited a second before allowing the room to go back to normal. "You can go to the dungeon, I will send word to allow you to take whoever you would like. I do not want any problems Alpha Winters." He said, smiling softly at me.

The building stopped shaking as I nodded once.

"Yet you call me weak." Xena growled unhappily at me.

Without another word, I walked to the office door and went out. I didn't stop for anyone as I went down the hall. Madoc was sitting on a small chair, where two guards were standing next to him.

The hits keep coming, why is everyone in Ireland getting on my freaking nerves. It's like they were bred to be annoying.

"What are you doing with my Delta?" I growled, shoving the guard that was closest to him against the wall.

My hand was on her throat, squeezing enough to bring my point across. "This gives me grounds to kill you."

My entire body felt tense, the need to find my mate was nearly overpowering. I was angry. I was worried. I was everything, all at once. I just needed to chill out. No I just needed my mate and to get out of this terrible country.

The guard didn't react as she looked down, refusing to look me in the eye. "I apologize Alpha... I didn't know what he was doing. So I wanted to make sure that he was safe." The guard informed, her cheeks burning red.

I looked at her before she returned her attention to Madoc.

Ah they're mates.

Madoc's eyes were on the guard, I growled and threw her to the ground. "Go wait for me in the cars. Tell the rest of the guards that I will be out in a few minutes. You two." I pointed at two of my guards. "Come down to the dungeon with me."

I opened the large heavy oak door, before heading down the spiral staircase. I grabbed onto the railing as I inhaled sharply. Dark energy immediately circled around me, and it felt like my power was draining slowly. Almost like I was suffocating.

"Are you alright Alpha? I think that we should get you back to Scotland." One of my new guards, Martin, spoke to me.

His hand went to my shoulder before I shook it off and continued to walk down the steps.

"I'm fine, I feel an odd energy here... Like something is suffocating me," I explained, shaking my head slightly as I stood at the bottom of the staircase.

My guards stood behind me as someone came out of the shadows. I shook my head again as I looked around, I honestly don't think I could fight someone in this state.

"They do that on purpose... It's a barrier that is specifically made for special wolves like you and Seth..." The male said, with a kind smile.

THREE

Xena goes completely silent in my mind. I couldn't stay silent, then my people would know about him... About what he was for me.

My safety net.

The one thing I knew I didn't need. But still I thankfully took it because I felt like I *needed* it.

"No it's in the past. No one is going to know unless we tell them. Move on Scarlett. Stop thinking. Our mate is here. He is what is important." Xena assured me.

But I heard it, the slight tremor in her voice. She was annoyed, stressed, and anxious.

Goddess I need out of this horrible country.

I looked at him in surprise. "I-... I didn't know that you were here." I said as I walked towards where he stood.

Alex has always been good at hiding. I guess it's something that made me like having him around. *The adrenaline.* Goddess. The adrenaline made me feel alive.

I hated how much I craved it. Needed it.

"I've been here since we last saw each other... I've been trying to find a way out for Seth and his little brother. I'm glad you're here Sc-..." Alex said, before looking at the guards behind her. "Alpha Winters... I assume that you are here for the only two prisoners that Pete keeps at the Packhouse?"

Xena stiffened at his words, and it took everything in me not to punch Alex. The only two!? At the packhouse? Goddess. What is wrong with this pathetic waste of space male?

I nodded, keeping my head high and my shoulders back as I walked with confidence. Head high, shoulders back. Chest puffed out. It was a pathetic attempt at showing my dominance. But something wolves respected.

I had never been to The Bloody Rose Packhouse dungeon before, but I knew in my heart where to go. "Yes. I have high belief that this is where my mate has been calling out to me Alex. I heard a howl; and I knew it was him... I just don't..." I started to explain before we stopped in front of a cage.

The darkness here in this specific spot made me feel like I had a crushing weight on my chest. The pain amplified and it felt like I was cowering away from my father again.

"You think that you will ever amount to anything! Even your children will be pathetic and worthless! I should sell you. Maybe the only thing you're good for is making me money when I sell you and your bastard children!" My fathers voice rang through my mind.

It took everything in me not to shutter. That was a long time ago. He's dead. I killed him.

"We're safe. Stormy is safe. Grayson is safe." Xena repeated to me, her strength made me feel safe.

I stumbled slightly before I caught myself. Dark energy was radiating off of the cell, the energy was weakening me.

"We aren't monsters, just because we have different powers. Doesn't mean anyone has the right to keep us locked up." I growled as Alex opened the cage.

No one has the right to treat us differently because we're stronger than them.

Two wolves were cowering in the far corner of the cage, one large black and white wolf. With a smaller gray wolf laying directly on top of him. I inhaled sharply as I rushed into the cage. I fell to my knees before them, a weak whimper came from the wolf laying against the iron ground.

Pain ran through my legs, the iron burned my skin. But it wasn't bad. For me. I was used to pain.

"You're okay... You're safe now. We're going to take you away from here. You and your brother. You will be okay... I promise you. I need to pick you up. I know you won't be able to talk, but I do need to pick you up to get you out of here." I informed the wolf, looking at Alex. "Pick up his brother. I will get him."

The first step is getting him and his brother out of here. And the next is getting to the cars. And then out of this stupid country.

Alex nodded in understanding, walking into the cage and gently picking up the smaller wolf. The larger wolf started to whimper at the loss of his brother.

"I know... I know... But I promise that you will be with him soon. Nothing bad will happen to him nor you." I promised, before gently picking him up into my arms.

I bit my lip hard, he was so light. I feel his bones.

His fragile, obviously easily broken bones. I was trying my best not to add to his pain.

"We will be heading to Scotland... Where you'll be free to do whatever you like..." I continued to talk as I walked out of the cage and went to the spiral staircase.

With every step I took, he whimpered in pain. His whimper made my entire body stiffen, I tried to keep my body from reacting. But it was impossible, his pain was my pain. I frowned as I took slow steps.

My muscles didn't burn, they didn't hurt. The only thing I felt was the overwhelming need to get him out of this country.

And burn it to the ground.

"Do it do it! They deserve it! It will show the world that we aren't someone to be messed with!" Xena yelled in the back of my mind. Goddess.

I want to. I want to watch it burn and grin as I see the anger in Pete's face.

Once in the packhouse, I immediately went to the exit. I slowly allowed my power to go through his body to allow his body to heal faster. And hopefully give him some relief from the pain he feels. I look down and see black veins rushing through my forearms. But I didn't feel the pain.

"We're almost there..." I promised the wolf in my arms.

"I know what you're thinking. It's working. You just have a high pain tolerance because you're the Queen." Xena told me.

And it took everything in me not to grin. She was my biggest supporter. And I wouldn't have it any other way. I went immediately to the exit, refusing to wait for anyone.

As I walked out of the packhouse, I couldn't help the sigh of relief that rushed out of me at being outside.

Step one. Done.

Step two. Getting him and his brother to my country.

"Alex, you will be taking my car to Scotland. You can follow either me or the guards SUV. As I will be taking one SUV for myself and my male." I commanded, causing everyone to jump to action.

The male whimpered as I opened the trunk to the closest SUV and gently placed him in the back. Whoever had the seats already down and ready for me deserves a raise.

I hated not being able to hold him, soothe his pain. But I gotta get him out of here.

"It might be a little scary back here... But I want you to know

21

you're safe…" I explained, bending down to speak softly to him. "You, Alex, your brother. You guys are all safe now and under my protection. I know you are probably scared and don't understand what I'm doing… But I'm an Alpha, Alpha Scarlett Winters of The Winterfall Pack."

He just looked at me, whimpering when I reached out to pet his fur. I immediately retracted my hand.

Rejection seeped through my body and I just stared at him. My mate doesn't want me to touch him. I just… I just want to help him. How can I explain that to him?

"They must've really messed with him." Xena told me, frowning in the back of my mind.

I know that. But that doesn't calm the anger I feel at knowing he doesn't want me to make him feel better. It's an unrighteous anger, but it's my anger to feel.

"I won't touch you… But when we get to Scotland… I will need to carry you into my house." I told him before closing the trunk.

I rolled my shoulders before heading to get in. Everything will be fine. It has to be.

What I want to tell him is I want to touch him. Show him he's safe. But I can't freaking do that. I tried to calm myself because I knew just how bad it gets when you're finally safe. I couldn't let anyone touch me for weeks after I killed my dad. I was just in a constant state of fear that me killing him was fake. That it was a dream.

"Goddess I'm gonna die if he won't let us touch him for weeks." Xena told me.

And yeah, I get it. I will too, but I'll respect his decision. He needs to know he's safe, and he needs his time to heal.

Once I was in, I turned the SUV on and drove off quickly. "I'm going to try and keep it as smooth as possible… But I am sorry if it gets bumpy." I told him as I continued to look back at him while I drove.

He was laying there, his large head on the floor of the SUV. He was staring at the trunk, his breathing shallow.

My car was behind me, and then the other SUV behind it. I breathed in deeply, as I tried to calm my nerves. "Everything will be fine..." I said aloud, but I didn't know who I was saying it to.

Me... Or him.

After a while, what seemed like an eternity, I pulled up to the packhouse in Edinburgh. I parked out front, before quickly getting out and heading to the trunk. I stilled for a second, knowing I needed to be strong for him even when I feel like I'm breaking apart.

"Fake it till you can punch someone in the face and make yourself feel better." Xena told me and I rolled my eyes.

But I knew it would make me feel better.

A kind smile came over me as I opened the trunk. "We're here... In Scotland... I'm going to have your brother taken to the hospital." I explained to him.

I think his name is Seth? I need to ask Alex to make sure.

Seth. Goddess just his name makes me melt.

He looked painfully up to me, a soft whimper escaped him. It looked like he was crying, I went to cup his face but hesitated. I can't touch him yet. I just can't see that fear flash through his eyes at my hand.

"I am going t-..." I started before I was interrupted.

Maybe I'll punch Alex in the face.

"I second that!" Xena nodded.

"Alpha Winters... I wanted to inform you that Max shifted

into his human form on the ride here... We will be taking him to the hospital at your command." Alex said, his arms were behind him as he looked down at his feet.

"Take him to the hospital, make sure no one speaks to him until I say so. I need to care for his brother and Max deserves time to heal and adjust to a new life. Away from torture and pain..." I said, sighing softly as I didn't take my eyes off of my male. "Do you know his name? I would like to talk to him and call him by his name. And not accidentally call him the wrong name. I know you said Seth... But there were two wolves in the cage."

Or well I want to call him by his right name. Or I could totally just call him my male.

Alex smiled softly. "His name is Seth. But I do think he would like for you to call him yours. He may need some time to adjust, but I know him. Seth would like that a lot." He told me, grinning at the surprised look on my face.

He knows he's my mate?

"How did you know?" I asked, struggling to contain my facial expressions.

Everything seems so amplified. I can't control anything right now. "I..."

"You don't have to make up stories, Scar... I know you. I know him. We had a past together, something that I will never forget. No one has to know... But I know you guys are mates. It's why you came to find him, it's why you saved him. It's how he called out to you. I know you both. Just give him some time." Alex told me with a wink, before a wink to Seth.

I smiled kindly.

"If he knew Seth was ours. Why didn't he come to us?" Xena asked, and I knew what she was feeling.

She wanted to kill him. But I need to focus on the task at hand.

"Make sure Max has everything he needs, and most importantly make sure he's safe and doesn't get overwhelmed by everyone. Once Seth is feeling up to it, I will send word for Max to come see his brother." I nodded to Alex.

Before I narrowed my eyes on the small group of males in front of the packhouse.

I swear, I can never get anything done around here.

"Let's have some real fun with this." Xena growled, and I felt my body shake with anger.

It's always one thing after another.

"I will stay here while you go deal with that." Alex chuckled.

I walked over to the group, my eyes shining with my power. The power that I held soaked the air around us, and this time. I didn't hold anything back, if they want to come for me. They're going to struggle.

"And what can I do for you gentleman? I do believe that we don't have a meeting set up for today. So why are you interrupting my busy schedule?" I called out over the chatter of the men.

Everyone quieted down before a tall scrawny man walked to the front of the group. He looks familiar... Like someone's kid I saw years and years ago. Jason? I think.

"We have come here today because we want you to step down from your position as Alpha. You have left us again, unguarded in search of only you know. You are not fit to lead us and protect us." The man said, causing me to smirk evilly as I took a few steps to stand in front of him.

"Oh this is gonna be grand!" Xena grinned, waiting patiently for me to give her control.

I didn't have to turn around to feel his eyes on me. I couldn't just fully lose control in front of him. That would just make him more scared of me.

"And you use all these men to make me scared? I smell your

fear, I smell everyone's fear here. Are they only here because you want to try and become Alpha, Jason?" I asked, looking at the men behind Jason.

They refused to look me in the eye, casting their gaze down to their feet.

That just gave me pride, they still knew I was the Alpha. Not everyone in this group is stupid.

Jason stood up straighter, keeping his head high. "Wow. No words to say Jason? I thought you were here to force me to step down. I wouldn't mind seeing that, I do love a good fight. I haven't had blood on my teeth for so long." I growled, my eyes slowly turning a darker shade of purple.

Xena was waiting for her moment to get out.

"I could lead this pack better tha-..." Jason started before I reacted quickly.

My claws came out and I sunk them into his throat. He gasped, his eyes wide as he went to grab my throat. Oh he's so pathetic, I see him flinch with pain as I sink them further into his neck.

"For your treachery against your Alpha. Jason I sentence you to death. You will be remembered as a traitor and nothing more." I told before ripping his throat out.

Jason's blood splattered onto my face and neck before I let his body drop to the ground. I tilted my head at the cowering group in front of me.

"That would've been more fun if you let me do it." Xena complained, plopping down in the back of my mind.

"Submit to me, or face the same death as Jason." I ordered, knowing they wouldn't be able to tell me no.

My power filled the air causing the few men left to drop to their knees.

"We submit to you as our Alpha. You have protected us since

you were just a child and we believe in you as our Alpha." The group said in unison before I walked off to the SUV.

That's what I thought.

"Lame! I wanted a fight." Xena growled, and here I thought she wanted to stop the fighting.

"I want them on guard duty for two months. Constant shifts. I will not allow stuff like this to stand." I ordered Madoc, before he quickly ran off.

Alex smirked slightly.

"That will never not be hot." Alex laughed, causing me to roll my eyes.

He will never stop, I'm going to need to tell Seth about us sooner rather than later.

"Don't make me punch you in the face. Go make sure Max is okay." I ordered before gently taking Seth into my arms.

He whimpered at the touch before he calmed. Good he calmed down, or I was gonna cry. I frowned, closing my eyes and transporting us to my house.

This is going to go so badly.

"I agree." Xena groaned at knowing what I had to do.

He needed to shift, and I'm going to have to make him.

I walked him into my home gym. He started whimpering immediately, his heart rate escalating. And now he knows what's going to happen.

"You're such a moron." Xena teased me.

I swear, somedays I wish she was an actual person so I could punch her too.

"I know my love... I know you're worried and scared... But this will help you. I promise. I'm going to set you down, and then I'm going to need you to shift into your human form. This way I can help you... It is going to hurt a lot, and I don't know for how long..." I explained as I got down on my knees.

I paused, not wanting to let him go. I just wanted to hold him and make everything better.

"He won't let us. Like you said. He needs time." Xena told me.

And I knew she was right, doesn't make me hate it any less.

Reluctantly I placed him on the ground, he immediately started to whimper from the loss of contact. And here I thought that he didn't want me to touch him. Did I really take a lot of his pain away?

"I know my male... I know. I wish I could take your pain away completely... But as soon as you turn into your human form, I will be able to help take your pain away. I want to help heal you... I want you to be safe. But for that to start, I need you to shift into your human form. Can you do that for me, my love?" I asked as I sat down in front of him.

Being in his human form, it will help make things easier.

Seth whimpered, trying to shake his head no. I frowned, rubbing the back of my neck.

My whole body screamed to help him, I itched with the need to hold him.

"I really don't want to order you... But I don't know if you can even shift to your human form in this condition. I don't want to command you, but I might have to. Would you be okay with me ordering you to shift into your human form?" I asked, trying to keep my voice from breaking.

I have to be strong. He whimpered his answer, trying to move away from me. I bit my bottom lip hard.

"That hurt." Xena whined, I didn't like him moving away from me.

"I wish there was another way around this... I really really wish that there was. But in order to help you... I am going to have to command you. Just this once I promise." I told him.

Just this once and never again.

"So Seth... Shift." My command rolled through my words, before rolling into his injured body.

He whimpered painfully, his body aching as he started to shake.

And immediately I hated this more than I did before.

CHAPTER
FOUR

The sounds of bones breaking filled the gym. I cringed at the sound before I forced myself to focus. Not on the sounds of his pain and cries, but on something else. *Anything* else.

"*Yuck. Why does it have to be so loud?*" Xena asked, flinching when we heard a specifically loud crack of a bone.

I feel like he is resisting the shift. I have to figure out something.

"Seth. I told you to SHIFT." I ordered, pushing my full power at Seth.

He cried out, moving slightly as a sudden scream filled my mind. And a same still anger filled my body, the same anger I felt a thousand times since I turned fifteen.

"*Please! Please! Make this stop! Stop making me do this!*" My males voice cried out to me.

I bit my bottom lip, tears welling in my eyes. I tried to show my strength. But being this close to him... Unable to help his pain. It broke my heart. I laid down in front of him on my belly, my eyes shining purple.

I felt Xena sharing in control, showing her power to try and give him some assurance that we're both here. I don't know if it would even work.

"I can't stop this... You're so close. Stop fighting my command. This is the toughest part, allow yourself to listen to my command. It will help you, I just need you to trust me a little bit... Show me just a little bit, and I will show you afterward that you can trust me... Can you do that for me? Allow me to help you?" I asked softly, my powerful eyes staring into his dim red eyes.

He looked over my face before weakly nodding yes.

"He's trying! Yay!" Xena shouted happily.

A baby step is better than nothing.

"I am going to put my hand on you... I'm not going to do anything. I'm just going to place it gently on your fur, I will be able to help take your pain that way. It will also help you to feel my order more directly. Are you okay with that?" I asked again, moving slowly to not frighten him any more.

It's like treading lightly around prey. He nodded again, closing his eyes. His body tensed, feeling me move next to him.

Eventually I can hold him... Eventually he will let me comfort him... Everything will be better eventually.

I looked at my hand, I saw it was shaking. Crap I need to stop shaking, I can't be shaking in front of him. He'll think I'm scared.

Which I am... But I'm not scared of him. I'm scared of losing him... Of him dying. I have never been more scared of anything in my life.

I closed my eyes as I willed my hand to stop shaking. "I'm going to put my hand on your side now... Again, it's just going to rest on your body, with no pressure at all. Just a light touch." I explained, before gently placing my right hand against his side.

I bit my bottom lip hard, trying to keep myself from growling with anger.

It's worse than what I thought. I feel just how fragile his bones are, and just how easily I could accidentally break them.

Seth tensed under my touch, his body flinched as my hand was resting on his ribs. He kept his eyes closed, whimpering softly. That painful whimper that made me want to put him in a bubble to make him feel all safe and warm. I frowned, looking over his form. Closing my eyes, I allowed my power to flow into his body.

Slowly so I didn't completely freak him out. I allowed my power to drift into his body to help my command take root.

"Seth... Shift." I growled at him, my wolf dancing around in my mind, itching to take control and go rip out Pete's throat.

I wanted to rip his throat out too. He whimpered, trying to get away from my command. He bared his teeth in a growl; before his eyes opened and looked at me.

"He's fighting our command which is both a good and bad thing." Xena told me, she stood still finally just watching Seth.

I wish he would just give into my command, it would help with this whole thing.

I focused on his body, sensing where his pain was. It was very rare that I could do this. But I'm hoping to be able to do it. I licked my lips as I slowly pulled the pain from his body into mine. After all I could take it, he doesn't need to. Black veins started to go up my arms, it was the pain in his body going into mine

I had to peek my eyes open to watch. His bones started to crack and shrink faster; his black fur slowly fading away to show pale human skin.

Seth was shaking, his skinny fragile body curled into a ball to protect himself. He couldn't take his eyes off of me. I quickly took my hand off of his side as his skin was ice cold. His heart rate was high, as he looked into my eyes.

"He's scared... But he's hopeful?" Xena said softly.

I closed my eyes for a second, I couldn't be the reason that he was so scared. Could I?

"Can I pick you up?" I asked, causing him to shake his head no.

He struggled but managed to back himself into the corner of the gym. He continued to look at my face, before looking at the blood that was splattered across my skin.

"You really are a moron! You should've washed yourself." Xena growled at me.

And suddenly this is my fault!? How is this my fault!

"I know you're scared... But you're not in Ireland anymore. You're in Edinburgh Scotland. You are safe now, you and your brother Max are safe. He is just getting checked out by the doctor before he comes here. Would you like me to care for your wounds? I could move you to a comfortable bed and then wake you when your brother gets here?" I offered, my voice smooth as I looked at his eyes.

Smooth... Even... Don't show my emotion. Even though I know the air stinks of my anxiety. I can't help it! I'm freaking out.

"Oh the big bad Alpha is freaking out. Dipstick." Xena told me, in her condescending way, growling softly.

I nearly gasped at her tone. She's being condescending! Why are you fighting me Xena!

"I could get you clothes for after you're feeling better. We're at my house, no one comes here besides me. So you don't have to worry about anyone seeing you naked and healing from everything you endured." I sat cross-legged, letting him as much space as he needed.

His heart was slowing down as he studied my body, his eyes reading every inch of me.

I felt his eyes trace over my body, and I willed myself not to flush at the motion.

"Who... Are... You...?" Seth asked with a slight struggle, his voice cracked from years of no use.

I smiled softly, giving him a slight nod of understanding. My eyes never once left his. Don't show weakness.

"My name is Scarlett Winters... I am the Alpha of The Winterfall Pack. My pack is in Scotland, and I have based the main place for my pack in Edinburgh." I told him, studying his face as he looked confused. "As I'm sure you're wondering... Yes, I am an Alpha... Not by birth, because I am the second born in my family... I killed my father for this position. But that story is something that can be saved for another time."

I flinched at my own words, I needed to figure out a way to talk that doesn't continue to scare him.

Seth's eyes were wide at my words, a whimper came free. I frowned. "I guess I shouldn't have told you about that part yet... You're safe with me. I promise you're safe... I would never hurt you. There are a million reasons why I did what I did... And I will tell you all of the reasons when you are feeling up to it. Now... Can I move you to a bed and dress your wounds?" I asked softly.

He shook his head yes, I sensed reluctance in his decision. He looked down at his knees as they were pressed tightly to his chest.

I stood up immediately and walked over to where he sat. I bent down and gently took him into my arms. Seth whimpered softly, tensing at my touch before his body relaxed into my hold. That holds promise. He looked up to my face, a shaky hand reached up and gently wiped away part of the blood that was on my cheek.

My entire body warmed at that simple touch. Maybe he's not so scared of me?

I instinctively leaned into his touch, the warmth of my tan clear skin was welcomed. Or at least I thought it was.. "I have you now...

I promise you are safe. Once your brother is cleared from Doctor Hunter, I will have him brought here where he can stay until he decides to leave." I reassured as I walked us into my bedroom.

I knew it was the most comfortable bed.

"I... Have to... Stay?" He questioned, his voice rough and soft as he looked at me.

I shook my head no, gently placing him down on the bed. Even though it would kill me if he left, I couldn't force him to do anything. Xena whimpered, but she knew I was right.

"If you don't want to stay here, you don't have to... I can start making arrangements for you and your brother and Alex to stay in a different house if that makes you the most comfortable." I forced a smile before I walked into the bathroom and grabbed the first aid kit.

He watched me, I could tell. I just need to focus, one thing at a time. I quickly washed my face, and changed into a random shirt I had in here.

It was better than nothing. I couldn't go back in there with blood all over me. I'm hoping it will show me trying to bring him comfort.

"Ohh the big bad Alpha is panicking!" Xena taunted me.

I swear I wish I could punch her in the face.

I walked back into the bedroom and sat down on the edge of the bed and opened the box. "It looks like most of your wounds are burns... They should go away as you eat and rest. I am going to just apply some ointment onto them. It's something that I make, it's herbs so it won't sting. It will prompt your healing to be faster." I explained, opening the same jar before putting some on her finger.

Seth inhaled sharply as my finger spread the ointment over a burn on his arm.

I had to breathe deeply, the feel of the scarred burned flesh. It sent waves of rage boiling through my veins. Which of course made Xena want more control.

"Please..." He whimpered, biting his bottom lip.

I whimpered, frowning at him. I wish I didn't have to do this, but he needs some help with his healing.

"I know it hurts... It will help I promise. It's going to hurt more before I can make it all better." I told him.

I want to help him, but I feel like I'm failing. "I'm trying my best to be as gentle as possible. I promise this will help... Maybe instead of talking, you can try speaking to me in my mind like you did before?"

Seth watched as I put ointment over the burns and cuts that needed it, and wrapped the other more worse ones. I wanted to look at him, but I needed to keep working. One thing at a time.

"Why do you care? About me and my brother? What made you come?" He questioned, his voice filling my mind.

I paused for a moment as I looked at his eyes, reading his confused expression.

How do I explain this without pressuring him? How do I explain he's the one thing that kept me going all these months? How do I explain I would have burned Ireland to the ground to get him?

"For many reasons I care... For instance, I was in a very similar situation to you before. Another reason is I don't believe in torturing someone because they are different... And you are a wolf. You don't deserve that. Neither does your brother. The iron. The magic that seemed to be draining us of our power.

That was torture... And it's not something I think you deserved. Neither did your brother. I may be ruthless to my enemies but I'm not a monster," I spoke softly to him.

I placed my hands on my jean-covered thighs. I wanted to hold him... But I knew he wasn't ready for that. "And there are more reasons too... But nothing that you have to worry about.

Right now, all you need to concern yourself with is healing and resting."

I looked at my hands on my thighs before bringing my eyes back to his. They weren't shaking anymore, so that was a good thing. *"I have done nothing to deserve this... My father has the power and the right to torture me for what I had done."* He said, tearing his eyes away from me.

Pink flushed across his cheeks as he looked at his bare skinny body.

"Oof, if he wasn't so hurt. That blush would be adorable." Xena said, watching intently.

"You are the heir to The Bloody Rose Pack. One day if you decide, that pack will be yours." I frowned. "He doesn't have the right to torture you."

Instinct led me to reach over to hold his hand, but he flinched. I quickly withdrew and placed my hands back on my thighs. I need to get a handle on myself.

"You don't know what I did. I don't know if I'll ever be able to explain to you what I have done. Can I see my brother? I want to see if he's okay." Seth asked, one comfort I had was that he could talk to me through my mind.

He looked at everything in the room but me. I nodded, I reached into my nightstand and took out my phone.

After sending a message to Madoc, I placed my phone back on the table. "Your brother and Alex will be here in a few minutes. I am having my Delta go and have someone escort them here. I doubt your father will try anything, but I want to make sure you all are as protected and safe as possible." I explained, standing up and moving to sit at the end of the large bed.

My entire body felt tense, the need to hold him close was nearly overwhelming. If I give him space, everything will be okay. I have to believe everything will be okay.

He shifted his body, making him as small as possible. He brought his knees to his chest as his body shivered as he slammed his eyes shut. His whole body showed he didn't feel safe. I frowned, getting off of the bed and heading over to kneel on the side. I just want to help him.

Xena was fighting against me, and I struggled for control. I needed to keep control, I can't add more stress onto him.

"I want him!" Xena yelled at me.

And the thing is. More than anything... I wanted him too. But I couldn't live with myself if I pushed *us* on him... And it end up that he never wanted me in the first place.

"Please... Please tell me what I can do... Let me help you. I don't want you to be in pain. I want to help you if you'd let me... Please..." I begged, my deep brown eyes, slowly starting to turn purple.

It was inevitable. Xena was going to take control sooner or later. And her making my eyes purple, it was her way of showing that she was there. Seth shook his head no, refusing to open his eyes. I would do anything to make him feel better.

"Just leave me alone. I just want my brother." Seth said, whimpering as his voice filled my mind again.

It felt like my heart shattered into a million tiny little pieces. I looked at him, nodding slowly before standing up and bringing my deep purple comforter over his shaking body.

My body was tense as I forced my legs to take me out of the bedroom and into the hallway. Xena lost it, I felt her power swirl around me. And I knew I wouldn't be able to stay in control for much longer.

My vision started to blur as I struggled my way out to the living room. The air felt heavy, the room felt too small. I needed out, I felt her claws sinking into my consciousness. She wanted control, she would take it. I flinched when I heard the door open.

I was fighting, and I guess my body was taking a toll with it. I needed to go running. It would help clear my head.

"It would help if you would let me free dipstick!" Xena snapped, and I nearly gasped as I felt like I couldn't get air into my lungs.

The room started to spin, I didn't even know who came through the door.

"Scar..." He, *Alex*, spoke softly.

He stood in the doorway, he was scared of me. I knew it. I felt it, he along with everyone else is scared of me. And I get it.

I didn't reply as I landed on my knees, tears threatening to fall. My arm broke as I growled out my pain. I forced my eyes closed as I refused to let the rest of my body shift. I willed my arm to go back into place. But it didn't.

"I want my mate! NOT Alex!" Xena howled.

I want him more than anything, but I can't put that pressure on him. I won't do that to him.

Alex ran back to me, landing on his knees in front of me. No he needs to go. "I need you to look at me Scar," Alex said, his blue eyes bright as he looked at me with concern.

My body was shaking as I was breathing heavily. I hate this, I felt my entire body cry from the pain.

It felt like I was that little kid again... Begging for her daddy to love her and not hurt her anymore. Maybe this isn't in the cards for me. Maybe after all my sins... Maybe I just don't deserve a mate. And just that thought, made my body ache at the possibility.

"I need... You to... Run..." I growled out, my voice was deep.

My eyes glowed purple as I finally opened my eyes to look at him. Fear crossed over my features, pain flickered across quickly after. I didn't want him, but I didn't want him to get hurt either.

"You and I both know that I'm not doing that. I have never left you... I only left the once because you made me go. I never wanted to... And you know that... I'm not scared of you, I'll never be scared of you." Alex promised, slowly taking my hands in his.

I looked at him, studying his face as I nodded slowly.

Xena was fighting against me before she watched Alex. *"He isn't scared of us? Well he's about to be! If the world wants a Ruthless Queen let's show them how ruthless we can be!"* Xena yelled, growling her anger to me.

"Breathe... Breathe Scar... Feel the warmth of my skin against your palms... Hear my voice. I am not scared of you, you shouldn't be scared of yourself." He spoke calmly to me.

I bit my bottom lip, tears slowly starting to fall as my breathing calmed down. I looked down at my legs. I feel like my whole world is crumbling around me.

"I... I can't do this..." I whispered, my voice cracking as I couldn't bring myself to look at him.

Alex intertwined our fingers together, a slight frown overtaking his face.

Feeling his hand in mine... It feels wrong. It feels like I'm cheating on Seth. My body felt ice cold.

"What can't you do, Scar?" Alex asked, the scent of confusion filled the air around us.

I looked up to him finally, tears streaming down my rosy cheeks. My eyes were swollen and puffy as I tried to contain myself.

"I'm not made for this. I'm not made to be a mate, I am an Alpha. I have to be ruthless, I can't show these emotions. I just met him and already my heart is his. That is so stupid of me to say, he owns me. I would've given up everything to save him and he doesn't want me to help him." I sniffled, my hands shaking in his.

Xena suddenly became quiet and I didn't like it.

"I understand that he has gone through a lot, I know he has... But I just want him to be okay. I want to help him, I want to be there to take away his pain. But I can't do that. I'm the she-wolf who took over her pack and I can't do this one simple thing!" I growled, my anger coming back.

Alex held my hands tightly, not letting me slip away from him. My anger about everything, I just wanted to kill Pete for doing this to my mate.

"You can handle this Scar. You are the Alpha Female. The only one in the entire world, you can handle anything. I've seen you take down a group of fully grown men when you were just six-teen. I have seen you lead battles and lead them to victory. I have seen you talk about politics with grown men that looked down on you.

I have seen you force alpha males into submission to get what you want and what your pack needed. This will not be your downfall, Seth went through a lot... It is not my place to tell you about what he went through. But one day, he will open up to you. I know him, and I know this is something he has always wanted.

Give him some time... He just needs to adjust... I'm here Scar, I am... You aren't alone, you don't have to handle this alone." Alex reassured me as he reluctantly let go of my hands.

He opened his arms up before I moved closer to him. Tears streamed down my face again as I wrapped my arms tightly around him.

My first friend... And at a time the only person who understood me.

"I don't know what I'm going to do if I lose him. I won't be able to handle it if he leaves me..." I cried into his chest, plastering myself to his broad chest.

He frowned, running his hand gently through my hair. If I closed my eyes tight enough, I could beg the Moon Goddess to give me Seth. To allow me this blessing.

"I know Scar... I know you are worried and in pain right

41

now... But I know you. I know you can handle this. You got this... And I'm right here, just like I will be for the rest of our lives..." Alex spoke calmly to me.

The vibrations from his voice caused me to smile with the comfort he brought me. In this moment I needed that.

"You need Seth. Not some off brand." Xena snarled, unhappy obviously.

Alex let go of me and gently brought my face up to meet his. "You have this... You have everything. You can handle anything..." He reassured, leaning forward closer to me.

My breath hitched in my chest, I froze before pulling away before he could kiss me. My first everything will be Seth's.

"Let me kill him now? Please? I said please. I never say please!" Xena asked me, suddenly happy again.

And even though I wanted to throat punch him. I couldn't kill him.

"No. No. Alex. We can't do this. Not anymore... I... I have Seth I need to worry about now. He's my... He's my mate, even if he doesn't know that we're mates. I can't betray him like that... Alex..." I said quickly, scooching away from him on the hardwood floor of my living room.

He nodded in understanding, placing his hands on his thighs.

"I understand Scar... I'm sorry, I don't know what came over me. I promise that won't happen again, I shouldn't have done that." Alex apologized, smiling at me.

I crossed my legs, rubbing the back of my neck slightly. Everything about Alex trying to comfort me seems wrong now.

"It's alright... But do you think he'll come around? That he'll want to be with me?" I asked softly, looking at him now.

Alex nodded in confirmation. I want him more than anything.

"I think he will... I think he needs some time. He went

through some terrible stuff because of his dad. But he always used to talk about his mate and how he couldn't wait to meet her. And I think he will be ecstatic that you are his mate. A hot, powerful, independent Ruthless Queen." Alex winked at me, causing me to laugh.

Always trying to push that boundary.

"I hope so... I don't want to lose him..." I spoke softly, looking out of the large window in my living room.

Or as Xena said...

The world will be shown what an actual Ruthless Queen looks like.

CHAPTER
FIVE

After a while, Alex and I were sitting in silence. I couldn't move, I couldn't bring myself to do anything.

So I sat there, until there was a soft knock on the door. I breathed in deeply as I stood up, heading to the door so that I could let Madoc in. I opened the door, letting him walk in with the large box of clothes that he got for me.

"I wasn't sure what I was supposed to get... So I got jeans, sweatpants, shorts, various t-shirts, and hoodies. I got a lot of sizes because I wasn't sure. And then as usual I didn't tell anyone what I was doing per your orders." Madoc informed, bowing his head in respect to me.

I couldn't help but grin as I took the box.

Sometimes I wonder why I picked him, until he does stuff like this. His willingness to help me no matter what I asked.

"Thank you Madoc, I appreciate this. I know this isn't what you are usually used to. But I didn't want to leave my house. So I appreciate your willingness to always help me." I said kindly, Madoc beamed with pride.

I knew Xena wanted to tease him, but I wouldn't let her.

"I would do anything for you Alpha. I am your Delta, I am happy to do anything you need me to do." Madoc smiled, bowing his head again. "Do you need anything else Alpha before I head home for the night?"

Alex was trying to hold back his laughter. I shook my head no, I don't know why Alex is laughing right now.

"It's because Madoc is a tad bit of a suck up." Xena explained with a slight shrug.

"No, I will text you if I need anything. Thank you." I said before Madoc left and made sure to shut the door behind him.

I waited a moment to listen in, I'm not sure of what I want to do. I want to go with Seth. But I know he doesn't want that.

"That poor kid loves you so much, he just wants to make you happy." Alex started cackling, laying on the floor clutching his stomach.

I couldn't help but giggle at his laughter. Alex's laugh was just so contagious.

"Everybody wants to make me happy, I am the Alpha after all. And not just the Alpha, but the only female Alpha in the entire world. I am special, some even think that I am going to be remembered as the one who changed the world for the better." I smiled, looking out of the large living room window.

Darkness had fallen quickly, giving me a slight frown.

"It feels like centuries have passed since we were sixteen, two young children trying to figure out the world... And here I am, still running my pack... And you becoming a part of my guard apparently." I said, stretching as I looked toward the hallway where my bedroom was.

I just want to be in that room with him. "I don't even know if he wants me to check on him..."

"Do it. Don't ask questions." Xena told me.

And I knew she meant well, but I couldn't just pressure him. I've felt pressured, and I refuse to do that to my male.

"Check on him if you'd like... I know you though. You want to be there, but sometimes you can't always be there. You are the Alpha, you can't just have Grayson take ov–..." Alex started before his cheeks turned red and he looked away from me.

I growled, my eyes glowing brightly once more. I'm gonna kill him.

"Let me!" Xena shouted, her anger made mine seem like child's play.

"Yes, Alex. I am the Alpha of my pack, I wouldn't just hand my pack over to my brother while I cared for my mate. My pack runs smoothly, I don't have to constantly be in the packhouse with everyone. Everyone knows that if I am not around, they can just go to Grayson or Madoc. I have made it where my pack runs amazing even if I am not there one hundred percent of the time.

And as you saw, the people who try to deny me. Or try to tell me that I can't rule my pack, I kill them. I have grown into the Alpha destiny wanted me to be. So I do not need your advice on this. As I told Seth, you can stay here for as long as you'd like. I have plenty of room, and I will be sending Madoc to get me things tomorrow for you guys." I explained as I went down the hallway and to my bedroom where Seth was sleeping.

Don't wake up... Don't wake up...

I quietly opened the door before walking inside. Seth was laying under the sheets, tossing and turning as he whimpered in his sleep.

"What is he whimpering about?" Xena asked, whimpering softly.

I don't know, but I want so badly to find out.

"Scarlett... Save me... Please..." His voice was weak, breathy as he panted quietly.

I walked over closer to him, getting down on my knees on his side of the bed. His claws were out, clutching at the blanket that covered his naked body. I frowned as I took in his sweating form.

I feel wrong looking into his mind. But I at least needed to wake him from this nightmare.

"Seth... My love... Wake up... Please. You're okay, you're safe. No one will ever hurt you again..." I soothingly said, gently squeezing his shoulder to try and wake him.

He gasped, breathing heavily as his eyes opened. His brown eyes seemed to darken as he stared into mine.

He's okay. I think? I don't think he's scared of me. Or maybe he is?

"You are safe... No one will ever hurt you again. This I promise you, and I never break my promises. Would you like some food? I could make it and bring it in here for you to eat? That way you can be right by your brother?" I offered, reluctantly moving my hand off of his shoulder.

He looked over my face, before nodding slowly.

I couldn't help the small smile that crossed my plump red lips. He's not scared of me! I take that as a win! Yay!

"I am going to pick you up again... And then I'm going to carry you out to the kitchen." I informed.

Seth inhaled shaky as he nodded at me, a nod is good. It's good, I have to believe that. I stood up, gently picking him up into my arms, quietly walking out of the bedroom. He stared at me, and I willed myself not to blush.

I felt his eyes on me, and I felt my body warm in response.

"I do have clothes here for you if you would like to put some on. You don't have to of course. I just thought that it would bring you some comfort." I explained, walking into the kitchen.

He nodded softly, looking around at the house around him.

"Are the nods a good thing?" Xena asked. "Why does he keep nodding and not speaking to us?"

I don't know but dang it Xena I don't need this self doubt right now!

Once we were in the kitchen, I gently placed him on a chair at the kitchen island. He groaned, inhaling as he winced. And I'm assuming that's because I'm not holding him? He keeps wincing everytime I put him down. So it could be the loss of the connection? Of our bond?

"Are you alright?" I asked worriedly, as I started to take things out to cook for him. "You can talk to me in my mind..."

In my mind it will be easier for him, giving him less pain. And I am hoping and praying to the Goddess that blessed me with him. That it will help him see that we are mates.

He nodded, leaning most of his weight against the granite island. *"I hurt... Everywhere... I don't know why I'm here... I don't know why you saved me. I don't understand what's happening. I don't understand why you care... Are you the wolf that I have been calling out to?"* His voice filled my mind as I looked at him.

I tilted my head slightly, trying to think of the right way to form my response.

I care because you are the only thing in the entire world that gives me hope. The one person that keeps me sane, and makes me feel like I can be more than what I am.

"You are here because this is the safest place in Scotland... I am the strongest wolf here, so I can protect you the easiest. I saved you because you didn't deserve a single thing your father did to you. I care because of things you don't have to worry about right now... Do you remember who you were calling out to? Or are you just assuming it's me because I am the one who saved you?" I asked, placing a bowl of cut-up fruit in front of him.

I always had a bowl in my fridge at all times, it was something easy for my siblings to grab. I guess it became a habit. Seth slowly went to put a piece of strawberry into his mouth.

He looked at me again. His skin was already gaining some color back from just being out of the cell. I looked into the fridge, grabbing the steak out.

"I remember trying to call out to my mate... I didn't know who she

was... But I begged her to save at least my brother. Hopefully me, but at least my brother. He deserves a better life than that... I know I did a lot of things that put me into that position. Which I regret, I just wanted to save him. So many things went wrong though." Seth shivered at the thought as he watched me make him a large steak.

I nodded, showing him that I was listening to what he was saying.

I know the feel of that... A lot of things went wrong after I took control of my pack. But that's not important right now.

"I feel safe? Comfortable... I feel like I am okay. I don't even know why I feel this way. Does this mean that you are my mate? Why don't I feel anything then? Other than this safe, comfortable feeling?" Seth questioned, his body involuntarily shaking slightly as he continued to eat from the bowl in front of him.

Oh he knows! He knows! He knows! It took everything in me not to squeal with excitement. This means that things are working out well! I can't and shouldn't get my hopes up. He still has every right to reject me.

"Goddess don't even say that. It makes me want to have a panic attack." Xena cringed at the drastic change in my thoughts.

I smiled, my back was to him, so I closed my eyes. "Yes... We are mates. But I know you went through a lot, I don't know how much you went through. And I don't need to know right in this moment... I'm not expecting anything from you. I don't want you to feel forced into something you don't want..." I said, my voice cracking as I plated his steak and shut off the stove.

He stared at my back, I felt his eyes on me. When I turned around he couldn't hold my gaze so he looked down at the bowl in front of him.

I couldn't help but frown as I placed the steak in front of him. "Be careful... It's hot..." I told.

Last thing I need is for him to burn his tongue. That would freak him out.

"I don't know what I want... I don't know who I'm supposed to be... I can't feel anything besides pain right now. Pain and hunger... I want to feel more, something in me has always called out for you. I never understood it, and then... I heard you out here with Alex..." Seth told me, his soft strong voice filled my mind.

I frowned, watching him start to eat the steak I made him.

"Alex always finds a way to really screw us over." Xena growled.

And now I wish I let her punch him in the face.

"I have been the Alpha of my pack for ten years. Nobody really liked that me being fourteen and a woman... Well, a female at the time since I was still a kid. Was running the pack. The only friend I had was Alex... I don't want you to worry about that. When you're stronger we can talk about what happened between him and me then." I informed, leaning against the counter as I watched him.

He looked up at me, his mouth full of his steak. Fear crossed his features causing me to frown.

If I could, I would go back in time and change that. I... I never thought it would end up like this. My mate was scared that I would pick *Alex* over him. When I see Seth for who he is. A powerful Alpha that needs some help resurfacing.

"You're right. We could kill Alex to help with his stress?" Xena offered, sounding way too pleased by that suggestion.

And I would be lying if I said I wasn't tempted.

"I was alone, my brother and sister didn't understand the pain I was going through. And then walked in Alex, he was alone too. We were close, very close friends. Nothing serious happened between us, I promise you. We both knew that we weren't mates so nothing could happen between us. And then I met you, and nothing else matters to me now." I offered with a soft smile at him.

He swallowed thickly, before rubbing the back of his neck embarrassed. Why is he embarrassed?

I keep digging a bigger and bigger hole for myself. I couldn't help but groan slightly.

Seth couldn't bring himself to look me in the eye as he asked the question. *"You guys were together intimately?"*

"Ew! Ew! That's just gross." Xena gagged at the thought, and I cringed at the thought.

Yeah... With Alex? I would rather die a virgin.

I shook my head no, before heading to the fridge and grabbing two bottles of water. I opened them both before placing one by him.

"No, it wasn't like that. We were together, but we never had sex. Goddess, why are we talking about this right now?" My cheeks burned red with embarrassment at talking about my inexperience.

A small smile crossed his face before he quickly made it disappear. *"Thank you for telling me... I think I just need a little bit of time... I don't want you to think I'm not grateful for everything because I am... Thank you for saving me and my brother's life... I just need to think about a lot before I can give you a direct answer.'* Seth tried to explain as I nodded in understanding.

It's why I wasn't going to pressure him Xena! But with her silence, I knew she felt guilty for even suggesting pushing past his boundaries.

"You take as long as you need. I am not going to rush you or pressure you into anything. When you are ready, you are ready. I do not want you to push yourself into something you're not ready for." I smiled lovingly at him, as he downed his water.

I didn't know he was that thirsty.

Seth was about to stand up but knew that he wouldn't be able to make it back to the bed. *"Can you help me please?"* He asked, still not looking at me.

I nodded, heading over to where he was sitting. A tiny flower of hope blooms inside of my chest. This is going better than I thought.

"I'm going to pick you up now before I take you back to the bedroom," I told him, waiting until he was ready for me to pick him up.

Seth nodded weakly before I gently took him back into my arms. It took everything in me not to cringe at his bones against my skin.

"I am trying my best to not go too fast because I don't want you to feel any pain," I told him, gently carrying him back to my bedroom.

He rested his head against my chest and closed his eyes. Warmth spread across my skin from that action, and I had to bite back the excitement.

"Thank you for saving me..." He told me quietly, keeping his eyes closed.

I couldn't help the smile that spread across my face. I quietly walked into my bedroom and gently laid him down on the bed. I'm hoping the food will help him sleep better.

"Sleep well, my male..." I spoke softly to him, before covering him back up with my blanket.

I leaned down, pressing a gentle kiss to his forehead. I allowed my power to wash into his body, causing his skin to return back to the normal tan. I wonder if he was tan before? He inhaled deeply, my power made him drift off into sleep easier.

I smiled softly, tucking him in.. After I made sure they were asleep, I brought back some of the clothes that Madoc had brought for me. At least they had freedom to shower and change if they wanted. With one last look to a sleeping Seth, I left the bedroom and went to a guest bedroom that was right beside mine.

"The woods would be better than this." Xena grumbled.

Yeah... I'm beginning to agree with that. But no one can see me sleeping in the woods again. Ugh I don't need people thinking I'm fully crazy.

I rubbed the back of my neck as I walked into the room. It wasn't terrible. I just never really made this as comfortable as I should've. "This won't be forever... I will be back in my bedroom when he is ready..." I told myself as I started to get ready for bed.

CHAPTER
SIX

T he next morning, I woke up in a cold sweat. My heart raced as I looked around the room.

I groaned, covering my face. I can't breathe fully for a second as I look to make sure it wasn't my nightmare.

That same cold nightmare of me laying in the snow, freezing to death. But that cold is nothing compared to this cold. The cold in my body at the knowledge my mate is in the next room. *Choosing* to not lay with me.

"I can't do this." I mumbled to myself, before forcing myself out of bed.

I changed into a pair of ripped blue jeans and a cropped black tank top, it was the only items of clothing I had in there. It wasn't anything different from what I typically wear.

I went to the bedroom door, this guest room. Will never be my room. It won't bring me comfort. As I walked out of my guest bedroom, I hesitated at my bedroom door. I want to check on him, to make sure he's okay. But I don't know if I can handle him flinching and asking me not to touch him.

"I just want to help him feel better." Xena whimpered, begging silently for me to let her free.

I want the same thing, I just can't force his hand.

"He's still sleeping if you want to go check on him..." Alex whispered to me, he was in a pair of black gym shorts and nothing else.

I looked at his shirtless form and it took everything in me not to growl. I rolled my eyes as I walked out of the hallway and made my way to the kitchen.

I'm not doing this today. I'm not fighting with anyone, I just need coffee. Tea. I need vodka. Anything to get me started for this day, cause so far it sucks. My back hurts, I'm stiff from that uncomfortable bed. Sleeping on the forest floor would've been better.

"See! I don't know why you don't listen to me. I'm a genius." Xena growled at me softly.

I couldn't help but snicker at her teasing me. I do need to listen to her more. I mean after all, she is the only reason I've made it this far.

"I want to... But he asked me for space. I need to give him the space he asked for, no matter how much I hate this." I informed as I started to take things out of the fridge to make breakfast.

Pancakes maybe? I'm not sure.

Alex resumed towel drying his hair, his chest glistening. I had to turn away, he's still trying to push me. "I don't think he would be mad if you sat in there with him while he slept." He offered with a shrug as he sat down at the kitchen island.

I turned to him and shrugged. Oh how I wanted to do that everytime I tossed and turned. Which was like all night. I really need a shot of something. Adrenaline? I feel like that would be best.

"Could we actually do that?" Xena asked, tilting her head at the thought.

"I can't push him... I want him to be comfortable and feel safe. Me invading his space and privacy would not be good." I frowned, looking at the herbs I had.

I couldn't help but grin as I started to pull out random herbs to make a healing tea. I've always sucked at it when it comes to myself. But hopefully it'll work for him.

"I don't think he would mind... He's not used to being... Weak." Alex said.

My body stiffened at his words.

"Weak!?" Xena growled, starting to thrash around as she wanted control.

Alex is pushing me. And I'm about to let Xena teach him a lesson. My growl was loud, the glass cup in my hand shattered as my fist tightened around it. My eyes were purple as I turned to him. Xena needed to show her power.

If looks could kill. He would be dead.

"Don't you EVER call him weak," I growled, blood dripped down my hand to my forearm, then slowly fell to the floor below.

I watched it, rolling my eyes slightly. This day just keeps getting better and better. "He is stronger than YOU realize. He is stronger than YOU give him credit for. How about you try going through what he did! How about you try feeling what he felt in that cage for YEARS!" I snapped.

Alex's eyes widened as he looked at my form.

I don't know why it was such a shock to him. This is what he gets for testing me.

"Punch. Him. In. The. Face." Xena snapped at me.

And I'm just about to do that.

I was shaking slightly as I slammed my fists down on the counter. "You EVER talk down on him again. And so help me Alex I will break your neck." I snapped, my power soaking the air around us.

He immediately started to whimper and bare his neck to me in submission. Xena growled inside my mind, it wasn't good enough for her.

And to be fair, it wasn't good enough for me either. I wanted him to pay for calling my mate weak.

I looked down at my right hand, seeing the glass shards still stuck in my palm. I guess that's why it was bleeding so badly. I sighed, slowly picking out the shards and throwing them in the trash. I felt his eyes before I even knew he was in the room.

Goddess I just keep making a fool out of myself in front of him. My body tensed before looking up, my eyes immediately finding Seth's. My cheeks burned red as I put my hands behind my body. I was hoping they would heal before I had to do anything with him.

"He doesn't need to be scared even more." Xena winced slightly.

I wanted to wince, but if I winced. He might think something is actually wrong. When I didn't even feel the glass go into my palm.

"I was going to bring you Breakfast in bed... I thought that it would be good for your brother and you to finally have someone take care of you." I offered, biting my bottom lip.

He nodded, looking behind him. And I so badly wanted to be that person to take care of him.

"I felt your pain... Are you alright?" Seth asked, his voice in my mind.

He was leaning painfully against the wall, dressed in baggy gray sweatpants and a black hoodie. Max walked out from behind his brother, he wasn't in nearly as bad of condition. And while I wish neither one of them were in pain. I knew Seth was happier knowing Max was less hurt.

"Hi Alpha..." He said shyly, casting his gaze down to his feet.

I smiled softly, rinsing the blood off of my hand and arm

before drying it with a towel. I walked over to them, gently taking Max's face in my hands and looking at him. I don't want him to call me Alpha. Not now, not ever.

"I promise you... You don't have anything to be scared about...You are safe here, I won't let anything happen to you or your brother. And you don't have to call me Alpha... You can call me Scarlett." I smiled kindly, before kissing his forehead gently, allowing my power to race through his body.

Seth was watching us, a soft smile on his face.

"Oh yeah! Adding up points for him!" Xena howled inside of my mind.

Yes!

Max gasped, his eyes opening and shining brightly at me. He hugged me tightly, closing his eyes as he rested his head against my chest. "Thank you for saving us! Thank you!" He cried into my chest.

I frowned as I gently rubbed his back, holding him so I didn't hurt him. This reminds me of when Grayson and Stormy were younger.

"You are safe... Thank you for allowing me to protect you..." I spoke softly, biting my bottom lip as I looked at Seth.

His cheeks were a soft shade of pink, as he was looking at us. Something sparked across his eyes, but it quickly disappeared. It disappeared too fast for me to even think about what it was. Max sniffled, wiping his tears as he let go of me.

"Why don't you go sit down? I was just about to make breakfast." I offered, as he nodded and eagerly went to go sit by Alex.

He gulped, struggling to keep himself standing. My body reacted before I could stop it. I rushed over to him and held him up. My eyes widened at my action.

Oh crap oh crap oh crap. I should've stopped myself!!

"Oh oh oh shut up! Listen to him!" Xena said, her over-positivity would be the death of our hope.

"I am so sorry, I should've asked you if it was okay that I helped you." I whimpered softly, he leaned his weight into me.

Seth studied my face, before quickly looking away. I bit my bottom lip, I struggled not to blush at just him looking at me.

"It's alright..." His voice was soft in my mind.

I walked him over to the kitchen island and gently sat him down. He held on tightly to the island top, is he dizzy? I thought that he was doing okay? Or well as okay as he can be? I went back to cooking once I knew he was okay. I tried my best to focus on the task in front of me.

When suddenly I heard Seth cough slightly, causing me to frown and quickly get him a cup of cold water. I should've thought to get him some water, I can't believe I forgot that.

"I guess we really are out of practice with taking care of people." Xena offered nonchalantly.

Ugh I'm screwing this all up.

"Are you alright?" I asked, kneeling beside him and looking at him intently.

Seth brought his gaze to me for a second, before gently taking the cup into his hand and turning away. His cheeks burned pink and I swear to the Moon Goddess. It's one of the cutest things I've ever seen.

"I'm okay... It hurts a lot to talk..." Seth told me, a small smile crossed my face as I stood up.

He watched as I went back to the stove and plated the three omelets before serving them. I'm glad that he's at least trying.

"Be careful you two... It's hot. And if you can't eat all of it. Don't worry about it, I don't want you to eat yourself sick. I just know this will help you gain some weight and strength back." I said, looking between Seth and Max.

I got some water for Max as well before Alex whined.

"And what about me?" Alex asked, feigning heartbreak.

I rolled my eyes, starting to make myself food. At least I cooked him food.

"You are not injured, therefore not my responsibility to care for you," I growled, flashing my purple eyes at him.

Xena wasn't happy with him, and sometimes neither am I. "I allow you to stay here because it brings Seth and Max comfort. Don't test my kindness."

Alex frowned, starting to eat his food. My chest filled with warmth as I heard Seth's soft chuckle. And I knew that I wanted to hear that again.

"This is really good... Thank you for caring for me and my brother... And for putting Alex in his place... It means a lot to me." Seth said, looking down at his plate.

I smiled at his words, starting to eat the food that I made for myself. But what he doesn't know is that just being here with me means the world to me.

"After breakfast... I'm going to need to check on your wounds if that is alright with you... If not, I can have someone from the hospital come to check you out." I told Seth, looking directly at him.

I didn't want him to think that I even had interest in Alex. He blushed, looking at me for a spare second before looking down at his empty plate.

"I think it's so cute how flustered he gets." Xena giggled softly, watching in silence.

I'm shocked that she isn't trying to take control..

"I really don't want to leave the house... And I don't want to have anyone come here... Obviously, this is your house so it's your choice..." Seth spoke softly to me.

When I heard his stomach growl, I wished I had made him more food.

"I like to think of this as our home... Your comfort is what matters most to me..." I spoke back to him.

Something about talking like this is extremely intimate. His cheeks burned at my voice. I giggled softly before I looked at Alex.

"Clean up for me." I ordered Alex, before smiling kindly at Max. "Feel free to watch some TV or do whatever you like... I just need to tend to your brother's wounds."

Max nodded before heading to go to the living room.

I didn't wait for Alex to reply, I just picked Seth up and walked back to my bedroom. He frowned slightly as he just rested his head against my chest. I felt his sadness and smelled his anxiety.

I walked into the bedroom, before shutting the door with my foot. I used to have to do this with Stormy when she picked fights. I'm out of practice, but I'm sure it's like riding a bike.

Seth sniffled, as I sat him down on the toilet seat before grabbing my first-aid kit again.

"What's wrong, my love?" I asked with a frown.

He finally looked into my eyes as tears slowly fell down his face. I hated that he was crying, I bit my bottom lip as my heart ached.

"What's wrong?" I asked again, sitting down in front of where he was.

His bottom lip trembled as he looked down at me. If he says me being here. I'm going to die.

So many things... So so so many things..." He said, whimpering softly.

I frowned, reaching to take his trembling hands but I hesitated. I didn't know how to comfort him. He wrapped his arms tightly around himself, trying to keep himself from shaking more. I wish he would let me hold him.

"I don't understand what's wrong..." My frown deepened, and I placed my hands on my thighs.

I wanted my hands to be on his thighs but I guess this will have to do.

"I wasn't supposed to be like this. I was supposed to be an Alpha. I was supposed to be strong, I was supposed to be taking care of you. Not the other way around." Seth looked at me fully now.

He watched my eyes so he could see if I was lying.

"How can you look me in the eye and tell me you want me? I am not an Alpha. I am not a Beta. I am nothing... I can't give you anything. I can't prompt your rule as Alpha."

I nodded, listening to the words he was saying. Even though I didn't need him to prompt my rule, I understood his worries. I smiled softly, as I reached up to gently take his hoodie off. He lifted his arms to help me, before looking at me again. I placed my hands on his bare torso, I allowed my power to slowly flow into his body.

Hopefully this will give him comfort. Xena was quiet, and at this moment I was happy for that bit of silence.

"I want you. I don't care that you aren't a Beta. I don't care that you aren't an Alpha. You are everything to me, I don't need you to give me anything because I can give you everything. I don't need you to prompt my rule as Alpha. I can do that myself... You have gone through a very terrible thing.

Something I know you aren't ready to talk about. I just want you to take your time to heal, to process everything. You don't need to worry about anything right now. The pack runs itself pretty much, or my brother handles everything pretty well without me... I am here to help you heal from everything." I smiled kindly at him before I looked over the wounds on his torso and arms.

I'm shocked that he's healing so quickly. "Look... You're already healing."

Seth looked down at his torso, his brows lifted in surprise. He shifted on the toilet seat slightly.

"I didn't know you had a brother..." He spoke softly, watching as I stood up to put the first aid kit back.

I nodded slightly as I sat down in front of him again. I took his hand gently, keeping my eyes locked on his. Seth inhaled sharply as my power overwhelmed his senses.

"Cool it." Xena snapped at me, and I immediately withdrew some of my power.

I didn't even realize I was giving him too much.

"I have a twin brother named Grayson, and a little sister named Stormy. I used to have an older sister but she is long since been dead. My older sister's name was Hayley and she was our father's favorite...

It's not something I wanted to tell you about right away because I know how people handled me telling them about it. But I killed both my father and my older sister to protect my little sister and my twin brother... When I was born, it angered my father... Apparently, he was a nice man before me and Gray were born.

But I never saw that side of him, only Hayley did. We can talk about that another time, it's not important. But he was abusive, neglecting... It was bad enough that my mother actually left shortly after Stormy was born... So I somewhat understand what you went through..." I spoke softly, gently rubbing my thumb over his hand.

He watched my finger move, gently squeezing my hand.

Oh how I wish I could hug him. Just that gentle squeeze of his hand gave me more hope for the future.

"I don't want to go into detail about what happened right now. But I took most of the abuse from my father... That's why Max was laying on me so that he wouldn't get burnt by the floor or the bars." Seth offered, forcing a sad smile. *"He is the one thing that actually matters to me. He didn't deserve any of that... I knew I did."*

I frowned again, leaning up slightly so that our faces were at the same height. "I want to know everything you are willing to tell me. But you don't have to tell me right now... You don't have to tell me anything you don't want to. Would you like to go sit outside for a while? Maybe that will help you feel better?" I offered, smiling still as I didn't let his hand go.

Sunlight should help with his healing.

"Is this because you want to go spend more time with Alex? I would understand. He was a part of the guard in my pack. He's strong... He's not fragile." Seth frowned, looking away from me.

Fear and self-doubt evident in the smell of his emotions. I shook my head no, I will not stand for him talking bad about himself.

"I just thought that being in the sun would help you feel better. We could go sit out in the living room and watch some TV. Or we could sit in the bedroom and watch some TV. Or you can tell me that you don't want me to be with you right now and I will give you your space. And my love... You are not fragile. You are not weak.

You went through something so terrible and you made it out alive. You protected your brother, you kept him as safe as you could. You will never make me see you in another way. You are strong... You are powerful. And if you decide one day that you want to take Ireland back. I will be there with you to take back what is yours." I squeezed his hand gently, trying to bring his gaze back to me.

He forced a smile at me, shrugging slightly.

"They didn't want me. They watched what my father did to me for years and they didn't do a single thing to stop it..." I stared out into space, sadness in his eyes.

I would do anything to take that sadness away from him.

"If you would like me to, I would burn Ireland to the ground for you." I grinned, and Seth looked back at me in surprise.

But I'm not in any way joking.

"I'm only somewhat joking. If you wanted everyone dead from that country I would do it no questions asked." His smile was slow as his cheeks heated.

"I'm still happy to do it!" Xena shouted, anger boiling inside.

I wanted Pete to burn, I wanted him to pay for what he's done. But that will come in due time.

"Maybe we could go on a small walk together..." Seth offered, causing my eyes to light up with excitement.

I stood up, and gently took his hands. Xena howled with excitement as she ran around in the back of my mind.

"We could just walk outside to where I have some outdoor furniture. I don't want you to overdo yourself. You just were saved yesterday." I smiled at him, helping him put his hoodie back on. "I don't want you to be cold."

He smiled softly as I helped him stand up.

"This is happening! This is happening! Yay!" Xena howled with happiness.

I can't believe this is happening!

"I feel you pushing your power into my body... I feel strong when you keep your power running through me." Seth told me, causing me to giggle softly.

I was slowly helping him walk out of the bathroom before we were heading to the door that led outside. I was honestly scared to let go of him.

"I just wanted to help give you some strength... I did the same for your brother." I smiled, gently leading him to my back deck.

He gripped onto my arm tightly as he stepped through the now open glass door. "I'm not going to let you fall... I've got you."

Seth looked at me, he was slightly shorter than me since he couldn't stand straight. I gently sat him down on the large wooden rocking chair. Before getting on my knees in front of him. I would never let anything bad happen to him.

"Thank you for caring for my brother... You didn't have to. But thank you..." Seth smiled at me, his cheeks burning red before he looked away.

I stood up, gently kissing his forehead and pushing my power into his body again. It was a habit, something I never wanted to lose.

"You don't have to thank me. I would do anything for you, and your brother. I take care of my own." I told him, before sitting in the chair next to him.

I looked out to the woods that surrounded my house. Seth slowly began to rock the chair as he watched the treeline. I looked at him, before frowning slightly.

"He seems so stressed out." Xena whimpered softly.

"I had this house built because I was the guardian of Stormy and Grayson... They deserved a safe place to grow up without the harsh words of my pack, belittling me in front of them. Most of my pack hated me for years because of what I did... We're secluded, but we're safe." I tried to calm his worries.

Seth forced a smile, giving me a slight nod. I did anything to make my family safe.

"It was a very beautiful house..." He spoke to me, not sparing another glance at me.

Alex and Max walked out next, sitting in the open chairs that were there. I couldn't help but slump slightly at the way he didn't look at me.

"They're already being inappropriate out here," Alex said with a teasing smile.

Seth shot him a glare, growling softly at him. He quickly whimpered in apology. I grinned at Seth, before turning my focus back to the woods.

Will I ever understand this male? Not giving me attention one second and then the next standing up for us? I'm lost.

"I don't think that Seth likes it when you talk like that." I shrugged slightly, as I leaned back against the chair.

It started rocking slowly with my movement. Max laughed slightly, smiling at his brother.

"I like it when he stands up for us!" Xena was excited, and honestly so was I.

"I think this is going to be really good for us Seth. Her pack seems great, Alex has told me a little bit about it already! I think it would be great for us if we stayed here!" Max said, positivity filling his voice and the air around us.

Seth smiled tiredly at his brother, before nodding slightly at him. Max looked confused, frowning as he looked from Seth to me. I wish I had something to comfort him.

"He'll be okay, he's just healing still from everything that you guys went through. You don't have to worry little wolf. He just needs some more time before he can talk." I said positively, trying to calm him down.

Alex smirked at Seth.

"Would you look at that Seth, you've got the one and only Alpha Female in the whole world wrapped around your finger already." He grinned, causing Seth to smile again before he shut his eyes.

Xena suddenly made my entire body stiffen, why was she freaking out?

"How about we just sit..." I started before I stopped and stood up.

My body was tense as I saw a wolf walking towards us slowly. No.

"Alex, take Seth and Max inside now and keep them there." Alex quickly got up, helping to get Max inside.

Seth's eyes shot open, his heart racing as I stood in front of him.

"Nothing will take him away from us." Xena growled.

"I need you to trust me. You're okay. I won't let anyone hurt you, I will protect you." I told him soothingly.

A growl rippled through the air as I looked at the wolf.

CHAPTER
SEVEN

"I came for Seth and Max Knight." The male growled, continuing to walk slowly towards us.

Towards *him*.

This isn't happening. I growled again, shifting into my six-foot-five-sized black wolf. My transformation was effortless as my body shifted without fighting.

"Time to show this male that anyone who comes for our mate dies." Xena growled, as I let her take control.

I stood protectively in front of my deck, my massive paws spread apart in a fighting stance.

When the wolf didn't stop heading towards me, I took off running at him. My body was larger than the other wolf. My power was stronger, no one could stop me.

I growled again, baring my fangs.

He didn't stop, and I knew he wasn't going to. When I got close enough to the wolf I sunk them into the wolf's neck.

My eyes glowed brightly as I ripped out his throat and let his dead body drop to the ground. My body was shaking with anger as blood dripped from my fangs. But then I put things together.

The wolf didn't fight. He just ran at us. He didn't try to get free. He let me rip out his throat? This wasn't an attempt to take my mate and his brother. This was to gauge what it took to get me to lose control.

"And we walked right into that trap..." Xena said with a groan. *"But I don't regret a single thing."*

Seth was staring at me, his body was shaking as he watched me stalk up to the porch. He's scared of me. Of what happened. They sent that male to put a wedge between us.

My paws barely fit on the steps as I walked over to him. His breath hitched in his chest as he kept his eyes on me. I sat down in front of him, lowering my head to look him in the eye. I just need to show him that he's safe, that I would never hurt him.

"He's safer here than anywhere else." Xena growled at me.

She was stressed. I was stressed. This wasn't a good sign.

"Hi..." Seth spoke softly to me, biting his bottom lip in nervousness.

I looked him in his eyes, before bowing my head in respect to him. His hand was shaking as he brought it up to my furry head. *"Are you going to hurt me?"*

Feeling his hand brush through my fur made me want to twitch with excitement. It brought a feeling of love that shot through my entire body.

I growled unhappily, closing my eyes as my body shifted back into my human form. My transitions were always quick and painless, have been that way since I was a kid. My skin was tan and clear as my back was in view to him. I looked up to him, a soft smile on my face.

Hopefully this will show him that I trust him, and I would never do anything to hurt him. Or with my luck, this will just stress him out even more.

"I would never hurt you... And Xena... Adores you as much as I do." I told him, I was confident in my body.

As I was in the presence of my mate, I didn't need to wear clothes. Seth looked down at me, his cheeks burning red as he quickly looked away.

"Ohhh he likes what he sees." Xena giggled with excitement.

"You don't have to worry about anything... I don't mind if you look at me. But if you aren't ready for that, let me go get dressed, and then I can bring you back inside." I offered, watching him as he didn't look at me.

He simply nodded his answer when I stood up. Baby steps. I don't want to overly push him.

I couldn't help the frown that slipped across my face when I walked into the house. I made quick work of heading to my bedroom and quickly throwing on random clothes. I looked down at myself, before rushing to head back outside where Seth was sitting. It was just a hoodie and shorts. But anything is better than nothing right now.

He looked lost in thought as he rocked gently in the chair. His face was pale, sweating as he sat there. A pang of pain shot through my chest. I did this to him. I should've thought things through. I should've known it was a test, I should've put Seth inside.

"Did I scare you?" I spoke softly.

I sat down on my knees in front of him before placing my hands down on my thighs. Xena was quiet in my mind, I knew she was thinking of what is going to happen next. I can't believe we screwed up this much.

"You... You killed him so easily... What stops you from doing that to me?" Seth asked, his body shaking still.

I frowned, my eyes softening as I looked at him. His fear is because of what I did.

"What stops me from doing that to you is because you are my mate... And I love you. I would happily give my life to protect yours. He was sent here to gauge how quickly I was going to lose control of myself... I played right into his plan. I'm sure Pete sent some low-ranking wolf to trespass to see if I would send him back to Ireland.

Or kill him right where he stood. He wanted you, and I wasn't going to let that happen. I should've put you inside before I fought him. So I am sorry about that... I didn't mean to scare you. I just wanted to protect you, my love..." I spoke softly, looking at him now.

He hugged his knees to his chest.

And I would do anything to take that pain from him. That fear from his eyes. I just thought I was protecting him...

"I don't want you to die..." Seth spoke softly, tears welling in his eyes. *"I don't want to die either... I don't want to cause more pain than I already have."* His eyes were shut, as I stood up and picked him up.

He hasn't caused me any pain.

'He feels responsible." Xena whimpered, wanting to help him.

I wanted to help him, but at this point. I don't know how I'm supposed to help him. Everytime I try to help him, it just makes everything worse.

"You are not a bother to me... You will not die. I will not die... You are not a pain to me. You will never be a pain. I want to protect you, I want to love you. I want to be everything for you and give you a break from the pain you have had for such a long time." I told him soothingly, he struggled against me before I tightened my arms around him.

I sat down on the deck, holding him to me. He continued to fight me, as his body trembled in fear. I am not going to let him go.

"Please... Please let me go." He cried into my chest, tears streaming down his face, wetting the front of my shirt.

I closed my eyes as I began rocking us slowly. I had to close my eyes, because feeling him fight against me killed me inside. I just wanted things to be okay. With him. With us. With everything.

"I know that you don't want me to let you go... Please don't be scared of me... Please, I know I don't have any place to ask you for that... But please don't be scared of me. I would never hurt you or Max... I swear to you on The Moon Goddess that paired us together." I whimpered, holding him to my chest as I pressed my nose to his hair.

I inhaled his scent.

His scent that brought a sense of peace through my body. I have to believe everything is going to be just fine. I need to be positive.

"Everything will be fine. He just needs some time." Xena told me, even though I could tell that she didn't believe what she was telling me.

Seth clutched onto me as he refused to open his eyes. *"I don't want you to hurt me... I don't want to be hurt anymore. I can't handle anything else."* He pleaded with me, his body was slowly stilling in my arms. *"Promise me you won't hurt me... Promise me you will protect me... Promise me that I am yours..."*

I stopped rocking us as I looked down at him, my heart stopped for a brief moment. Just hearing the sadness and despair in his voice broke my heart even more. "I promise you I won't hurt you. I promise you I will protect you. I promise you that you are mine. I promise you the world... I promise that if you ask me for anything I will give you anything I can...

I promise to love you and protect you. I promise to help you through this tough time if you would let me... I promise you everything, my love... I promise you to protect your brother like he was my own. I promise you, I promise you, I promise you." I told him soothingly, my power flowing through his body giving him more strength.

Seth looked up at me, not saying anything as he studied my

73

features. I stood up, walking into the house. Alex was about to say something to us but decided against it, thank the Goddess. I didn't need to deal with him anymore. I licked my lips slightly as I brought us into my bedroom. Making sure to shut the door behind us, I walked over to the bed. I was about to place him on the bed before he shook his head no.

"Did he just tell us no?" Xena asked, staring at him with wide eyes.

He did. But I kind of like it.

"What do you mean no?" I asked, tilting my head at him.

It's kind of hot that he said no. I don't like hearing the word.

"Why are you putting me in here?" Seth asked, he still hasn't used his voice.

I couldn't help but smirk slightly as I looked down at him. My brother is going to come over here, and I know for sure. Seth has had enough excitement for one day.

"Maybe not." Xena said, as she was pacing around in my mind.

"I know my brother is going to be coming over here to check on me after the incident. And I am going to need to talk to him about some political stuff. And about security at our territory border. And I might get angry so I don't want to scare you even more." I informed, sitting on the bed with him in my arms.

He looked confused, but I thought that I was being pretty straight forward?

"But you're calm right now?" Seth asked, looking at the wall before stealing glimpses of me when he thought I wasn't looking.

I smiled softly, looking out of the glass wall to the woods. Oh how that easily changes.

"It's like the flip of a switch. We can be pretty crazy out of control." Xena started laughing in my mind.

But the thing is she isn't wrong.

"I have mastered controlling myself, so I'm not angry right now. I'm not showing you my anger because you are not the reason I am angry. I am angry at your father and angry that he thinks that he can try to come and take you away from me. I am angry at the actions of him hurting you. But you... My love. My Male.

I am not mad at you. I would never be mad at you, and I know you are in a delicate place right now. I don't want to add to that trauma and pain by showing you me getting angry." I smiled, looking at his face as he was practically sitting in my lap.

Which I'm okay with. "Would you like me to get you some food before Gray comes over?"

Seth shook his head no, he bit his bottom lip hard before looking at me .

"I want to be in there with you when you talk to your brother about my father... I know him... I can help you with his tactics to defend against his attacks." He told me, stress caused his body to tense.

I frowned, rubbing his back gently.

"He's pushing himself... I don't think it's a good idea." Xena said, her pacing was getting more rushed.

I don't think it's a good idea either. But if he thinks he's ready... I can't tell him no.

"You don't have to do this Seth... No one is expecting you to help us with your father. My general can handle planning for the upcoming battle... I can figure something out. You deserve your own time to heal, to grow away from him." I looked over his face, trying to read his features.

I kept him as close to me as possible. His body molded to me, as he looked to the woods.

If I tell him no then he'll think I'm trying to keep him sheltered. I want him to grow. I just don't know if he's ready. I don't know if I'm ready.

"I can't be afraid of him forever... I don't want to see him. But this is my problem that I brought to you. You wouldn't have even known about me... About what I went through if I didn't call out to you. I need to fix this issue. This is one thing that I can fix." Seth said frowning as he was starting to get lost in his thoughts.

I tilted my head, wanting to ask more questions but I didn't want to press the issue.

"You're so whipped for him. But I don't blame you, he's adorable." Xena told me, and it took everything in me not to laugh.

She was trying to taunt me and then immediately agreed that she was the same.

"I don't see this as your problem. I see this as my problem that I took to handle. I don't want you to think of anything right now, because you already have gone through so much. This is my problem now. This isn't yours. I made the decision to take you. I made the decision to find you. I made the choice to take you into my pack.

I don't regret a single thing. I would do it a thousand times, I would burn the world to the ground to find you. I wouldn't have stopped until I found you. When you are better, you can ask my brother. I had my pack search every country, every pack until I got you in my arms." I told him, frowning slightly as I looked down at his face.

I would have killed anyone and everyone to get him in my arms.

"Yeah!" Xena cheered in my mind.

"I think I can do this with you..." Seth said, his voice sounding unsure.

I couldn't help the smile that crossed my face. He was trusting me. Baby steps. Maybe everything will turn out okay.

"Tell me when you are ready for this to be over, and I will immediately bring you back here. You are in control of every-thing that happens. You decide when you are ready to leave your comfort zone. I am just here to make sure that everyone listens to you." I smiled, standing up with him in my arms.

He frowned slightly as I walked out of my bedroom. My office was down the hall, I walked to the office before heading straight to my desk.

He will sit in my chair this time.

My office was large, and dark, bookshelves lined the walls. Different books lined the shelves, along with various pictures of me and my younger siblings growing up. He watched everything that he passed before I gently placed him in my desk chair. One day I'll add our pictures up there.

Seth was about to protest before I shook my head no. "I don't want you to try and argue with me. I see us as equals... I don't see myself as higher than you just because I am the Alpha of the pack." I told him with a caring smile before Grayson walked into the office.

Grayson smiled kindly, bowing in respect. "Good afternoon Alphas." He smiled. Seth's eyes widened at his greeting.

CHAPTER
EIGHT

"**G**rayson... This is Seth Knight, my mate, therefore your Alpha. I assume you already know about the male that came here to try and take him back to Ireland." I said, standing beside Seth, but my eyes were on my brother.

I was hoping this subtle form of showing his power would help him.

"I heard from Madoc about him so yes. And I assumed since you were so bent out of shape on finding him that he was your mate. It's a pleasure to meet you Alpha Seth Knight. I'm Grayson Winters, Beta to Scarlett. And yes, I didn't hear about him until it was far too late. Did he say anything about why he was sent?" Grayson asked, sitting down in the chair in front of my large wooden desk.

Seth looked down at his hands, struggling to maintain eye contact with anyone. I mean he barely even made eye contact with me. But it was slowly getting better.

"I'm sure it will get easier for him over time." Xena told me, and I could sense she was trying to make me feel better.

But we needed to make him feel better. That's what's important.

"All he said was that he wanted Seth. I refused, I told him that he could leave or face me. He decided to continue to walk toward us. But he did this on purpose, he didn't fight. He didn't say anything, I think this was Pete's way of seeing how fast I lost control regarding Seth's condition and him being here.

I played right into his hands with that one, but I could sense the wolf's fear. He didn't want to do this, but my thing is. How would Pete know what happened? I could've sent him to prison. I could have sent him back to Ireland with a message. How could he have known I would kill him?" I asked, my mind racing to try and figure out every possibility.

Seth looked up at me, his cheeks turning pink before looking down at the desk. I looked at him, tilting my head slightly.

"What was that all about?" Xena asked.

All I had to say was I wanted to know too. All I know is that I messed up, I played into his hands. Just like he wanted me to.

"There are many possibilities..." Seth informed softly. I looked at Grayson now as he shrugged slightly.

Next time this happens, I need to be level headed. But when it comes to Seth... I'm not level headed. Goddess. I don't know what I'm supposed to do.

"Maybe he was betting on how everything used to be..." Grayson said, his eyes drifting down to Seth before up to me.

He was asking for permission to speak, so I nodded, silently answering his question. "How you used to lose it very easily... Maybe he was hoping that seeing Seth in his condition would make you so on edge that anything and everything could set you off.

I think he's grasping at straws, trying his best to get you on the edge of a cliff. He trespassed on your territory. If Pete tries to start a war because of you killing someone from his pack, then we will win. We are stronger, we have a better army. We have the better Alpha. There is nothing to worry about Scar..." Grayson said, smiling kindly as he tried to calm me down.

I didn't even know that he knew I was seconds away from marching into Ireland and killing Pete. All of my problems would be solved.

Seth tilted his head slightly, rubbing the back of his neck. *"I don't think that's what he wants. I think he wants to see if he can make you lose control. I think he wants to see if you would give up on me and Max and quickly give us back. He's testing your power... He's testing your strength. He is testing your love for me."* He explained, looking out the window.

A frown overtook his face as he refused to look at anyone.

What Seth is saying makes sense. If I gave up Seth now... He could turn that against me. Although I would never ever give up on Seth. But if I did, Pete could use that to try and paint me as a horrible Alpha who doesn't love her mate.

My body tensed as I closed my eyes. I inhaled sharply, biting my lip before I exhaled. And here is the moment that things change, and I have to prepare for war.

"I want the security around the border to Ireland doubled. I want to be prepared for anything that happens. And I want to know anything that happens, I want our spies in Ireland to report how frazzled Pete is getting with me not giving Max and Seth back." I informed, steadying my breath.

I felt Xena itching for control, her stress of needing to protect Seth, nearly outweighed mine. I gripped the large black leather chair as my claws started to come out.

"I want out!" Xena shouted at me, anger boiled through every inch of my body.

And I struggled to keep in control.

Grayson nodded. "Of course Alpha, is there anything else you would like before I go? I believe that you might've messaged

Madoc about meeting with the general? I could have him come here to meet you. Although I don't think that will be the greatest idea..." He spoke softly, standing up as he could sense my uneasiness.

I need to dismiss myself, I need to go for a run. And everything will be okay.

"I want Ireland to burn to the ground. I want to rule their pack, and kill whoever I have to. No one tests me, tests my power, tests my strength. No one will ever test my loyalty to my mate ever. I will kill whoever comes at me to show that I will not be messed with!" I growled, my body shaking with restraint. My anger fueled Xena and it was just making things worse.

"Pete will burn in hell for coming for me and thinking he could win!" I gripped the desk, before forcing myself to let it go, my eyes glowing brightly.

Xena was fighting for control, fighting harder than she's ever fought before.

"Scar... Breathe." Grayson spoke softly, his head bowed in surrender to his Alpha.

I snarled as my features changed, my power was soaking the air around us causing him to whimper. My vision started to blur, and if I didn't get a handle on myself. I was going to lose control completely.

"You will not tell me what to do! I don't care if this puts a target on my back. No one will come for me and survive. And especially no one will come for my mate and survive." I snarled, my body shaking as I held onto the desk now.

My claws came out as they scratched against my desk. Well looks like I'm going to need to buy a new one. "I will burn this world to the ground before someone thinks they can control me."

Grayson bowed his head in respect, subtly motioning towards Seth. Seeing that motion. Something clicked inside of me and Xena gave me back control.

I shook my head slightly before my eyes turned back to brown. He was whimpering in the chair, his knees hugged tightly to his chest as he had his eyes closed.

No no no. How reckless am I going to be!

"Don't hurt me... Don't hurt me, please... Please, I beg you... I didn't mean to disobey you! I wanted to protect my brother!" Seth whined to me, as I frowned.

I groaned silently, I'm going to make him reject me. And then my life will be over.

"Ah! Don't put that thought into my head!" Xena whined in my head.

I didn't want to think about it, but it's a possibility.

"You may leave us, Grayson... And do not breathe a word about this to anyone." I ordered, causing him to nod and quickly leave.

I got down on my knees in front of where Seth was sitting. I didn't mean to scare him, I wish I would've listened to my gut and made him stay in the bedroom.

"My love... You could've told me that this was getting too much for you... Can you open your eyes for me... Can you look at me? You are safe. You are not in Ireland anymore, no one is going to hurt you. Not me... Not anyone. I'm here now, nobody will mess with you anymore this I promise you. I promised you that you were safe. Do you not believe me?" I asked soothingly, wanting to comfort him but I didn't want to scare him further.

And it was a real possibility that by touching him, it could make things a million times worse.

Seth shook his head, before opening his eyes so he could look at me. *"Don't hurt me! Please!! I beg you! I will do anything you want!"* He cried to me, his voice still in my mind.

He fell out of my chair, before struggling to run off to hide. I watched him for a second before going after him quickly. I can't believe I did this again.

"Please Seth... Please let me explain!" I begged, when I touched his body.

The soft skin of his arm, I wished I was holding him. I accidentally transported us into my large shower. I cursed under my breath as he cowered against the shower wall. My chest felt tight as I watched him.

"Don't speak the words. Don't speak the words." Xena repeated in my mind.

And I found myself wishing for the same.

"I can't take it again. I can't get hurt again. I don't want to get hurt anymore. I just want to be safe." Seth whimpered, shaking his head slightly. *"I want to be alone please!!"*

I don't want to leave him when he's like this... He's terrified of me. My heart raced as my worst fears were coming true. My mate was scared of me.

I frowned, tears welling in my eyes as my heart ached. "I don't want to leave you like this. I don't want to leave you when you need me." I told him softly, my voice cracked as I sat in front of him.

I could hold him, everything would be okay. Maybe...

"I want you to leave me alone! You're just like him! You're going to hurt me like everyone else has! I can't be loved, no one can love me! I just need to be left alone! I want to be left alone!" Seth yelled at me.

My eyes widened at his volume. I nodded, standing up slowly. I wanted to tell him that I loved him, that I needed him. But I need to listen to him.

Xena was whimpering in the back of my mind. The pain of the possibility of rejection radiated through my entire body. I can't do this. But I have to.

I couldn't bring myself to say anything else as I opened the glass door of my shower and walked out slowly. He started sobbing as I left, his body shaking violently with his sobs. I looked at him one last time before walking out of the bathroom.

Everything in me wanted to go back in there and hold him. Hug him to my body, and make him realize that I love him. That everything was going to be okay because we had each other.

But he made it entirely sure that he wanted to be alone. And as much as I hated it, I had to listen to him. With Xena being quiet, I knew she knew that I was right.

When I made it out of the bedroom, I stumbled into the wall as my vision blurred. I growled as I struggled to get outside. I'm scared of what I might do if I don't get outside. Xena was starting to panic, my body felt too small.

The walls of my house felt like they were closing in. I feel like I was suffocating by the scent of my mate who doesn't want me. Alex was in the living room on the couch, he quickly stood up at seeing me.

"Scar..." He spoke softly.

Max looked up, before quickly heading off to his brother. I shook my head no, my eyes frequently changing from brown to purple and then back again. My vision went from color to black and white, and I knew this could get bad.

"No... No... Not this time." I was breathing heavily.

Alex walked over to me and my entire body flinched. I was backing towards the door before I opened it and ran out. The rain poured down and thunder struck as I quickly shifted into my wolf form and took off running into the woods.

If I run, maybe I will pass out. If I run long enough, maybe the pain will go away. Maybe I will figure out some way to fix everything. To heal him and make him realize that I loved him and that I just had a hard time showing it.

I needed him.

CHAPTER
NINE

D ays seem to drag on... It feels like an eternity since Seth asked me to leave him alone.

But in reality I know it was only a couple of days ago. I can't sleep, when I close my eyes, I'm haunted with dreams of my past. Of my father telling me that this was going to happen.

He told me that if I was Alpha... My mate wouldn't want me. He would be scared that I would hurt him, or he would hate that I was powerful. Maybe more powerful than him.

"He seemed so hopeful. He seemed willing to give us a shot, give this a shot." Xena whimpered.

She was taking this hard, I'm grateful she hasn't tried to take control. I sighed as I looked at the woods in front of me. When I wasn't home, I was here. Figuring out the new training center for my warriors.

I have known for a long time that we needed an extension, a better place to train. But I'm thinking that a new building is the best idea. The old one could be transformed into an orphanage where we can find better homes for children.

"So on no sleep, what are you planning on doing here Scar?" Alex questioned me, I sighed as I rolled my shoulders.

I mean he has a point, I can't do much. My entire body is screaming at me to get sleep. But the only thing I can manage is short power naps.

"I am planning my new training center. I think it will be a good new space for the place. They can run through the woods surrounding it. I think it will be nice." I explained, smiling softly at the drawing I had in front of me.

Before I frowned as I processed the image, my lines were shaky. The words I have written are barely readable.

I really hate not being able to sleep. I can't function. At least not anymore, I was too spoiled. I should've kept myself on the little sleep schedule I had when I was first Alpha. Xena snickered in the back of my mind. I'm sure she's thinking about the energy drinks, the sparing.

It was a sight to behold. I was a mess, and no one knew about it. Or if they knew, they were too scared to say anything about it. Perks to being the Alpha I guess. I shook my head, coming out of my thoughts as Alex came to stand in front of me.

"You can't keep doing this to yourself Scar. It's dangerous. You could really hurt yourself. Let me talk to Seth. Explain to him how much this distance between you guys is hurting you. I know he's feeling bad, he wants you with him. He's sad that all you do is cook them food and then you leave." Alex whimpered softly.

I knew he was just worried about me, but for some reason. His worry just made me angry.

I growled, slamming my sketchbook closed. Someone can decipher what I was trying to say.

"You can't push him into wanting me around. I did this. I knew I should've kept him in my bedroom, but he wanted to try. And I wasn't going to stop him. So no Alexander, you can't talk to him about this. I'm fine. I'm perfectly fine, I can handle this. The pain, the little sleep. I can take it. He needs his own time to heal." I snapped at him, standing up from my seat on the fallen tree.

It was old, maybe I'll have it taken to my house and I will have a bench made out of it. It seems historical almost, like I need to leave it be. Alex whimpered beside me.

"I don't like it when you call me by my full name! It makes me feel like I'm in trouble! And I don't like that feeling." He whined. "I'm just trying to help you both. It'll end up killing you both if you continue like this much longer!"

I sighed again, starting to head down to the lake. And of course, he followed right back. I needed my space, and I didn't want to hurt him.

"I know you care Alex. But I was just using your full name so you knew I was being serious. I don't want to hurt you, but if you continue like this. I might have to. Seth needs his space to heal, I feel bad that I made him snap like he did. I pushed him... Too much too fast. And I need you to realize, I'm doing this for him. All of his power was taken away from him. His choice. I'm giving his choice back to him." I tried to explain.

Is he listening? Probably not.

"I want to punch him in the face." Xena snarled, rolling her eyes as she laid down in the back of my mind.

Yeah... I'm about ready to punch him in the face too.

"So do I have this right? You are punishing yourself with solitude from your mate? Because you think distance will somehow help him get through his torment? Make that make sense to me. Because it sounds like you're being stupid." Alex taunted me, he was testing me.

Maybe I should just remind him how easily I can lose my cool.

I allowed Xena to take some control, my eyes glowing purple.

"My my my Alex. Taunting me? You really think that's the best idea?" I asked, narrowing my eyes at him.

My skin felt like it was vibrating with the need to punch him. To inflict this torment I'm feeling inside on another living soul. That makes me bad, but in this moment. This pain needed an outlet, or it would swallow me whole.

"Use it for a reason. Just like when we were younger. Use your anger to keep yourself as Alpha." Xena reminded me.

As if I needed reminding. I'm not going to just attack someone for looking at me, no matter how much I might want to some days.

"You and Seth are a lot alike. Taunting seems to work well for the both of you. It makes you have to make a move. I know how to play you Scarlett. You may be the Alpha but to me you're an open book. One I have read and analyzed before. I know you woman, I know how to push you." Alex growled, a hint of playfulness in his voice.

He stepped in front of me, his face an inch from mine. I glared, my body tensing in preparation for this fight.

I couldn't help but crack my neck as I kept my eyes locked on his. He thinks he knows me? He thinks he even knows an inch of me? Yeah. The only thing he knows is the pathetic child I used to be. The one who needed someone, I don't need anyone.

Anyone... But *him*. My heart ached at the thought of not being with my mate. He could easily choose to reject me. And those words would absolutely kill me. I'm not prepared for it. And I'm begging the Moon Goddess to allow me to keep my blessing.

"You think you know me Alex? I was a child when you and I were friends. I grew, I've learned. I'm completely different than I was then. You don't know me. You most certainly don't know him. Trauma makes a person different. And he is allowed to take the time he needs to heal from what he needs to. Neither you nor I will force him to make a choice before he's ready. Now. This is your only warning. Get out of my face before I put you in your place." I snapped at him, my voice dripping in the anger I felt.

Xena was prepared, she always was for a fight.

Alex actually had the audacity to smirk at me. "What are you going to do about it? The Scar I used to know wouldn't have let me get in her face. She would've already had me on the ground. So maybe you've grown and changed and learned. But during all of that. Somewhere along the way, you lost your edge. You became soft." He told me, and I lost it.

I grabbed him by the neck, before I threw him to the ground. He landed with a groan as I walked over to him and stood above him.

"Me? Soft? You're going to see that I'm anything but soft." I snarled, leaning down to punch him as hard as I could in the face.

I didn't want to kill him, but I was the Alpha. This level of disrespect he has for me won't be tolerated.

I backed away from him, allowing him to stand up. I'm not weak, I won't fight someone who isn't prepared for a battle. "As an Alpha you learn when to show your strength and when to show mercy. You are my friend Alexander, I allow you to do much more than anyone else." I sighed, this fight was going to be far too easy.

"You allow me cause you like me. You want me. You don't want him, admit it." Alex taunts, and my growl was loud causing it to vibrate through the woods around us.

His eyes widen as I advance on him, throwing another punch to his stupid face. I can't kill him.

"You could." Xena grinned.

He's my mate's best friend. I can't kill him no matter how much I want to.

My vision was turning red, black, and white. All I saw was Alex fall to the ground and me climbing on top of him. Hit after hit after hit. I felt his bones cracking under my fist, his blood and my blood splattered across my skin.

"He's mine! He's mine! He's all I want! You don't get it. The pain!" I scream at him, letting out all of my anger.

At him. At not being able to hold Seth to tell him everything was going to be okay. At not being able to sleep. At the males in this world that wanted to kill me. At everything.

"I want him more than the air that I breathe. But I can't force a decision on him that he doesn't want. I had that on me before, and I won't let that happen to my other half!" I yelled, but when I went to hit him again.

I felt arms wrap around me, they struggled to haul me away from Alex's barely conscious body.

"Scar stop! Calm down!!" Grayson grunted, his arms tightening around me.

My body stiffened, Xena was angry. I was angry. But not angry enough to ever hurt my twin. I stopped moving, but Gray still held me. He was scared to let me go, probably thinking I was going to kill Alex.

And a huge part of me wanted to kill him. He brought anxiety to my mate, and I wanted to calm Seth. But if I killed his friend, it would make things worse between us.

"Brother... I am in control." I told him, breathing out.

Inhaling as I tried my best to get my heart to stop racing. He reluctantly let me go, but he didn't step away from me yet. I am in control.

"Yeah because we can't kill him." Xena huffed, she was annoyed with the situation.

Well so was I. Maybe finding someone to spar with would be a good idea. Grayson wrapped his arms around me again, almost as if he knew what I was thinking. Heck. He probably did know what I was thinking.

"You're going to go on a nice long. LONG. Run to calm yourself down. Because I swear if you do go and try and spar. I will send everyone home. I don't know what's going on. But you don't need to be taking it out on people who don't deserve it." Gray whimpered, reluctantly letting me go.

I had to turn around slowly, he was scared of me... I bit my bottom lip hard.

"Gray... Do you think I'm going to hurt you?" I asked softly, I don't think I am prepared to hear this response.

He frowned looking down at his feet.

"I don't think you're going to hurt me. But you in this state scares me. It reminds me of when we were younger. You fought a lot, you barely slept. You barely ate. What is making you feel this way?" Grayson asked, rubbing the back of his neck slightly.

I hated the smell of anxiety, and I hate that I'm the reason for his anxiety even more. I couldn't bring myself to look at him.

My heart was breaking even thinking about speaking the words. My mate doesn't love me. My mate doesn't want me. And it's breaking my heart. Just the thought of him rejecting me is eating me up on the inside. I'm scared if he speaks the words of rejection I will actually die.

I shifted my weight from one foot to the other. "I... Um... Seth is not in good shape. Mentally or physically..." I told him, swallowing thickly as I spared a glance at him.

I saw worry and fear written across his face. And I wish I could take that away from him.

"You guys seemed okay when I spoke to you the other day..." He trailed off, looking down at Alex before back at me. "Did he...?"

I sighed. "No... It's not Alex. Seth is just dealing with a lot right now. You know, people deal with trauma in different ways. I don't know what he went through, I just know that it's a lot. He doesn't want me around. I'm not handling it well, but I'm okay. I'm fine. I can handle it. Everything will be okay brother. It has to be." I told him, trying my best to sound positive.

But with one look at my brother. I knew he didn't believe me. And I don't blame him, especially with my panic attack that he saw. I frown as I looked at Alex, I walked over to him and gently picked him up into my arms. Well I guess this isn't the first or the last time the doctors will see someone that I beat up.

This is going to be a funny conversation. Grayson just looked at me as I was still staring down at Alex.

"You don't have to be okay... That's a lot to handle at one time Scar... Let me take him to the doctor while you go for a run or a swim. The woods have always brought you comfort and peace. You don't have to handle this all alone. I'm not a kid. I can help you." Grayson told me, gently taking Alex away from me.

I nodded, looking down. Just seeing his worry on his face, it will make me cry.

"Thank you twin brother... I will go for a run. I need to clear my head. I can't think straight. But I promise I'm gonna be okay. I know you aren't a kid, but no matter how old we get. I'll always see my younger twin that I need to protect." I teased softly, giving him a smile.

It was small, but I was hoping it gave him some relief. He chuckled, shaking his head slightly.

"You are like twenty seconds older than me." He rolled his eyes, causing me to laugh softly.

He hated being the younger one. I walked away, before giving him one last look.

"Careful brother. You sound like you might want to be the older one. And then you would be the Alpha. I thought you didn't want to provide heirs?" I teased him, but his eyes widened at my words.

"You are the best Alpha. For our pack and for the entire world. You handle it wonderfully, I wouldn't be able to do it. I don't want to do it. Just hearing you try to explain Alpha meetings to me makes me very confused. So no thank you, and children are a no for me." Grayson laughed, starting to walk away. "I prefer to be a bachelor! Everybody loves the hot twin of the Alpha they can't touch!"

I laughed, before I started to jog. I don't know why I ever thought I couldn't go to my brother with this. I didn't want to be the weak one, that needed to be comforted by her twin. But no matter what he always finds a way to put a smile on my face. And I don't know if he knows how thankful I am for him and his ability to calm me down.

I started to pick up pace, before allowing Xena her freedom to shift. She growled and this time... I allowed myself to drift into that darkness. Maybe the one thing that would give me peace in these ever stressing times.

I welcome the darkness. And pray that one day soon my mate will make his decision. Because if I continue to overthink, I'm gonna snap.

CHAPTER
TEN

The next few days were progressively getting harder and harder. I couldn't sit still, my house smelled like Seth.

I loved his scent, but knowing that I couldn't hold him. Couldn't see him, it nearly killed me inside. Correction, it was slowly killing me.

Each day I woke up, I died a little more inside.

I watched the storm brew outside as I was cooking everyone their dinner. It's what I did everyday, made sure they had food and then I left. I wanted to care for Seth, without pushing my luck. Xena wasn't talking to me right now, she was mad. And I didn't blame her.

"I could talk to him..." Alex offered, causing me to scoff.

I rolled my eyes and forced a smile. I appreciate his kindness, his worry. But he needs his space, no matter how much I hated it.

"I appreciate that, but no. He wants his space, no matter how much it hurts me. I need to give him that space." I frowned, there were dark bags under my eyes.

My skin was pale, my body ached as I placed the bowl of cut-up fruit in front of him. Alex frowned at me, I don't think I want to hear what he has to say right now. I already feel bad enough.

"So you barely sleep, and you barely eat. You spend all of your hours either at the packhouse or outside doing Goddess only knows what. You need to continue to take care of yourself, Scar. Your pack needs you." Alex frowned as I began to set the table.

I shrugged slightly as I placed bowls for the spaghetti I made them.

My pack needs me? That makes Xena stir. It feels like he's trying to say I'm not taking care of them. Everything I do is for them.

"I take care of my pack. That's what I do at the packhouse. I plan for the upcoming war against Ireland. I am constantly doing stuff for my pack because they come first. They have to always come first. You don't have to worry about my pack. Everyone is safe, everyone will continue to be safe." I assured, placing the noodles and sauce on the table.

I turned to Alex as I shrugged off my hoodie.

The wind, the rain, the power of the storm. It will feel nice against my bare skin. I'll let Xena out to run for a while, we'll check on the border security. And maybe go sleep at the packhouse, cause I don't think I can stand to sleep in this house alone again.

"Everyone will continue to be safe besides you." Alex sighed.

Is he finally realizing that I'm not going to change my mind? Alpha's are known to be stubborn. And well, because I'm a female. I had to be extra stubborn.

"I am a powerful shadow wolf. I will be fine, thanks for caring Alex. I hope you guys have a good dinner." I smiled sadly as I went to the back door.

I opened it, closing my eyes for a second as the cool evening air hit my bare skin. I was in very ripped jeans and a black tank top. Because it's the easiest thing to shift through.

I sighed as I heard Seth and Max walking into the dining room. I knew that it was then that I had to leave. I quickly shut the back door before jogging down the steps of my deck. Xena whined in my mind, I knew she wanted to go back there. But I couldn't. He asked for space, and I'm giving him his space.

No matter how much it hurts me.

With tired feet, I forced myself to take myself away from the place I wanted to be most. I ran now, running to the place where I felt the most safe. The one place I knew I could calm down. I went to the water, my eyes tearing up.

Goddess I hated how much I was crying lately. I never cried this much before Seth. I didn't think I would cry this much finding the one person who was supposed to love me.

"Why me?" I called out to the woods around me.

I knew no one would answer me. I stopped moving when I got to the river that was near my house.

"I do EVERYTHING!" I yelled, pointing at the full moon. "I do everything you ask for! I never complain! I never question what you want! I never disobey you! I killed my father, and my older sister when I could've taken my siblings away from all of this! I could've taken Seth and Max away from all of this!"

I continued to yell my frustrations, knowing it wouldn't help anything in the long run. It would help only slightly. And only for a little while.

"I always thought about my mate... I always thought when he came into my life. Everything would be better. And it's been a little over a week, and my heart feels broken." I sat down on the ground, crossing my legs as I covered my face.

I've never felt this alone in my entire life.

"I feel alone, I don't think I've ever felt so alone. I knew that relationships were hard... I know that in some cases you allow wolves to reject their mates. But please... Please if you're listening to me. Please don't let him reject me. I know I have no room to ask for something like that. Because I know he went through more things than I know.

But I need him. I won't be able to do this without him." I sniffled, tears slowly falling down my face.

I finally looked to the moon again, my eyes drifting down to the water below. I used to find this peaceful, talking to the moon Goddess like she's actually listening to me. I used to think that she was. But now... I just feel lost and abandoned. "I just want to help him, and I don't know how to. Am I being pushy and overbearing?"

I hugged my knees to my chest, closing my eyes now. "You're the only friend I have... Everyone else hates me for what I've done, but I would do it again for you. Because I trust that you have my best interest at heart." I bit my bottom lip, my body tensed as I opened my eyes.

I feel someone... They are near.

Xena stirred in my mind, but other than that. She didn't say anything... I don't like the silence.

I heard something around me, I jumped up to my feet as fast as I could. "This is my private space. Who are you and what are you doing here!" I growled out, my eyes glowed purple as I scanned my horizon.

I stopped, narrowing my eyes at a large Rowan tree. And then his scent hit me like a ton of bricks. It's Seth...

"Seth..." I spoke softly, I couldn't hide the hurt in my voice.

It pained me to not be able to spend time with him. I saw a frown on his face when he walked out from behind the tree. Seth rubbed the back of his neck as he looked at the full moon. Why does he seem nervous? It's like he's acting like I followed him out here.

I've been giving him space. Does he want this space to himself now too? I don't want to give it up, but I would if it gave him comfort.

"That seems like a bit of a harsh welcome..." Seth told me jokingly, I wonder when he would try to talk to me, using his voice.

I couldn't help but chuckle at that. I didn't mean for it to be harsh, I just wasn't expecting him to follow me.

"He's trying to tease! This is a good thing!" Xena said, and just at his nearness.

She was perking up. I don't need her getting my hopes up.

"It wasn't intended to be harsh. I just figured you would still be eating dinner." I explained with a shrug, before sitting back in my spot.

I kept my eyes on the water in front of me, wanting to make him more comfortable. I knew if I continued to look at him, I wouldn't be able to control myself and I would hug him to me and never let go.

"I was... But I wanted to come and see you. You haven't been eating with us... You just make our food and then you leave and don't return. I only see you as you leave..." Seth walked closer to me, standing beside me now.

I noticed he had gained some weight back. At least he must be eating. That's a good thing. He sat down beside me, looking at the moon.

"Yes... It's my responsibility to care for you. Even if you would like your space to heal and gain your own comfort in this new place. I overstepped and was overbearing, I'm sorry. I just wanted to help you heal... And I wanted you to be okay with me." I spoke softly, my tired eyes were on my knees.

Could I show him this weakness? This exhaustion I felt. I knew my pack saw it slowly getting worse. But they never asked about it. He stole a glimpse at me, tilting his head slightly.

"You weren't overbearing... You weren't too much... I just haven't felt love since I was a young child. I didn't understand how someone could love me so much and not expect anything in return. It was some-

thing I have been craving for a very long time, I cried out to you every chance I got.

I didn't have much strength. I mean I still don't, but it's slowly getting better. I gave everything I had to my brother because I knew even if I died... Something in me told me that you would still protect my brother." Seth tried to explain, his cheeks turning pink with his frustration.

I looked at him, looking into his eyes as I studied his features. Just hearing his pained voice makes my body ache.

"You didn't tell me where you were... You just told me that you were in danger and then continued to cry out to me. I'm not mad of course, I just would've saved you a lot faster if I knew where you were. I promise you that Max will have everything he ever wants or needs. He is a part of the Alpha's family after all.

And while my brother is the only other family in the country right now... Everyone will know that Max is family. And everyone will know that you, no matter what you decide, are a part of my family as well. So you will not be bothered." I smiled tiredly before looking at the moon again.

He looked at my pale hands, noting the slight tremble in them. I didn't even notice they were shaking, I just thought that was my imagination. He frowned before he gently took my right hand in his.

Just feeling his skin touch mine, sent energy shooting through my body. I inhaled softly, I struggled with controlling myself. I can't hold him. But I can take this, and hold his hand. I looked down at our joined hands before I looked into his eyes. This is happening.

Xena practically squealed in the back of my mind. I felt her start to get more energy, and I was just hoping she didn't force a shift right now.

"I didn't mean to hurt you so badly... I couldn't handle everything. Your love... The fact that you were wanting to care for me and take

care of me. The way your eyes lit up when you looked at me like I was the only thing in the world that mattered to you..." His voice was soft in my mind as he intertwined our fingers. *"I feel and felt pathetic... I was barely able to talk. I couldn't and still can't speak... I didn't want you to get so tired of me that you gave me back.'*

Seth closed his eyes, listening to the sounds of the woods around us and the water in front of us. I gently squeezed his hand, allowing my power to flood into his body. Since I was so tired, I knew it wasn't much. But I just wanted to give him some comfort.

"I can't believe he thinks we would give him back." Xena growled with frustration.

People deal with trauma in different ways.

"I would've never given you back... I want to care for you and take care of you. My eyes lit up when I looked at you because you are the only thing in the world that matters to me. I love my siblings... I love my pack... But before I met you, I couldn't feel anything. I felt numb and like I was going through life without a purpose.

And then one night... I heard your voice. I knew you were in trouble and every time I went to try and connect more with you. Everything would go black and I would lose you. That first night I heard you, it sparked something inside of me. And I knew it would never die down until I finally had you in my arms... Until I finally had you safe." I said with a small smile, I couldn't take my eyes off of him.

His skin heated with my close proximity, the soft flush of his cheeks. Everything about him was absolutely adorable. He gulped, his adam's apple moving with the motion.

And now that I got to be this close with him again. I don't think I could ever keep myself away.

"Nope! Because he's mine. And you got to be a moron once, and

now he's holding our hand. So this is happening! Get on board baby!"
Xena howled with excitement.

I tried my best not to giggle because of her.

"I tried so hard to connect with you... To tell you about where I was. But you felt the magic in that cell. It felt like if I spoke the word Ireland, that it was just going to kill me. Maybe that's why I can't talk..." Seth said, shrugging slightly.

He looked at me, his eyes roaming over my face before they landed on my lips. My heart started to race as I watched him look at my lips. Oh Goddess. This is gonna happen. He's gonna kiss me. I'm freaking out.

"Shut up and stop panicking! You're Alpha Scarlett Winters! You are an adult woman. You've got to put your big girl pants on! Unless you like it when he takes control?" Xena teased me, and my cheeks heated at the words.

"Haha you like to be dominated!" Xena taunted. *"I don't blame you. Goddess that's gonna be the hottest thing I ever did see."* She practically sighed at the thought.

And it's taking all of my self control to not flush like I'm a teenager. I absentmindedly licked my lips as I watched him watch my lips.

His cheeks burned red before he looked back up into my eyes.

"Scar... I..." Seth started, his mind stalling as he looked back to my lips.

My heart sank, please don't let him push me away again. I can't take it. I won't survive.

CHAPTER
ELEVEN

My heart was beating rapidly as I watched his eyes intently. My breathing was slowing down as my body froze with anticipation of his next move.

He looked back up to my eyes, a small smile spread across my lips. This is actually happening! Yay!

"What do you want..." Seth spoke softly, he shifted his body closer to mine so our legs were touching.

And just with that small touch, my entire body jumped into overdrive. *"Because I want a lot of different things..."*

My cheeks burned red as I looked at his lips. Should I make the first move? "I... I want so many things... I want you to kiss me. But I don't want to pressure you. I don't want you to kiss me because I want you to kiss me. I want you to kiss me out of your own free will." I said, my voice a whisper.

He smirked slightly, biting his bottom lip. I felt like my entire body was shaking, but not out of anxiety. But excitement.

Seth took his hands and cupped my face gently. My eyes started to glow purple, Xena showing her power.

"I have been dreaming about this for a long while... I remember

hearing about you right before my father had me imprisoned. This fourteen year old powerful she-wolf killed her father and her older sister to take over her pack... Who knew ten years later we would be sitting here..." He spoke to me, his thumbs rubbing over my cheeks gently.

I couldn't bring myself to say anything, I just stared at him in shock.

The rain started to fall, pouring down around us. My hair darkened as I kept my eyes on him. "I always believed I would find you..." I spoke softly, looking at his eyes before his lips.

Xena was sitting on edge waiting for it to happen.

"This needs to happen!" Xena howled with pure excitement.

"Good... Because I never stopped praying for this hot Alpha Female to save me..." Seth smiled at me, before leaning closer and kissing me on the lips.

My eyes widened, before they shut and I leaned into the kiss. Power from our bond shot through each other's body as he slid his tongue across my lips. And if I thought I felt alive before, that doesn't even compare to what I feel at this moment.

I opened my mouth, allowing him to slide his tongue into my mouth and explore it. I moaned at the feeling of his tongue dancing with mine.

I moved closer, wrapping my arms around his back gently before straddling him. He wrapped his arms around me, before changing his mind and placing his hands firmly on my hips.

Seth broke away from the kiss, panting as he nipped at my bottom plump lip. I growled in approval causing him to chuckle.

"That was... Incredible..." He licked his lips slowly, his eyes trained on mine. *"I want this... It might take me a little bit to under-stand what I'm supposed to do as a mate. But I want this... I want you. I'm sorry I freaked out... I should've talked to you. I was having a really bad flashback and I couldn't take everything..."*

I smiled lovingly at him, cupping his cheeks gently. "It's

something that we can learn together... I don't know what you've heard about me... But I am not the most loving person. And there is a reason for that." I said softly, my eyes back to their regular brown.

The rain continued to pour around us, causing Seth to shiver. I felt hot, so hot. I barely even felt the rain. "We should get you back to the house."

He couldn't stop himself, he snuggled against my warm chest. *"How are you still so warm?"* Seth asked, I smiled at him.

That is a story for another time.

"I can explain everything when we get you changed." I told him, reluctantly standing up before helping him to his feet.

Seth tilted his head slightly, he was confused. Don't ask the question I think he wants to ask.

"He's going to ask." Xena snickered in the back of my mind.

I knew she always found it funny that we couldn't transport.

"Can't you just transport us to the house?" He asked, his eyes roaming over my soaked body.

My cheeks burned red with embarrassment. This is going to be just great.

"I... Can't... Not right now, maybe I can transport us around soon." I informed, gently taking his hand as I led him back to our house.

Seth squeezed my hand, maybe he understands? Hopefully he understands.

"What do you mean?" Seth asked, as his eyes were on me.

He kept pace beside me as we walked down the path. I sighed, frowning slightly. I'm a bit on the out of control side.

"It's a long story... A long complicated story. I will tell you everything. I just don't think you're ready for it right now." I explained, bringing him closer to me to try and warm him up.

His cheeks burned red at the closeness. I wrapped my arm around his waist, his black shirt clung to his thin body.

Even thin... He's still the hottest person I've ever seen.

"I still don't understand how you're so hot." Seth told me, as I grinned at him.

His eyes widened as he looked at me. It's cute how embarrassed he gets. *"I... Um... I meant that in your body temperature. But you are hot too..."*

I giggled, pointing to the house that came into view. "I will talk about everything once we get you warmed up. And thank you my love. I think you're hot too." I grinned, picking up my pace as I brought him to the door that led to our bedroom.

If he stays cold and shivering for too long, he'll get sick. And I don't want that.

"I thought of everything to make things easier." I smiled, before opening the door for him and letting him go in first. " Would you like me to leave the room while you get changed?"

Seth walked into the massive bedroom, before shaking his head no. I don't want to push it.

"You can stay... It's alright..." Seth told me, his cheeks were pink, his lips were turning blue from the cold.

I frowned as I looked at him. Shouldn't he be much warmer?

"I would think so?" Xena whimpered, and I knew she was worried.

"How is your healing coming along? Why are you still so cold?" I asked, my eyes studying his entire body.

He struggled with stripping off his soaking wet clothes. I quickly shut the door before rushing over to help him. My skin was warm as it brushed over the pale skin on his torso. His body instinctively leaned into my warm touch. He's ice cold.

"I don't know why I'm so cold. I think it could be just because I don't weigh enough." He said with a soft shrug, sitting on the bed so I could lift the wet shirt off of his body.

I looked directly at his eyes, not wanting to make him feel uncomfortable.

"I hope you know that I didn't leave the house because of you... I didn't trust myself to stay here without being overbearing towards you. I didn't think that I could stay here and not constantly check on you or want to take care of you." I tried to explain as I got down on my knees in front of him.

He struggled slightly as he lifted his thin hips up so that I could shimmy his pants off of him.

I guess it was kind of about him. I couldn't smell his scent and not feel pain about my mate not wanting me. But I'm not telling him that.

"I still don't know why an Alpha wants to take care of me. Shouldn't I be taking care of you?" Seth asked, as he tilted his head slightly.

I smirked up at him as I saw he didn't have any boxers on. Okay so he's getting braver.

"Or he just doesn't like the feel of clothes since he was in his wolf form for so long. But I likey the less clothing." Xena offered.

I tried my best not to snort at that.

"I enjoy caring for you. So no, no you shouldn't be taking care of me. I want to take care of you, I enjoy it. I love taking care of the people that I love. I mean I think I'm pretty good at it, especially since I've been doing this since I was a young child." I smiled at him as I stood to my feet.

I was always super confident, so I stripped myself of my clothes. Leaving them on the floor by the pile of his clothes. I'll deal with that later.

I walked over to the other side of the bed and climbed into it. Seth turned around on the bed so he could face me, his movements were slow. Maybe the cold was getting to him?

I slowly moved closer to him, allowing our bare skin to touch. I immediately felt warmth flood through my body, and I wondered if he felt the same.

His cheeks burned red as he continuously eyed my bare body. He swallowed thickly as he studied me.

It was super slow, like he wanted to memorize my curves, my tan perfect skin, my patch tattoos that were scattered along my body. His eyes continued to go up, to my breasts, a smile crossed his face as he saw the tattoo in between them. My first tattoo. My most important.

"S.K..." Seth said softly, without thinking about it he ran his finger along the delicate cursive letters. *"You marked yourself... Even when I wasn't here... You put a claim on yourself... My initials."*

My cheeks burned red again as my skin heated even more under his touch. I couldn't help but bite my bottom lip as I looked into his eyes. "I had these dreams when I was a child, they were super weird. But I would always see S.K. everywhere in them. So when I became the Alpha of my pack, one of the first things that I did was get it tattooed." I explained, smiling as he finally looked at me.

Or well my face at least.

Seth growled suddenly, his eyes turning a dull red. He bared his fangs, showing his disliking towards someone looking at me naked. I took his hands in mine, gently squeezing them. He whimpered suddenly, his eyes shifting back to brown. I was confused at the drastic change and I wanted to know why he flipped so easily.

"Hey... Hey... Look at me. You're okay... You're okay. You don't have to worry about any guy seeing me naked. One of my childhood friends did, she was interested in tattooing so I told her I would let her try on me." I looked between his eyes, trying to calm him down.

Seth's body started to shake, before he grabbed onto me and hugged me tightly. Did I hurt his feelings? I don't know what I'm doing wrong.

TWELVE

"*I don't know how to express to you how much it means to me that you went through such great lengths to stay faithful.*" Seth practically whispered to me, holding himself against me.

I pulled him away slightly, just to look him in the face. He is the thing that means the most to me. That first moment I laid eyes on him, I knew he was mine.

"I would like to tell you about how I came to be in the Alpha position if you are ready to hear about it... I know that me killing in front of you scared you, I just want you to know how I came to be who I am." I told him, moving closer to him so I could keep my arms wrapped around him.

He studied my face, before looking into my eyes. I want him to know me, the real me. Since this is going to happen.

"*You don't have to tell me if you don't want to...*" Seth told me softly, but I shook my head no.

I leaned forward and kissed his lips once. His cheeks heated up again almost instantly. I love how easily he blushes.

"*It is absolutely adorable and I need more of it.*" Xena howled with joy.

I loved that this is us now.

"This whole thing started before I was born, a prophecy started I think about a month before I was born. It stated.

"The second born of the line of Winters shall be the heart of the pack. And will be the first female shadow wolf in hundreds of years. Her strength will be unmatched as she breathes new life into the land"

I think as people continued to tell others about the prophecy, it kind of got shortened and changed a little bit. But you get the jist of what it's about. I am the second born of the bloodline. My sister Hayley was the first born, everybody thought that she would be the Alpha. But when me and Grayson came around..." I breathed in deeply, biting my lip slightly before I willed myself to continue.

It's going to be okay. He needs to know this, even if it scares him more. This is what made me into who I am.

"He wasn't doing very well. Apparently when we were born, I somehow breathed life back into him? They put us together in a plastic little crib, and when I touched him a bright purple wave of power washed through the land. Apparently everybody started to feel stronger. So everybody started saying how they wanted me as the Alpha instead of Hayley.

This angered my dad, angered Hayley... He did everything in his power to see if he could take my power away from me and give it to my oldest sister. After a year, my mom got pregnant with my sister. And things continued to get worse from there.

When I was four... My mom left. She couldn't handle the abuse from my dad, she couldn't handle watching him treat us the way he did. So I became a mom at four. Once my mom left, it's like it made my dad lose his mind.

Everything became so much worse, the abuse. Both physical and mental... The neglect. I did everything I could to make sure my siblings were safe. I took care of them, I stole food. I took the abuse as much as I could handle. I was put into the hospital several times, I slipped into a coma twice." I paused, closing my eyes for a second.

Maybe I was waiting for him to tell me to stop. Maybe it was too hard for me to talk about. But I needed him to know that he could trust me.

"And each time... The land around me started to run into chaos. There were heavy storms, plants and crops died. The sun didn't come out... It was like the land knew I wasn't healing and needed as much power as I could get.

When I woke up the second time, I was eight years old, everything calmed down. I first shifted into my wolf form, her name is Xena by the way, when I was eight. Most wolves don't shift until they are fourteen. I didn't have any choice because he was going to kill my little sister Stormy." I wiped my cheeks, tears were slowly starting to fall down my face.

Seth frowned, wrapping my legs around his waist and pulling me into his lap. My entire body lit alive at the small action. I could get used to this.

I sniffled as my eyes were slowly turning purple. Xena shivered, hating that I was bringing this up. "I came home from the hospital, and I saw Gray on the ground... He was barely alive. And my dad had Stormy pinned to the wall by her throat. She was trying so hard to fight back, but she was so small. She wasn't nearly as strong as our dad. Before I knew it, I shifted and I took him to the ground and I put him in the hospital where he belonged. Hayley was laughing at us, so I decided to put her in the hospital too.

I moved Grayson, Stormy, and I to a small cabin into the woods far away from the city. But of course my dad always found a way to abuse us still. Thankfully Stormy and Grayson weren't on his mind. He was hellbent on killing me..." I stopped, breathing deeply.

Seth tightened his hold on me. I can't cry. I've cried enough over this.

"By the time I was fourteen, I knew I had to kill him. I didn't know what to expect after, but I couldn't let it go on anymore. One night I told Gray to keep an eye on Stormy... Because I was going to make everything better.

I marched over to where my father and my sister were living, and since I have the power of shadows. I was silent when I went in. I went to Hayley's room and I slit her neck in her sleep. And after I knew she was dead, I went outside. I knew that I couldn't stop there..." I inhaled slowly, tears continuing to fall.

My voice cracked, this was the trauma that led to the build of the Ruthless Queen. He rubbed my back gently, kissing random spots of bare skin to try and comfort me.

I felt whole at this moment. My mate was holding me, and I felt like I belonged. What could be better than this? Even if I was exposing a lot of my dark past.

"I confronted my dad... I knew he would never change. I don't think he could ever truly change. I challenged him to the Alpha position, and of course he couldn't say no. It was a brutal match, but I was stronger. I was smarter, he let his anger blind him. And I had my mind on protecting my little siblings.

"*I can't wait to rip your throat out.*" He told me... And I could see that his plan was to burn me and my siblings alive. He shifted, his shift was slow. Mine was fast, I shifted and before he could finish his shift I disappeared. And I reappeared by him, I sunk my teeth into his neck and ripped out his throat.

His body dropped, and that was when I noticed that a lot of my pack was there watching the fight. They said it was disrespectful and disobedient that I killed my father and older sister. The ones who used to want me as the Alpha, showed me that they didn't believe in me at that moment." I scoffed, rolling my eyes.

I thought I got over it. But I guess I didn't. I wish my pack trusted me and gave me strength in that moment.

"Wolves challenged me for the position that I earned by myself. They decided to fight me, and I killed them too. After what felt like hours... I finally showed my pack that I was the Alpha and nothing would be changing that. They outcasted me mostly, they didn't want me to be a part of anything.

They let my siblings do whatever they wanted, even though Grayson pretty much stuck by my side while Stormy went off and did whatever she wanted to do. They would whisper about my ruthlessness... My anger... My mercilessness. No matter what I did, they didn't support my decisions until I started to force Alpha males to submit to me.

When they realized that a teenager was running the pack better than any adult male could. They started to call me The Ruthless Queen... They called me coldhearted. They submitted to me through fear of dying. And I didn't care, because this is the pack that let my father abuse us for years.

They didn't care, they just wanted to submit to their alpha and not think twice. Well now here I am, I process things a lot faster than someone should. I knew that guy that was coming for you wasn't going to fight me because he knew he was going to die... I have the world scared of me. Because they think I'm a wildcard, and to be fair... I can be one.

But throughout my whole story... Gray and Stormy... They were always safe. They were always well taken care of. They were always protected. Because I did all of it, to protect the ones I love. I wanted to keep them safe, just like I want to keep you safe. You are safe with me my love... I would never hurt you.

And I don't want you to be scared of me. I just want you to know that you are my top priority... And that won't change... I will protect you from your dad..." I told him, rubbing the back of my neck slightly.

Seth's eyes were slightly wide as he listened to what I was telling him. Crap crap crap. It was too much at once. I should've just stuck with the highlights or whatever.

"Wait wait give him trust! I think he's good!" Xena said, watching with a nervous excitement.

Please please be good.

"I'm so sorry... I know that is such a stupid thing to say. But I am so sorry that you had to go through all of that... I don't know how you handled it. And I'm sorry myself... I... I am trying my best to know that I am safe. I... I just went through a lot with my father." Seth forced an uneasy smile as I tilted my head at him.

Is he going to tell me what he went through?

THIRTEEN

"We don't have to talk about your dad if you don't want to. I didn't tell you about my story to make you tell me yours. I just thought that it was going to bring you some comfort knowing that I wasn't going to hurt you. And that all the stories that people say about me are not true." I spoke softly, not wanting to pressure him into speaking.

He stared at the wall of my bedroom, his eyes scanning over the various picture frames and books I had in the room. I sense his worry, and I hate that he is forcing himself to talk about this.

Xena was standing on edge, watching quietly as the events unfolded before us.

"I know I'm safe with you... I guess even after being here, it's still hard to believe that I'm finally safe and away from my father and my pack... Ya know, he wasn't always mean and abusive. He was a loving dad, a loving Alpha. He was the best... Something snapped in him when I turned nine... I don't know what happened, I think it had to do with my mom dying.

I had these very bad black outs when I was younger. I couldn't control Reign... That's my wolf's name by the way. But I would get so angry where I would destroy the room that they managed to lock me in. Most of the time they couldn't even lock me in a room. They had to block off a part of the woods for me to have my episode and then let me pass out by myself.

This gave my father happiness, he thought it would show the pack that I wasn't someone to be messed with. All the other kids I would go to school with would make fun of me for being out of control.

Which of course only made matters worse. I got into trouble a lot, but of course being the heir to the pack, I didn't actually get in trouble. However, I was a troublemaker, my dad knew this. My mom knew this. Everyone knew this but no one was stopping me. Every bad thing I did made my dad so proud of me." He paused, and I figured he just needed a moment.

A moment to collect himself. If his story was as bad as I thought it was... He needed a moment and I was going to give that to him.

"I hate myself for saying that I liked that. I liked causing trouble because I felt proud when my dad was proud of me. It gave me this sense of pride and confidence when I saw the other kids were scared of me. My mom was so disappointed in me. I still remember what she said to me.

"My sweet, sweet boy... You are so much better than this. One day you will be such an amazing Alpha and I hope and believe that you will learn you don't have to gain their obedience by making them scared of you. You will find your mate one day, and she will either be the cause of your happiness or the cause of your undoing...

And with the she-wolf you are destined to be with. You're going to need a lot of patience for that one. I have heard stories about her..." *She told me, and at that point in time I thought she was crazy. I didn't think she actually knew who you were, but she did, the moon goddess showed her who you were. It didn't stop me though, I craved the attention of my father and the only way I got it was by acting out."* When Seth paused, I watched his adam's apple bob with his swallow.

I'm not going to lie, it's kind of cute that he thinks he has to be embarrassed because of his past. I like that he was the troubled wolf. Just like me.

"One time it was on my ninth birthday... I lost it completely. I don't know why, all I remember is I blacked out and when I woke up... There was blood everywhere and my mother's body was on the floor.

My dad blamed me, and rightfully so. I still blame myself for it happening. I should've had better control over myself. My mother was an angel, she was the sweetest person you would've ever met. She always tried her best to calm me down. She tried to help me learn ways to work through my anger, but nothing ever helped. With my father's constant bickering at me, pushing me to be better and better, I just became worse... And worse.

I always felt this pressure to be better, to be the best of the best. I think that's why I had so much anger. I guess I still have this anger in me, at the situation. At my father for everything he did... At myself for killing my mom, even if I didn't mean to. I did everything I could to make him happy, but nothing was ever enough. I was just happy he didn't push this pressure on Max...

But after my mom died... My father took out his anger on me. It was like the life was out of his eyes, like nothing else mattered now that his mate died. Everything in Ireland turned dark, and I think that pack could sense his darkness. I can't remember a lot of what happened during those years.

I spent most of it beaten up or protecting my little brother. I did everything I could to make sure that he was safe, but I knew in my heart that we had to get out of there. As time went on my father continued to get worse and worse. The abuse and neglect got to a point where I was struggling to survive because I gave all of my food to my brother." Seth paused again.

And with his scent. I knew he was upset... That he was about to cry. Maybe this will be good for him... Good to get it all out in a safe place. I wrapped my arms around him and held him to me.

"When I turned fifteen, I heard about you. Something in me called to you, so I thought that I would be able to escape with Max to Scotland. I had everything planned to leave, but someone gave information to my father and he about killed me. When I woke up, I was in that cell. Max was there with me.

My father was spewing some crazy rant... I could only make out part of it.

"The Moon Goddess might have given you a powerful destiny, but boy, I am ending that right here right now. I refuse to give my pack over to you! You're pathetic and out of control! You even drove your own mother to leave."

It didn't make sense to me, and it still doesn't. I saw my mothers dead body, I cried and mourned over her. We buried her, I just thought that he lost his mind. Well I guess I thought he continued to lose his mind. Nothing got better after that, everything got worse. I didn't even think that was possible.

I tried to be defiant... I tried to show him that I could be an Alpha... I said that you would come for me. Which I shouldn't have said that... Because he used that against me, he would taunt my dreams and turn them into nightmares. He would show me, me losing control and killing you like I killed my mother.

I blacked out a lot of things that happened, I guess it's my own way of trying to protect myself. I wanted all of it to end so badly. I never thought that things would get better. I tried to be positive, but after a while... After hearing that I was unlovable. That I didn't deserve you. That I could never make you happy.

After a while I felt like it was my truth, being beaten and starved. I wasn't strong, I couldn't protect you. I still can't protect you, and I know that you said you don't care that you want to care for me, but I feel like I'm a burden to you. I'm scared..." Seth told me, his body shaking as tears streamed down his face.

My heart ached as I listened to what he was saying. How I wish I could just remove those bad things and save him from this. Or literally go back in time and save him from the torture. I whimpered and hugged him tightly to me as I rubbed his back. If he wanted to talk about this, the least I could do is hold him and tell him everything is going to be okay.

"I'm scared of being so dependent on you... And then one day you decide that I'm not worth the hassle. I'm scared that you are just doing this out of obligation... I'm scared of a lot of things. And it's not your fault... I promise you I don't blame you. But please... I'm begging you. Don't give up on me.

Don't leave me, I just need some time. I need some help to learn how to be a good mate and a strong male. I just need someone to love me... And for once not give up on me." Seth begged me, holding me as tightly as he could manage.

And I hugged him back just as tightly. *"I tried my best and my best wasn't good enough. I don't think I could ever be good enough."*

I couldn't help but growl as I gently pulled away so that I could talk to his face. My beautiful mate. I hate that he was put through all of this.

"My love... He took your power away from you to try and belittle you and our connection. He tried to kill your power but that's not possible. You are the Heir to The Bloody Rose Pack. I don't know what prophecy he is referring to, and I could look into it if you would like, but you are not pathetic nor are you weak. You deserve all of the love and happiness in the entire world. I wish I could've gotten to you sooner. You deserve me, if either one of us didn't deserve the other. I wouldn't deserve you. You make me happy, right now. Even though we are exposing our scars and inner demons to one another...

You make me happy. Because you are showing me a side to you that not many people know about. And you are looking at me like I'm not some crazy monster that is running the pack. I am so sorry that you went through all of that. I wish I could say more, but I am so sorry. I promise you he will never lay another finger on you. He won't get into this territory.

I will never leave you. You take all the time in the whole world. You need to heal on your own pace, I just would like to help anyway I can. Your best is good enough, it's more than good enough. Just sometimes you can never make someone happy. They just take and take and take without thinking of anyone else." I told him, cupping his face as I gently wiped his tears.

I felt like my heart broke hearing his story... And when we mark. Seeing it... That's going to hurt more.

"It's going to kill him even more, having to relive all of it." Xena whimpered, I hated that he had to relive it.

"I love you. That will never change. This I promise you. You don't have to say it back, but just know that no matter what. I will always love you." I smiled softly, as his eyes were red and puffy from crying.

He smiled sadly as he looked over my face. He's just heart-breakingly handsome, I hugged him a little tighter.

"Will you stay with me tonight?" He asked, his voice was deep and husky causing my eyes to widen. I swallowed thickly as I looked at him.

"Wow." Xena said, shocked.

Did he just? Was that his?

CHAPTER
FOURTEEN

I stared at him. "Did you just..." I was stunned by his voice.
I honestly haven't heard anything sexier. His voice was like honey and whiskey, and everything good in this world. Seth tilted his head, confusion written across his features.

"Would you rather me talk like this?" Seth asked, he frowned slightly.

I shook my head quickly. I think I would die if I didn't get to hear his voice again.

"No no no... Just your voice... It's... It's wow." I told him, I gulped slightly as my cheeks burned red.

I need to get a grip on myself. I gently cupped his cheeks in my palms, praying to the Goddess that he couldn't smell my arousal.. "I would like to hear your voice again..."

Seth smiled softly, moving slightly so that our bodies were pressed tighter together. "I don't know why you want to hear my voice. It's nothing special." He told me, his eyes trailing over my bare body.

He couldn't help but shift slightly as his cheeks burned red with how flustered he was.

My whole body heated even more. He wants me. He wants me. It makes butterflies flutter in my belly.

"I... I... It is special... It's the voice of my mate. It's the best sound I have ever heard." I said, my voice was soft, softer than I would like, as I giggled. "It's okay if you are aroused by the sight of me being naked... I don't want you to feel ashamed."

Seth cleared his throat as he looked into the dark forest. "I... I don't want you to think that I only value your body. And I know that's not a very masculine thing to say but it's the truth... I remember as a child these wolves walking around town. They were so happy with each other, so in love.

I want that for us. So I don't care if it's not a very masculine thing to say. I don't want you to think that I only value you for your body. I value you for your heart... Even though it was going to hurt you. You took time away from me to give me space to process things." He told me, coughing slightly as he rubbed his throat.

Maybe all of this talking was too much all at once. I smiled, nudging his throat with my face to rub my scent on him. Xena rumbled in approval.

"I know that you don't just value me for my body... But I don't want you to feel ashamed for feeling aroused. We're mates, we're supposed to be with each other. Now if you get turned on by some other female." I informed, gently pulling his face so I could look him in the eye. "I will kill them."

Seth couldn't help but chuckle at my seriousness. At least he knows I'm not joking.

"And you being the Alpha, you can very easily do that and not get in trouble." He said with a smile, his voice cracking slightly.

I frowned, reluctantly untangling myself from him. He needs to drink some water.

"I would do it if I get in trouble or not." I shrugged, walking to the mini fridge I had in my bedroom.

I grabbed two water bottles and walked back to the bed. "I am not the greatest vision of calmness..."

Everyone knows that, everyone knows to also stay out of my way.

Seth watched as I climbed back into bed. "I once thought I would be like that... I guess I just never thought this would ever happen. Would I even be able to be the person I was supposed to be? The Alpha? The male everyone wanted to be?" He asked, frowning as he took the bottle from me gently.

It's a question I understand.

He wants to be an Alpha. I wanted to be an Alpha. In so many ways we're alike. But also in so many ways we're not. I wish things were different.

I couldn't help but sigh. "I know that you will be able to get to be the person you want to be. I don't think that you should worry about what others think. And you most certainly don't have to worry about needing strength. Because I am here, no one is going to make you do anything you don't want to do." I reassured him, gently taking his hands in mine again.

He couldn't help but inhale as he felt my power roll through his body again. My power is his power, and when we mark it will be easier to give him it.

"It feels as though you're the only one thing that is keeping me alive... Your power keeps me awake and moving. But the last week without feeling your power in the house... Without feeling your protective energy. The nightmares, the fears all came swirling in my mind and it felt like I was drowning..." Seth said, staring at our intertwined fingers.

He rubbed his thumb over my hand gently. That sent a pang of regret to circle through me.

"I'm so sorry my love... If I knew that my distance would hurt you. I would've never left, I just thought that it would make things easier on you. After you told me to leave, I didn't think that you wanted to see me." I frowned, squeezing his hands gently. "I just wanted to give you power back. I wanted you to feel like your orders and demands were being listened to. I thought it would make you feel better."

Seth looked at my face now, tilting his head slightly. "You... You left because you wanted to give me power back?" He asked, his eyes softening.

I smiled slightly, my cheeks turning pink. I don't know why that's so hard to understand. I would do anything for him.

"Your dad took your power away... He took your will away... He took your choice away... I wanted to try my best to give that back to you." I told him, nodding slightly to confirm my answer.

I know he doesn't think this, but he's the best thing to ever happen to me.

"I am an Omega... You put yourself under an Omega?" Seth asked, his eyes drifting over my face to study how I was feeling.

I always had a problem with showing my emotions. I guess it was a fail safe. I shrugged. I wish he thought better of himself, so I'm frustrated. I guess? I really don't know.

"I don't think you're an Omega... As I feel my power warming your body, I feel something..." I said, releasing one of his hands so I could place my palm on his chest.

His skin heated under my touch, his heart started to race. His skin felt so much hotter, but with this skin-to-skin contact.

I feel something deep inside of him. Right now it's small, but I can feel it growing. It's like a little seedling of power. His Alpha strength finally growing into something much bigger. "I feel something deep inside your body, a power that has long been hidden."

"That's also thanks to our power!" Xena added in quickly, she was obviously super excited.

We're going in the right direction. I'm finally allowing myself to hope that this will actually happen.

My hand started to glow purple, my power going directly into his body. The glow slowly disappeared as it moved along his skin. "I don't know how you feel that. I don't even feel that." Seth said, looking down at my hand before looking at my face.

Oh! He's talking about the core of his power, or the seedling. There are many names for it.

"I think that you feel it during some moments. Like when your adrenaline is up. Like with Alex being around? Do you feel anything?" I asked, smiling softly. "He seems on edge around you now... Like at one moment something will tick you off enough where you will kill him."

Seth blushed, biting his bottom lip. I wonder what he said, or what happened between them.

"I don't like that he was with you before I was..." Seth frowned, rubbing the back of his neck nervously.

I smiled, laughing softly at his expression. His shy expression is so cute, I love that he is starting to really get protective of me.

"My love... You don't have to worry about him... Do you want to know about what happened between me and him?" I asked with a frown.

He looked at my face. As much as I would love to never talk about this, I know it has to be done. Sadly... My body stiffened as I didn't know how he was going to react to this.

"You don't have to tell me the story if you don't want to. I just don't like that he was here for you before I was able to be." Seth gulped, his face paling.

My face immediately softened as I took in his expression. Goddess help me please, I hate that this is happening so quickly.

"I am not mad at you. I am not upset with you. It's not a very interesting story... One day I was trying to burn off some energy so I was running around near the border. I said that I was checking on the security of the border line. Which a part of me was, but most of it was just me running and trying to cool Xena down.

I don't know why she was so mad, I guess I've just always had a lot of power and energy that I could never really handle. But anyways, this average sized brown colored male wolf came barreling into me and took me to the ground. He was running from something, and I never understood what until now.

I think he might've been running from your dad, but when whoever was chasing him saw it was me. They stopped and turned around and went back home. But we got close that day, so I took him back to my house. And we just started talking, he didn't know I was the Alpha so he talked to me like I was any regular wolf." I paused, wanting to make sure he was okay before I continued.

Today has been a big day for trauma dumping.

"When he found out I was the Alpha, nothing changed. And I guess I liked that, he wasn't nice to me because he wanted something. He was just nice to me because I was a wolf and I deserved the kindness. He doesn't know the whole story about my father and my sister... I don't want the whole world to know.

They would look at me like I was damaged and broken, and not like the Alpha I am. But we got close for about two years. He was my best friend, he was always there. He was the only person who could calm me down from a panic attack or a black out. But he was nothing more than that...

I knew I had a mate, and I wasn't willing to risk losing my mate because I didn't want to feel alone. Alex made me feel safe and comfortable, but I never looked at him more than my best friend. We weren't exactly dating, but I guess it looked like that to everyone around. I didn't feel like correcting them because I didn't care.

I was sixteen when I met Alex, so it was just young pups

doing what we did best. We were causing trouble and trying to find a place to call home. Alex never told me much about his family, but when he asked to stay in Scotland I didn't say no." I explained, shrugging again like it was no big deal.

But it was a big deal... He was the first one who looked at me like I was more than an Alpha. That I was an actual wolf. Seth stared at me, his eyes wide and his mouth slightly open.

"Too much too soon?" Xena asked, wincing slightly.

I think so...

"Does... Does that mean that you never...?" He asked, but he couldn't bring himself to ask the full question.

I smiled, kissing each of his cheeks before taking his hands gently. Seth will be my first for everything.

"No... I never kissed him. I never had sex with him. I didn't want to take that away from you. I always had my heart and mind set on you." I assured him, he grinned at my words.

He wrapped his arms around me again and hugged me. He relaxed against me, making me smile slightly. This is what I like most, us being like this.

"Thank you for that... Thank you..." Seth smiled, leaning his forehead against mine. "I have another question."

I nodded, silently telling him to continue. What could his question be?

"Can we kiss some more?" Seth asked, his face lit up like a young pup in a candy shop.

I started laughing at his innocence, Goddess I am truly blessed.

"Of course." I smiled, leaning forward and kissing him.

FIFTEEN

The next morning, Seth had his head resting against my chest. I had my arms wrapped around him, holding him against me. I had been awake for a while now but didn't want to disturb his sleep.

He looked so sweet and innocent, I just wanted to give him that safety. He inhaled sharply, trying to sit up but was trapped by my arms.

"Let me go! Let me go!" Seth whimpered, struggling against me.

I frowned, immediately letting him go as he sat up. I didn't mean to cause him pain.

"Look at me... My love... Look at me." I spoke softly, sitting up slowly so I wouldn't scare him.

He's obviously not fully awake yet, so I don't need to test my limits. He looked at me, his heart racing. He frowned, his eyes watering as he looked down at his lap.

I wish I could take away his bad memories, give him the peace that he deserves.

"It feels so real..." Seth sniffled, shifting closer to me. "It always feels so real when the memories haunt my dreams... I'm sorry." I gently cupped his face, smiling softly.

"He's adorable when he thinks he's in trouble." Xena snorted inside of my mind.

"You have done absolutely nothing wrong... You didn't scream, you didn't move around in your sleep. I think it's your body's way of trying to save you from the nightmare. Did you have it for a long time before you woke up?" I asked softly, opening my arms up to hug him.

He rested his head on my chest, closing his eyes. When he lays his head on my chest, everything feels right in the world.

"For the most part... I was dreaming really good. We were just laying in a field, we weren't talking. We were just enjoying each other's company. And then my dad suddenly appeared and he had me pinned down..." Seth was starting to panic, his breathing quickened. I immediately wrapped my arms tighter around him.

I don't know how I'm supposed to help, but I want to.

"Hey hey... You're okay. You're safe. Don't worry... I won't let anything or anyone hurt you. Me and you... It's just me and you." I reassured, slightly rocking us on the bed. "You don't have to talk about anything if you don't want to. You are in complete control."

Everything is going on his schedule, I want him to know that he has the power. He has the control.

Seth held on to me, clutching to me like... Like I'm the only thing that makes him safe. "I want to tell you everything... It just hurts a lot." He whimpered to me.

I rubbed his back gently. I understand that more than I care to admit.

"In your own time you will tell me, I am in no rush. But for starters... How about we go and get some breakfast? I can hear Max in his bedroom, he's still sleeping. I want to make him some for whenever he wakes up though." I told him, smiling softly when he looked up at me.

He nodded, reluctantly letting me go so we could stand up.

"If we lived alone, I would've just walked out naked." I teased him, wanting to calm him down. Anything to get his mind off of things.

"I don't think that we want Alex to die. And I don't want you to overdo yourself and kill him." He couldn't help but chuckle as he slowly put on gray sweatpants and a hoodie.

I pulled on gray shorts, and a black t-shirt. It was the easiest thing to shift out of.

Seth looked at me, a soft smile spread across his face. "Alex and I used to be close before I was locked away... Now I don't very much like him." His growl was low, barely registerable.

I smiled, walking over to his side of the bed.

"He's getting possessive!" Xena practically squealed.

And I don't remember the last time she was this excited.

"It's okay... I'm yours." I assured him, taking his hand before leading him out of the bedroom.

He intertwined our fingers, and I felt his eyes on my hips as I walked. "Do you just want me to pick something for breakfast?"

Alex got up from his spot in the living room and followed us to the kitchen.

Exactly what I needed.

"What are you cooking for us, mama!?" Alex grinned, sitting dramatically in a chair by the kitchen island.

Seth's growl was low and rough as he sat down beside him. I smiled as I looked at Seth. My focus is Seth. Nothing else.

"Have you been liking what I made you? I can make strawberry pancakes again?" I offered with a kind smile.

Seth nodded, his cheeks burning as he looked at me. I've been trying to get new things into his diet, so far he hasn't told me he hated anything.

"Yes, please... Thank you." He spoke softly to me.

Alex looked at him completely shocked. I nodded, getting into the fridge as I started to get things out to prepare breakfast. I made sure to get the chocolate milk out because I knew Seth liked it.

"Wow!! Would you look at that! The Alpha speaks!" Alex taunted, a playful grin on his face.

Seth kept his eyes on me, his body was tense at his friend's teasing. I don't know if I need to intervene yet or not. "I am swooning in my seat! Such a hot hot voice!"

I rolled my eyes, placing a cup of chocolate milk in front of Seth. "Milk is good for your bones." I informed, smiling as I placed a purple metal straw in it.

He smiled, bringing the cup closer to him to take a sip.

"But I didn't get anything sexy mama," Alex said, he continued.

Seth growled louder this time, his eyes beginning to glow red. I looked at him, and couldn't help the grin. He's growing in his power. I feel it, even if he doesn't yet.

"That's enough," I growled at Alex, my voice showing a warning.

I placed a large bowl of randomly cut fruits in front of Seth. "I just like a lot of fruit, there's a story behind it. Maybe for another day, it's not anything bad."

He smiled, gently taking my hand and bringing it to his lips. I inhaled sharply, when his lips pressed to the back of my hand, sparks shot through my body.

"I didn't think that was going to be as hot as it was." Xena whimpered in the back of my mind.

That was the hottest thing ever. My heart was racing as I just watched him.

"Thank you, pretty girl..." Seth told me, looking directly into my eyes.

The red was prominent in his brown eyes. I froze at his words. The way he said pretty girl! It really made me weak in the knees. I blushed, biting my bottom lip. When he let my hand go, I went back to making the pancakes.

I had to pause for a moment, Xena was running around in my mind. Wanting to get out and claim Seth. Just because he called me pretty girl doesn't mean we can mark him without consent. And that's not something she wants to hear.

Seth's body tensed again as I moved away from him. I leaned against the counter to watch him. Alex smirked at him. "You know she likes to eat a lot of fruit because it makes her puss-" He started before he was cut off.

Seth grabbed him by the neck, tightening his hand around his throat to cut off airflow.

"You finish that sentence EVER and I will rip your head off of your body and use it as a football." Seth snarled, baring his fangs.

My eyes widened at the interaction in front of me. Alex was gasping for air as he nodded, fear made his eyes wide.

"Oh my Goddess! Did you see that!" Xena howled with excitement, and I had to press my thighs tightly together.

Heat and need flushed through my body.

With another growl, Seth let his friend go before shoving him off the barstool. He slammed his hand on the island, his body tense with anger. I kept my eyes on Seth, my mouth was slightly open. I don't even know what I'm supposed to reply to that.

"I need to get out of here. I don't like being trapped." Seth told me, licking his lips as he eyed me.

Does he smell my arousal? My cheeks heated at the way he was looking at me. "Come with me."

He started walking to the door that led to the back deck. I eagerly followed after him, taking my hand in his.

I kinda like being bossed around by him.

Seth opened the door, his eyes glowing red. He walked out

first, I was quick to follow suit. He was practically shaking with the anger he felt. It vibrated through his body, I smelled it. I didn't know he could get this mad.

We walked down the deck, heading to the woods that surrounded our home. "Alex is just teasing you, my love... You don't have to worry about him. Nothing happened between us... I told you that. I don't know why he's acting like this." I told him, trying to calm him down.

I don't want him thinking I was lying to him.

Seth shook his head no, he gulped before stopping abruptly. "He's doing it to be a jerk. He's doing it to get a rise out of me. He's doing it because no matter how much I hate it. He had you first. I know nothing happened... But there were obviously feelings there. He wouldn't have tried to kiss you.

He wouldn't have come here with you if he didn't love you." Seth growled again, his eyes glowing brighter now.

I frowned, listening to him as he ranted. "He wouldn't be doing this to me if he didn't want you for himself."

I looked into his eyes, my eyes slowly turning purple. Xena wanted to show her support to her mate, and I let her. "I never thought of him in that way... I loved him like a best friend. And nothing more than that. I've always loved you." I assured him, frowning slightly. "You're mine... And I'm yours."

Seth grabbed me and pinned me to the tree. My heart skipped a beat as I watched him.

A grin crossed his face. "Say it again..." He whispered again, his lips inches away from mine.

My cheeks burned red, I eyed his lips. Ever since our first kiss, I haven't been able to stop thinking about his lips. The electrifying kiss. And the need to kiss him again.

"I'm yours..." I told him, and before I could say anything else.

Seth crashed his lips to mine, kissing me deeply as he

brought his hand slowly to my right leg and hiked it up. He used his other hand and brought my hands above my head.

Our bodies were pressed tightly together, lips moving in sync with each other. I leaned forward trying to deepen the kiss as I opened my mouth. He eagerly slid his tongue into my mouth and swirled it around my tongue.

CHAPTER
SIXTEEN

Seth reluctantly pulled away for air, he rested his forehead against mine staring into my eyes. His eyes slowly went back to brown, showing Reign has calmed down. My cheeks turned pink as a shy happy smile spread across my swollen lips.

"Wow..." I panted, trying to catch my breath.

He brought his hand up to my face, gently cupping my cheek before running his thumb over my lips. And just his little touch sent a wave of need through my body.

"You taste amazing..." Seth smiled, his body still plastered to mine. "Does it turn you on when I kiss you in front of Alex? Showing him you're mine and no one else's?" He questioned, gently rubbing my thigh that he was holding, caressing the soft flesh.

I bit my bottom lip, my eyes flashing purple to him. My heart started to race as I struggled to keep Xena down. She was excited at this change in our relationship.

The strong scent of arousal filled the air around us, causing me to laugh nervously. "Yes... I.. Yes it does." I answered him honestly.

Seth nudged my nose gently, before nipping it. Oh Goddess help me now.

"What was it that you said to me baby? Don't be ashamed that I turn you on. It's a normal feeling for wolves to be turned on by their mates. But let's get this clear, I'll brutally murder anyone else you find attractive." He told me, letting me go before taking a few steps back.

I was still leaning against the tree as I watched him. I was stunned, I didn't know how to reply. "Wow..." I repeated, before reluctantly stepping away from the tree towards him.

He grinned, waiting for me to take his hand.

"Come take a walk with me. Alex can make Max breakfast." Seth stated simply, before taking my hand and not leaving me with any choice.

I intertwined our fingers as I walked beside him.

As we walked down the path together, I started to lead him away from the house; towards the town nearby. I couldn't help but roll my shoulders as I looked around us. Something isn't right...

"What's happening?" Xena asked me, but I felt her stress levels rise.

"What's going on inside of that beautiful mind of yours?" Seth asked, gently squeezing my hand to bring me back to the present.

I laughed nervously as I intertwined our fingers together. I can't tell him about my off feeling, that would just make him nervous.

"Well... A lot. But I thought you should know something." I frowned, biting my bottom lip as my body tensed slightly.

He looked at me for a second before wrapping his arm around my shoulder to pull me closer to him.

And I felt complete at this moment. Here with him. Everything would be okay. Even after I told him of what made me the Alpha of my pack.

"You can tell me anything... It's okay..." Seth spoke softly to me, gently rubbing my bicep to help me relax.

I gulped, he has to hear this. And hear it from my lips, and not whatever other people are trying to say.

"Well... When I was a child... My father was very old school in a sense. He actually had arranged for me to be married off to the now Alpha of Spain's pack... The Flames of the Woods, I think. Well that was the last Alphas decision to have the pack named that. But that's not the point of this whole thing.

I thought it would be a good idea to tell you that Link is here right now. Nothing happened between us of course. We were both extremely loyal to the idea of our future mates. Well I killed his father so now technically it's my pack but I'm letting him run it. I wanted to focus on this pack... The Winterfalls.

But yes... I wanted you to know that Link is here right now..." I told him quickly, looking at him to see his reaction.

I didn't know how he would react to knowing someone like Link is here. He looked at me, his eyes darkening to red as he growled.

"So I see everybody got to be with you before I had the chance." Seth growled, his jealousy had a powerful scent.

I smiled looking up to him, gently rubbing my head against his chest. I don't know why I loved his jealousy so much.

"My love, you don't have to worry. I'm yours." I smiled, giggling softly. "There has never been anyone else for me. I believed in what all of the myths say. We are two halves of one whole. All mates are! I held onto that hope. And here we are... Where I'm falling more and more in love with you by the days past.

I can see you, the you you think you hide. Your kindness, your love, the way you want to make sure your brother is always okay.

Not to mention your protective nature, your possessiveness. Your kisses. Everything about you makes me happy. I love you and no one else." I told him, wrapping my arm around his waist as we walked.

I wanted him to know that I loved him for everything.

Seth smiled softly as he looked down at me . "I love you more than you know. I don't like that you had Alex and this Link character. But when I was younger, I heard about you. This powerful beautiful young female who fought tooth and nail to protect her siblings and her people.

The fierce power behind the powerful Winterfall pack. The strength behind everyone in this country. I saw it that day you first saved me... And I continue to see it to this day while you care for me and love me. Even when I screw up like too many times to count." He told me, holding me close.

The large trees covered us in a peaceful shade as we continued to walk. I don't think I've ever been so calm before.

"How about this? We play random questions. Just to get to know each other better?" I offered, trying to lighten the mood.

He nodded, although he was confused. "Okay... Like how old is Max?"

"He is twenty three. How old is Grayson and Stormy?" Seth asked, bumping me gently.

I smiled, he caught on quickly.

"Grayson is my twin, so he's twenty four. Stormy is two years younger so she's twenty two. What is your favorite thing about me?" I asked.

His cheeks immediately darkened as he shyly looked away from me. "You can answer honestly. I'm not going to be upset."

"He likes our body." Xena snickered in the back of my mind.

"I... The hornier part of me wants to say your boobs. But the more respectful part of me wants to say your heart. How you're always so giving and caring. You put everyone and everything above yourself. Wish you wouldn't do it all of the time. But it's something I love about you. What is your favorite thing about me?" Seth asked, stopping to look around us.

He's the cutest thing I've ever seen.

"One of my favorite things about you, besides your body, is the way you love, your loyalty. The way you smile so brightly at Max when you think no one is looking. The way you watch me as I do something. You're so shy I think that it's super adorable." I grinned, nuzzling my nose against his neck.

He chuckled, moving his head to the side to give me more room.

Seth narrowed his eyes as he looked into the woods. He gently tapped my shoulder before motioning into the woods. "I think someone is out there..." He whispered to me.

And that simple statement caused my entire body to freeze.

CHAPTER
SEVENTEEN

"Goddess woman! You are complaining that I saved you from getting attacked by some out of control she-wolf? I will never understand you." A male voice groaned out in the nearby woods.

Lincoln? What is Link doing out here?

"It's not that! I had everything under control, and you came stomping up like a big pouty Alpha and man handled everything!" A young wolf whined out.

Octavia? My brows knitted together as I looked at Seth.

I'm sure he'll send me a text message or something, if it's important.

"It doesn't seem to be important... I'm sure Link can handle everything." I informed, wrapping my arms around him.

My chin was resting on his chest as I kept my eyes on him. "I want to be here in this moment with you."

Seth smiled before kissing my forehead. "I want to be in this moment with you too. But I don't think that's going to be possible." He told me, motioning to the four black SUVs pulling up to us.

I groaned as I reluctantly let go of him.

"I swear I never get to have any fun anymore." I growled softly, forcing a pleasant smile as the males got out of their cars. "Can I help you gentleman with anything?"

What is happening in my pack today?

"Oh! My apologies Alpha Winters." A tall, tattooed male said, bowing his head. "We were just looking for our Alpha. Alpha Woods. We saw him run off into these woods. After a she-wolf, he had wanted to go back to Spain. So that's why our cars are here. I hope we didn't frighten you guys. My name is Antonio..."

"I'm Alpha Winters, and this is Alpha Knight. I'm pretty sure Alpha Woods is having a bit of a problem with his mate." I laughed slightly, nodding my head towards the sound of the yelling.

Seth crossed his arms, standing behind me as he eyed Antonio. I feel his anger radiating off of him, it was kind of cute.

"We can just wait for our Alpha and our soon to be Luna in the car. I didn't mean to interrupt your conversation with Alpha Knight. It's a pleasure to meet you." Antonio said, finally acknowledging Seth's presence.

"I would say the same. But considering you haven't taken your eyes off of my mates breasts. I don't much like you." Seth growled, wrapping his arms around my waist and pulling my back against his chest.

Ooh... Okay. I like this. I couldn't help but giggle as I bit my bottom lip. Antonio chuckled awkwardly, turning to look into the woods.

A young tan female with long wavy brown hair came walking out of the woods with a groveling male right behind her. "I didn't mean to upset you! She was just yelling at you and starting to get physical and I didn't want you hurt! Can you really be mad at me for that?" He grumbled, behind her as she had a grin on her face.

Would you look at that. Him being such a simp for his girl.

I laughed listening to them."Well well well. How the mighty have fallen. Who knew an Alpha can whine like that?" I teased him, causing his cheeks to burn red.

I took a step towards them but Seth growled and pulled me right back against his body.

Okay so maybe this is all too much for him right now. I should excuse us, and head back to the house.

"Good idea!" Xena told me.

"Oh and you say how the mighty have fallen. Who knew an Alpha Female could fold like that?" Lincoln teased me right back, smirking as he looked up at Seth. "I take it you're Alpha Knight. Seth Knight. The world thought you were dead."

Seth growled, baring his fangs at him. "Yeah, here I am. Living the dream with my woman. Laying with my mate naked and doing everything. You wish you could do with her." He licked his sharp fangs as he eyed him.

It took everything in me not to snort at his antics, I love possessive Alpha Knight.

"Looks like your mate doesn't like me. But if you were me, you would've fell for her too." Lincoln chuckled. "I'm Alpha Lincoln Woods by that way." He told Seth, looking directly at me to provoke him.

Seth rolled his eyes as he leaned down, kissing my bare neck. I gasped at the sudden electricity that shot through my body.

I pressed my thighs together as I struggled not to whimper. I needed him more and more as the days passed. But I won't push him. And when I felt his teeth graze against my neck where his mark would lay one day? My knees nearly buckled out from under me.

Octavia pouted, crossing her arms as she walked to one of the large suvs. Lincoln groaned, rolling his shoulders.

"I swear that woman is going to drive me insane. I stop a

wolf from punching her in the face and she's whining like I just killed her favorite dog." He rolled his eyes. "What is with her? Oh that's right. She's freaking like six years younger than me."

I giggled at his anger and Seth nipping and sucking at my neck. I squirmed against him, and I felt Seth grin against the soft flesh.

"She will get over it. Octavia Spencer has gone through a lot. But never once accepted my help. She needs you. Don't let..." I moaned as Seth scraped his teeth along my delicate skin.

That simple action sent my heart racing. My cheeks burned red. "Don't let her attitude deter you from your bond with her."

Lincoln made a face at us. "This is disgusting. I have my mate. You have your mate!! Why are you doing all of this in front of me!! Yes we had a past but nothing happened. She is the one person who gave me my pack. So yes I love that woman, but in a she's my big sister type way and nothing more! Stop doing that in front of me!" He groaned, covering his face. "You'll make more problems for me with Octavia."

"Good. Hopefully you'll go to Spain and stay there." Seth growled at Lincoln, his eyes flashing red.

I nuzzled back against Seth to try and calm him down. Xena rolled over laughing at his remark. I love this man more and more everyday.

"Hey, what the heck is your problem? I haven't done anything but promote her rule. We both made it completely clear to each other that we wanted our mates. Not each other. Besides, how much do you actually know about her? What makes you actually love her?" Lincoln snapped, his grey eyes slowly turning blue.

I groaned, rolling my eyes as I leaned against Seth.

I'm going to give him a chance to say something, if not I happily will.

"Let's see. I know she puts her family first. I know one of her favorite things to do is walk in the woods. She enjoys reading, preferably paperback. Her books look disgustingly tragic so she reads a lot. I know her bra size, her clothing sizes. I know what makes her angry.

And let's see, one thing that makes me love her is that she could have had ANYONE in this entire world. Male female. She could have her pick. She could still have her pick. But she wakes up everyday and she chooses me. She cares for me when she doesn't have to. She gives me the power to make me feel better, when she doesn't have to.

Another thing... Is the way that she looks at me like I'm her everything. Like I can do no wrong in this world. She gives me strength to see another day when frankly sometimes I don't want to. But most of all, she cares for my brother like he is her brother. She is the most loving person I've ever met. And the only person in the entire world who puts me first." Seth glared, narrowing his eyes at Lincoln.

I smiled as I looked up at him. "I didn't know that you noticed all of that..." I said softly, only keeping eyes on him.

Seth nodded, smiling lovingly at me. He noticed all of that? I didn't think he was paying attention.

"I notice a lot of things that I don't say." Seth told me, before kissing my forehead.

Lincoln smiled at us, heading over to the awaiting SUVs.

"I would hug you goodbye Scar. But I don't want to get my head bit off by your mate. Seems like he's going to be a possessive one. Have fun, and text me if you need me." Lincoln said, opening the door and looking inside. "I will not be getting in a different car. This is my car!"

I laughed at the start of their argument, before turning my focus back to Seth. I wrapped my arms around the back of his neck. Time to show him I notice things too...

"Another thing I love about you is that even when you're

scared and anxious... You still find confidence to show that I'm yours. You didn't think twice... You just looked at him and wanted to show that I was yours. And that no one could take me away from you.

I love how you can look at me like I'm a person... Like I'm just me and not Alpha Winters who needs to do everything and anything to keep the pack afloat. I'm just Scarlett when I'm with you. A she-wolf who loves her mate for giving her a chance even when he was scared to do so." My eyes watered as I hugged him.

I can't remember the last time I've been hit with so many emotions. Love, happiness, safety... He rested his head on top of mine as he wrapped his arms around me.

"I love you more than the stars in the sky... And one day I'm going to be able to explain to you all the ways I love you. Right now I kind of suck with my words." He chuckled, gently bringing my face away from his chest.

He cupped my cheeks gently to wipe away my tears.

With the soft glide of his thumb against my cheek, waves of love and calm peace washed through my body. He was my center in the universe.

"This is the face of my mate... My Alpha... The one person in the world that I would burn the world to protect. No one can touch you but me." Seth smiled, leaned down to capture my lips in a kiss.

I smiled slightly before leaning into the burning passion.

CHAPTER

EIGHTEEN

As we walked down the path together, I continued to spare glances at him. I just wanted to know what he meant by feeling trapped. Was it because of what I was doing?

"Did you really mean that you felt trapped?" I asked softly, worry eating at me.

I feel like I might be sick. Seth closed his eyes and inhaled deeply. I wonder if he found peace in the woods too?

"In a sense I did... I think your house is amazing. It's really wonderful and beautiful. Now that I can walk around without much help, I feel like I need to go outside. The walls just feel like I'm in that cell again and I hate the feeling. I never got to feel the sun on my skin... I never knew what day or time it was.

I didn't know what was happening and when it was happening. Now that I'm free... That I'm safe. I can't help but be outside. When you were gone for a week, I would sit out on the deck that was connected to the bedroom. I would watch you walk into the woods and then you wouldn't return for hours later.

Sometimes I slept out there, because being in that house

without you..." Seth inhaled sharply, his eyes getting lost in front of him.

I gently squeezed his hand before moving so I was under his arm instead. I didn't want him to tell me if he wasn't ready.

"You don't have to continue if you don't want to..." My voice was soft, full of the love I had for him.

I watched him intently, wanting to catch any change in his features. He shook his head no, tightening his grip on me.

"No... It's fine. I need to stop pushing away everything and start to deal with it. I felt like I was in that cell again... Without you in your house I felt trapped. My father would always taunt me with your scent, he'd say you came but didn't want to take me with you... It was one of his ways to really mentally break me.

Max thankfully didn't want to meet his mate, I mean being a young child... They don't really think about that. I think I was the only one who thought of that, I thought of the family I would one day have. My father took that as one of my many weaknesses.

I wasn't ashamed that I wanted kids or a mate... I wanted to show them love and a happy home. Something I didn't have when I was young... He used the thought of you coming to save me to taunt me..." Seth gulped, his face paling at the memories that swarmed his brain.

I frowned, whimpering slightly as I led him to a clearing in the woods.

That way we could talk, and I would be able to comfort him properly.

Once we were there, I pulled him to sit down on the ground. I sat down, letting our legs touch. "My love... He used the thought of me coming to save you because he knew. I am kinda crazy sometimes and call war if I get angry enough. I would've called war, I would've burned Ireland to the ground if he didn't give me you.

I never visited Ireland before the day I brought you home. I couldn't really leave my territory because other Alphas from packs would come and try to take my spot. I wouldn't have left you... Is that what you were dreaming about earlier?" I intertwined our fingers.

The feel of his skin calmed my nerves, and I was hoping it would do the same for him. Seth looked around us, noticing the clearing.

"This is what I was dreaming about..." Seth informed, randomly laying back and dragging me on top of him.

I giggled as he wrapped his arms around me, holding me against his chest. "And then my father randomly came... He grabbed you away from me before pinning me down... I woke up after that... After him telling me that one day you would get sick of me."

I leaned up only enough to look him in the eyes. "I will never get sick of you... Nothing will ever make me change my mind about you." I assured him, leaning my head back against his chest. "This is what I've always dreamed about..."

Being here in the one place that centered me with my mate. And now that I'm here... It feels like a dream come true.

Seth closed his eyes, allowing the sun to beat over his skin. "I feel like you're giving up so much for me... You should be leading your pack... Not laying out here with me." He frowned, his heart skipped a beat.

And I didn't like that, I would do anything for him. My growl rumbled in my chest.

"Kiss him, tell him that this is us now." Xena yelled at me in the back of my mind.

Oh she's not happy with me.

"I have built my brother up enough where he knows that I am the rightful Alpha to this pack. Everyone knows that if I want a break that they can go to him. And being the great twin brother he is, he will inform me about stuff that needs my attention. I don't need to be at the pack house leading the pack, when I lead it amazingly from here.

What I want and what I need is to be here with you. I want and need to help you heal. And if that means we lay out here everyday for as long as you want, then so be it. I don't want you to feel stressed or like you're trapped." I told him, my eyes closing as I listened to his steady heartbeat.

I could just fall asleep out here with him. I don't think I've ever felt so relaxed.

"I want you to be here with me too..." Seth smiled, his body relaxing against the soft grass. "I don't think I've ever wanted something more in my entire life." I giggled, looking up at him. I'm glad he's calming down again.

"And here's to think that I thought you wanted my kisses more than anything in the entire world." I teased him.

Seth grinned, flashing his fangs at me before flipping us around so that he was on top of me. He licked my cheek, creating a loud giggle from me.

It sent shocks of pleasure throughout my entire body.

"Your kisses are like my air. I need them." Seth told me, before kissing me softly.

I needed more than that.

I wrapped my arms around him, pulling his body down onto mine. My hand went to his head, threading my fingers through his soft brown hair. He practically groaned into my mouth from me caressing his head.

Seth rested his forehead against mine, his eyes closed as he breathed in my powerful scent. "Roses and vanilla... Even being deep in the woods. Your scent... Your uniquely powerful strong scent is the only thing I can register." He whispered against my lips, his tongue darted out to swipe across my lips. "And yet... Your mouth tastes like pure honey."

I felt pleasure swell in me at his compliments, and Xena was fighting more and more for control. Maybe we should just let our wolves meet finally.

"I like that idea!" Xena shouted, and I had to bite back my laugh.

My cheeks warmed again, my eyes shining purple. I started to blink rapidly, trying to control myself. Everything was starting to turn red, and I didn't want to lose control in front of him. "Don't worry... I like your purple eyes. And I like Xena too." He smiled softly, opening his eyes.

They were blazing red. It seems like Xena and Reign wanted to meet each other.

"Your scent is a powerful unique scent of rose and whiskey. And something very... You... And I don't know how to explain it. It's just something so addicting to me and I can't get enough of it. And your mouth... It tastes like pure sugar, and I want as much of it as I can get." I tried to explain to him but I didn't know if it made sense.

My fangs peeked out. Seth couldn't help but chuckle.

"I absolutely love the sound of that." He told me, leaning down to kiss me again before my body tensed.

Someone is watching us. I immediately flipped us around, my eyes glowing brightly as I narrowed my eyes at the woods.

I see them standing out there, but they're masking their scent.

"Someone is out there..." I whispered to him, keeping him under me as my body was preparing to shift.

It's time for Xena to shine.

"State who you are! Because I know you are not my pack!" I shouted.

CHAPTER
NINETEEN

I stood up quickly standing in front of Seth. He was starting to freak out as he sat up, keeping his eyes on me. I felt his gaze on my back, but I refused to not stand in front of him.

"I need to protect him." Xena growled, but thank the Goddess that she let me stay in control. *"For now."* She grumbled.

The older female had her hands up, stopping once she fully came into view in the clearing.

"I didn't come here to start a fight." Her voice rang through the silence around us.

Seth's body stiffened, his eyes shooting straight to the woman. I smell his fear. Does he know who she is?

"You are trespassing on the Alpha's private territory. You should've gone to the Packhouse like my people would have directed you." I snarled, my body going rigid as I felt Seth's anxiety.

He stood up, standing behind me.

A million questions ran through my mind. But the one I needed to focus on was who she was, and why she was causing Seth so much anxiety?

"I apologize for my interruption Alpha Winters. I heard the news of you saving some people from Ireland... I escaped there a very long time ago." Her voice was sweet, silky, and smooth as she didn't move from her spot.

I growled again, my power soaking the air around us. I don't care for her excuses, I don't want to hear it.

"If this has to do with my pack members that you have a problem with, you can go speak with my Beta. He will schedule you with a time where we can talk. And talk privately." I ordered, my body shaking with restraint.

I wanted to rip her apart, I didn't like her being here. Seth's body was shaking as he reached for my hand.

I gently took his hand, intertwining our fingers. I was flooded with his worry. Was it because of me? Xena growled, and as I felt my anger rise. I knew she wanted control.

"I will not ask you again. What is your name and what is your intention for coming here?" I demanded, my voice turning deep as Xena was closer and closer with taking control.

Seth stepped closer, pressing his body against my back. He's definitely trying to keep me in place. Which I mean he's the only one who could ever hold me back.

"My name is Emily Rosewell, but before I left my mate... My last name was Knight." Emily told us, I felt Seth stiffen again and I knew I was going to put an end to this.

One way or another. I growled again, my eyes glowing purple. Xena was lending me her power, but let me stay in control.

"Leave. Now." My command drifted through the air, forcing Emily to run off quickly.

I turned around, immediately wrapping my arms around him and holding him as tightly as I could. I will never let anything bad happen to him. He had to bend over slightly, but he placed his head against my chest.

151

"Shh... You're okay. You're okay... You are safe. I won't let anyone hurt you." I assured, rubbing his back as he cried into my chest. "I will make her leave... You do not have to speak with her if you don't want to. The power is in your hands."

Seth held me tightly, his body shaking with his sobs. "I don't understand... I don't understand. She was dead. I saw her dead body, my father told me I killed her. I thought I killed her." Tears streamed down his face as he slammed his eyes shut. "I don't want to do this."

No one is going to make him.

I picked him up, teleporting us back to our bedroom. We appeared on our bed, Seth refused to let me go, clinging to me like I was his life force. He shook his head, suddenly letting me go. Is he going to shift? Maybe a run will help him feel better. I feel helpless in this situation.

"None of this makes sense," Seth told me, standing up and passing the bedroom. "None of it does! She was dead. She was dead in front of me. I saw her body, I think I saw her body?" His breathing was quick.

I stood up quickly, watching him pace. Everything in me wanted to hold him, but I didn't want to overwhelm him.

"Think back to that night... What do you remember? Describe the body..." My voice was even and calm as my eyes never left him.

I'll be here if it gets to be too much for him. Seth ran a shaky hand through his hair as he couldn't stop moving. I felt his energy vibrating off of him.

"I was angry... I hated seeing everybody so happy while I was hurting inside. I felt alone, I was getting angry so I went into the gym to blackout. I figured that everyone would just leave me alone. I saw my mom walk in, and that just made me start to panic.

Fear made my vision blur, I begged her to give me space. But she just kept telling me she wasn't scared of me. That by giving me space, it's adding to my fears. But the thing is, I wasn't scared of myself. I was scared of what I didn't remember. She told me my fears were what was making me blackout.

Which I guess made sense because I always was scared that I would never find my mate, and I'd never be truly happy like everyone else. Her talking just made everything so much worse, it made me ticked. She was trying to calm me down, but one day I would be her alpha. I didn't think she had the right, but as my mother, she of course had the right." Seth paused, and I was waiting to see if he would continue.

He had every right to stop. To not continue, this was a rough story.

"I blacked out, I must've shifted when I did... Because when I woke up, I was shivering and curled into a ball in the corner of the gym. There was blood everywhere, claw marks, and a body torn to shreds. My father came in screaming at me, saying that I am an uncontrollable monster. That I would be cursed for killing my mother.

There was too much blood, the body that was in the gym was too torn up for me to tell who it was. I hung on my father's every word so I automatically assumed that the body was my mother. Because she was nowhere to be found after, and the whole pack went into mourning for her." Seth shook his head, his eyes shifting from brown to red rapidly.

His memory slowly piecing everything together, I can see it on his face. The slight flinches. The slight anger. I stood in my spot, letting him do whatever he needed to do.

"There are so many pieces I'm missing... It's like they are there but I can't see them. I can't figure this out." He rambled, his heart racing as he ran his hand through his hair again. "My father wasn't always the nicest guy with my mom... But in the

end, they would always hug and make up. I can't figure this out."
Seth couldn't stop, his mind was obviously racing.

This was not a good idea of mine.

"You're an idiot." Xena snapped at me.

How did I get stuck with the wolf that is rude to me?

"Oh my Goddess... Oh my Goddess..." He stopped pacing, he swallowed thickly.

I walked over to him quickly, my eyes scanning over his face. I know he's in pain, but what did he figure out?

"What's wrong? What's happening?" I asked, cupping his cheeks gently. "Are you okay?" Seth shook his head no, his eyes watering.

"I had to tell my little brother that I killed our mother... And this whole time... It was a lie. I didn't kill our mother, but why wasn't she there? Why didn't she stop our father? Why did she leave her mate and her children and her pack? None of this makes sense. Why was I blamed for her death?

Max was mad at me for a while, but in the end, he came around. He said he didn't blame me for something that the Moon Goddess gave me. He always told me that it was out of my control, and I shouldn't feel bad. But I did... I of course blamed myself for our mother's death. He deserved to have her there growing up. And I thought I took her away from him.

I was outcasted after that, which of course just made my anger issues worse. No one wanted to be around the wolf who got so angry that he killed his own mother. The one who gave him life. I guess I didn't blame them. Why did this all happen to me... To us? My brother didn't deserve that... I... I didn't deserve that?" Seth was rambling, his body was shaking involuntarily.

I frowned, wrapping my arms around him. After a moment, I felt his arms wrap around me slowly. Before nearly crushing me to him. His eyes were shut tightly as he inhaled my strong scent. "You do not have to talk to her. You don't have to tell your brother if you don't want to. You don't have to do anything you don't want.

The power is in your hands, my love. You are in charge of what happens... You make the decision. And you decide when or if it happens." I assured him, reiterating that he was in complete control of what happened.

I closed my eyes, holding him tightly. He has the power of me behind him. No one will dare try to deny me.

Seth gulped, moving with me to sit down on the bed. He brought me into his lap, refusing to let me go. Not like I wanted to go anywhere anyways. "Can I think about this for a little while? I... I don't know how to feel about this whole thing. I don't know what I'm supposed to do." He sighed, laying back on the bed, staring up at the ceiling. I laid down with him, knowing my body pressed to his was comforting for him.

I nodded, frowning slightly as my stomach growled with hunger. "You take as long as you need." I promised, keeping my head on his chest.

A soft knock came from the door. Seth covered his face, his body tensed under me. I could tell by the scent that it was Max.

"It's okay... I can handle this..." I explained, reluctantly getting up and sitting beside him. "Max... You can come in..."

TWENTY

The door opened slowly before Max walked in. His eyes were at his feet, as he slowly shut the door. Immediately I knew he felt bad for listening in. But he has a right to know.

"I'm sorry for listening to your conversation. Wolf super hearing and all..." Max said softly, he couldn't look at us.

Seth frowned, reluctantly sitting up and moving to sit beside me.

"It's okay... Come here. I want to talk to you." Seth asked him, patting the open spot in front of where he had his legs crossed.

I held his hand, intertwining our fingers. It was my way of silently showing that I had his back, showing my confidence in him.

He needed that right now.

Max walked over to the bed quickly and sat down in front of us. "Is what you said true...?" He looked to his brother, searching his eyes.

Seth frowned, rubbing the back of his neck nervously. I shifted slightly, looking at Max now. So... I guess I'm going to start this.

"We don't know for sure..." I started, turning my focus back to Seth.

He shook his head, before inhaling deeply. Did I overstep? I think I overstepped.

Crap.

When he exhaled, it came out shaky. Seth forced himself to look Max in the eye. "All we know is that she trespassed, so Scarlett has every right to punish her as she sees fit. As the Alpha, she could banish her from ever stepping foot in Scotland again. But she's leaving that decision up to me..." He gulped, looking at our intertwined fingers before looking into my eyes.

I smiled kindly.

"And I am thinking about it... I was going to process it a little more before I brought the complicated situation to you. There are a lot of black holes in the story... Things I don't understand. Things I do understand... Some things are coming back to me, but I don't think I'll understand it fully until I talk to her." Seth told him, his heart racing as he looked at his brother.

I bit my bottom lip, trying my best to support my mate. But I worried that I wasn't doing it right. Xena wasn't helping me by being oddly quiet.

Max nodded in understanding. "I thought that you said she was dead...? You said that you blacked out because of something you didn't want to talk about. And when you woke up, she was ripped apart." Max asked, tilting his head slightly.

I shifted closer to Seth, putting my legs over his crossed ones. Touching helps. Right?

Seth forced an uneasy smile, putting his free hand on my bare thigh. His calmness came through our bond, and it brought me peace. I needed to bring him peace right now. Dang it, I'm sucking at this.

"I thought she was... You know I would never lie to you. You're my best friend, I've always protected you. I've always put you first, I wouldn't take your mother away from you." He tried to explain as he looked at Max.

"What are you feeling about this whole thing? Do you want me to talk to her before she can talk to you? I would really not like for you to meet with her alone." Seth told his brother.

Max nodded, taking his words as an order. I looked at Seth, smiling softly at him. I'm glad they were working through this.

"You guys can take as long as you want while making this decision. Or if you would like, I can talk to her before you do to see if I can get the story out of her?" I offered, looking between them now.

Seth growled, shaking his head no.

"Oh? I like this." Xena told me, bouncing on her paws.

"As if I'm letting you go see someone that I know next to nothing about," Seth told me, leaving no room for discussion.

My cheeks burned red at his words, and a small smile crossed his face.

"OH! He likes it too!" Xena howled now, running around with excitement.

Her excitement made me fidget in place.

"Okay okay... It was just an offer. I didn't mean anything by it. I just thought things would be easier that way? She can't do anything to me without risking death." I smiled innocently, trying to ease his anger.

He snarled as I giggled resting against his chest. Max watched us with a smile on his face.

"I'm happy that you're so happy Seth..." He grinned at his brother.

Seth looked up at him, his cheeks burning red. His embarrassment is adorable.

"I..." Seth started, Max shook his head slightly.

"I'm not saying anything about it, you deserve this Seth. You put yourself through so much for me, you deserve to be happy and to put yourself first finally. Scarlett makes you happy, and I can see that. Please... Let yourself have this one thing. Take this for you." Max grinned at him, causing Seth to smile down at me.

"You are always going to be welcome here. I don't want you to think that I'm going to kick you out just because I am with your brother now. I look at you as my brother now." I smiled at Max, keeping my body pressed against Seth.

And what I was saying is the truth.

"I really appreciate that Scar... Oh, wait, if I call you Scar am I going to get choked?" Max teased him.

Seth chuckled, shaking his head slightly.

"There was more to it than that. No, I won't choke you if you call her Scar, because I know you aren't meaning it in a bad way like Alex is." He smiled at his brother. "But if you try to steal my woman, I might just have to choke you." Seth teased him back.

Both Max and I started laughing. And I know he's telling the truth.

"Seriously though, what are we going to do about... The woman you might think that could be our mother." Max asked, fiddling with his fingers as he looked down.

Seth sighed, looking outside into the woods.

Max must've been too young to remember his mother.

"I don't know, kid... I really don't know. I know you want an answer, you want me to tell you that I have a plan. But I don't... I'm sure I'll have to meet with her. But I don't think that I want to... If you want to know about her I will do it... But I... I just don't know." Seth answered truthfully, frowning slightly.

"I can have her put into a temporary housing facility until you want to see her. It could be weeks, it could be months. I don't care how long you guys need. Whatever I can do for you guys... Just tell me. I want you to help you guys in any way you need." I told, trying to sit up but Seth tightened his arms around me.

He didn't want to let me go, and that made my heart beat

faster with love. I've never felt this before, but I welcome it. Max gagged dramatically.

"I could go without you guys being disgusting in front of me." Max gagged again, turning away from us.

I shook my head, before rolling my eyes. He sounds like Grayson.

"Are you mad at me Maxxy?" Seth asked softly, his eyes watering.

He couldn't bring himself to look at anyone, so his gaze stayed on the woods. I looked at Seth, sensing his sadness and his body tense underneath me. I nuzzled against him, doing my best to calm him down.

"I was mad for a while... But I was upfront with you about it. I'm not mad anymore, more frustrated with the whole situation." Max tried to explain his thoughts.

Seth was shaking slightly as he reluctantly put me on the bed beside him and stood up.

Crap.

"I've... I just... I gotta go. I'll be back." Seth said, gulping as he quickly made his way to the door that led outside.

Max frowned, worry crossing his features.

Double crap. If Seth knew he made his brother feel bad, it would make things ten times worse.

"Did I do something that upset him? I didn't mean to! I... I never wanted to hurt him." Max whimpered, his eyes watering as he watched his brother walk into the woods.

I frowned, cupping Max's cheeks gently. I kissed his forehead before looking into his eyes. Hopefully I can fix this.

"You didn't upset him... I think there is something deeper that he doesn't want to talk about with you. But it's not your fault. This whole situation is messed up, and it's even more now that he has to deal with this after being saved.

Why don't you get yourself some food? I'm sure Seth and I

will be back soon. He just needs his time to deal with his emotions and in the woods is where he thinks best." I informed, smiling lovingly at him.

Max nodded, a sad small smile spread across his face.

"Okay..." He said, but I was already on my way outside.

I jumped down from the deck, following Seth's strong scent into the woods. I would always be able to find him. My eyes were glowing purple as I looked everywhere around me as I ran. Is he hiding?

When I found him, he was sitting in that same clearing. Seth didn't say anything as a sob shook his body. I frowned and walked over to him. I wish I could take all of this pain away from him.

"It's me..." I said softly before sitting beside him. "Do you want to talk about what's happening?"

Seth hugged his knees to his chest, he shook his head slightly. "I just want it to be us. Why can't it just be me and you? Things were so simple, laying here like we were the only thing in the world." His voice cracked, swallowing thickly. "Everything that has happened since you saved me... I just wanted you to hold me. But I couldn't bring myself to ask you..."

I frowned, nodding in understanding. I kept my eyes on him as I waited for him to continue.

TWENTY-ONE

"I don't understand..." He told me, watching his body shiver.

I frowned as I wrapped my arms around him and rested my head on his shoulder. His mother is still alive?

"I beat myself up... For years about her death. I blamed myself, I told myself that I wasn't worthy of a mate. I told myself that I deserved the torture... The abuse. I felt like I deserved it for killing my own mother. The one woman in my life that I adored, I hung on her every word. And I slaughtered her like she was nothing.

My father used that against me, I called to you when I first was thrown into the cell. But then he told me that I didn't deserve you for what I did. After hearing it so much, I believed it and stopped calling for you. Until I knew my father would kill me one day and I had to get out of there.

How can you want me after I tell you that? How can you look at me and see someone you want to spend the rest of time with? I am out of control." He whimpered, leaning his body into me gently.

I frowned, rubbing his back softly. I wish I could take away all of his pain. I closed my eyes as my power washed into his body.

I hope this will be able to calm him, and calm me. Because every inch of my body wanted me to go and rip his mother apart for what happened to him.

"I like that plan!" Xena shouted loudly in my mind.

"My love... My sweet... Innocent... Adorable... My Male... Even though we haven't had that much time together. I just... I don't know how to explain it. I feel like I've known you my whole life. I know your heart, you didn't want to hurt your mother. And well come to find out, you didn't hurt your mom.

Although I don't know what happened after you blacked out, I know you went into the gym to protect everyone. You thought you were a monster because of your dad. But I don't see you as that. I see you as strong, powerful, brave... I see you as loving, caring, protective, and kind... I see you as the strongest person I have ever known.

You didn't have to protect your brother but you did. You didn't have to starve for your brother, but you did. You care so deeply about those around you, that when you think you messed up... You beat yourself up for over a decade. I see you as handsome and strong. And I hope one day you can see yourself the way I see you." I told him, smiling softly as I turned his face to look at me.

I don't know how else to show him that he's my everything.

Seth's eyes were glowing red, tears continued to stream down his face. He whimpered, sniffling as I gently brushed away his tears. "I feel pathetic. I can't protect you like you protect me. I'm not giving you anything. And you're giving me everything." He tried to look away from me, but I wouldn't let him.

I hated him speaking like this about himself.

I growled softly, my eyes turning purple. "Don't turn away from me. You're not pathetic. I don't need you to protect me, I can protect us both. You have already given me everything by being here... By letting me help you through this. Please don't push yourself to get over something so traumatic." I said softly, my eyes slowly turning brown again.

His bottom lip trembled as he nodded slowly. My heart skipped a beat as I looked at him.

How could someone so perfect think he's... Not?

"I just don't understand, I know I was a troubled kid. But I didn't mean any harm, I couldn't handle everything. The training... The power. The anger I felt. Everything was too much and I felt overstimulated at an almost constant rate. Just like I feel now... Everything feels like it's drowning me, and then when I feel your touch.

Everything calms down and I feel at peace. Even for a moment, I feel at peace." Seth explained, closing his eyes as his body stopped shaking.

And when he started to relax, so did I. Finally.

"I don't want you to leave me, I know I'm being emotional right now..."

I smiled, shaking my head slightly. This is all completely normal. "You're not being emotional. You are trying to process your trauma, you're slowly healing. It gets easier, but sometimes things just trigger you and that's the process. You heal at your own time, dealing with it how you see fit. I am at peace here with you too.

And knowing that I can help you by just sitting here with you in my arms. It makes me feel good knowing I'm helping you. You make me feel calm and at peace from the raging anger I feel." I told him, trying to calm him down.

Seth started laughing, opening his eyes so he could look up at me. Little does he know that most of my anger is to his parents.

"You really know how to make me smile huh?" He asked, leaning back only enough to see my face clearly.

I smiled, kissing his forehead gently. It's something I try to get as much as possible. His beautiful smile melts my heart.

"Sometimes all we need is someone who can hold you and tell you everything is going to be okay. Which my male... My love... Everything will be okay, maybe not today. Maybe not tomorrow, but one day it'll be great." I told him, gently placing kisses all over his face.

Pouring out all my love into each kiss.

"Everything will equal itself out. With good there will be bad times, and with bad times good times will be right out around the corner. And I know laughter is the best medicine, so baby... Sometimes I will make random jokes, but it's all in good fun. But just so you know, I do tend to have pretty bad anger problems. But that's a story for another day." I grinned at him, winking and flashing my fangs.

I have a lot of stories, some I know he won't like.

Seth smiled, darting his tongue out and swiping it across one of my pointy fangs. And I tried my best to bite back my moan at the pleasure that shot through my body.

"I'm glad I have you by my side. Thank you for making me feel better. What do you think I should do about this whole situation? I know what Max secretly wants but he'll never tell me that to my face." He asked, rubbing my bare thigh.

I leaned back, laying down on the soft grass.

Seth laid his head on my stomach, as he continued to rub my thigh. "I don't know what you want to do. If I were you in this situation, I would want to kill my mother for abandoning me... She left you with a monster, just like my mother left me with a monster. But what you want to do could be different than what I would do.

Even if you don't want her dead, like you said. I could banish her, I could make sure that she never steps foot near you or Max again. I could imprison her, there are a lot of things that I could do. But in the end, the decision is up to you. You tell me what you want, and I will make that happen.

The power is in your hands." I told him, gently running my hand through his hair.

A lazy smile spread across his face, he felt the vibrations from my voice through my stomach. In this moment, it's just us and that's all that mattered.

"What if I wanted to talk to her? Would you be there with me? You won't leave me alone will you?" Seth asked, his voice wavered slightly as his fear sunk in.

I growled playfully. As if I would ever let him face her without me.

"Does he think we're not completely obsessed with him?" Xena scoffed in the back of my mind.

That's what I'm saying!

"I would never let you be alone with someone that I don't know. I don't know what she's capable of. And I made you a promise, I will always protect you. No one is going to hurt you while I'm around." I smirked slightly, licking my lips. "I'm a bit of a wild card, so who knows. Something she says might just set me off."

I might be teasing him, but I'm totally serious. I could easily give Xena control to bite her head off.

"Oh oh oh! Do that! Yeah yeah yeah do that!" Xena cheered at the thought.

Seth started laughing again, his body shaking with his laughter. "I guess that makes two of us. I haven't shifted since I shifted back to my human form. Or well since you helped me shift into my human form. I am sure Reign will not be too happy that I haven't let him out to run around. Or to meet you yet." He said, laughing slightly again.

"It sounds to me like we're a perfect pair." I said, running my hand through his hair again. I'm obsessed with touching him.

"One day, we can let our wolves out to play a bit. I'm sure they'd love that." A sudden growl rippled through me causing my cheeks to burn red.

Xena!

"What can I say. I want to play. And you're taking forever to LET me out!" Xena growled at me.

"Sorry..." Seth looked up at me, his chin resting against my stomach.

His eyes were sparkling playfully at me.

"What was that about?" Seth asked with a teasing grin.

I couldn't stop blushing. This is going to be great to explain.

"Xena is very down for the idea to play, and she isn't patient. But today is about you, everything is about you and what you want. You can stop trying to change the subject my male. I want you to continue to grow, but if this is your way of asking me to deal with the situation. You won't like what I want to do." I told him, winking at him again.

He started laughing again, rolling over onto his back. I'm so happy he's relaxing.

"I won't lie... I want you to handle the situation. But I know I won't be able to have you handle everything forever. I have to stop putting things off..." He sighed, putting his hands behind his head as he looked up at the sky.

"I don't mind handling everything for you... I just don't want to be pushing." I explained, rolling over onto my side so I could look at him again.

My head rested on my hand as I watched his chest moving. I'm obsessed with him. With touching him. With talking to him. Everything about him makes me obsessed.

"I know... I don't think you're pushing. I think it's nice... I haven't had someone wanting to take care of me in a very long time... You give me the strength to do stuff on my own and I appreciate that. I think that I want to talk to her, at least for Max." Seth told me, opening his eyes slightly to look at my reaction.

CHAPTER
TWENTY-TWO

I smiled at him, leaning forward and kissing his cheek. "We can do that tomorrow. Today we are going to get you some food, and we're gonna continue to relax. You also have to talk to your brother because when you left he was pretty upset." I explained.

This is the only thing I will push.

Seth sighed before quickly turning us around, pinning me to the ground underneath him. "I can tell him and talk to him when we get back. But I would love to stay here with you." He whispered against my lips, his eyes directly on mine.

I gulped, staring at him. My heart rate escalated as I was stunned.

I... I like this turn. *"Oh... I do too."* Xena practically purred to me.

"Why is it that you are the alpha... *My Alpha*... Yet you are under me. Letting me pin you to the ground. My Alpha... My Mate. My woman. Why are you letting me do this... Does this turn you on?" His voice was a low growl, his eyes turning red.

He gently ran his hand up my bare thigh, before going up my shorts.

My skin felt like it lit alive at his touch. Goddess I needed him so bad. I inhaled sharply, my eyes bright purple. I couldn't bring myself to say anything, my mouth opened but no words came out. I don't know what to say. All I can think about is his hands up my shorts. If he just moved over a little...

A smirk crossed his face, his fangs growing as he traced my plump red lips with his thumb. "I could think of something I could do with this open mouth of yours." He whispered, looking at my powerful eyes.

I whimpered, causing my cheeks to burn red.

Who knew he would be able to have me wrapped around his thumb so easily?

"I did. You simp." Xena teased.

"Oh, my Goddess," I said, embarrassment written all across my face.

He chuckled, sitting beside me now.

"Maybe I do feel good enough with myself now..." Seth told me, I just laid there and watched him for a second.

My brain froze as he stared at me. Goddess I need to get a handle on myself.

"How... How did you..?" I tried to form a correct sentence but I couldn't.

I laughed nervously, covering my face. An Alpha shouldn't be acting like this. "No one has ever got me so frazzled before."

He grinned, gently prying my hands away from my face.

"I like being the only thing that gets you frazzled baby." Seth smiled kindly at me.

He pulled me to sit up, his stomach growling with hunger. I frowned, looking at him intently. I should've made him eat.

"I wish you would've eaten before we left. You are still

healing and need as much food as possible." I told him, standing up and pulling him to his feet.

As I kept my hands in his, I let my power flow through his body. And I was blessed with his husky laugh.

"I really don't feel hungry, right now all I feel is your power running into my body. It makes everything feel like it's getting lit alive." Seth told me honestly, following me in the direction of our house.

He intertwined our fingers together and pulled me so that I had to walk beside him. "Why can't you teleport?"

This makes me feel like we're equal. And I do really like it. This makes me hopeful.

I frowned, rubbing the back of my neck with my free hand. "I can... Sometimes. Very rarely can I teleport. Most of the time when I try to teleport, I either don't go anywhere or I go to the opposite place of where I want to go. I can't control it, so I normally just run everywhere or I drive." I explained, biting my bottom lip.

He tilted his head as he looked at me, his curiosity piqued.

I hope that he doesn't make fun of me for this.

"Why can't you control it? I thought that Alpha's were supposed to have perfect control?" Seth asked, squeezing my hand gently.

I swung our hands slightly as we walked down the path together.

"Yeah, they are supposed to... I shifted when I was young... So my power is a little different, I have a bit more of a struggle with controlling myself than other Alphas do. Which is fine, everybody thinks I'm a wild card so they don't want to get on my bad side. Especially with one time, I teleported and I appeared randomly in Italy and scared the Alpha there.

I made up some story about how I just wanted to see if I was welcome whenever I decided to show up. And you should've seen the scared look on the Alpha's face, it was hilarious. But I went to a specialist, you could say. She told me that there is a great power inside of me and that it awoke sooner than it should have.

I still don't understand what she meant by that, and she refuses to tell me what it's about. But she's an elder, and as much as I can throw my power around. She talks to The Moon Goddess, and I really don't want to get on the bad side of her. I used to think that because of everything I did...

That The Moon Goddess didn't bless me with a mate. But now I know that's not true and I'm just thankful that you're alive and you're healing. And that I can finally have you in my arms." I explained, smiling up at him.

He smiled down at me, kissing my forehead gently.

His smile brought a sense of comfort to me... Something I thought I didn't deserve.

"I honestly thought the same thing... But now my mother is alive and I know it's not true because you're here with me. Even though I tried to push you away, you didn't let me. And I quickly found out that distance from you makes me want to die even more than I did locked in that cell." Seth told me, wrapping his arm around my waist and holding me against his side.

I smiled, my cheeks turning pink.

Xena growled with her anger, telling me she wasn't happy that we haven't had sex yet. She made my need known. And I tried my best not to shift uncomfortably.

"The distance between us killed me too... But I knew what it felt like to be powerless... And you had to deal with so much more than me. I just wanted to try and help give you some power back. Even if it isn't everything, I just thought that it would be nice for you at least. I don't know I tried." I laughed nervously, causing Seth to grin.

We walked up the deck to the back door. Before we went

inside, Seth stopped me. I looked at him, with a tilt of my head. "Are you okay my male?" I asked, looking intently at him.

Just that claim over him made my heart beat faster. He was mine. And everyone would know.

Seth smiled, cupping my face gently. "Thank you for putting me first... Thank you for going below your rank to make me feel better. Thank you for caring about me. Thank you for feeding me and housing me... Thank you for taking care of my brother. Thank you for being you..." He whispered to me, before kissing me deeply.

I instinctively wrapped my arms around the back of his neck, as he pinned me against the side of the house. His hands went to my hips before his left hand slid down lower to my thigh. He gripped it roughly causing me to moan into the kiss. He growled possessively, hiking my leg up so that he could press himself against me.

I moaned again, feeling him rock against me. I need him. So bad.

Seth slid his tongue into my mouth, swirling it slowly around my tongue. I submitted to his dominance, my body pressed tightly to his taller form.

Alex whistled. "That's what I like to see!" He shouted from inside of the house.

Seth reluctantly pulled away from me, panting as he rested his forehead against mine.

"You... Just taste... So amazing." Seth whispered to me.

I smiled, my cheeks turning a shade darker as I was trying to catch my breath.

Holy wow. That was.... *"Fantastic."* Xena finished my sentence.

Yeah it really is.

"You taste... Like the best thing I've ever had in my mouth." I told him. Seth smirked, cocking an eyebrow at me. I licked my lips slowly, smirking back at him.

"I haven't had you in my mouth yet, but I am sure that I will absolutely be addicted to it too." I spoke inside of his mind.

Seth swallowed thickly before he shifted, reluctantly placing my leg back down on the deck. The strong scent of his arousal mixed with mine filled the air. I started blinking rapidly, my eyes turning a powerful bright purple. Xena was fighting against me, trying to take control. But she needed to calm down and stop it.

"Hey... Hey." He said softly as he took my hands gently. "Don't freak out. I liked it... I want more. I want you... I just... I want to be stronger first so I can properly take care of you." I calmed down, smiling up at him.

"I want him." Xena growled.

"Sorry..." I blushed, embarrassed.

Seth nodded in understanding before we walked into the house. Alex and Max were already sitting at the kitchen island. Did they not eat? And were they listening to us?

"Do none of you know how to cook?" I asked, reluctantly letting Seth go so he could go sit with the others.

I started to take random things out of the cabinet to make us lunch. Seth sat down beside Max, looking at his brother.

"I... I wanted to say I'm sorry about my reaction earlier... I hope you know that it isn't your fault. Your reaction to me killing Mom is one hundred percent completely understandable. And your reaction to finding out that she is still alive is understandable too. I don't blame you for a single thing... I just am having some trouble with controlling myself right now. I feel like everything is very overwhelming and I didn't want to lash out at you. I'm sorry for making you upset, I'm working on being better..." Seth told his brother, his body tense as he reached over and hugged him.

Max hugged him back, smiling happily.

I smiled as I watched them. I'm glad that I was able to save both of them. I took the bowl of fruit out of the fridge and placed it in front of them.

"Scarlett explained to me what was happening before she left. I'm just glad that you're okay and calm now. I meant what I said, you deserve to be happy. I don't want you to beat yourself up over what happened in the past. We're here now, and we're safe. I trust Scarlett will keep us safe." Max said proudly, letting his brother go so he could dig into the fruit that I had just placed in front of him.

"You three are a part of my family. I will protect you and care for you all. Nothing will happen to you here, I promise you." I assured them, winking at Seth.

He smiled at me, watching as I was starting to make spaghetti. Everyone seems to like it, so I thought it was a safe bet. Alex looked over at Seth.

"Is it true about your mom? If so... What are you going to do about it?" Alex asked, causing Seth to sigh.

He closed his eyes, breathing in deeply to still his racing heart.

"You are not alone. I'm right here." My voice rang through his mind.

Seth opened his eyes with a smile, looking at Alex now.

"I have come to the decision that I will meet with her. I'm assuming probably tomorrow. I want you to stay with Max and protect him. I don't trust her and I don't know what she is doing here, or what her plan is. I was going to meet with her today but *My Alpha...*" Seth said, his voice going slightly deeper.

I sucked in a breath at his words. My whole body heats when he says it like that. "Has told me that she wants to care for me first."

Max was too lost in his food to pay attention but Alex gasped dramatically. "That is DISGUSTING!" Alex gagged, covering his face.

Seth and I started laughing hysterically.

"I will take care of you in all ways... I can't wait till the day I can really take care of you." I practically purred in his mind.

Seth gripped the countertop in front of him, his eyes blazing red at my words. I smirked slightly, looking over my shoulder to watch him.

"Two can play at that game, my mate." Seth growled in my mind. I smirked, winking at him again.

CHAPTER
TWENTY-THREE

The next morning, I just wanted to lay here. Wrapped in his arms, under the blanket without a care in the world. My heart feels happy. I feel happy here. For once in my life, I actually feel like I belong.

"How did I get blessed so much?" Seth spoke softly, running his hand through my hair gently.

I inhaled, blinking a few times as I looked up at him. I didn't know he was awake. I smiled tiredly, I felt Xena stir as she lay in the back of my mind.

I'm happy that she is giving me this moment.

"I would ask the same... You are my greatest blessing." I told him my truth, kissing his bare chest. "Why are you up so early?"

Seth laughed nervously, looking outside now. I felt his anxiety, and I wanted to take it away from him.

"I am really nervous... I don't know if I even want to hear what she has to say. In the end, she left her two kids with a monster... And possibly blamed me for her death..." He told me.

And I should've known that. "Would anything even help with that? What could make that better?"

I frowned, sitting up to look at him better. "In all honesty. Nothing will make that better, in the end she left you. She abandoned you and your little brother. No excuse will ever make up for that. She can talk all she wants, but nothing will make that better." I told him, taking his hands gently. "But you don't need her... Everything is going to be okay. With or without her."

"I still say we should just kill her. Save him and Max from any further pain because of her. She left them. She has no right to be anywhere near them," Xena growled, showing me her displeasure.

I felt that same way honestly. But it's not my choice to make.

Seth forced an uneasy smile, squeezing my hands gently. "I just feel like visiting her... Seeing what made her leave is going to hurt more than I need." He explained, frowning slightly at the thought.

I moved to straddle his lap, my legs easily fitting on either side of him. Maybe I should take this choice from him.

"You don't have to meet with her if you don't want to... If you don't want Max to know that you didn't want to speak with her... I can take the blame. Say that I didn't think that meeting with her would help either one of you guys so I banished her. Or something like that, but I will take the blame. After all, I'm the Alpha what I say goes." I told him with a teasing smile as I shifted my hips slightly.

Xena is waking up, and I need to run off this energy. Seth growled, gripping my hips tightly.

"You are a hot little brat, I hope you know that." His voice was deep, his eyes blazing red.

I couldn't help but giggle as I leaned forward and kissed him softly. Oh I like his confidence.

"Only for you am I a hot little brat." I told him, grinning happily.

He chuckled, shaking his head.

"That is what I like to hear. I assume you want us to eat

breakfast before heading over to the packhouse?" Seth asked, moving my hips against him. I bit her bottom lip, my control over Xena slipping. My eyes started to turn purple.

If I don't have sex with this man soon. I might die.

I licked my lips, before looking back down at him. "Of course." I said, panting slightly.

Seth smiled, reluctantly letting my hips go so that I could get up. I need this man.

"Maybe we could get in the shower first?" Seth offered, scrunching his nose up. "I think I smell."

I started laughing, shaking my head before getting off of him.

Look at him making jokes now.

"I'll get our clothes while you go and get the shower started." I smiled at him, climbing off of the bed before heading to the walk in closet.

Seth watched me for a few minutes before reluctantly getting off of the bed.

Since I was able to get clothes for the both of us. I followed him into the bathroom. He looked at everything again, laughing at the size of the shower.

"I know that I've seen this before... But that shower is big enough for a wolf." He told me, slowly stripping himself of his pants. I inhaled sharply, my eyes drinking in his bare body in front of me.

Seth stepped out of his sweatpants, smirking slightly as he looked at me. I was staring right at him. Oh Goddess, am I dreaming?

I couldn't snap out of his, my eyes were glowing purple. He grunted, biting his bottom lip.

"Scar..." Seth spoke softly, opening the glass shower door and stepping inside.

I was shaking with restraint, my claws dug into my palms as

blood dripped to the floor. The pain didn't even affect me. "Why don't you join me...?"

I growled, stripping out of the sleep shorts, panties, and sports bra I had on. I walked over, opening the shower door and walking in. My body was shaking still, Seth grinned as he turned on the rain shower.

"*Let me out!*" Xena growled, needing the control.

"Why are you looking at me like that baby?" He teased, smiling as he watched me.

I licked my lips. My body looked as if I was stalking her prey. And I kind of am.

"The real question... Is why are you testing me? Why are you pushing me to lose control? When I would give you whatever you ask for." I told him, growling softly.

The water cascading around us, my hair nearly black as he reached over and pushed it behind my ears.

"Because..." Seth spoke, biting on his bottom lip.

He shifted in place slightly.

"I want to do something. Between me and you... While it's us in this private moment. I want to submit to you." I told him, keeping direct eye contact.

"Scar... Baby. You don't have to submit to me. I'm not expecting that. In fact I should submit to you.." Seth started, trying to stop me.

But I sank to my knees before bowing my head to him in respect. He needs to know that yes we are equals. But I'm not afraid to give him more power.

"I, Scarlett Rose Winters, Alpha of The Winterfall pack bow down to you... Seth Knight, Heir to the Alpha of The Bloody Rose Pack. I promise to love you. I promise to protect you. I promise to obey your every command. I promise you that you are My Alpha. My King. My Mate. For the rest of my life and till the end of time." I said, before looking up at him with bright purple eyes.

Seth's eyes watered as he bit his bottom lip again.

"I submit to you Alpha Knight. As long as you will allow me to..." I told him, watching as he got to his knees in front of me.

My body nearly vibrated. Things are changing for us. I love this.

"I..." Seth swallowed thickly. "I, Seth Knight, Heir to the Alpha of The Bloody Rose Pack. Accept your submission... But also I submit to you... I submit to Alpha Scarlett Rose Winters, Alpha of The Winterfall Pack. To protect, to love, to obey your every command. I promise to you that you are My Alpha. My Queen. My Mate. For the rest of my life and till the end of time." Seth told me, leaning his forehead against mine.

I closed my eyes, letting my power flood his senses.

"I promise that no one will ever take you away from me. For I would burn the world to protect you because you Seth... You are mine." I promised, holding his hands now. "I promise you that you won't be disappointed in me as a mate."

"I accept you as my mate." Seth breathed out, when he opened his eyes they were a bright red. "I accept you as my Alpha. I accept you as mine. As long as you will be mine in return. There is no other female for me... There is only you."

I smiled, a single tear fell down my cheek. "I accept you. I accept you as my everything. Of course I do. There is no other male for me. Only you. Just like there will be only you for the rest of my life."

Seth wrapped his arms tightly around me, holding me against him. I closed my eyes as the water fell down around us.

"You are my everything." We said in unison.

When I pulled away, Seth frowned.

"I just want to take care of you." I smiled, reaching for my shampoo to wash Seth's hair.

He chuckled as he let me bath him. "Such an Alpha you are." He teased.

"I will bite you." I growled.

When I was done washing and conditioning his hair, Seth turned around and stood up, wanting to take care of me now too.

"Oh my Goddess..." He repeated, not knowing how else to explain what he felt. "That was... Incredible." Seth groaned, remembering it.

I smirked, licking my lips as I rinsed the shampoo out of my hair. I'm glad I could make him speechless.

"I enjoyed it." I winked at him, before offering him the conditioner.

Seth walked over to me and pulled me against him. I knew he wanted to finish rinsing my hair. I like the thought that he was going to smell like me.

"Do you want me to..." His cheeks burned red, causing me to giggle.

He kissed my shoulder.

"I love taking care of you, so I don't want you to worry. You take your time. I'm not worried about anything." I explained, scrubbing my body with my rose scented body wash.

Seth started to wash my back before attending to himself. I watched as his hands scrubbed against his growing muscles. It was like a dance.

"I'm going to smell like you." He told me, scrubbing his body slowly knowing that I was watching him.

"I like that you're going to smell like me." I smiled, rinsing off the last bit of soap before leaning against the wall.

I crossed my arms over my breasts, watching as he teased me with a show. He knows what he's doing to me.

"*Oh I like confident Seth.*" Xena panted, I pressed my thighs together.

Seth let the soap rinse off his body before shutting off the shower. "I want you to smell like me too." He told me.

I opened the shower door, allowing the steam to follow us out.

"I don't think that will be a problem." I giggled at the thought, drying off with a purple towel.

Seth looked at the color scheme of the bathroom, using a towel to dry off his hair. He was using a black towel. I maybe had a little problem.

"Is everything in the house purple and black? Or well... Dark colors and purple?" He asked, watching as I started to get dressed.

I had on a purple lacey set, before shimming into a pair of black ripped skinny jeans.

"I... Yeah. I might've gone a tad overboard. It's my favorite color." I laughed, rubbing the back of my neck. "We can change whatever you want."

Seth was still naked, his cheeks flushed as he looked at the pile of clothes on the counter.

"I really like it, I just never noticed before." He informed. "It still feels weird having to put clothes on. I hope that goes away."

Seth started to pull on the hoodie and sweatpants that I had gotten for him. Until we could go shopping, this is what I had.

I smiled, pulling on a cropped t-shirt. "That is why I got you a baggy hoodie and sweatpants. I figured since you haven't been in your human form that it would make you more comfortable." I told him, kissing him softly. "Let's get you some breakfast."

"Yes I would love that." He smiled, following me out of the bathroom and bedroom, and then to the kitchen.

I started laughing as I went to the fridge.

Max and Alex were outside, play fighting. Seth smiled, sitting at the island. "I feel like maybe one day, they are going to move in together." He said, watching his brother and Alex for a moment, before turning his focus back to me.

I smiled as I started to make an omelet for him. "I can see

that, I'm sure Max will end up finding his mate too." I explained, before getting him a glass of apple juice.

Seth laughed looking at the cup I placed in front of him. "You know... I am an adult. I don't need apple juice or chocolate milk." He teased me, causing me to blush.

There is nothing wrong with apple juice or chocolate milk.

"I didn't think it was childish, I like this stuff." My cheeks burned red as I got into the fridge again.

I took out the bowl of fruit, frowning slightly as I saw it was empty. "Alex needs to learn to take care of himself."

Seth chuckled, shaking his head slightly. I'm getting a little annoyed with him.

"That's Alex for ya." He shrugged.

I sighed, waiting impatiently for the omelet to be done. "Are you nervous about today?"

I looked up at him. "Yeah... I'm nervous. I don't know what's going to happen, and I guess I just like to know everything I possibly can." I shrugged, fiddling with the spatula. "I worry about what this might do to you."

Honesty is the best policy or whatever.

"As long as you are by my side I can handle anything." Seth smiled, trying to steady his nerves.

I put the omelet on a plate for him, before placing it in front of him.

"I will be right there with you, I won't leave your side." I promised, pulling out the leftover dinner from last night.

I started to eat the hamburger, letting him start to devour the food in front of him. He deserved the fresh food.

CHAPTER
TWENTY-FOUR

After we ate breakfast, I drove us to the packhouse. Everyone was crowded around, no doubt wanting to see Seth. It wasn't the best kept secret. But when he wants to meet everyone, we'll plan something.

I revved the engine of my Bugatti causing everyone to move out of the way. I pulled into my parking spot, before parking and turning my focus back to Seth. He was trying to hide his emotions, and wasn't doing a good job.

"You don't have to do this if you don't want to..." I reassured, reaching over to take his hand.

He gulped, looking back at me now. And I can see the emotions all over his face. He didn't want to do this.

"I have to do this... No matter if I want to or not. I have to." He said, inhaling and holding his breath.

He exhaled slowly to calm his racing heart. I smiled, nodding as I unbuckled and got out of the car. Seth waited a minute before closing his eyes. I turned to look at him, smiling softly.

"I can do this." He told himself, I could read his lips, unbuckling and stepping out of the car. "Is your car a push to start?" Seth asked, wanting to change the subject.

I nodded, taking his hand gently and tapping my front jeans pocket. I typically have them on a lanyard around my neck.

But I don't want to have anything that could be used to choke me.

"They are right here." I informed, squeezing his hand as we walked up the steps to enter the pack house.

Whispers could be heard all around us as we walked through the building heading towards my office. I was used to the whispers, but he wasn't. This day was going to be hard on him.

Seth's body tensed as he looked at everyone who was whispering about us. I frowned, sensing how nervous he was. I growled, my loud voice caused the pictures frames on the wall to start to shake. In an instant everyone stopped talking.

"I always like doing that." Xena laughed in the back of my mind.

"Why do you guys think it's even remotely okay to whisper about your Alphas? Go back to whatever you were doing. NOW!" I ordered, immediately everyone started to rush around to go back to their duties.

Seth seemingly relaxed a little when everyone stopped watching us. I opened the door to my office and let him go in first.

I froze for a second. Am I going to end up having him do that for me? I shook my head, that thought would be for another time.

Seth started to pace from each side of the room. I shut the door behind me and went to my desk. "There is still time to cancel." I informed, sitting on my desk as I watched him pace.

That's healthy right? I'm not sure honestly. "You can cancel whenever you want to, even if it's while she's in here. You just tell me."

Seth walked over to where I was sitting, nudging my legs apart so he could stand in between them. "I know... I'm just freaking out. I don't want to know but at the same time I do." He said, leaning his head against mine.

I nodded in understanding, before kissing his lips gently.

"I am here. You have complete control over this situation... You have all of the power." I repeated, looking into his eyes. "I am going to be right here. Throughout the whole thing. Guards will be outside of the door. Guards are positioned around our house. You and Max are completely safe."

I allowed my power to flood through his body, I was hoping it would help calm him.

Seth nodded, his eyes looked down at my chest. "Sleeping against you... Is something I find very comforting. I hope you know that." He told me, grinning softly at me.

I laughed, motioning for him to sit behind my desk.

I truly love how confident he's getting. It's sexy.

"She's right outside of the door." I smiled, reluctantly getting off of my desk.

Seth gulped before heading to sit in my desk chair. I smirked looking at him. "I didn't think that would be as hot as it is." He laughed, cracking a smile at me.

"*That's hot. Like bend us over our desk and spank us hot.*" Xena told me, and I tried my best to not laugh at her remark.

But just thinking about him spanking me made my thighs clench together.

"Are you ready?" I asked, walking to stand behind him.

He nodded, silently giving me an answer. "Come in!"

Immediately guards walked in, dragging Emily in. I nodded to the chair in front of my desk, making the guards place her in it. "I will call for you if I need you." I told them, they nodded and left the office quickly.

Emily looked at Seth, causing me to snarl.

Oh no she doesn't. No one gets to look at him.

"You will not look at him, you will not speak unless you are spoken to. You will answer his questions honestly, and if you lie. I will know and you will be punished accordingly. Do you understand?" I asked, crossing my arms as I stood beside Seth.

By me standing behind him, it's my nonverbal way of showing my submission to him being an Alpha. My alpha.

Emily nodded, looking down at her legs. "Yes, Alphas." She said instinctively.

Seth reached for my hand, holding it tightly. I allowed my power to rush into his body, giving him my strength to use.

"Tell me why you did it..." Seth said, his eyes glowing red with anger.

I intertwined our fingers and ran my thumb over his hand gently. I will know when I need to put a stop to this.

"What do you mean?" Emily asked, her cheeks burning.

Seth growled, slamming his free fist on my desk. Ohh... I like this.

"Don't play dumb! You know what I mean! Why did you do this! Why did you leave your children? Why did you blame it on me! Why did you change your last name! Why did you leave your mate!" Seth shouted, a deep growl echoing through the room.

Emily whimpered in submission to the Alphas in front of her. I gently placed my free hand on Seth's shoulder.

"There is no excuse... Your father was a mean man. Not just to me... Not just to you... But to the pack too. He didn't care about anyone but himself. The only thing that he cared about was turning you into someone just like him. I tried my best to show you true love and happiness. I tried to let you show your emotion.

But you hung on every word your father said. I don't blame you, that's what a child is supposed to do. But as time went on... He just would get worse and worse. I couldn't handle it... I couldn't handle your power. You would force me to submit to you, which just showed that you had more power than your father.

But he forced you into submission time and time again. He made you feel like you had to be just like him. I didn't want your dad to do that to your brother. I tried to make him stop... But after a while... I found love in another... Aleckzander Williams... We fell madly in love." Emily started but Seth cut her off.

Oh... Talk about a plot twist.

I let him go, knowing he was going to stand up. He stood up, his nails digging into the wood desk underneath his hands.

"I don't know what we're supposed to do here." Xena told me honestly.

"You slept with my BEST FRIENDS dad!" Seth growled out, his eyes glowing brighter as his body shook with restraint. "You cheated on dad! You caused this!"

Emily whimpered with fear. I went to stand beside him, wanting to be prepared for anything. I needed to protect him.

"It wasn't like that at first! You were one... Your power was already so powerful!" Emily continued.

Seth was breathing heavily, the room around us started to get even hotter. Power radiated off of him in waves.

Okay I need to put a stop to this.

"You made him into the man he is. His mate cheated on him with his BEST FRIEND!" Seth growled out, his body practically vibrating with his anger. "You LEFT your child to be raised by his father ALONE. And then went back to your mate and had another KID! You made me the way I am! I needed you there but every time I needed you you weren't there!

It all makes sense now, you left. You left me and Max and Alex with Pete! You left your children! Alex didn't have a family! He grew up ALONE!" Seth was breathing heavily, his arm started to break slowly but he didn't care.

I gently placed my hand on Seth's, a silent signal that I was right there. With that touch, I pushed a wave of calm through his body.

Emily whimpered, her body shaking with fear. "I.." She started again, but he wouldn't let her talk.

"My mate has informed you you will speak when spoken too! I didn't ask you a question! So be quiet! Why did you come here!" Seth ordered, his power making me stumble slightly from being so close to it.

Emily gulped. My vision blurred. I didn't know he had that much power.

"Your father is looking for me. He wants me dead. I thought you would be happy that I came back." She tried to explain.

Seth slammed his hands on the desk again, the wood cracking and splintering from the force.

"You will leave Scotland and NEVER return. If by some mercy from the Moon Goddess you escape my fathers anger, you will live your life in exile. If you ever step foot in Scotland again, you will be killed on sight." Seth ordered, growling. "Guards!"

Immediately the guards opened the door quickly and rushed in. They grabbed her, before looking right at Seth, awaiting their orders. "Escort her to the border and MAKE sure she leaves. If she comes back to Scotland, kill her on sight. No questions asked." Seth ordered.

The guards nodded, dragging Emily to the door.

"Please! Please Seth please! I'm sorry! Please give me a chance!" Emily yelled as she was being dragged down the hall.

Seth was shaking, his eyes turning a darker shade of red. I grabbed him, holding him close.

That all... Happened really fast.

CHAPTER
TWENTY-FIVE

"Y ou're okay... Everything is okay." I assured him, rubbing his back gently.

He whimpered, biting his bottom lip as he sunk into my hold. That... That was a lot of information.

"Don't be insensitive." Xena growled at me.

"Alex is my half-brother..." Seth said, swallowing thickly.

He started to shake, even more, breathing heavily as his eyes started to dull. "What's happening!" He was starting to panic.

Is he going to turn?

"Yes... But that is okay. Because you guys are practically brothers anyway. You don't have to worry about that. Because all of you are safe now." I assured, continuing to rub his back gently.

I can't tell if he's going to turn or not. I can't feel Reign. Seth sniffled, shaking his head slightly as he looked down at the desk.

"I broke your desk... I'm so sorry." Seth frowned, his body still shaking in his hold.

I couldn't help but laugh. Oh he's the cutest thing.

"I'm not worried about the desk my love. Things can be replaced." I promised, squeezing him gently.

He was starting to cry now, his body shaking more violently. He tried to back away from me, the scent of fear filled the room.

Why is he scared?

I reluctantly let him go, as his body was slowly disappearing. "Seth baby please, calm down. You're panicking." I said, about to grab him to stop his power.

"Someone's taking him!" Xena yelled at me.

"Don't let him take me! Don't let him take me please! Please!" Seth begged before he disappeared.

I growled angrily, Xena taking control, I disappeared right after him and appeared in front of him in Ireland.

No one takes what's mine.

Pete chuckled evilly, crossing his arms at me. "And here I thought you were going to give up on him. Why not give me my children back?" He asked, glaring at me.

I snarled, baring my fangs. *He has no right to call them his children.*

"This is a sign of treason. You forcefully taking my mate out of my territory. I can kill you for this. But I am willing to leave here today, giving you your life." I growled, standing protectively in front of Seth.

He was shaking with fear behind me, clutching tightly to my shirt.

I need to get him out of here. "Agreed." Xena said.

"I think this is more fun though. Me getting my sons back. Where is Max?" Pete asked, walking towards us.

I started shaking, my restraint slipping. I reached behind me, holding Seth's hands gently. I needed to be calm for him.

I could do this.

"You're going to be just fine. But I need you to trust me, I'm going to send you back to our home." I explained to him in his mind.

His body tensed at my words. *He's not going to like this... But it has to be done.*

"*What about you! I can't leave you here with him!*" Seth was freaking out, as he didn't want to leave me.

My body tensed at his fear, my eyes staying on Pete. I need to focus. But I won't be able to focus with him here.

"*I am not giving you a choice in this my male... This is what I need to do to protect you. You will be safe in our house and I will be home soon.*" I told him reassuringly before I transported him back to our house.

I licked my lips before cracking my neck. Time for the real fun to start.

"You don't even know what I can do. Why are you starting this fight, Pete? When you know I will win without a doubt?" I asked, circling him slowly.

I eyed the crowd of wolves gathering, I rolled my eyes knowing what was going to happen.

Is he seriously going to have his pack do his business? Typical.

"You came here. Demanding something that isn't yours. Seth and Max and Alex are mine, and I want them back. Bring them back and I will not call a war on your pack." Pete growled at me. "Leave now to go and get them, and you will walk out of here unscathed."

I sighed, obviously bored with the conversation.

"*I get to fight!*" Xena yelled happily in my mind.

And I know that's exactly where this is going to lead.

"Here am I, thinking that you would fight me like a man. Instead of getting a group of your soldiers to do it for you." I sighed, my body shifting into my wolf form quickly.

My fur was pitch black, and the only thing that was standing out were my bright purple eyes. I bared my fangs again, my body tensing as I stood in a fighting position.

Let's do our thing Xena.

"Whoever draws the first blood gets control of Scotland

when I win it!" Pete yelled, looking at the people who surrounded me.

My eyes darkened with mischief, allowing the small male to run at me.

"For my alpha!" He hollered, shifting into a small red wolf before charging at me.

I ran at him, opening my jaw and clamping it around his throat. I growled, ripping it out. Blood dripped off of my teeth as I eyed Pete. My power rolled off of me in waves, and the wolves around me slowly dropped to their knees to show their submission to me.

"Pathetic! All of you!" Pete yelled, growling with frustration.

He shifted into his wolf, overweight and a deep red, he was about a foot shorter than me. I pawed the ground, my large paw sunk into the muddy grass.

Pete ran to me, growling as he snapped his teeth at me. I jumped out of the way, biting into his side. I growled with pain as he swiped his paw at me. My eyes turned a shade darker, the world around us turning darker. The sun went behind clouds as the light started to disappear.

"This ends." Xena told me.

And I allowed her to use her true power. Using the shadows to get what we needed.

"What's happening!" A young wolf whined.

This caused me to smile with pride.

"She's doing it! She has the power of the shadows!" Another wolf claimed. "Run!" They screamed, running for their lives.

"Such a pathetic, weak little pack. Just like their Alpha." My voice boomed through the air around us.

Shadow figures started to pop up around us, lurking towards where Pete stood. The strong scent of fear filled the air as he started to panic. "What is it, Pete? Are you scared of the young she-wolf who took over her pack when she was a child?"

I taunted, walking around him again. He watched me, his eyes dulling in color. He growled, his claws started to glow red. As I was walking in front of him again, he moved fast. Swiping his heated claws through my side. Immediately I felt a burn sensation shoot through my side, he burned me. I whimpered, stumbling slightly before reacting.

I gotta focus. For Seth. I need to protect Seth. This is for Seth.

I sunk my teeth into his side, ripping out another hunk of flesh. Pete growled, falling onto his side. I looked at my side, the shadows slowly disappearing as I saw black blood drop to the ground below me.

I need to get home. This isn't good.

The sun shined brighter as the grass started to die where my blood fell. I took off running as fast as I could manage, everywhere my paws touched killed more land. This is what Pete gets for crossing me.

"I will kill you for this Scarlett! You have cursed my land!" Pete yelled after me, slowly shifting back into his human form.

I shook my head slightly, my eyes slowly turning to brown as I raced through the woods.

Xena fell asleep quickly, and I just needed to get home. Get home and then everything will be okay.

With every step I took, more of my blood fell to the ground. My vision blurred slightly as I pushed my tired legs faster. I felt Pete's venom race through my veins, stinking Ember wolf venom. Muscle memory took me home, I inhaled sharply seeing the border to my land coming up.

Home... We're almost home.

I practically jumped over the border, I wanted to fall to the ground. But I knew that if I fell, I would look weak in the eyes of my pack. And I wouldn't get up again.

I need to get home. For Seth. For Seth.

I started to slow down as I was heading to my house. My eyes drooped slightly as I was happy that I picked to build my house deep into the woods.

Safe. It's safe.

Seth was fighting with Alex. "I am going after her! I don't care!! I need to make sure she's okay! I know something is wrong!" He shouted, shoving Alex away from him as he walked down the steps of the deck.

He was going to come after me?

"Scarlett can handle hers–..." Alex started, his eyes widened as he saw me emerge from the woods.

Seth looked confused before he turned his focus to where he was looking. My Male...

He's okay... He's safe. I slowed down to a walk, I didn't have the energy to run anymore.

"Scarlett!" Seth yelled, running to me.

I was limping slightly before I collapsed on the ground. He slid to a stop beside me, his eyes wide as he looked at my side.

I laid my head on the ground, staring up at him. I wanted to tell him I was okay. But I couldn't get the words out.

"Why... Why is it black? Why are you bleeding black!" He was freaking out, gently placing his hands on me.

I looked up at me, closing my eyes as I allowed myself to shift into my human form. He quickly took me into his arms, picking me up.

I wanted to whimper as pain shot through my body. But as quickly as it did, I felt it go away. It was from his touch. He's healing me.

"Please... Don't be scared... I'm... Okay..." I was breathing heavily, but still, I was trying my best to calm him down.

Seth growled, his eyes turning red as he rushed me into the house.

"Don't try and take care of me right now! You're really really hurt, I don't matter right now. You're bleeding and it's really

really bad." Seth said, his body shaking as he carried me to the master bathroom.

I whimpered as he placed me on the toilet seat. His eyes widened at me.

Oh no, my vision blurred as the pain got ten thousand times worse when he wasn't touching me. I wanted to puke.

"Just... H-hold me." I asked, forcing an uneasy smile. "I-it makes the pain... G-g-go away."

Seth gulped, biting his bottom lip as he gently placed his hands on my thighs. I inhaled sharply at the way he took my pain away.

"But I need to stop this bleeding... I need to do something." He looked down at my side, seeing that I was still bleeding profusely.

I don't like looking at my own blood. I shook my head slightly, closing my eyes. I'm going to pass out if I look at it.

"Keep your eyes open! Scarlett! Keep your eyes open!" Seth shouted, shaking me slightly.

His power crackled across my body, Xena sparked awake and a rush of power hit throughout my body. I gasped, my eyes sparking to life.

"Wha-... What did you just do?" I asked, looking at him.

TWENTY-SIX

"I don't know, but I need you to tell me how to help you heal. This doesn't look like how it should." Seth looked at my side, his face paling as he watched black smoke coming out of the long gashes.

Oh that's not a good thing.

I inhaled when he placed a hand on my side, I slammed my eyes shut. I wanted to whimper, but then I felt his healing energy and my whole body felt better.

"I don't know... I underestimated your father... He underestimated my power, my anger. And for sure underestimated the extent of what I would do to keep you with me." I told him, forcing my eyes open.

I smiled mischievously. "I poisoned the land."

I wanted to laugh. But it hurt to breathe, so laughing was off the table.

Seth looked intently at me, he didn't understand. I need to tell him.. "None of that is important, I need to heal you. Please focus... Please tell me what I can do to help you heal faster." He said to me, he moved his hand away from me.

The pain amplified and I couldn't think straight. I whimpered, grabbing his hand and placing it back on me. And that relief washed over me again.

"I am assuming that he tried to poison me..." I inhaled sharply, biting my bottom lip. "There is a way where you can help heal me. But I don't like it." Seth tilted his head slightly, looking down at my side.

Focus. Keep focusing.

"I would do anything to help you feel better." He whimpered, fear lacing his voice.

His hand slowly started to glow red, and I moaned with relief. I closed my eyes, leaning back against the toilet. I felt his power twirling around me, holding me tightly to give my wolf a break.

"You could drip your blood into the gashes... There aren't many cases of a Ember wolf poisoning a shadow wolf. But from what I've heard, the blood of a Ember wolf can cure the poison of a Ember wolf." I inhaled sharply, opening my eyes tiredly. "I will heal eventually... It's not that deep. The poison won't reach my heart." I tried to reassure him.

I just need to sleep. I'll feel better in the morning.

Seth growled at me, his eyes flashing red. If I wasn't so tired, that would've turned me on. "Stop trying to tell me you're okay. You're not okay. Your blood is black, there's black smoke coming from the claw marks, and there are black veins coursing from the wound. So, no. Baby... You are not okay. And you don't have to be okay." He snarled softly, allowing his claws to come out of his right hand.

Before quickly flashing three deep claw marks into his left wrist.

I didn't want him to hurt himself. But Xena is not waking up. I don't know what I'm going to do.

He inhaled at the pain, turning his wrist over so the blood

could drip into the wound. I closed my eyes, a few tears slipped down my cheeks. I forced my eyes open as I watched him stare at the wound.

He's not going to like this next thing. But it has to be done. I have to protect him. I have to protect everyone.

"I need to go to the packhouse," I told him, smiling sadly at him.

Seth snapped his focus back at me, his eyes still glowing red. Uh oh... He's mad at me.

"Yeah right, after this at least scabs over you're going to lay in bed until you're healed." He told me, glaring slightly at me.

I smiled, my dimples showing slightly. He's hot when he's mad. Not the time to say that but I had to admire his stern look. The way his jaw ticks.

Everything about this man was attractive.

"I have to see Gray... And Madoc... They have to know what's happening. Pete declared war by taking you, he doesn't think I'm going to strike back. I have to... And I have to strike back harder. He wants Scotland, and now he knows I want Ireland for what he did to you."

My skin slowly gained some of its color back. I felt his power holding me down and I just wanted to sleep. Seth looked down at the gashes, his wrist healed up as the claw marks started to scab over.

"That can wait, he wouldn't fight back again so soon... Would he?" He asked, placing his palm back over the healing wound.

I frowned, my brows knitting together. I have no idea. But I know I need to be prepared.

Is it possible to be dead tired and wide awake at the same time? I feel like that.

"The truth is, we don't know. We don't know what he's going to do. I felt this power in Ireland... He is grabbing at straws, the wolves submitted to me. Everyone saw it, Pete couldn't kill that many people without someone throwing a fit and overthrowing him. It took a lot out of him to try and poison me..." I explained, holding his hand gently. "Can you help me wash up please?"

Seth nodded. "Do you want to take a bath? Or a shower? I don't think you should worry about Ireland... You poisoned the land anyway. Doesn't that mean that the land will die if the land isn't surrendered to you?" He asked, I winced as he went to lift my body off of the toilet seat.

He frowned, hating that I was in so much pain.

"I didn't think about that. But thank you, I'm so sore." I told him truthfully. "I don't need to take a bath or a shower... I can wait till tomorrow. I don't want you to force yourself to do something you don't want to do."

Seth moved closer to me, cupping my face gently. Our faces were just inches apart. I want to be everything for him.

"I want to care for you... I want to protect you. I want to love you. I want to help you heal. I want to help make things better. I want you to know I am here. Please... I know you're in pain. I don't want you to be in pain. Let me do something... Anything..." He whimpered, before kissing me gently.

I leaned into it, kissing him back for a moment.

Kissing him feels natural. But I can't help but worry that I'm rushing him into this.

"I just never wanted you to feel rushed into something..." I told him softly, resting my forehead against his.

Seth smiled, his eyes sparkling with mischief. What does he have going on in his mind?

"Well the other day in the shower was amazing, really sold the whole thing for me." He told me jokingly.

I started laughing before pain shot through my body. I clutched my still healing side.

"Ouch, ouch don't make me laugh!" I giggled, smiling at him.

He gently cupped my face with his large hand. His large. Loving. Hand.

"I'm sorry my love... Let me run you some bathwater... And then I will consider letting you talk me into letting you speak with your brother and your Delta." Seth said, standing up and heading to the large Amethyst crystal bathtub.

I smiled, watching him for a second. I can't believe he just lied to my face.

"You're a terrible liar. Don't get my hopes up." I smiled as he bent slightly.

Seth made quick work of getting the water turned on hot. The water looks delightful... I hope it helps.

"You're right." He told me, standing up before smirking as he saw me staring at him. "I am not letting you go see your brother and Delta today. I don't necessarily like your Delta anyway. Can I try something?" I nodded, waiting for him to come pick me up.

I have to brace for the pain, it's mostly gone due to his blood coursing through my body.

"You are free to do whatever you want. Except if you want to do anything to me, I would like a rain check because it hurts to just sit here." I told him, trying to lighten his mood.

Seth frowned, looking at the shelves I had filled with different herbs. Some of them made me want to sneeze.

"I wasn't going to do that because I know how much pain you're in... I remember when I was young. I would get hurt sometimes cause I had too much self-confidence and fought people bigger than me. That's not even the point of this whole story. My mother would show me different herbs to use to help prompt healing.

Based on everything that you have here... You tried to do the same thing? Did it ever work for you?" Seth asked, grabbing different jars and sprinkling some of their contents into the water.

I sighed, shaking my head no.

"I tried... But it never seemed to work out. I could heal my brother and my sister just fine. But when it came to me... It's like something was keeping me from healing. So I tried to get into the whole herb thing. Yeah, it didn't really work out for me." I laughed, I was obviously embarrassed.

Seth shook his head slightly, stripping himself of his clothes. My cheeks turned pink as he got down on his knees in front of me.

How did he go from being so insecure to just being naked right in front of me? Not that I'm complaining.

Seth gently placed his hands on my thighs. "There was a myth... I didn't believe it. But it was said that sometimes, a wolf will refuse to heal herself because their inner wolves don't feel complete. Only complete healing could be done when mates are connected again." He explained, standing up and picking me up gently.

I tried not to whimper at the sudden movement. With every movement, I felt it... Hard. It nearly took my breath away.

"I'm sorry... I'm trying to be as gentle as possible." Seth told me, climbing into the bathtub and gently placing me in front of him.

I inhaled softly, leaning back into his chest. I felt my body numb when I was submerged. Thank the Goddess.

"Oh, Goddess I didn't think that would feel as amazing as it does." I said, closing my eyes.

Seth smiled softly, gently braiding my long brown hair so that it wouldn't get wet. I leaned completely against him, letting him wrap his arms around my front.

"You do too much my love... You deserve to have someone take care of you. I know I'm not the strongest wolf yet... But I do want to take care of you... And I hope that you will let me..." Seth spoke softly, gently caressing my body.

I sighed, refusing to open my eyes. I just wanted to stay in this moment forever.

"When you had a childhood like ours... You learn to do too much. You learn to be everything so your little siblings don't miss the parents they didn't have. Being right here... With you. In this tub... I am at peace, I think we can do some good things together." I told him, smiling as I finally opened my eyes. "I think we could do a lot of good things together."

Seth chuckled, shaking his head slightly. "I am at peace here with you too. We're such a perfect match, we both make dirty jokes to make the other feel better."

He smiled, holding me tightly against him. I giggled at the feeling of our power mingling in the water. It's like dancing across my skin, I love it.

"Sure. I'm totally joking." I laughed. "Tomorrow... We will have to meet with the general." I frowned, Seth groaned.

CHAPTER
TWENTY-SEVEN

The next morning, I was sleeping soundly on my side until I woke up. I was pressed against Seth, he was like my own personal form of pain relief. Suddenly he woke up with a start, his heart racing as he looked down at me. Even with my eyes closed, I felt his on my body.

I opened my eyes as I looked up at him. He opened his eyes again to look at me.

"What's wrong?" I asked, wincing slightly as I went to sit up.

He shook his head, wrapping his arms around me and keeping me against his chest. What rattled him so much?

"It's just a nightmare... Same ol' same ol'... Don't worry about anything." Seth told me, trying to act like everything was fine.

We are so alike in that aspect. I looked up at him, letting my body press to his.

I'm not letting him move past this topic till he tells me.

"What nightmare?" I pressed, frowning slightly as I knew something was wrong.

He closed his eyes again as he leaned against the headboard.

"This time... It was different... I was the Alpha of Ireland and you were right by my side. I didn't think anything of it. Every-body was happy and loved that I was the Alpha, and things were prosperous. The sun shined brighter... The food tasted better. Everything was better..." Seth started, his cheeks turning pink.

I tilted my head in confusion at him. How is that bad?

"I don't see how this is a nightmare?" I asked, trying to understand.

He laughed nervously, opening his eyes to look down at me.

"We had kids. I don't know how many, but there were a lot of them. It was the happy family I always dreamed about... We were out in the field together, that one that we were laying in when my mother found us. So our territories were joined together and it was peaceful. But everything turned dark...

A young she-wolf, a lot like you actually... She was head-strong, powerful, and beautiful... She was just like a mini-you. She went running off into the woods, and my father grabbed her. I don't know why it was a nightmare, my entire body felt cold. I saw his hands on her, grabbing her throat like he did to me so many times.

I felt utterly useless..." Seth told me honestly, closing his eyes tightly at the memory.

I frowned, moving up slightly so I could lay on his chest better. I wish I could just protect him from all of those nightmares.

"It's okay baby... You aren't useless. You are powerful and strong... You are wonderful. We don't have any babies yet. And just so you know, I want a big happy family too." I told him, kissing him softly to ease his worries.

Seth smiled into the kiss, wrapping his arms around me again.

I wish Xena would wake up, I don't know how to handle this without her.

"How is your side doing?" Seth asked, shifting so that I was laying down and he was hovering above me.

I smiled up at him, my eyes sparkling slightly. And that answers my question.

"It's fine, I'm perfectly healed," I told him, smiling innocently.

Truth is, my side hurt a lot with every move. But I was hoping he believed me. He growled, sensing my lie. "It's somewhat sore." I finally told him the truth. Or somewhat of the truth.

"Somewhat sore." He huffed, pulling up my hoodie and frowning as he looked at the bruise on my side. "Maybe we can postpone talking to the general?" I frowned, taking his hands gently.

"Every second that I don't plan my revenge on Pete. Is a second that he gets ahead of me. Is a plan that he could plan to take my pack... My territory... I worked too hard and too long for me to hand over everything I built to him." I told him, kissing his hands gently.

I'm fine. I have handled so much worse.

"I promised you I would protect you, and I'm not gonna switch on that because I'm a little sore. I've been hurt far worse than this before."

Seth nodded, his frown stayed on his lips. "I understand... But I don't want you getting yourself killed for me... I don't want you getting hurt because of me." He told me, his eyes turning red.

I could never leave this pretty face.

"I'm not going to get hurt... But I need to make sure my family is safe. And that's not just my blood family... That's you, Max, Alex, and my pack... I have to get Gray to find Stormy and get her back to Scotland. I don't trust Pete, I feel like he's going to use her to get to me... I can't let my little sister get hurt." I told him with a soft smile, my eyes sparkled.

I felt Xena shifting inside, and I was hoping she would wake up fully."You can come with me."

"What about Stormy?" Seth asked, trying to change the subject.

His heart was racing as he leaned against me. He was scared... And I didn't know how to ease those fears. I could die. But I was going to try my hardest to stay alive.

"When things were good, I had the world scared of me. Stormy told me that she didn't want to stick in one place, now that our father was dead. She wanted to explore, I understood what she meant. So I let her go, I told the pack she was going to different packs to make appearances on our behalf.

But I haven't heard from her in months. I've been searching the entire world for her, but Stormy knows how to hide. If she doesn't want to be found, she won't be found. Which is irritating me because I don't know if she's safe. I don't know if she's dead. Actually, I take that back, I can feel that she is still alive.

But I just want to know where she is... Who she's with. I don't know a single thing about what she's been doing. It's like she dropped off the face of the earth. I don't like it, and I also don't like that I'm going to have to send Grayson out to find her himself." I sighed, groaning as I sat up.

Seth whimpered softly, helping me move quickly so it didn't hurt me.

I could moan at the relief he gave me. Each day it will get easier.

"Why do you have to send Grayson out to find her? Why don't you just order for her to come home through the pack mind link?" Seth asked, knitting his brows together. "I'm not trying to be mean or anything... I just don't understand what's going on."

I laughed softly, keeping my hand on him. He's my pain relief and I'm soaking it up.

"I am not upset with you. I just don't know a lot of information other than what I've already told you. Grayson and Stormy...

They... They got even closer when I became Alpha. I sadly didn't have as much time for them. I made as much time as I could, I just didn't have all of the time to spend with them anymore.

We were all super close before everything escalated. But they got even closer, which is something I loved to see. But Gray knows how Stormy's powers work better than I do. He knows how she hides, he knows the signs of where she's been. He can bring her home better than anyone else. I don't want him out there alone, but I know if Stormy senses more than just Grayson; she will run even more.

She is very sensitive and doesn't really like people. But it's fine because I love my sister for who she is and I would never change her. But yeah, I would prefer to not send anyone out alone. I don't trust Pete, and I don't know what he's got going on." I told him honestly, standing up with a slight growl of pain.

Having all of my siblings here in my territory will be good. I'll be able to know that they're safe and won't have to worry. Seth got up beside me, hurrying to grab me shorts and a hoodie to put on. New ones at least.

"I wish you would just let me take care of you. I understand that you would want your siblings safe, after all that's what I would want to. I mean that's what I do want, as you can see." Seth laughed nervously, gently placing me back down on the bed. "I just want for you to heal."

"I'm sorry my love... I just am very used to being the main person taking care of everything. I just wanted to go and make you breakfast. I think Max is still sleeping." I told him with a soft smile.

Seth smiled back at me, gently pulling down my sleep shorts before putting on my gym shorts.

I felt Xena growl with pain, but I tried my best to not tense. I didn't want to make Seth feel any worse than what he already does.

"I can make you breakfast... I know a little about cooking. I don't think that it would be terrible. But I think that he is still sleeping, I don't hear him moving around out there. But I know how it is being the person to take care of everything. But you've been taking such good care of me, I want to take care of you now." Seth explained, standing up and gently lifting the shirt I had on off of me.

I watched as his eyes drifted down my body, and a blush crept up my neck.

Ohhh how I wish we could do things. But I can't.

"Thank you... For helping me. For wanting to take care of me." I spoke softly, biting my bottom lip.

Seth's cheeks burned red, forcing himself to look up at my face now. At least he likes what he sees.

"Thank you for sticking with me." His voice was barely a whisper, he helped me put on the hoodie.

I inhaled sharply as his hand grazed over the bruise. "I'm so sorry."

Oh help me now Goddess.

"It's okay, really. It just still hurts a bit." I smiled, taking his hands and standing up. "Maybe after this whole thing, you can bathe me again."

Seth laughed, shaking his head as he helped me to the door. Nothing matters as long as he's touching me.

"I didn't think that you would like it that much." He smiled, his arm wrapped around me gently.

He was being careful not to touch my bruise. "Is that okay?" I nodded, kissing his cheek gently.

"It doesn't hurt anymore." I told him.

Seth grinned, opening the door, startled as he saw Grayson standing there.

"Oh! I'm so sorry!" Grayson quickly apologized. "I didn't know you guys were... I'm so sorry Alpha."

CHAPTER
TWENTY-EIGHT

I couldn't help but laugh painfully as I held onto Seth. Gray looks so uncomfortable. "Stop making me laugh." I said, clutching at my side.

Seth held me up, feeling the slight poison in my bloodstream still. It feels a little more than slight, I just know that it's draining me a bit.

"What's wrong?" Grayson asked with a frown, eyeing me. "I felt something yesterday... I came by and Alex said that you were busy and couldn't talk. You didn't leave the packhouse yesterday. What happened?" I smiled, reaching over to squeeze my brothers hand.

"First off. I'm okay... I'm still a little sore. I feel like I was hit by a car repeatedly on my side, but I'm healing. I was going to tell you everything when this one would let me out of here." I smiled teasingly at Seth.

He still hadn't spoken a word, he kissed the top of my head. At least he hasn't ran, or cried. I'm so proud of him.

"At least he cares about you!" Grayson offered with a positive energy.

He nodded, motioning for me to move over so we could walk through. Standing hurt. So I want to sit down. Grayson nodded as we all walked to the kitchen together.

I'm just impatiently waiting for Xena to wake up from her nap.

Seth gently sat me down on a chair at the kitchen island. I squeezed his hands gently, leaning my forehead against his. "I'm okay..." I repeated, feeling his fear and anxiety.

He forced an uneasy smile. I know he doesn't think I'm okay, but I know I am. I'll be okay.

"I... I know..." Seth said, before kissing my forehead. "I'm just worried about you... I can't stand the thought of losing you."

I love hearing his voice in my head.

I watched as he went to search around the kitchen for random things. What is he making? Grayson looked at us, tilting his head slightly.

"So what happened?" Grayson asked, breaking the room of silence.

I snapped my focus to my brother. He's probably going to be seriously mad for this.

"Like I had told you... We were going to meet his mother. Everything was going okay, all things considered. I won't go into details about it, but Seth made the decision to banish her after learning some things. I completely gave him full control of the situation, so I backed his order. Not that I needed too, everybody is slowly learning that he is my mate and has equal power.

But he disappeared, which is weird considering I don't think he can do that. But it turns out his dad forced him to go to Ireland... I of course followed after him. Pete wants Seth and Max and I told him no. Seth, Max, and Alex are a part of our pack now. I want them protected no matter what happens to me." I started before Seth's growl interrupted me.

My cheeks turned pink as I looked at him.

I felt Xena slowly start to wake up. I knew he would be the one to wake her up. And turns out I was wrong. Seth was going to be mad at me, not Gray.

"Nothing is going to happen to me. I am fine, I'm going to be just fine. But I fought Pete... He wants me dead. He wants Scotland for himself so we fought for a while. I didn't know that he was still in touch with his Ember wolf form. But he does and he scratched my side, it was pretty bad honestly.

But I poisoned the land with my blood, I think soon people from The Bloody Rose Pack will be venturing here to submit to me as their Alpha." I continued, before Grayson started laughing at my story.

I couldn't help but smirk. I didn't think it was possible, until I did it.

"Shut up, you did NOT poison Ireland!" Grayson laughed, holding his stomach from laughing so hard.

Seth turned around, placing the freshly cut bowl of fruit in front of me. My heart skipped a beat, he remembered the fruit?

"Why is that such a shock?" Seth asked, turning his attention to Grayson.

"There was this old legend about fighting Alpha's. That if a neighboring Alpha spills his..." Grayson laughed nervously. "Her... Blood. Spills her blood on their land. That if the pack believes in her so much, that her blood could poison the land until she is given the pack. Everything would die off slowly, starting with the plants, before going to the animals and people.

I knew she was capable of doing that, I just never thought she would actually do it." He chuckled, shaking his head slightly.

Seth nodded in understanding, turning his focus to me now. I never thought I would actually have to do it. But here we are.

"Eat. Or I won't." Seth threatened, growling softly at me.

I bit my bottom lip, I like it when he growls at me. I giggled, eating a piece of strawberry in front of him.

"He should growl at us more often." Xena yawned.

And I could shout with excitement. She's awake. Everything would be okay.

"I am eating I am eating." I told him, starting to eat more as he went on to make pancakes.

This man is everything to me.

"So what are we going to do?" Grayson asked, smiling at my happiness.

I don't think I've ever been this happy.

"You're going to get Stormy, no one has been able to find her. And I'm hoping that you will be able to. I don't want you to go alone though, take someone with you. Someone that Stormy gets along with. Pete called for war. He took my mate, and I'm going to take his territory and his pack for it. I'll take his life for what he thought he could do to me.

But yes, I will meet with the general in a few days when I'm healed. I can't do much, I still feel the poison in my body. For now though, I need you to tell her to keep the army ready, ready for anything. Pete is going to try something, but I don't know what and I don't know when. I feel like he might be going for Stormy first...

Using our amazing little sister to bend me to his will. It'll never happen though, she's too smart. But I still want her safe, and the safest place for her until this whole thing is over is to be in Scotland." I informed, causing Grayson to nod as he started to write a note in his phone.

"I will take care of everything... Do you need anything? Do I need to send the doctor over?" Grayson asked, staring intently at me. "I hope you're being nice to him."

My jaw dropped as I stared at him. Seth laughed quietly, shaking his head as he placed a few large heart shaped pancakes in front of me.

I need to be super extra like he's being for me. And I can't believe my brother would say that.

"I am nice!! I have been very nice to him!" I whined with embarrassment.

Grayson started laughing as I playfully smacked his arm. I would never be mean to my mate.

"I'm just saying, you tend to be a bit harsh." He winked.

I blushed as Seth bent down to kiss my forehead. The touchiness is amazing, I crave it.

"I think she is absolutely perfect just the way she is." Seth told us, leaning against the counter as he watched me eat.

These are amazing. Grayson smiled, taking out his phone and taking a picture of us.

"I am so glad that you guys finally found each other. I am going to head out so I can go get things squared away for when I go and find Stormy. I'm sure she's completely fine, you know how she is. Sometimes she just likes her private time. Maybe she found a pack she really likes and has started to make friends." Grayson shrugged, standing up.

Seth and I looked at him. "No she hasn't. You're trying to indirectly say she found her mate and hasn't brought him back here yet." I laughed, about to stand up before Seth growled at me.

Ah okay someone's mad mad at me.

"Okay okay okay, I'm not going to stand up." Seth nodded in approval.

Dang it. I wish he would call me a good girl.

Xena snorted with laughter in the back of my mind.

Grayson started laughing hysterically. "Who knew an alpha she-wolf would be so quick to submit herself to her mate." He teased, before he eyed my expression.

I growled, flashing my fangs at him. Can I bite him? I kinda wanna bite him.

"Don't start with me. When you find your mate, you will understand how it feels." I snapped slightly.

Seth moved closer to me before kissing my cheek. Just that kiss made me feel so much better.

"I'm going to leave before I get my head bitten off! I truly love you, my sister and my Alphas! Next time I will try my best to not interrupt you guys' private time." He continued to tease before he quickly left the house.

Seth couldn't help but chuckle at the interaction.

I know we have a kind of... Unique relationship.

"I haven't submitted publicly..." I blushed, watching as he took a pancake from my plate. "But I was going to talk to you about that..."

Seth tilted his head, studying my face slightly. "Okay... I don't know what you're talking about..."

Eventually it needs to be done... I just need for him to be ready.

CHAPTER
TWENTY-NINE

I shifted uncomfortably. "I hate doing this to you so soon. But it's something we're going to have to talk about..."

I frowned slightly, looking at his eyes. He looked down at the plate in front of me.

If things go as planned, we will take control of his pack and then... We're going to need to make a choice about who will submit to who.

"Is this about you submitting to me in front of everyone... Because if it is, I don't..." Seth started before I grabbed his hands and squeezed them gently.

I know it's not something he wants. But we need to decide sooner rather than later what we're going to do.

"In your pack... It is customary for the mate of the Alpha to publicly show their submission to their Alpha... I am not expecting you to take control of your pack. But I want you to know that you are my equal. I don't see myself as higher than you..." I spoke softly, kissing his hands as I locked my eyes with him.

"I don't know what I want. I don't want you going for Ireland if it's going to get you killed." He told me, his body shaking slightly with fear. "You looked like you were going to die. I thought you were going to leave me... I... I..."

I frowned, standing up quickly and hugging him tightly.

Xena whimpered, as she watched our interaction. I wish I could make him realize that everything was going to be okay.

"I got hurt... But I wasn't going to die. I promise you, I'm okay... I'm sorry for scaring you, I didn't mean to. But I am going to go for Ireland... I don't trust your dad, I do think he's going to continue to come for you and Max. And I won't let that happen, I know for a fact that there is tension in Ireland.

I felt it when I forced people to submit. Things are changing... I feel it in my bones. I know that makes no sense, but I do know that there is something brewing in Ireland. I wish I could send someone over there to see what's happening, but it's not safe." I told him, biting my bottom lip.

It would make things so much easier if I knew what was happening.

"If I knew that for one hundred percent certainty that you and Max would be safe. I wouldn't go for Ireland."

Seth nodded in understanding, he kissed my hands gently. "I just want you to be safe... That's all... And I agree with you. My dad won't stop until he gets what he wants. And in this situation... He wants us dead because of me." He gulped slightly, his eyes sparkling red as he tried to control himself.

"It would be super hot if he didn't control himself." Xena grinned.

"I don't want you to submit yourself to me in front of everyone. You've already gone through so much... Adding in showing submission to me. That's not necessary... Your pack just knows rumors and myths about me. They don't know me... They know you though. They know you are the heir to the pack.

They will want you as the Alpha, they won't want me to be the Alpha. But it's your choice, if you want me to run your pack then I am completely okay with that." I told him, kissing his cheek gently. "No one is going to make you do anything you don't want to do."

Especially me. I'll figure something out if he doesn't want to be the Alpha of his pack. I'll make them submit to me.

"I don't know... I would love to be the Alpha ya know? It's been what I wanted since I was a child. And now... It might be petty, but I want to show him that I can be a better Alpha than he could be. I want so badly to prove to my mother that I could've been enough to keep her in my life.

I want the life I always dreamed about. I want our kids to have a safe space... I want so many different things." Seth explained, his cheeks turning pink. "But if you want to be the Alpha of The Bloody Rose Pack. I don't mind submitting to you. I know you wouldn't hurt me like my father did. I trust you."

I smiled at him, kissing him softly. "I completely understand, you are going to be an amazing Alpha. Pete will die. If you change your mind at any time, just tell me, baby." I told him, smiling at him.

Seth was about to reply before he stumbled slightly. "What's wrong?"

I wanted to get up, but I knew I wouldn't be able to catch him in this state.

"My vision..." He said, as he grabbed onto me and we both blacked out.

When we woke up, we were standing in an empty field together. "What's going on?" Seth asked immediately, his eyes wide as he looked around.

I don't like the feeling of this.

"I think that this is a meeting from the Moon Goddess..." I spoke softly, I looked at the world around us. "This is a field in Scotland... It's the place I killed my dad."

Seth turned his focus to me, looking at me intently.

Why are we at the field that I killed my dad?

"Why did she bring us here? Where is she? What is happening? Why did she make us blackout? Why did she make me blackout before you?" Seth fired off question after question.

I couldn't help but laugh quietly. I don't have the answers to the questions.

"Okay okay hold on there firecracker. One question at a time. I don't know why she brought us here, I don't know where she is. I don't know what is happening. I don't know anything other than what we experienced together." I told him, intertwining our fingers together. "We just have to wait and see what happens."

At least we have each other.

Seth held my hand tightly, walking forward now as he wanted to explore. Explore it back then... Since he's seen this place before.

"This is where you killed your dad?" He asked, looking at everything.

I nodded, waving my hand slowly before two shadow figures appeared.

"This has gone on long enough! I won't let you hurt us any longer! It's not our fault mom left you!" A young me screamed out before running at my father.

I turned away, my face paling at the memory. This is the day that my life forever changed... I couldn't stop moving forward after this moment.

"You didn't have to show me if you didn't want to... I would've seen it when we marked." Seth spoke softly, his cheeks turning pink.

I looked at him, surprise written over my features. Did he just say that? Did he really do that?

"Did you just...?" I asked, my eyes were slightly wide. "We hadn't talked about that before... We kind of skipped over that."

Seth's cheeks turned a shade darker.

"I figured we had to talk about it eventually." He told me, looking

at the bright light in front of us. "I'm assuming that that's the Moon Goddess..." I frowned looking at him.

"I wish she would've given us more time..." I pouted, before forcing a smile as I turned my focus to the Goddess in front of us.

"My children." The Moon Goddess' voice was sweet and angelic. "The time has come where I must give you a bit of information."

Seth was stunned as he watched her, he swallowed thickly.

"What do you have to tell us Moon Goddess? Are we doing something wrong?" I asked, holding Seth against me.

Don't take him away from me... Please. I just got him. I wanted to beg. I wanted to get on my knees and beg her not to take this away from me. Seth looked down at me, closing his eyes before pressing a kiss to the top of my head.

Fear made my heart race. I wanted to wake us up. But when the Moon Goddess wanted to talk to you. The Moon Goddess was gonna talk to you one way or another. I can't do this. I don't know what I'm going to do if I lose him.

"You both have done nothing wrong, my sweet children. But there is some information for you to know before things progress." The Moon Goddess spoke, walking beside us now. "There is a reason that I brought you here. This place holds significant meaning. Do you feel the power that courses through the ground?"

"Of course... Why is that?" Seth asked, looking at the Moon Goddess now.

I squeezed his hand gently. It's my power... I feel my power flowing through the Earth beneath us.

"I would like to know that too," I added in.

The Moon Goddess laughed quietly.

"I thought you would've understood Scarlett. This place is where you sealed your destiny. This is where you made everyone know that you are a blessed from me. You have listened to everything I have said, and have done everything I requested. But this place is a sacred land, *this is the place you gave all your trust to me and allowed me to seal your destiny.*

This is the place where everything will change when the time comes. As you know, I will not be able to give you all of the information. But I will give you something to help you." The Moon Goddess spoke, motioning to the healthy forest around us. "A wolf will be born from those who used to be enemies... With the great power of both breeds, her eyes will be two colors, showing her unique power and abilities.

She will have power that is unlike any other and will either bring the world to peace and into a new era. Or she will be the cause of the world's destruction. A new breed will come alive, and show the world their true strength.

The event you think of will not end in the way you imagined it to... But the end will be surprising in the greatest of ways." The Moon Goddess explained, stopping to give both of us a look.

Seth looked like he was processing everything, trying to figure out the puzzle. I looked surprised at her, my eyes slowly turning purple.

What did she just say?

"A wolf will be born of those who used to be enemies..." I said, my mind slowly piecing everything together.

"I have given you everything that I can give you my children. I know with this guidance, you will one day understand everything. I trust that you will be able to figure out how this will benefit you. I wanted to give you something that shows you that even though you guys have been through a lot. That I am here and I am looking out for you." The Moon Goddess smiled, bowing her head slightly to us.

Seth and I bowed back, staring in shock at her.

"For now this is goodbye my children..." The Moon Goddess explained before disappearing.

Almost immediately Seth and I woke up, we were laying on the floor. I was on top of him as he instinctively wrapped his arms around me. What the heck just happened?

"Oh, my Goddess..." Seth said, staring at me in surprise.

I tilted my head in surprise.

"Why are you looking at me like that? I mean I know I'm laying on top of you. Is it because you are getting turned on and aren't prepared to take things further? If so tell me and I can move." I flushed, my body instinctively squirming at the thought.

He chuckled in response, shaking his head no.

"No no no it's not that. And if the shower the other day didn't show you that I'm willing to take things slow then I don't know what will." Seth explained, looking at my face again. "I am just thinking about the prophecy... I think that I might know what it means."

THIRTY

S eth stood up with a slight groan, he kept me in his arms as he walked to our bedroom. I looked at Max's room before I looked at Seth. I haven't seen Max yet today.

"Where is your brother?" I asked, obviously confused.

Seth opened the door to our bedroom and walked in. He used his foot and kicked the door shut before walking to place me on the bed.

"I'm sure that he is with Alex, they have been liking to explore. I saw them walking into the woods before you woke up." Seth explained before sitting down beside me.

I shifted to the middle of the bed before looking at him intently. I want to know about this vision, I need to know what he thinks.

"So explain what you think the little vision thing meant," I told him, sitting cross-legged so he could sit in front of me.

His cheeks heated as he looked at me. Why is he so embarrassed?

"I feel like this might make me sound a little crazy." Seth laughed nervously, biting the inside of his cheek.

I reached over and squeezed one of his hands.

"I don't know... But it's making no sense to me." Xena said, tilting her head in the back of my mind.

"I don't want you to be nervous, I don't think you're going to sound crazy. Just tell me what you're thinking of." I smiled, making our legs touch since he was sitting cross-legged in front of me.

I want us to be open and honest with each other.

"Okay just stick with me okay. So the prophecy said that it would be a wolf born of enemies. Enemies mean anything at all... A new breed of wolf will show the world their true power. Enemies that are wolves.

Legend has it that shadow wolves and Ember wolves are enemies. I know it's ironic considering us. But that's not the point, she said that it's a new breed of wolf. Meaning, two powerful wolves that are enemies, breeding, and mated together. I feel like this is trying to talk about our children.

Think about it, it would make sense! It would make a lot of sense! Because our kids would technically be a new breed because of the two breeds coming together. And two-colored eyes? That could be their wolf's eye color! And now that I'm saying this out loud, it makes no sense because I can't figure out why the moon goddess brought us to the specific spot." Seth explained, trying to figure everything out still.

I looked at him, before nodding slowly. His eyes widened when I didn't say anything. I just... He figured all of that out in like? No time?

"You can tell me I'm being crazy, I just wanted to try and make everything make sense," Seth said quickly, biting his bottom lip hard.

I frowned, leaning forward and kissing his lips softly. I feel horrible about myself, I should've said something.

"He's okay." Xena whimpered to me.

I just worry about him.

"I just needed a moment to understand everything. It makes a lot of sense, so I'm not saying you're wrong. I'm just saying this whole thing is confusing. Because what does the field where I killed my dad have to do with anything? Other than it being a powerful piece of land because of the emotions that I had that day." I told him, smiling slightly as I looked over his face.

Seth sighed out in relief.

Is it too much to ask for me to have one day where a new prophecy isn't coming up to stress me out?

"I was thinking about that, what if my dad tries to do something here? Maybe he thinks that you will not want to go to that area because of everything you endured there? I could go to Ireland and se–..." He started before he quickly stopped as he saw my features change.

My eyes turned a powerful dark purple.

"Over my dead body would that happen." Xena growled.

I'd rather lock him in the house before letting that happen.

"Don't say that, you're not going back to Ireland until Pete is dead. You're NOT stepping anywhere near that territory until he's dead and I stop the stupid curse." I growled, my body tense at the thought. "If you can't stand the thought of me dying, why do you think I can stand the thought of you dying? I spent years hearing your screams, feeling YOUR pain! I could never understand what was happening but now I do."

Seth looked at me, surprised at my outburst. I'm surprised at my outburst too..."I'm sorry... I didn't mean anything bad. I just want to help you in any way I can, this is all happening because of me. I feel responsible." He frowned, holding my hands gently to try and ease my worry.

I frowned, I feel like the worst mate imaginable.

"I'm sorry for the sudden outburst. I should've calmed myself before acting like that. I just... Pete got to me. And I'm scared of not being able to protect you. That's why I sent you back here that day. Everything is just a lot and I don't know what I'm supposed to do. I need Stormy here before anything escalates.

This means Alex will need to step up as Delta since I know Madoc won't be able to handle things." I sighed, putting my legs around his waist and pulling myself into his lap. "Things are going to start moving very fast. I need to know if you're going to be okay."

Once things start. Things will continue to move quickly, and I won't be able to stop it. Or slow things down.

Seth wrapped his arms around me, putting his head on my shoulder. "I don't know if I'm going to be okay with things moving fast, but I know I won't have another choice. I think I can handle anything if you're right there to help me through it. I know, you probably would've loved someone else as your mate.

Ya know an Alpha that can handle situations like this... And I hope one day I can be that Alpha for you... Even though I know you're an Alpha in your own right and don't need me to be an Alpha for you. But I would love to be everything you need." He told me, his voice soft as he looked out of the glass wall staring out into the open. "I need to keep Max protected from all of this..."

"Of course... I promise you that nothing will ever happen to you or Max again. And Seth... My love. My male. My mate. You are everything to me, you mean so much to me already. You are everything I've always wanted or needed. I love you for who you are, I don't need you to be an Alpha for me.

I don't mind taking care of everything and handling every-thing. I just want you, I want you in any station you are. I want you to be mine. I want you to be my mate. I would never ask for anyone else. Because your heart, your love, your personality.

Everything about you draws me in. And I don't want you to put yourself down.

You went through something absolutely terrible, and I am here for you. Please believe me when I tell you that I want you. I want you for who you are, not just because you are the heir of the bloody rose pack. But because you're an amazing brother, friend, and mate. You are trying so hard to put everyone else before you.

And I'm here to put you first to show you that you are perfect." I explained to him, gently pulling away to look him in the face.

I need him to know I'm telling him the truth.

"You are my everything, you are perfect and I would never ask for anyone else. Because you are the most perfect and the greatest blessing in my life. You are already the man I want by just being you." I promised, kissing him gently.

Seth growled in approval into the kiss, he had me pinned to the bed quickly. He kissed me hungrily, sliding his tongue into my mouth.

Seth pinned my hands above my head, his eyes glowing red. "I can't wait to have your belly swollen with my babies." He growled possessively before his eyes widened.

My whole body heated at his words. Did he really just say that? I smiled as my arousal scented the air around us.

"*Oh that's so hot.*" Xena whimpered, and I knew we couldn't hold off marking forever.

"I... I-..." Seth laughed nervously, biting his bottom lip as he tried to get off of me but I wouldn't let him move.

I wrapped my legs around his waist and pulled him down against me. No way he's backing down from this. I won't let him.

"I think that is the hottest thing I've ever heard you say to me," I told him with a soft smile, I scraped my nails down his bareback gently. "I can't wait to see you all hot and bothered because I'm pregnant. It's going to make my boobs big."

My boobs. My stomach. I wonder how I'll handle being pregnant.

Seth's eyes drifted down to my chest, his cheeks tinted before looking back at my eyes. "Bigger." He corrected.

I tilted my head at him.

"What?" I asked, wanting him to clarify.

What is he talking about?

"Bigger. You said it's going to make my boobs big. It's going to make your boobs bigger. Your boobs are already big, that's the thing, they are perfectly round... Perfectly perky... Perfectly big...." He trailed off, his gaze drifting back down to my covered chest.

I giggled, gently pulling his face up to look at me. I swear I fall more and more in love with him as the days pass.

"My eyes are up here my love." I teased him, causing him to grin at me.

"I can't help it!" Seth kissed my cheek. "Everything about you screams perfect... Everything about you screams mine mine mine. Including that sexy tattoo in between your perfectly beautiful breasts." He shook his head slightly, trying to keep his focus on the conversation.

I laughed quietly, smiling at him. I flashed my fangs at him, growling playfully.

"I am gonna need you to put a tattoo on you that claims you as mine. But I do think that I would prefer the bite mark." I teased him, he shook his head with a smile.

"Good job at throwing it in the conversation!" Xena praised me.

"I can't wait to bite your neck to show everybody that you belong to me." He growled against my lips, before crashing his lips against mine again.

THIRTY-ONE

Three months passed, the weather had changed from warm sunny days to chilly and cloudy. I can't help but have a bad feeling about this...

I rubbed the side of my face as I stared down at my desk. Grayson was standing in front of my desk, looking down at his feet.

"The weather is taking a toll on us... It's telling us that something bad is coming. I don't know what it is, but I need you to go to the guards at the border and tell them to be on high alert." I said, rubbing the side of my face.

The exhaustion was written all over my face.

I haven't been sleeping well. Xena is antsy, her power is making me hyper constantly. Not to mention... As days pass by, Seth is getting progressively more touchy. Which I adore, but it's been a long time... And we haven't marked yet.

It's driving me crazy to say the least.

"But nothing has happened in three months...? What makes you say something is going to happen now?" Grayson asked, looking at me intently. "Have you slept?"

My twin knows everything.

I rolled my shoulders slightly, a soft annoyed growl was sent to my brother. "Because Stormy is coming in today... And I feel like when she comes in... It's going to bring in a lot more than just her. I'm sure Pete will see this as me preparing for a war. Or he will think I'm scared and take this as a sign that he could win the fight." I sighed again, licking my lips slightly.

Anything is possible with that wildcard.

Grayson frowned, worried about me. "I don't like that you look so tired, Scar... You need to take a break... You need to mark Seth. In the end, you know it will make you both stronger as a result..." He spoke softly, not wanting to anger me.

I breathed in deeply, fear flashed across my eyes.

"*I want him!*" Xena growled.

I bit my bottom lip, she was mad. And that doesn't bode well with my anger problems.

"I know... I know what you're saying. I'm listening to what you are telling me, and I appreciate your concern. But this has to be up to him, I have to give him back the power his father took from him for so long. I can't force this upon him because of my fight with his father..

The moment I found out Seth was in Ireland. The moment that I took him out of that hellhole. All of his problems became mine. All of his issues became mine and I am so okay with that. This is my battle now... It's not his concern. I will talk about it to him and see what he thinks." I said, standing up from my chair.

Grayson nodded, walking to hug me. I would do anything to be able to wipe the worry off his face.

"I just can't lose you okay?" He whispered to me, hugging me tightly.

"You won't. I'm going to be fine. We'll all make it out of this. Everything will be better." I told him, kissing his forehead. "Now go and warn the guards at the border for me. I have a meeting with Alex soon." Grayson nodded reluctantly, heading to the door and leaving.

I sighed as I sat down in my large office chair.

"If it comes down to it. I am going to burn the world to the ground." I told myself, looking at the maps and graphs in front of me.

Seth walked into the office next, before closing the door behind him.

"Hey, baby. I missed you." Seth said with a happy smile, striding to the desk with confidence.

I looked up, surprised to see him. I thought he was working out?

"He should be locked in the house." Xena growled her displeasure.

And for the last time, I remind her. That's plan B.

"Hey, my love. I didn't know you were going to come to see me today. I thought you were working out with Alex?" I asked, circling in my chair as he came to stand in front of me.

He kneeled down, studying my face.

"I thought you said you were sleeping through the night... I've noticed the last few nights you're running around again... You flinch and twist and turn before you go outside and run off into the woods. I wasn't going to say anything, but you haven't brought it up yourself..." Seth trailed off, his eyes softening.

I smiled tiredly, licking my lips slightly. Dang it. I thought that he was sleeping when I left.

"I feel something bad coming... I can't explain it, or how I know. It's like I can sense something in the land, the weather isn't normally like this..." I frowned, my eyes flashing purple.

Xena wanted control, wanted to talk to him. But I won't let that happen until she calms down.

"She's fighting me."

He frowned, nodding in understanding. He gently placed his hands on my bare thighs.

"How about I help with that? Do you trust me, baby?" Seth asked, looking up at me.

My cheeks burned red as I felt his hands creep slowly up to my hips. What is he doing?

"I trust you with everything." I told him with a nod.

He grinned, flashing his fangs at me.

"What is he doing?" Xena asked, hyperfocusing on him.

I laughed looking at him. "What are you doing?" I asked.

But he didn't answer, he got down on his knees in front of where I was sitting. What is he doing?

"I need a skin to skin contact with you for this to work... If we've marked before now I could've done it easier. But we haven't and we're not getting into that. Anyways!" He asked, gently placing his hands on my bare thighs. "I'm going to try and let my power go through your body. To calm your senses. To have Xena know that she's safe."

"This is weird... But I like it." Xena growled softly in the back of my mind.

I nodded, listening to him talk. "I didn't know that's something you were able to do. I didn't know you were strong enough to do that yet."

Seth grinned. "I'm about ninety percent sure it's because Alex is making me mad by the way he's talking about you. But I don't know for sure. I just know that I want to try. I want to try and make you feel better."

I tilted my head slightly. "He's doing it on purpose you know... To push you. To push us. To make your adrenaline spark to make you more possessive of me."

I didn't want him to hate Alex. He was just trying to help.

Seth smiled, kissing my cheek. "I know this... It still doesn't stop it from being annoying. You're mine. And no one else's. I hate the fact he was here before me. I hate the fact he was able to calm you down and I wasn't. He doesn't need to keep shoving it in my face over and over again." He growled, his eyes glowing red, showing Reign was with us.

I giggled, wrapping my arms around him and hugging him tightly. Seth sat down on the floor and pulled me into his lap. This has always been so comfortable.

"You are the only one I care about. The only one who I need. The only one who has ever been able to calm me down." I promised, kissing him softly. "You are my male..."

There was no one else in the world for me.

"Just like you are my female." Seth growled in approval. "Ah stop distracting me." He shook his head, closing his eyes so he could focus.

I wanted to make some sort of joke. But before I could I gasped when I felt his power flood my senses, wrapping around my heart and calming me down. I immediately felt at peace. I felt calm. Like nothing could hurt me. My body sunk into him, my eyes closing as I sighed in relaxation.

"That's my good girl..." He praised, as he gently rubbed my back.

I hummed, my eyes closed as I didn't want to move from my spot in his embrace. "You can sleep... I've got you baby... I will forever have you."

"I love you." I told him tiredly. "I love you."

Seth kissed the top of my head, "I love you more than you realize my female."

Alex walked into the office and headed straight for a seat by my desk. He didn't say anything, just watched us sit together on the floor.

Seth closed his eyes when he opened them. I had a pair of his gym shorts on and I was sitting on his lap. "I didn't think that would work." He grinned proud of himself.

I smiled, leaning into him completely. I like that he's growing in his power. I should just wear his clothes, since he keeps changing me out of mine. Alex smiled, taking out his phone and snapping a picture.

"I love this for you guys." He looked at the picture on his phone, making sure to send it to me.

Seth wrapped his arms tightly around me. He had gained a healthy amount of weight and muscle in the past several months. I closed my eyes, listening to the sound of his steady heartbeat.

His perfect heartbeat. His arms around me. Nothing else matters.

I jumped at a sudden knocking on the door. I groaned, rubbing my eyes as my body refused to move. Seth frowned, rubbing my leg gently. "Come in!" He called.

Grayson walked into the room, his head was bowed with respect.

"We have activity at the border..." His voice was low, his body tense.

Great.

THIRTY-TWO

I tried to sit up but Seth wouldn't let ME move. "No. She needs sleep. If it's not anything important, you can handle it with Alex." He growled, flashing his red eyes at Grayson.

I frowned, looking at him. I wish I could relax, but I can't. Not now. And not for a while.

"I have to go and handle this... Afterward, we can go home and we can watch a movie with Max and sleep." I smiled softly at him, wanting to calm him down. "You can come with me. If there was a fight I would feel it. Is there a fight, Gray?"

I at least believe I would feel it. I always feel anything on my land.

Grayson looked up, smiling softly at me. "No... Stormy is here. She's not alone, there's... I don't know how to explain it. You just need to come and see." He said, smiling wider.

Seth growled, showing his unhappiness with this.

I don't think that he believes me that everything is going to be okay.

Alex stood up, smirking slightly. "She is the Alpha after all. In more ways than one." He teased Seth.

I couldn't help but blush at his words, knowing exactly what he meant.

"Seth isn't going to like it." Xena snickered.

"You obviously weren't paying attention before. I will happily do it again." Seth smirked, standing up with me in his arms. "I'm driving you." He stated, before heading to leave the office.

He shouldn't be carrying me in front of everyone. But I like it...

"I can walk," I told him, even though I just laid my head on his shoulder.

He chuckled, shaking his head slightly as he opened the door and walked into the hallway.

"You can walk, but I can now carry you. And I would very much like to carry you." Seth explained, shrugging as he went for the exit. "I know you will need to stand on your own at the border. But until then I'm going to hold you as much as possible." I smiled, before looking up at him.

"Thank you... I'm sorry I haven't been sleeping. I just feel like I can't sit still." I frowned, looking out as I watched us leave the packhouse.

He licked his lips slowly, heading towards my Bugatti.

"I... Is this because we haven't marked yet? I know I haven't spoken about it... I would like to... I really would. I just..." Seth stumbled over his words, his cheeks heating up.

I gently pressed a kiss to his cheek.

He's so cute when he's nervous.

"Don't force yourself into something okay? I would wait until the end of time for you. I don't want you to pressure yourself." I told him before I yawned. "I'm a bit too tired for anything anyway."

Seth opened the passenger door before placing me gently on the seat. After buckling me in, he quickly jogged to the other side of the car and got in. I turned to look at him as he took my hands gently.

"I want this... I want you... I guess I just... Goddess, I don't know how to say this." His cheeks burned red. "I wanted to be the strong guy I always thought I was. I wanted to be able to protect my mate... Protect my child when I would one day have them. I wanted to be the world to my one-day family...

And with this whole thing happening, I can't help but feel responsible. If I would've stuck out with my father if I would've just sent Max to you... All of this would've been handled long ago. I don't think it would've been this bad. I just wanted to protect you... Be able to fight to protect you. Protect you enough where you could sleep through the night.

I feel like I'm failing you... I wish you would sleep through the night with me. I wish I could be enough to protect you. I didn't want to be a failure." Seth told me, forcing an uneasy smile as his body was shaking with nerves.

I frowned slightly as I listened to him talk.

My heart broke as I listened to him. I love him with every-thing in me, I wish he didn't feel like a failure.

"My love... My King... My male... My mate... My Alpha. You are not failing me. I want this too, I want you too. I love you for who you are... Not for this version of yourself that you think you have to be. I think you're insanely attractive, the sexiest person I've ever laid eyes on. These muscles are hot, but what I think is truly hot is your heart.

You try your best to put everyone before yourself. You care for your brother... Everything about you makes me happy and full of love. But my love, you are not a failure. You went through some-thing no one should ever have to go through. I want to help you see that, I know right now...

I'm a bit stretched thin. I feel like I'm failing you by not protecting you good enough. I want nothing more than to sleep through the night with you. I love sleeping beside you... I love feeling your body wrap around mine, holding each other tightly. I spent so long being the main person doing absolutely everything. I just want to have a future with you. That's all I want." I smiled, kissing him lovingly.

I reluctantly let his hands go so I could cup his cheeks. *"You are all I want."*

For the rest of time... He is all I want.

Seth kissed me deeper, sliding his tongue into my mouth. I felt his hand go through my hair before gripping my hair at the base of my skull. A harsh knock interrupted us.

"It's not fair." Xena whined.

"You are all I want." He repeated my words, before starting the car.

He took a deep breath before pulling out of the parking space and driving toward the border. "I hate driving. I love your car, it's beautiful and it reminds me of you. But Goddess I hate driving, it's stressful.

And ya know all I'm thinking about right now is that if I crash your one-of-a-kind gorgeous car that you're never going to have sex with me ever." Seth told me honestly as he gripped the steering wheel roughly.

I started laughing, watching the way his muscles in his arms tensed.

"I'm gonna have sex with you. I'm gonna have a LOT of sex with you. If you crash my car, all I'm going to be worried about is you and if you're okay. I'll just buy a different car, it's not a big deal. A lot of packs want to get on the good side of me so I would just put a feeler out there and everything would be fine." I shrugged, reaching over and placing my hand on his thigh.

I felt every muscle in his body was tense. Wow... He's really stressed out. I squeezed it reassuringly.

"I trust you completely, don't worry my love," I promised,

leaning against the seat as I watched the scene go by. "Is it wrong that I am waiting for this nap? Ugh, it sounds so good. Me cuddled up against your strong warm chest. It's going to be great." I closed my eyes thinking about it.

I need to open my eyes, but I honestly don't want to. My whole body hurts.

Seth grinned, placing his hand on top of mine. "We're nearly there. Don't fall asleep, draw on my energy if you have to. I can handle it and I will be right there behind you okay?" He promised, squeezing my hand gently.

I nodded, forcing myself to sit up and reluctantly open my eyes.

"I just wanted to tell you that that possessive show of Alphaness back there was the hottest thing I've ever seen," I told him with a grin.

He chuckled before his smile faded at the crowd of people massed at the border.

"What is going on?" Xena asked, perking up.

"Oh, my Goddess..." He breathed out, slowing down so he wouldn't hit anyone.

What is happening?

"The Alpha is here!" Stormy shouted as she pulled a male out of the way.

Seth parked, making sure he had a clear way out if we had to leave early.

Is that... An elf? Xena growled in the back of my mind. And when I breathed in, I smelt it. *Elf stink.* Of course.

My eyes stayed on Stormy and the male standing protectively beside her. "She is mated to an elf," I growled, rubbing my temples. "I do not need this right now."

Seth frowned, turning off the car and quickly getting out so he could get my door. He walked over to my side and opened the door.

I stepped out and immediately everyone stopped talking. *"I am right here. If you have to, send your sister to our home. I'll have Alex go get Max so nothing happens."* Seth assured me, causing me to nod.

He went over to talk to Alex quickly. As I walked over to Stormy and hugged her tightly.

"I am so happy to see you're safe and you're alive. I'm sorry to do this." I said, turning my focus to the male standing by my sister. "Please keep an eye on her, things are turning here. Go to my house and we can talk more there okay?"

I forced an uneasy smile to Stormy. The male nodded, his eyes turning to Stormy.

"Of course, I was just waiting for you to get here before I left." Stormy smiled, before heading taking the male's hand and disappearing.

Seth stood behind me, his hand gently pressed to my lower back as I walked to stand in front of the mass crowd.

Everything is going to be okay. It has to be.

"My people... I see why you are here today... You are escaping the torment and wrath of the so-called Alpha you all have submitted to!" I spoke loudly, my shoulders were back as my head was held high.

I felt Xena send me her strength, and that mixed with Seth's comfort. I felt calm.

THIRTY-THREE

Seth smiled softly, his eyes looking out into the people. "I know you all must be worried... I don't want you to be scared. I'm not sure what kind of rumors that have been circulating in Ireland about me and the fight I had with your Alpha. But I stand here before you today to tell you the truth.

For years your Alpha has abused and neglected your heir for no reason. He did this because he is dark and ruthless. I know the same has been said about me, but I am merciful. I am only ruthless to those who try to show me that I am less of an Alpha because I am a woman. Many of you were there that day I fought Pete.

You saw that he took my mate, and your future Alpha male because he wanted to continue to abuse him. I fought to protect what is mine, and as a result of that, your territory has been poisoned. I want you to know that I welcome you into my pack and into my territory. As long as you submit to not just me..." I spoke clearly, looking at Seth for a moment.

Is he ready? I hope he is.

"There's no better time than now." Xena informed me.

And I knew that... He looked at me, his eyes glowing red.

"You don't have to do this..." His voice was soft and confident as he looked at me.

I smiled, cupping his face for a second before looking back to the crowd.

"You will submit to me and Seth as your Alpha here and now. You will earn yourself a place to stay... A pack to call your own... You won't have to worry about a single thing. Scotland is a safe space for everyone." I said, my eyes glowing purple.

They will know we are one.

"Thank you for your kindness Alpha!" A male stepped in front of the crowd before getting down on his knees. "We submit to you as our Alpha." Everyone slowly started to drop to their knees, baring their necks in submission to us.

I moved slightly so Seth was standing beside me instead of behind.

There's no turning back. War is coming.

"We will keep you safe from Pete. You will be okay here, you will thrive as I have thrived here." Seth called out to everyone. "I want you all to know that I am going to be a better Alpha than my father. I will not be harsh or mean like he was.

One day we will get Ireland back. One day we will move back to our land and everything will be as it should have been. But until then we are going to stay here with our amazing Alpha Scarlett." He promised, he motioned for everyone to stand up, and slowly one by one they listened.

"It's so hot when he is commanding people." Xena watched with obvious lust.

"To our Alpha's Seth and Scarlett Knight!" Alex yelled the crowd started cheering loudly.

Seth immediately looked down at me, my smile grew. I've never been happier than in this moment. My hands gently cupped his cheeks before kissing him.

"I am okay with it..." I promised him, opening my eyes to look at him.

His eyes started to water before he bit his bottom lip. I couldn't help but laugh, he's so cute.

"You want to take my last name..?" His voice was shaky as he wrapped his arms tightly around me.

I nodded my answer. I would like nothing more.

"Everyone head to the Packhouse, my Beta and Delta will help assist you in any way you need." I declared, keeping my eyes on him. "We have some other business to attend to."

Seth nodded, leading me to the car and helping me into the passenger side. He bent down, before buckling me in. "You are my everything." He told me, kissing my cheek.

Everyone watched, waiting for us to leave before they did.

Seth got into the driver's side, he started the car. "You don't have to take my last name if you don't want to." He told me, putting the car in drive and pulling out slowly to head home. "Alex kind of put you on the spot there... I'm not expecting anything."

I smiled as I turned to look at him. "I want to take your last name... I want to rebuild your family's legacy... I don't want everyone to look at the Knight family badly because of your father. I was going to talk about it with you when we talked about marking but it hasn't come up yet. Which is fine. There is a lot going on right now, and I don't think that it's going to get better anytime soon." I frowned slightly, rubbing the back of my neck.

I should've made it a priority earlier... Before things escalated. I just didn't want to push him.

"Wouldn't us completing the mate process help make you stronger? Well, make us both stronger?" Seth asked, speeding up slightly as he tapped his fingers against the steering wheel.

I was silent for a moment as I stared at him.

244

"He got you there." Xena snickered.

"Yes and no I guess..." I said, placing my left hand on his thigh. "Something could very well complicate things."

He looked confused, looking intently at me for a quick second before focusing back on the road.

It's a complicated situation to say the least.

"What do you mean?" Seth finally asked, placing his hand on top of mine.

He could feel my discomfort and stress. I still haven't figured out how to hide that from him yet.

"Because we're both Alphas... The chances of me getting pregnant after us marking are a lot higher. My heat will be amplified by your rut and vice versa. It's like the Moon Goddess desperately wants us to have kids since we're the first Alpha to Alpha couple." I shrugged slightly, biting my bottom lip hard.

He nodded in understanding, before parking outside of our house.

"It's gonna be the hottest thing ever seeing you pregnant. Everyone is going to know that you belong to me." Seth said, groaning slightly at the thought.

I giggled, leaning over to kiss him. I didn't think a breeding kink could be hot till right now.

"I think it's hot that you want me pregnant." I smiled against his lips, peering into his eyes.

He smiled, kissing me again before licking my lips.

"It's gonna be one of the greatest things to ever happen." He smirked slightly, before shaking his head. "But not until you sleep through the night."

Xena laughed so hard she actually fell down. I should've seen that coming.

I pouted playfully as he got out of the car. When he opened the door, I grinned at him. "What are you, my daddy?" I teased him.

He smirked, bending down slightly, his hand slid around my neck and just rested there.

My heart skipped a beat as I looked up at him.

"I prefer Alpha," Seth growled, his eyes flashing red as he kissed me roughly.

Just the taste of him made me hungry for more. I whimpered into the kiss, my body moving to try to be closer to him. He bit and tugged at my lower lip. "You're incredible." He groaned, unbuckling me and picking me out of the car.

I laughed, wrapping my arms around his neck. "I can't believe you just like to carry me around. Is Max here too?" I asked, worry-filled the air around us.

I didn't even think about that before I sent Stormy here.

"Max is at Alex's house while Stormy and her mate are here," Seth explained, walking into the house and making sure the door was shut after us. "You're not going to do anything but sit on the couch and I will go and get your sister and her mate." He instructed, heading into the living room and placing me gently on the couch.

I could moan at the comfort my body feels right now.

"Oh, we're right here." Stormy smiled cheerily as she strutted into the room, a male walking behind her.

She plopped herself on the opposite couch, the male following suit. Seth sat beside me, placing my legs over his as he kept his eyes on me.

"The possession, I love it." Xena groaned.

"It took you three MONTHS to get home?" I asked, growling slightly showing MY annoyance.

No call. No texting. No nothing. Stormy couldn't help but laugh at that.

"Yes... Well, Gray said that things weren't bad. That you wanted me home to keep me safe. But we were safe. So I didn't think anything by it when I heard about things escalating here...

246

About you POISONING Ireland!? I had to come back. This means war, they took your mate. I'm surprised that you didn't burn them alive." Stormy laughed, leaning into her mate.

Seth smirked, biting his bottom lip so he wouldn't talk.

Although I wish he would.

"Yeah, things escalated fast. He took Seth, and I poisoned Ireland in retaliation. He's gonna be coming soon, it's why so many people came here today. They probably followed you here, thinking that you would lead them to me. My borders are insanely secure for this type of thing.

I honestly thought that there would be a battle today, I think they were all so scared..." I started before narrowing my eyes at my sister.

Stormy's cheeks heated at the intense stare.

"What?" Stormy asked, even though her eyes were on her mate.

Seth growled, baring his fangs at the male. So obviously they aren't going to get along.

"*Stormy's pregnant?*" Xena asked, and sniffing the air confirmed my suspicion.

When it rains, it pours.

"You're pregnant... And your mate is an elf? Why didn't you tell me this?" I asked, looking at Seth as I felt his hands tighten on my legs.

He huffed, resuming messaging my legs to help me relax. But he's the tense one... I wonder what's got him so mad.

"*Probably because it stinks of Elf in here.*" Xena growled, showing me her annoyance.

"I didn't want you to be mad at me... So I thought I would come home and I would show you our baby... And then break the ice with my mate is an Elf his name is Kingston. He used to go by Poison." Stormy informed, nudging him to get him to say something.

"Stormy has said a lot about both you and Grayson. It's a pleasure to finally put a face to the name." Kingston said, shifting uncomfortably.

Seth leaned back against the couch, allowing his eyes to glow red to show his power.

Xena snorted, but I knew she loved his jealousy. I sunk deeper into the couch as this conversation was draining for me.

"We're not going to do anything to you Kingston. What matters to me is that you've kept her safe and happy throughout all the time you spent together." I smiled tiredly, I had to force my eyes to stay open.

"I think we should continue this conversation another day," Seth said, shifting slightly as he brought me fully into his lap now.

This is even better. I rested my head on his shoulder with a happy smile on my face. I can't wait to sleep in his arms tonight.

"No no... It's okay. I'm okay." I smiled, closing my eyes.

Stormy frowned as she looked at us.

"Why are you so tired? Why do you look like you're close to dying? Why is the weather so rocky?" Stormy fired off questions, causing Seth to growl unhappily.

I zoned out, his heartbeat calmed me and lulled me to sleep.

"She is the Alpha. Your Alpha. She is exhausted, she does everything so she hasn't been sleeping very well. The weather matches the seasons unless the Alpha is exhausted or unwell. So please, you are welcome to stay at our house. But I'm going to play a movie so she can get some rest." Seth growled his reply, and it was the last thing I heard before his arms tightened around me.

And I allowed myself to fall asleep.

THIRTY-FOUR

"Giving Seth part of the trouble isn't going to end badly. It will not only give him confidence. But our pack confidence in his rank as well." Xena growled at me.

I made a face at her. I hated when she yelled at me in my dreams. It was my only time for peace.

"I know you're right Xena... I know. But it's just hard for me. I haven't had someone to lean on besides you. I. We had to deal with everything. I know I need to give him some of my duties. I just don't want to overwhelm him." I frowned.

I hated this, knowing I was disappointing someone I care deeply about.

"Wake up. War is here." Xena told me suddenly.

But before I had a chance to reply I jolted awake.

My eyes glowing brightly. "No. No. I'm not ready." I said, sitting up quickly.

Seth looked at me confused before grabbing me and pulling me back against his chest.

"What are you not ready for? You're not making any sense." Seth told me, wrapping his arms tightly around me.

My eyes instinctively shut, craving the love. But I had to force my eyes open as I looked up at him.

"There is something going on at the border. I need to go there and stop it." I explained, trying to get up but he was stronger than me at the moment.

He stood up off of the couch, keeping me in his arms.

I need to go protect my people.

"I will handle whatever is going on at the border." He stated simply, heading out of the living room to our bedroom.

I didn't even know we weren't in our bedroom. He opened our door, and walking in, he made sure the door was shut behind us. "You need your sleep, you need your strength back. I need you to be okay, and right now you're not okay."

Seth laid me down in the middle of our king-sized bed, before tucking me in. "I need to do this," I told him, trying to sit up again.

If it's war... My people are going to need me. He growled, gently placing his hands on my shoulders and laying me back down.

"Let him do this." Xena growled.

As the Alpha shouldn't she want to protect her pack? On second thought, I'm not going to open that conversation cause I don't need her to be more mad at me.

"So help The Goddess who gave us life. If you don't lay down and let me handle this, I'll tie you to the bed." Seth's growl was low, his eyes turning red as he looked at me.

I like the sound of that. My cheeks burned red as I smiled at him. He couldn't help but chuckle, knowing by the smell that what he threatened turned me on.

"I can't put this pressure on you." I informed, frowning slightly.

Seth smiled, gently brushing a piece of my long brown hair behind my ear.

"Everything is going to be okay my love... I am not scared. I'm sure it's nothing, it's about time I start acting as an Alpha." Seth grinned, flashing his sharp fangs at me. "I gotta make the pack like me so they give me their blessing to be with you. Or maybe I'll defy that tradition and mark you anyway."

I giggled as he leaned over and kissed me softly.

His lips were my favorite, they're just so soft. Xena growled in my mind, warning me. I know I know. It will get continuously harder to refuse to mark my mate.

"I will be back as soon as I can, baby. Get some sleep... I'll wake you when I get back." He told me, he sat down beside me.

I knew he wouldn't leave until I fell back asleep. So I closed my eyes and allowed darkness to take me over again.

When I opened my eyes, I saw my home. But I thought I just fell asleep? And then I heard a little squeal and my heart skipped a beat. Was that what I think it was?

And right as I looked down, I saw two little kids run straight past me like they didn't even see me.

"It's because they can't see you Scarlett." Xena told me, but when I looked at her.

She was me... But I could sense her power. See that she was the Alpha. She was who I wanted to be... Who I once was before I let the things that everyone said to me get inside of my head.

"Why are you showing me this? Why are you showing me a dream I had when I was a teenager? When we first took control of our pack." I asked, tilting my head at her.

And she had the audacity to laugh at me. I glared, crossing my arms as I stared at the hotter version of me.

"Because you obviously forgot what we were told several times. That this is our future. No matter what happens to get to that point. This is what we are going to have. Or at least the beginning of it. But it won't happen if you refuse to make the first move to mark our mate." Xena snapped at me, and I wanted to whimper.

251

I know she has a point.

"I know! I know! Okay I get it Xena. You don't have to scold me like I'm a child. But you have to realize..." I started before she cut me off.

I really hated when anyone cut me off.

"Before you make any more excuses. I know what he went through. And we went through something similar. But instead of being in our adult years, it happened from when we were a child till we put a stop to it. Yes it's different, and I'm not taking away from what he went through. But look at how far he's come.

I needed to show you that he's ready. That's why I pushed you to let him deal with whatever is happening at the border. I needed you to see that he's ready. He's more than ready, and you're getting weaker. Every single day that you deny us what we need. We are getting weaker. And we need every ounce of strength we have to be ready for Pete." She told me, and I winced at her words.

"I know I can't hide anything from you... I'm scared okay? I'm scared. And I hate admitting that. Because I know we've already dealt with so much. And marking my mate shouldn't scare me. But what if he isn't ready? And I'm being too pushy. Or I'm forcing this decision on him. I love him.

We love him. I don't know if I could handle losing him. Handle him rejecting me and knowing that he was out there. With someone else. So I've been pushing it. So that he could actually tell me that this was something that he wanted. And you telling me all of this... I know you're trying to help me Xena.

But honestly I just feel like I've disappointed you..." I spewed out to her.

I should've told her this so long ago... But I just couldn't put this on her. She was so confident in our bond. And I just wish I was able to have that confidence in everything.

"You haven't disappointed me Scar... But I understand. Talk to him. Express to him what you are feeling. I wish I could give you my *confidence, because I know everything will be okay. You just need to learn to trust him more." Xena teased me with a wink. "Trust him with everything, just like you trust me."*

I smiled at her, before turning slightly to see the kids playing with each other. This is the future that I always imagined for myself. The kids. The mate. Everything in me wanted this. But I thought along the way with everything I've had to do to get to this point. That I lost that chance.

With the wars, the killings, the broken promises... Every wrong I did to protect the ones I loved. I would do it again, because they needed someone to hate. They needed someone to do the dirty work. So the world feared me. I killed those who told me no and I took what I wanted.

"You really need to remember we share a mind." Xena laughed, putting an arm across my shoulder. "And this is something we could still have. You know as long as you grow a pair and make the first move. Or you could easily just let me take control and I will do it for you." She grinned.

I laughed, shaking my head. "No. I will do it. I just have to wait till the perfect time." I teased her.

Xena snorted. "I truly hate you sometimes."

I shook my head with a snicker.

"You hate to love me." I teased her. "I will mark him, and soon too. Everything will be perfect, I promise Xena."

"Thanks Scar... I promise that it will make things better. And imagine how willing he is in bed." She teased more.

And I couldn't help but groan at the thought. I'm honestly so excited for this to happen.

But before our conversation could continue, I felt Seth's arms wrap tightly around me. Before I woke up.

"You're home." I smiled tiredly, barely opening my eyes to look up at him.

Seth smirked, kissing my forehead.

"Yes, I am baby... I told you I would be okay." Seth smiled, holding me to his chest. "I have everything handled."

My eyes closed as I held onto him. I love that he was able to handle it without getting hurt.

"What's happening?" I asked quietly, I kissed his clothed chest gently.

He gently rubbed my back, knowing I would be tired still. I'm always freaking tired.

CHAPTER
THIRTY-FIVE

"Things are escalating rather quickly," Seth explained, speaking softly.

And there goes me going back to sleep. I sat up quickly, staring at him. My heart raced, I knew this was coming.

"What do you mean things are escalating rather quickly? What happened down at the border?" I asked quickly, having to bite my bottom lip from yawning.

He frowned, taking my hands gently. As Xena woke up more, I felt her power going through me and was feeling more awake.

"Things are just escalating a bit quicker than we originally thought. Nothing happened down at the border, apparently, it was all planned by Alex and some guy named Zane. Or well not all planned by them because Pete sent them down here to start a fight. They started a fight while I went after Zane." Seth explained before my eyes widened at his words.

Crap I forgot to tell him about that! He couldn't help but chuckle.

"I guess I need to be informed about who our informants are," Seth smirked, shaking his head slightly.

I smiled, laughing with him. I read it on my desk, it must've slipped my mind.

"He's so nice, we are planning on getting his mate free from the dungeons in Ireland. We were going to do it before things escalated. But I guess we ran out of time." I said with a frown.

I hope Sadie is okay...

Seth held my hands gently. "I have that all taken care of, you don't have to worry about it." He told me, looking intently at me.

It's taken care of?

"It's taken care of?" Xena repeated my words.

"My love... What did you do?" I asked, trying to contain my worry.

He looked confused as he studied my reaction. Why is he confused? And why didn't he tell me what he did?

"I have a small group heading into Ireland to get Sadie back. Why? I thought you would be happy to not have to worry about this?" Seth asked worry etched into his feature.

I gulped, my heart raced. This is not what we planned. Crap.

"He was just trying to help." Xena growled at me.

I know that, but it's been a very long time since he's been around packs. He doesn't know that this could escalate things.

"If they get caught, that will give Pete grounds to march into Scotland. He will think that I went against the peace treaty and he will cause war. I mean we've been dancing around a war for the past few months anyway. But this will make the new pack members think that I did it on purpose." I was starting to panic.

Seth whimpered, cupping my cheeks gently to bring my face closer.

Just feeling his skin on my cheeks grounded me. My heart calmed, and I felt at peace.

"Alex and his team... They won't get caught. Alex knows that dungeon like the back of his hand. He knows to be quiet and not get caught. Everything will be fine, you don't need to worry. I'm sorry for not talking about this before... But I just wanted to help you. I didn't think it was that big of a deal." He frowned, kissing the top of my head gently.

I closed my eyes, leaning against his lips.

"No... I'm sorry for stressing out so much..." I trailed off, not knowing how to finish what I was thinking.

Seth leaned away from me, just to look fully at me.

"How about let's go away? I'll drive. Let's go to your small cabin and we can talk some more and relax." Seth offered with a caring smile, trying to get me to agree.

I looked over his face, my eyes widening as I began to think about what this could mean.

"What is it that you want to talk about there that you won't talk about here?" I asked, my worry was obvious.

Seth frowned, reluctantly taking his hands off of my face.

"It's not anything bad... But Zane did tell me some stuff about Pete. Like how he thinks we're weaker without finishing our mating bond. He thinks that you are weak because you haven't forced the issue yet... He thinks he can move in on Scotland before we have the chance to mark.

And we've kind of been beating around the bush, barely talking about it. But they have a point... Your brother... My brother... They have a point. We are going to be stronger once we complete the bond. We will have access to each other's power, we can sense when they are in danger. I mean I don't have to tell you everything because you're smart.

But I want to mark you... I know you're a strong independent Alpha that doesn't need me to protect you. But I do want to protect you, I want to be your mate, I want to be your male. I want everything... And I appreciate you giving me time to heal and process my trauma. But I've realized something because of you.

Our past doesn't define who we are. Just because my father

locked me up, beat me, and starved me... It doesn't mean I'm weak. It doesn't mean that you're going to leave me for Alex. It doesn't mean anything, because at the end of the day. I am the Heir of an Alpha. I am an Alpha by birth.

I know I can handle anything, and with you by my side I know I can take on the world. You are everything to me. I don't ever want to lose you... And marking you would be the greatest pleasure in my life... Please... While we can, please mark me. I can't stand the thought of losing you." Seth explained, biting his bottom lip slightly.

My heart skipped a beat as I listened to him. He's everything to me, and I hate that I've made him so upset.

"I just wanted the choice to be up to you... Your father took everything away from you... And well I just thought that by giving you the power... By giving you this back... That it would help you realize that you were safe in Scotland." I told him softly, looking up into his eyes.

They were bright red, causing my eyes to glow bright purple. Xena and Reign loved to pull at our powers.

"I know I'm safe in Scotland... I knew from the moment I laid eyes on you that I was safe. I loved you from before I knew you... But when you came to Ireland, I was scared. I shouldn't have put that against you, I should've sunk into our mate bond. I was just worried and I hated what this could do to me if you decided I wasn't good enough." He told me his truth, refusing to look away from me.

I frowned slightly, a soft whimper leaving me. I felt even worse.

All this time... I thought that I was doing the right thing. And I've been making him feel worse.

"You are my everything. I loved you the moment you started to call out to me... The moment I knew you were a real thing. I knew it was going to be hard on you. I don't blame you for a single thing. I just wanted to help you heal... Help you gain your confidence back. You are good enough for me. I never once ever gave up on us. I never will." I promised, squeezing his hands tightly as he grinned at me.

I don't know how else to tell him that he means the absolute world to me.

"So it is settled? We are going to your cabin?" Seth asked, his body bouncing on the bed, showing his true excitement.

I couldn't help but giggle. I felt his joy and excitement shoot through our bond and I wanted to bounce like he was.

"As long as you stop saying yours. It's not mine. It's ours. Everything that once was mine... Is now ours." I corrected him, smiling brightly.

He smirked, eyeing me mischievously. I know what he's going to say.

"Your Bugatti?" He asked me teasingly.

I was silent for a moment, thinking about my answer. I knew that was coming.

"Yes... Even my Bugatti..." I said, keeping that same smile on my face. He laughed, shaking his head slightly.

He could read me like an open book.

"I don't need to drive your Bugatti. I love it, but I don't need it. I think it's hot watching you drive it, or work on it, or honestly anything in general." Seth told me, grinning still.

When I didn't get up right away, he grabbed my hands and pulled me off of the bed. "Are you coming? You're moving so slow!"

I laughed, following him out of our bedroom. "I had like one second to process what you wanted before you were pulling me out of bed. I can't drive like this, I'm still tired." I told him, stopping abruptly as Seth pulled me into his chest.

"I want to take care of you... You've been taking care of me for... Well since you saved me. And even before you saved me, don't think I didn't feel you sending your power towards me when we had a connection." Seth picked me up so he could carry me. "It's my turn now to put you first. You can sleep on the ride to the cabin, and then I'll take care of everything."

I smiled at him lovingly, my eyes sparkling with happiness. "You really don't have to take care of me. I know traditionally in relationships that the female takes care of the male..." I trailed off, biting my bottom lip in worry.

Our relationship hasn't been like that. We've always taken care of each other. He frowned, heading out to the garage where the Bugatti was parked.

"I don't think that is right... I think that it should be fifty fifty. The male and female, or well whatever really. I think that you should take care of each other. And we're the first Alpha to Alpha couple, so we get to make our own rules.

I like to take care of you. I like to see you happy. I don't like when you work yourself so much that you end up like this. I need you. I can't lose you, I don't want to lose you. I love you." Seth explained his thoughts, holding me in his one arm so he could open the passenger door. "I need you to start giving me some of the burdens. It's not all on you anymore. I'm here now and I'm not going anywhere."

I can't believe that he can carry me in one arm. It feels like just yesterday where he couldn't hold his own weight up.

I smiled at him, cupping his cheeks gently and pressing a soft kiss to his soft red lips. "I love you. I will try my best, I am just really used to being in charge of everything. I'm not used to having someone who wants to take care of me... I'm trying my best. I don't mean to upset you." I frowned slightly, gently releasing his face from my hands.

Seth smirked, licking from my neck all the way up to my lips. I couldn't help but shiver at his actions.

I moaned at the pleasure that shot through my body. Seth's body stiffened, his eyes turning a shade darker.

"Scarlett..." My name came out as a strained growl, he forced himself to stand up, shutting the door before grabbing the keys.

He was shaking with restraint as he got into the driver's side and started the Bugatti.

I grinned. I loved making him lose control.

"You test my power... You test my restraint. And sometimes I really think you do it on purpose to see how much control I have over myself. Cause you're a hot little brat and you know it." His voice was deeper, rougher than usual as he pushed a button to open the garage door and backed out.

I giggled at him, leaning back into my seat as I watched him.

"I do really like to be a hot little brat, I enjoy seeing you struggle not to rip my clothes and claim me in front of everyone. It makes me feel good about myself." I smirked at him.

He laughed, shaking his head as he placed his large palm on my thigh.

"Get some rest... Because I don't plan on letting you sleep for a while after I mark you." Seth told me, his voice sending shivers down my spine.

It's something that I can't wait for.

THIRTY-SIX

When I finally woke up, I knew I was in my small cabin. It was a one-bedroom cabin, with a small bathroom, kitchen, and living room. I only used it for myself, so I figured I didn't need anything bigger.

I yawned, smiling softly as I looked down and saw that I was just in one of Seth's t-shirts. So possessive. I love it. I got up off of the bed, stretching as I padded out into the small hallway to where the noise was.

Seth was in the kitchen, making me something. His torso was bare, showing the scars that littered his back.

I sucked in a breath as I drank in his body, my eyes slowly moving down his body. His jeans hung low on his hips, showing the dainty cursive writing on his lower back.

'Scarlett Knight' Was written in beautiful writing. I grinned from ear to ear, before walking in closer to him. I wrapped my arms around him, kissing his back gently. "I love you... I love the tattoo..." I whispered to him, kissing his bare shoulder. "I love your scars... This shows my claim on you and I love it."

Seth grinned, looking over his shoulder. His hair was wet like he just showered so it hung down nearly covering his eyes. "I love you. I thought you would be asleep for a while longer." He told me, kissing my cheek with a grin. "You didn't wake up at all when I carried you inside."

Seth turned around, gently placing his hands on my hips. He lifted me up, placing me on the counter beside the stove. "I didn't think I was that tired. But I feel more energized." I told him, watching as he was making spaghetti. "How are you feeling?"

"I don't have a problem sleeping, because my hot, caring, loving, protective Alpha mate takes care of everything and never once has asked me for anything." Seth grinned at me, placing himself between my legs. "My Alpha Female who has constantly put herself last. My Alpha female who put herself at a lower rank with me to give me the power back...

My Alpha Female who came into my life, and I honestly thought that she was my saving angel because of her beauty... Because of her voice. My Alpha Female who moans, whimpers, and grinds against me in her sleep. Which I love and it drives me absolutely insane." He groaned at the thought.

I couldn't help but giggle as he pulled me closer to him.

"I didn't know that I moaned, whimpered, and grinded against you in my sleep. I never thought that you knew about those dreams." I said, my cheeks burning red as I looked at him.

I figured he would've found out about that when we marked. Seth laughed, smirking smugly as he went to finish the food.

"I am a light sleeper, have been since I was a child. And I guess that is a good thing since you keep leaving in the middle of the night." Seth told me, giving me a look. "So yeah, I heard you every time you had one of them. It was hard to keep control of myself. I guess more than one thing was hard."

I snorted at his joke. He grinned at me, smiling at my laughter.

Xena growled at me in the back of my mind. I know I need to ask him, she doesn't need to say anything.

"I can't sleep when I know something bad is going to happen. I feel the bad energy surrounding Scotland... I know something is coming. I don't understand it, and I'm sure it makes me sound crazy. But I just want to be prepared for everything that's going to happen ya know?" I shrugged, watching as Seth turned everything off.

I want to be able to protect him. I won't make it if he doesn't.

"It makes sense. You know the old saying... The power of the Alpha runs through the land. Your blood makes this land powerful. Your bloodline might have been darkened by your father but you're not going to let that stop you from making the world know that the Winters line won't be messed with." He assured me, picking me up off of the counter and carrying me back to the bedroom.

My body lit alive when he touched me, I was practically vibrating with need.

"Knight line... For at least us. I don't know if Grayson will have kids. And I also don't know if Stormy and Kingston will choose to make a new last name and a line for themselves. Stormy has always felt like the outcast... I tried my best to get her to know that she isn't. That she's one of us." I sighed, frowning slightly as Seth laid me down on the king-sized bed.

I freaking love this bed.

Just like at our house, I had a deep purple comforter that sunk with my weight. Seth stared down at me, his eyes darkening as he watched me look up at him.

"Can we not talk about our families right now? Unless you want to talk about the family I'm about to build with you right now. Goddess, just the thought of you swollen with my babies makes me want to come in my jeans." He groaned.

I couldn't help but giggle as he climbed on top of me. My smile faded when I saw his teeth come out.

"Seth... I-..." I trailed off, my heart racing as I didn't know what to say.

How do I warn him about what he's going to see?

"Yes, my love?" Seth asked, kissing my neck softly, teasingly nipping the delicate flesh.

"I... You're going to see a lot of things I didn't tell you about..." I gulped, biting my bottom lip slightly. "Some of the things I did I regret... But most of the things I did. I don't regret, but you're going to see and feel what I did while I did the things I did... And you're going to see a side of me that I have put away.

I found pleasure and happiness in the way I made people scared of me... I enjoyed seeing that they feared me because of my power and age. I lived for it... The way it felt when I killed them. I fed off of the negative energy... I thought I had to be that. I thought that I had to be a ruthless monster to get people to listen to me. I changed... I fought hard to change and do better. I... I just don't want you to see that and think of me as that..." I whimpered softly, as I averted his gaze.

I don't want him to hate me for what I've done.

Seth gently placed his hand on my cheek, moving my face so that I would look him in the eyes.

"I know you... I understand you... I know who you are. We all make mistakes. I regret pushing you away... I regret trying to leave instead of letting you come and save me yourself. I regret not being able to protect you from everything you went through. But I don't regret you... I want this. And I want you." Seth assured me, smiling lovingly at me. "You will see a lot of dark things in my mind..."

I had tears in my eyes as I brought him down and kissed him gently.

"I don't regret you... I want this... I want you..." I repeated his words, nodding softly as he looked intently at me.

He really is my everything.

"Everything will be okay," Seth promised me, kissing slowly down my face to my neck, where he made sure to leave a trail of hickies in his path.

I moaned as he marked my neck, arching my body up to meet his.

"I want my mark." Xena snapped in the back of my mind.

"Please... Stop teasing me." I panted slightly, a blush covering my cheeks as I turned my head to the side.

Seth had his one leg pressed to my core, my whole body needed him. I whimpered as I felt his teeth scrape against the juncture where my neck met my shoulder.

Where his mark would lay.

"I will stop teasing you." He whispered against my skin, before sinking his teeth into me.

I gasped, my eyes shooting open as I stared at the ceiling. My body arched into him as he locked his jaw so that I wouldn't go anywhere. Not like I would.

Seth's entire life flashed before my eyes, the years leading up to his abuse where he would draw my face repeatedly, his father's constant belittling. To the years of abuse, neglect, and bullying he endured afterward. The only constant thought he had was of me, even after he felt like he wasn't good enough for me.

Once his side of the bond was complete, he retracted his canines and slowly licked the mark to taste my blood. Seth couldn't help but moan at the taste, his eyes blazing a bright red as he looked up at me now. I was panting, sweating slightly as my purple eyes looked frenzied. Xena was running around in my mind, her energy amplified.

"You... You thought of me? Even through everything? You thought of me?" My voice was soft, barely a whisper.

He nodded with a smile, rolling over off of me to take his jeans off. I practically felt him throbbing against me.

"You were the one thing that kept me sane through everything. Even when I felt like I wasn't worthy of you. I knew that you would help me." Seth explained, letting his jeans and boxers sit on the floor.

He laid back down on the bed, pulling me to lay on top of him. He gently placed his hands on my hips, sinking his teeth into his lower lips.

"Maybe I should've waited to take my jeans off." He groaned, closing his eyes as he felt me drip onto him.

I giggled, straddling his hips. I inhaled sharply, my eyes glowing brightly as I peered down at him. He gripped my hips tightly, his body shaking with restraint.

Everything is looking up finally.

"I'm going to need you to not tease me. Because I can't contain myself anymore." Seth growled out, breathing heavily.

I smiled and leaned down as I placed my hands on his abs gently.

"I won't tease you..." I whispered against his ear, before moving quickly.

I allowed my canines to enlarge before I sunk them into the same spot on his neck. A powerful growl rippled free from him as my power shot through his body. He grunted, struggling to keep his hips against the bed as I remained on top of him.

His muscles strained, I felt his confusion and arousal zip through my body. I locked my jaw as I slammed my eyes shut. Seth gasped, as he watched everything.

My life flashed before his eyes, rushing from memory to memory. My constant fear of not doing good enough, from the young age of my mother leaving. I fought my entire life without a break. My memories continued to shift, before slowing down at the years of abuse I endured because of my father.

My body shook slightly with fear as the more painful memories played through my mind as well. The constant fighting from trying to keep my pack to the battles of packs wanting mine. My memories slowed down, before they stopped, showing that my side of the bond was complete. *Finally.* I retracted my canines, licking the blood up slowly.

Seth couldn't hold back, his eyes were dark with desire as he flipped me around so that he was on top of me. "Oh Goddess." He groaned, watching as I licked the blood off of my teeth.

He crashed his lips to mine, quickly sliding his tongue into my mouth to dominate the kiss. I moaned as I leaned up to deepen the kiss.

"Scarlett..." He breathed out, his heart racing as he lay beside me.

My whole body felt like it was on fire. I whimpered, shaking slightly with the pain of my heat rushing through my body.

"Please," I begged, my eyes fading to dark brown.

That was all it took to get Seth going again.

And I knew these next two weeks were going to be fun.

THIRTY-SEVEN

After two long weeks, my heat was over along with Seth's rut. Which don't get me wrong. I love Seth. But I'm glad that need and overwhelming heat is over with.

"It wouldn't have been that bad if you would've listened to me and marked him sooner." Xena reminded me.

For what seems like the thousandth time. I was hunched under the hood of my Bugatti, peering into my beautiful work of art. I've spent so long perfecting this car into something I could deeply love.

"Hey, baby." He said with a grin, walking over to me.

I saw him out of the corner of my eye. His shorts hung low on his hips as his torso was bare. He stood behind me, kissing my mark causing me to moan. I smiled, leaning back into him as he wrapped his arms around my waist.

A wave of love ran through my body, and I practically sighed at the feeling. It was something I never thought I could have. But here I am.

"Hey, my love..." I smiled, turning around in his arms and looping my arms around the back of his neck.

Seth smiled down at me, kneading my butt in his palms. I shook my head with a smile, he was so touchy. I loved it.

"What are you up to?" He asked, peering behind me, looking down at the engine. "You only work on your car when you're stressed out. What's wrong?" I sighed, leaning my body weight against him.

I didn't want to tell him what I've been feeling.

"I had a lot of fun during these last two weeks. It was the highlight of my life. But now that the fog has cleared, memories are coming back. I feel... The fighting..." I flinched, feeling another punch to my gut. "The terror... The pain. I feel it all. They are mad at me."

After the heat was over... Everything hit me like a ton of bricks.

Seth's eyes widened, tightening his arms around me tightly. "I need to stop this. They shouldn't blame you for this..." His voice cracked as he allowed his power to flood through my body.

His power made me feel drunk on adrenaline. "Why don't you stay here? And I will go handle this whole thing."

I sighed, frowning at him. "I wish... I wish I could just give that to you... But I can't. They already are mad at me. If I stay here and let you go handle everything. They will think that you are the Alpha now... And while you're my equal. I am their Alpha, they need to know that I am there right by their side. Or well, standing in front of them, leading the attack back on Ireland."

I trust him. I do. But I don't want him getting hurt for my decision. I chose this. He didn't.

Seth slid his hands down to my bare thighs and lifted me up. I wrapped my legs around his waist and looked at him. "I don't want you to think that I haven't loved every single minute with you. Because I have... But being the Alpha isn't easy ya know?" I said, kissing each of his cheeks.

He nodded in understanding. I needed him to know that he's everything to me. But it's not as easy as it looks being the Alpha.

"I understand... I know what you're saying. I have loved every single minute with you too... I think this was his plan... To push us into marking so he could have an open window to attack without you there to protect your land. Because you know that he can't face you head-on. Because there would be no fight, you would win.

He has already lost everything, his pack is diminishing. His land is dying... He went head to head with the first Alpha Female in hundreds of years. And he's losing. He's grasping at straws, and he pushed us... Well me into being terrified that by us not completing our bond that it would somehow make you weaker. He pushed me and I let him. I'm sorry about that..." Seth held me to him with one hand, while he used his other hand to shut the hood. "What were you doing to your car anyway?"

I nuzzled his nose gently, kissing him gently. "We needed to mark. It is something that we had to do, it will make us both stronger during this whole thing. They can't blame me for something out of my control. They wanted an heir, and this is the best way to get one for them. I mean I wanted kids, but they always pressured me.

I know he's grasping at straws, and with him doing this... This is scaring everyone. I don't blame them for being mad at me. But I wish that they had more faith in me. I've kept us safe for over ten years. I just thought that they would see me as stronger than this." I groaned, resting my head on his shoulder. "I wanted to do something, anything just to get my mind off of things... I wish we could stay here together forever without returning."

That's awful of me to admit. But he's my mate, so I can admit anything to him. Seth bit back a laugh, trying to remain serious.

"I would do anything for us to just have a simple life... I could build onto this cabin so we had room for our children. I mean I would already need to anyway when we decide to take a break. But our kids would have so much fun here. Goddess I hope you're pregnant. I can't wait to see your swollen belly." Seth groaned, his cheeks pink at his declaration.

I started laughing as I shook slightly in his hold.

"It's hot that he wants us pregnant." Xena growled, as she laid down. *"But not happy for me since I won't be allowed to play."*

I shifted several times a week, and sometimes several times a day. I'm not sure how I'm going to control myself. If I can even control myself enough to not shift when I feel the need. Pregnancy would effect me differently because of my status. I felt my head spinning.

"I can't wait to see you hard all of the time." I teased back, causing him to chuckle.

He walked over to the passenger side of the Bugatti.

"You say that like I'm not hard right now." He wiggled his eyebrows suggestively.

I laughed harder, shaking my head slightly. He's always prepped and ready to go.

"i love it." Xena huffed.

And honestly I did too.

"How about let's make the drive home and then have more fun? I'm starving and we don't have any food left." I pouted as Seth nodded.

He opened the passenger door and leaned down to place me in the seat.

"Of course. I want to care for you in every way." Seth winked at me, buckling me in before placing a kiss on my cheek. "Every way."

I blushed at his closeness as he closed the door. He jogged to the other side and got in. A grin plastered itself on his face as he heard the roar of the engine.

I laughed, shaking my head slightly as he backed out of the garage. "I didn't think you would love driving so much." I told him, leaning back in the seat as I watched the window.

At least he understands the love I have for my car.

"It's just something about controlling a powerful machine that makes me happy. It gives me a sense of peace. Working on this beautiful car with you gives me peace. Being with you gives me peace. I just wish that everything would be better for us." Seth frowned slightly, speeding down the road. "I want you to let me help you with Pete."

I growled unhappily. "No. I won't be able to focus with you there. I just need you to go with Alex and Max to the house and let me handle everything." I told him, rubbing the side of my face as my eyes started to shift colors. "I will be able to focus on the task at hand, knowing you are safely guarded."

Xena wasn't happy with Seth wanting to fight. She should trust me that I wouldn't let anything happen to him ever.

"No. I'm not doing that." Seth growled back, gripping the wheel tightly in his hands. "I am not standing back and letting you handle the situation that I started. And yes I know, you made the choice to save me. You made the choice to start this whole thing. But my father started it because of me.

Because I wanted to save my brother. I did this, I brought this to you. It's not your job to handle all of my problems. I'm not some helpless Omega anymore..." I smiled softly watching him drive.

"You've never been a helpless Omega... Not in my eyes. I saw a powerful, handsome, kind, loving, caring, protective Alpha who went through a lot. Someone who needed just a little bit of help to grow back to the Alpha I always knew he could be." I told him, reaching over to place my hand gently on his thigh. "I never once thought of you as weak..."

I always thought of him as powerful. Yes he maybe needed

some help, some confidence building. But he's always been strong in my eyes. My body tensed as my vision was blurring.

What was happening? Xena growled, the road in front of us darkened.

"I thought of myself as an Omega. A helpless Omega that had to deal with everything because he wasn't strong enough to stand up to them..." Seth sighed, pushing the gas pedal down, the engine roared with power. "I still feel helpless... I know you're just wanting to protect me and I love that about you. But I need to do this... I need to stand by you and protect you like you've protected me all of these months."

I whimpered as I saw my father in front of me. I need out of here.

I started shaking in my seat, my eyes flashing from purple and back to brown rapidly.

"Pull... Over." My voice was strained as my bones slowly started cracking.

I tried not to flinch as he swivered over to park on the side of the road.

Look at what you did to him! You lost it and killed your mate! My father screamed in my face, I closed my eyes with a wince.

No. No. Xena whimpered, cowering against the harsh words. I didn't kill him. I never wanted to hurt him.

Who I thought was my father reached for my hands. My eyes widened as I stared at him, I flinched away from his touch as I forced the door open and quickly unbuckled myself. My heart was racing as I got outside of the car. He's dead. Seth is dead. And it's all my fault. I wanted to scream, I wrapped my arms around my stomach.

I wanted to puke. My body felt numb. I can't believe I lost control and hurt my mate.

"No... No! I never wanted to hurt him! I can control myself!" I whimpered, falling to my knees as I stared at my hands. "I didn't mean to hurt him!" I sobbed, my body shaking.

I just want him to hold me one last time. Everything around me darkened further, my power slipping from my control. I bit my bottom lip.

Someone whimpered, dropping to his knees. "Baby baby what are you talking about! Let me hold you!" He begged as he gently reached for me.

No. If he wasn't my mate. I didn't want his comfort.

THIRTY-EIGHT

"I killed him... I killed him!" I cried out, wrapping my arms around my body as I rocked back and forth.

I looked at his dead form in front of me, and everything screamed at me that this wasn't real. But it felt real, I couldn't take my eyes off of him. He looked so pale... So lifeless...

My head shook slowly as tears streamed down my face. My heart was breaking.

"Who did you kill..?" A males voice was soft as he sat down in front of me.

He sounded like my mate. His voice wrapped around my body, but I fought against it's comfort. It's my mind playing tricks on me. It's my way of coping with what I couldn't handle. Everytime he would try to touch me I would flinch away from him.

"My mate... I killed him. I just wanted to protect him." I cried out, slamming my eyes shut.

I can't see his body anymore, I just want to wake up from this nightmare.

"I loved him with my whole heart. I don't know what I am gonna do now!" I whined, hugging my knees to my chest.

"Baby... Baby... I'm right here... I'm alive. You're okay... Just open your eyes and you will see that I'm here. What are you seeing right now?" The male questioned, shifting forward quietly.

But I could hear him. I shook my head no, I don't want to see his body again.

"I don't want to... I don't want to! I can't see what I've done! I don't want to see it again!" I refused again, shadows started to surround me.

I wanted them to swallow me whole. He grabbed me quickly, pulling me into his chest. "NO! NO! Don't do this!"

My body shook against him as he tightened his arms around me.

I don't deserve his comfort for what I've done. Xena whimpered in the back of my mind, she was trying to tell me something. But I couldn't hear her.

"Scarlett... Trust me. Trust me baby and open your eyes." He said, struggling to hold me as I fought against him.

"Stop fighting me!" Seth ordered, the power rolling through my body.

But this only made me angrier, I shoved him off of me and stood up.

No one gets to tell me what to do. Not anymore.

"I am the Alpha!" Scarlett growled, her eyes glowing a bright purple. "No one tells me what to do! I am Alpha Scarlett Knight! The first Alpha female in hundreds of years! No one is above me!" The shadows circled around me, darkening the world around me.

The male gulped, trying to contain his worry. But I could smell it. I hated the smell of worry.

"Scar... Baby... Please... You're scaring me..." He whimpered, staring up at me. "I didn't know that it would make you upset..." The male stayed in his place.

Why is he trying to appeal to my softer side? Doesn't he see that I'm a monster? I tilted my head slowly, it was like he was my prey. Why is Alex not running?

"Only one man in this world could have told me what to do and he's dead. Because I am crazy and I lost control." I growled, when my arm broke, I forced it back into place.

He watched me with wide eyes, studying my movements. Alex has seen me like this before, but still isn't scared of me.

Xena cried out in the back of my mind. And it must've just now hit her that our mate is gone.

"Baby... Please... I'm right here. I don't know what you're seeing... But I'm okay! You didn't hurt me!" Alex pleaded, standing up slowly.

I know I didn't hurt Alex... I hurt Seth. I hurt the love of my life.

I was walking slowly, the shadows danced around on my body. Two small wolves chased each other across my bare skin.

I felt my power overwhelming me. Someone elses power wrapped around my body. It's a power I don't think I recognize. Could this all be a nightmare? Could my mate still be alive?

"Can't you see? I lost my love... I lost my heart. The world wanted a Ruthless Queen, and the world will get one. They forced me into something I didn't want, and they caused me to lose my mate. And I will burn the world to the ground for what they did to me." I hissed out, watching as the wolves lay with each other before playing.

I don't know who the male is in front of me...

It looks like Alex. But if this power is messing with my vision. It could be anyone. His body was shaking with fear as he watched the black veins pulse through my arms. I was close to blacking out.

"Can't you see me... Standing in front of you? Pleading with you to look at me. But you're scaring me, baby... I know you wouldn't hurt me. But you're talking like a mad woman, what's wrong? Why can't you see me? What do you see when you look at me?" Seth asked, placing his hands gently on my cheeks.

It was freaking me out. How was a dead man talking to me?

I stared into his eyes, my eyes started watering again. Pain made my chest ache, I wish that he was alive. That he would hold me and tell me everything was okay. Xena was still quiet in my mind, and I didn't like it.

"I... I see my handsome... Beautiful dead mate... At the hands of his ruthless mate." I sniffled, my body trembled slightly.

I wanted to shut down and hide. But I couldn't do that. No matter how much I hurt I still had my pack to take care of.

"My Queen... I am alive... I am well... I am okay... I am right here. You didn't hurt me. You would never hurt me. I'm alive, I promise you this." Seth frowned, rubbing my cheeks with his thumbs.

His hands started to glow red, allowing his power to run through my veins. I gasped, instead of the strangers power in my body. I felt his. I felt him. He was alive! I didn't kill him!

My veins started to glow red, before fading back to their normal color. I inhaled sharply, my eyes widened as I stared at him. I practically cried out in relief as he was alive and well in front of me.

"Oh, my Goddess... I... I'm so sorry. I'm so sorry!" I hugged him tightly to me, putting his head against my chest. "I had no idea what was happening. But there is no excuse for how I was acting. I'm so sorry baby."

Xena was shaking in the back of my mind. This scared her just as much as it scared me.

Seth smiled, closing his eyes as he listened to my heartbeat. "I knew something must've happened baby... I think something or someone was messing with your mind. What were you seeing?" He asked, reluctantly pulling away enough to look at my face.

I was quiet for a moment as I looked away from him.

I hated to have to admit this to him. But he already seen it before.

"When I was younger... My father drilled it into my mind one day... One day I would get what's coming for me. I would kill the one person that I loved. The one person that loved me... He tortured me. He made me see my worst nightmare." My voice was quiet, my body tense. "It was a different nightmare each time... But the end result was the same.

I would kill you... In very brutal ways. The smell of your blood makes me want to vomit. Just the thought of me hurting you makes me want to die... I thought you were really dead there. All of it looked so real... It felt real. The pain... The emptiness... The realization that I killed the person that means the entire world to me.

It was so easy for me to give in to that power... That anger that I always feel. I let it drown me, I let it take control. I didn't think I would ever stoop to that level. But I did... And I liked it. I liked knowing I went back to that level of power I had when I showed the world my ruthlessness. What are you going to do if I have to turn into that wolf? The one who doesn't care about anything but getting what she wants? " My face paled as I looked at him again.

My eyes watered as I took in his stunned features. Seth frowned, kissing my forehead gently.

"He has already accepted us for our past. Stop being so surprised." Xena growled at me.

Someone's cranky.

"We're okay... I promise you I'm safe. Let's keep each other safe." Seth said, holding me to him.

I refuse to let him go. I needed him right here.

"You don't have to think about this if you don't want to. I trust you, and I know who you are. I don't want you to worry... And simple. If you think you need to show the world your ruthlessness. You can.

I know who you are at heart. I don't think you're a bad person for wanting the world to know you are the strongest wolf. But I would still like to be there for you. I think us being together that it will help things progress. I think seeing us together will make things better. It will show the world that we are one. And it will show my dad that he can't scare us." He tried to assure me as he kissed each of my cheeks.

I smiled, closing my eyes as I leaned into his comforting touch.

"Okay... Let's go handle this angry crowd." I forced an uneasy smile as I opened my eyes.

Although I just wanted to stay in his hold for the rest of my life.

"Are you going to be okay if I have to kill a few of them?" Seth couldn't help but chuckle.

"If they want to test you... They will pay the ultimate price for it. I'm not going to get scared. I promise." He reassured me, smiling brightly.

I frowned, looking away from him. But he was scared... Of me. And I never wanted that.

"But you were scared of me... Just a little bit ago. You told me that I was scaring you..." My voice broke, as I closed my eyes. "I didn't know what was happening... I just knew I wanted the world to pay for taking my mate away from me."

Seth frowned at my words, he gently placed his hands back on my cheeks and turned my face back to him.

"I know... But I wasn't scared of you. I was scared of what was going to happen to you. I was scared that something was seriously wrong and that I was going to lose you. I wasn't scared of you. Just of what was happening." He promised, his eyes drifting down to my lips before back to my eyes. "I know you. I do."

I just wanted him to know that he was safe with me. He was always safe with me. I would rather die than do anything to hurt him.

"I would never hurt you..." I promised, biting my bottom lip. "I feel like I'm failing at everything."

Seth kissed me, biting my bottom lip and tugging on it. I wanted to moan at the slight pain.

"You kinky alpha." Xena snorted in the back of my mind. *"I love it."*

"You're not failing at everything. Our lives are changing. We're growing with one another. You are learning to trust me and allow me to help with the pack and all of your responsibilities." He promised me, grinning proudly at me. "You handle everything without complaint. Now it's your turn to get a break."

I smiled, my eyes sparkling with joy. My power flooded the air around us causing Seth to tilt his head in confusion. He'll learn how to feel the fight that's coming.

"I... I feel the fight coming. It's instinct. Drown the weak in power and they submit before the fight even starts. Speaking of that... I have to tell you something." I told him, my cheeks turning pink.

Seth nodded. I gotta tell him about Sadie before I forget again.

"Okay... You're worrying me..." He said, his eyes going over my face as he tried to read my emotions.

I'm always stressing him out.

"He's going to have to learn to deal with it." Xena teased.

I'm happy she's calming down.

282

"You know Zane? And Sadie Arlington?" I asked, keeping direct eye contact with him.

Seth nodded his head yes. I wanted him to know that I wasn't lying.

"Well... She's my half-sister. And when I say my half-sister, I mean Stormy, Grayson, and my half-sister. A long story short... I found out about a year after I became alpha about Sadie. I tried to be there for her, but she just blamed me for her not having a dad. She didn't know about the abuse and neglect.

And frankly... She was a child. I didn't want to put that burden on her. We were all kids. And I had enough of ruining people's childhoods. So I kept it a secret. But by the time I told her about my father and what he had done to us... She hated herself. She hated everybody. So she left and she found Zane. Which she saved him from a human camp, but that's another long story for a different occasion.

Anyways... She is my half-sister. She decided that she didn't want the pack to know. And I respected her choice. The pack doesn't know. But Stormy and Grayson know, and now so do you. I don't mind if you tell Max and Alex. But I just don't want the whole pack to know. And I know they are going to try to throw everything at us.

We just have to be prepared, I don't know what your pack members know. And I don't know where their loyalty lay." I informed him.

Seth's eyes were wide as he processed what I told him. That's one thing I knew would be hidden deep within my mind. And I wasn't sure if it was information he remembered.

"Holy Goddess..." Seth said with a chuckle. "That's insane. I guess it all makes sense on why you wanted to save her. Even if she isn't a part of the family dynamic we have. Which now that I think about it is freaking weird." He said as he walked over to open the door for me. "I guess we make a good team."

Always the gentleman. I think it's adorable.

I laughed, getting into the passenger seat as he shut the door. Seth jogged to the other side and got in. "I can't get over how hot you are when you drive my Bugatti." I said, with a grin.

Seth smirked, revving the engine before putting it into drive and speeding off. It was one of the hottest things I've ever seen. And I wasn't ashamed to smell my own arousal.

"I love how your arousal makes me drunk because of the tiny car we're in," Seth growled, his eyes blazing red as his body tensed. "I think I feel the fighting... The tension... The anger... I feel it all and my power is pumping." He forced the car to go faster.

I giggled, smelling his arousal fill the air.

I feel like we won't be satisfied for a long while.

"I think that it's because we're one now. I mean we were one before when I saved you. But we weren't connected like we are now. So you can feel what I feel... And I feel it too... They're scared... They blame me... They blame us... Some are happy with the thought of a new heir. But most are angry about the upcoming war." I explained, biting my bottom lip as my body tensed.

I just wanted to do right by everyone. He reached over and placed his hand on my leg gently.

"We are here. We are together. Everything is going to be fine because we can handle whatever they throw at us, you hear me?" Seth told me, squeezing my thigh causing me to moan.

He groaned, his muscles tensing as he gripped the wheel. "Don't do that to me."

I'm definitely playing with fire. But the pain just shot pleasure all throughout me.

"I can't help it!" I whined. "The pain you give me just feels so so so good. It adds into everything you already do to me." I huffed embarrassed.

He didn't need to tease me.

For a while we rode in silence, just enjoying each other's company. I had my hand on his as I watched my window. Suddenly Seth started to slow down as he saw the crowding forming in the middle of Edinburgh.

This is fantastic.

"I didn't think they would have been this angry..." He spoke softly, slowing down even more as the crowd moved to let us through.

The Bugatti barely going five miles an hour. My eyes turned purple as a frown overtook me. This is worse than what I was expecting.

"We want to know what's happening!"

"Look the Alphas are back!"

"We need to know if we're going to die!'

"Are the wolves who came here for refuge will they be given back to Ireland!"

And a million other questions and statements were fired out from the crowd around us.

"I wish we stayed in the cabin." I frowned as Seth parked in front of the crowd.

He wanted to say something, but I was quick to get out of the car after he killed the engine.

I just wanted to get this over with.

THIRTY-NINE

I climbed on top of my Bugatti and stood up. Everything is going to be fine. I eyed the crowd in front of me and let out a sigh. Seth frowned as he looked up at me, I knew he was worried. But he's going to have to get used to this. He'll probably see it often. The crowd silenced with one hand gesture.

And I swear Xena growled in approval.

"I know you are scared... I know you are angry. I know you think I abandoned you. I was gone... And I am sorry for being gone for these last two weeks... I know you all have gone through a lot. Pete has put us through more things than he should have. But I promise you these last two weeks weren't for nothing.

I have marked my mate, which will give added power to our home. Added power to our pack! The Winterfall Pack is the first pack in the entire world. Hell maybe in history to have two Alphas! I don't want you to be scared. I don't want you to worry. I am back here, stronger than before because of my connection and link with Seth.

There will be a formal ceremony to introduce him properly as the Alpha of this pack. But that will come after I take Ireland.

286

After I take back what belongs to not just me. But what belongs to you and what belongs to my mate! Pete has given us enough trauma. Enough problems! I will end this. This I promise you!

I know that you have your fears. Your questions... And I will let you ask them now." I shouted to the crowd in front of me.

I eyed each and every one of them. No one will see even an ounce of fear on me, because I'm not scared. I know this is going to end. And end with me on top. Seth smiled as he stood beside the car in support of me.

"Are you pregnant!" A wolf yelled from the back of the crowd.

This seemed to get everyone's attention. Murmurs whispered throughout the people. I practically groaned at the question.

Why is it always that question?

"If you're pregnant then who will protect us! Stormy isn't back yet! No one can protect us!" Another wolf yelled out, as I nodded listening to them.

Before I could speak, Seth spoke up.

"That's hot though." Xena growled, smiling in the back of my mind.

"If she is in fact pregnant before the fight with my father comes. I will protect you. I will fight to protect you all with my life. I am your Alpha, and I know that you all don't know me very well. You've barely had a chance to know me before all of this started up... And I am truly sorry about that.

I came here under circumstances that I had no control over. But I fell in love with the peace and the love that I can feel in the land. Not only that... But I fell in love with your Alpha... The Alpha who has given anything and everything to protect us all. I understand you are scared and worried about what the future will bring.

But trust in your Alpha. We were gone to provide more strength to you... To you all. And when we get Ireland back. We will be even stronger! Thanks to your Alpha Scarlett!" Seth said, smiling as he held out a hand to help me down. "Our future is clear with her as our leader. While you are scared... She is our rock. She will protect us... And I will be right by her side protecting her and you all throughout the whole process."

I jumped down from the Bugatti, smiling as he wrapped his arm around my waist. "We are one today. We are ONE pack. We will be one territory! Ireland will be ours!" I yelled, causing the crowd to howl with excitement.

Xena's excitement flooded my veins, and I wanted to howl with them. But I didn't.

Seth grinned down at me, his eyes were filled with love and excitement. He crashed his lips to mine, wrapping his arms tightly around me and pulling me to him. I kissed him back, wrapping my arms around the back of his neck and leaning into it.

"Mine." Xena growled, and I was wondering why she wouldn't try to take control.

Hoots and hollers sounded throughout the crowd, starting with Alex. "YEAH Seth!! Get IT!" Alex shouted.

He growled, moving his hands down to my butt and squeezing roughly. I whimpered into his mouth, causing him to groan. He reluctantly pulled away, his eyes turning red.

There's the look I like to see.

"I wish we never left that cabin." Seth growled against my lips.

I giggled, my body practically vibrating with my adrenaline. The pack supported us as Alphas. It was flowing through the land, and right back into me. I felt amazing.

"Our pack has accepted you... This is us now. We are one..." I whispered against his lips.

My eyes never left his as the crowd stayed there, mingling among one another. I want us to be alone, I need us to be alone.

"We're having a party!!" Alex yelled, jumping on top of his Jeep Wrangler. "Down at the River! Let's go, everyone!" He jumped in front of the crowd, leading away from us.

"Do you even want to go to a party?" Seth asked, subtly grinding against me.

I laughed, kissing his sharp jawline. I just want to take him home.

"It feels like you don't want to go to a party. But I need to speak with them and make sure that they all have found places to stay. This will be much easier when we get Ireland... They can go back to their own homes and we won't be crammed together... But I do need to go and make sure I don't need to find anyone else places to stay." I smiled at him, keeping my body plastered to his.

He sighed, frowning slightly.

"You are no fun." Xena growled, obviously unhappy with my decision.

I'm unhappy with my decision too.

"Okay... We'll go. But we shouldn't stay for long. We haven't slept much these last two weeks, and you're under a lot of stress. You need your rest, especially with the fight coming up." Seth told me, gently kneading the flesh of my butt in his hands.

I nodded, the bags under my eyes were prominent. I just need a freaking nap.

"I know. But I had fun the last two weeks... Maybe after everything has settled... We can go back there and relax. I'm sure it would be a blast, considering how much fun we had there before. Maybe we could get a project car and work on it together since my Bugatti doesn't need any work.

Maybe a challenger? I think that would be pretty cool. Or it could be your car, and you can pick. I don't know but it would be special to do that together." I smiled, reluctantly pulling away from him.

Because if I didn't, we would definitely be going home instead of to the party. He smirked slightly, opening the passenger door for me.

"I knew you hated that I drove your Bugatti so much." Seth teased with a playful smile as I got in.

He jogged to the other side, before getting in quickly. I rolled her eyes, shooting him a playful glare.

"I hate it so much, so so much. That's why I let you drive my car and never tell you no. Because I hate that you drive it." I shot back, smirking slightly. "The one thing I do hate about it is that we can't have any fun in it because of its size."

Seth's eyes went wide at my words as he stared at me in shock.

I tried my best to not snicker at the look on his face. This moment is priceless.

"So you're saying that if we got a bigger car... We could have sex in the car?" He asked, his eyes glowing red.

I smiled, buckling up as he started the car. Of course I am, I would never joke about sex with him.

"Yes. Or honestly we could have sex on the hood of the car somewhere. It's not like people can say anything to us. We are the Alphas of our pack." I smirked as he pulled down the road, heading to the river.

"I really really like the sound of that." Seth grinned, speeding down the road. "I think it would be a lot of fun. It's like a scene out of one of those books you read."

My cheeks heated as I bit my bottom lip. I keep forgetting that he read those books. Or maybe he just saw them?

"I can't sleep well most nights okay. And when you first came here you didn't want anything to do with me. I didn't know what to do, so I read. And then I read a lot because I couldn't sleep. All I wanted to do was make sure you were okay. So I would go and get a book from my room and check on you.

I don't have a lot of free time." I was flustered.

I probably should've moved those books before putting him in there. Seth chuckled at my embarrassment.

"I didn't say anything bad about it. I think it's hot... This way I know what you like and I can better pleasure you." Seth smiled, proud of himself. "I thought you read books with kinks in them that you liked. So it was a real help to me."

Xena stared at him in shock. I didn't think he would've read them for me.

"Well who else would it be dipstick?" Xena deadpanned.

I looked at him, surprise written all over my face as I stared at him. He parked on the road, knowing I wouldn't want my Bugatti off the road. He gets extra points. Goddess I wish I could please him in my car.

"You read the books so you could know what I like? And how to pleasure me better?" I asked, my eyes slowly turning purple.

Xena wanted attention too, that whore. I probably shouldn't say that because she could make me uncomfortably turned on constantly. Seth turned to me and smiled.

"Don't test me because I'll do it." Xena growled. I was just teasing!

"Yeah! I didn't want to ask Alex because if he knew I would've had to kill him. But then I saw a book in your hand when you fell asleep on the couch. And I saw what page you were on, and it seemed like a pretty well read book so I thought why not. I don't think you knew this but I took that book and read the entire thing before you woke up.

I kept watch on you while you slept... And I feel like that's weird of me to say. But I was so intrigued by you in the beginning and I still am. I just wanted to know everything about you and I wanted to know why I needed to be around you. I'm still sorry I pushed you away, and I hope that we can move past that.

I was lost... I was stressed... I was feeling everything too much. I had no power and then all of a sudden you were giving me everything. I didn't know how to handle that and I'm sorry. I feel bad about it and I probably always will." Seth told me, frowning slightly as his eyes looked down at his thighs.

I whimpered, gently placing my hands on his face. I turned his face to make him look at me.

Nothing he did ever upset me. I understood his reasons, I might've not liked it. But I still understood it and supported it.

"I'm not upset my love... I know you were going through a lot. I just didn't know that you read the books I did. Because I know I can read some pretty dirty stuff. It's just an escape for me... Something that gives me peace. I don't blame you for a single thing. I am just happy that we're here now. That we're one. I don't want you to blame yourself for that.

Your father did this to you... You didn't do this to you. We're moving past this... Into a future where we can protect our kids from what happened to us." I smiled at him, kissing his nose before kissing his lips.

I need him to know that I love him so much, no matter what. Seth smiled, his eyes drifted down to my belly.

"I really hope you're pregnant... That would be hot." He grinned, changing the subject.

I started laughing as I shook my head. I freaking knew that was coming.

"I think it's going to be hot with you thinking it's hot." I smiled, getting out of the car.

Seth followed suit, following me down to where everyone was already dancing and drinking with each other. Well this should be interesting.

I wrapped my arm around his waist and stayed right by him. "I want everyone to know that you're mine." I growled, already feeling eyes on us. "Some of them weren't there today at the crowd..." Seth chuckled, placing his hand flat on my butt.

No one is going to take what belongs to me.

"YEAH! Or we're gonna kill them!" Xena howled, and I wanted to giggle at her excitement.

"Everyone will know baby. You don't have to worry." He grinned, walking over to where Alex was sitting on his Jeep Wrangler as Max stood beside it.

I followed after him, holding his hand.

"So where is your sister?" Max asked, looking at me. "Grayson is here... But we never see your sister."

I sighed in frustration. I don't even know what to do with her right in this moment. It's definitely too much to deal with.

"I believe that she is staying in a house deep in the woods. They have gotten used to their privacy I guess. The elf she is with probably has a hand in that and I don't like it... Especially with all the fighting going on at the border... But I don't want to push her into being a part of pack life... And I guess selfishly... I don't want to have to deal with another fight right now.

Especially with things being so tense in the pack... Introducing an elf into the mix... I don't want something else to deal with." I shrugged.

That's awful for me to admit. I love my sister and that she's happy. But elves and wolves don't mix. It's going to be a hassle and she knows it.

"Ya know, being the Alpha's best friend has its perks. Maybe I'll just have to eat you out underneath your desk and I'll get a pretty Bugatti next." Alex teased, causing me to laugh.

This is going to be fun. Seth growled, glaring daggers at him. Alex whimpered in submission.

"Seth gets hotter and hotter as the days go by." Xena growled with happiness.

"I was JOKING! I have never eaten her out, I wanted to. But she said no because she wanted to wait for you. So you should be happy, but now I have my sights set on someone else..." Alex said, his eyes trailing to a wolf sitting with her feet in the water and a sketchbook against her legs.

Seth followed his gaze, before his eyes widened. I followed after them, who is she?

"You think that's your mate! The doctor's daughter!" Seth whispered to him, causing him to shrug.

I looked between them. Am I supposed to know who she is?

"I have no idea what you're talking about." I said, tilting my head slightly.

Alex hopped off of his Jeep. Will someone tell me what's happening? Probably not and I'm just going to be confused through this whole conversation.

"In Ireland... We have this Supernatural hospital. It's huge. And many many creatures come to it to see our doctor. Doctor Hunter. Angels... Elves... Werewolves... Witches... You name it. They all came... But Doc's mate died in childbirth... And they say that it left his daughter Carter without the ability to speak." Alex informed, his eyes on the woman as she stood up.

Okay, so that makes sense.

"I heard that she can speak. She just chooses not to." Max added in.

Seth shrugged, his eyes locked on me. Pride swelled in my chest as he kept his eyes on me.

"I say I don't care because I have the hottest and the best woman in the entire world." He grinned, bending down to kiss my mark.

I giggled, as I placed my hands on his abs. I wish we stayed at home, we would've been having so much more fun.

"You should listen to me more often." Xena huffed in the back of my mind.

"I think I have the hottest and the best man in the entire world." I copied his words.

But I was telling the truth. Alex huffed, sipping his whiskey.

"Goddess. I just want to get drunk already." Alex huffed, downing the rest of his drink.

Max looked at Seth, smiling innocently. I'm never going to understand these people.

"Can I go talk to some friends?" He asked, excitement lighting up his face.

Seth couldn't help but laugh.

"You don't have to ask me for permission... You can go talk to whoever you want." Seth told him, causing him to nod eagerly and run off.

I frowned slightly looking up at him. I wish he knew that he was free here. I don't know how to help him.

"He's still not used to being free huh?" I asked, my eyes trailing to Max as he was talking to a group of guys around his age.

Seth's eyes were locked on his brother. At least I knew them, they were nice. And they knew better than doing anything to my family.

"No... He keeps asking me to do stuff... He broke a cup the other day, before we left to the cabin; and about had a panic attack because he thought he was going to get sent back to Ireland. I think the stress of the upcoming war is getting to him and I just don't know how to help him. He won't talk to me... He won't let me sit with him most times." Seth frowned, rubbing his forehead as he sighed.

I frowned, looking down at my feet.

The war will be over, and he'll never have to see Ireland again if he didn't want to.

Alex leaned against his car, the glow of the fire in front of him made his eyes sparkle. "He talks to me... He thinks now that you have Scarlett that you don't care as much about him. I told him he's just overthinking and it's a natural thing to do after everything he went through. But he worries that if he does something wrong or if he upsets you in any way that you will give up on him and send him back to your father.

I tried talking him out of this... But he is just stressed. I'm sure it's because he can feel the tension in the land. We all can... But the younger ones seem to be noticing it more... The kids talk to each other, they think they can't go and hang out. It's why I've been throwing a bunch of parties here. It gets them to relax a bit." Alex informed us, causing Seth to growl at him.

I frowned further.

He says that like this is all my fault. I blame myself already. But that's the Alpha's job to handle everything.

"It will be over soon... That's all I can say about that. And then Max will feel better. Everyone will feel better. Everything will be better." I smiled, trying to stay positive.

Seth was no doubt blaming himself, so I don't need to be taking any attention away from him. Seth grunted, his eyes turning red as his body stiffened.

"None of this is your fault... Max needs to work through his trauma just like you did... And you still do..."

"I know..." He sighed, looking down at me with a soft sad smile.

Alex stiffened up as Carter slowly walked closer to us. Her eyes were on Seth. I noticed this immediately, I straightened up my power soaking the air around us.

"Oh oh we should kill her if she touches what's ours." Xena growled, obviously not liking her.

Frankly, I don't like her either.

I leaned back against the black Jeep Wrangler. His body was tense as his arms crossed over his chest causing his muscles to tense and untense repeatedly. Should've just went home.

"Hey..." Carter said, staring at Seth.

I growled softly, standing in front of her. I don't like her at all.

"Hey!" I said, overly happy. "I'm Alpha Scarlett Knight." I introduced myself, making sure to use my title.

So she knew who she was messing with. My power caused Carter to wobble slightly. I drew on Seth's power to make it even more sure she would know that we're one.

"I'm an omega. I'm Carter." Carter introduced herself, her eyes were still on Seth. "He's my Alpha." She said, referring to Seth.

Alex couldn't help but laugh softly at her words, he shook his head slightly. Seth didn't speak to Carter, his eyes on me.

"Can we kill her... Now?" Xena asked.

And I want to. I so badly want to.

"And that is where I stop you. I am the Alpha of this land. So I am your Alpha, unless you would like to go back to Ireland. I will gladly drive you there and throw you back to the scum where you belong." I growled, baring my fangs at her.

Carter looked taken back at my words. Her eyes drifted to Alex now, immediately her cheeks heated as his eyes locked with hers.

So they are mates. Which means I can't kill her.

"I just wanted to speak with my Alp–..." Carter started before I had her by the neck.

I pulled her in, getting in her face. This ends here and now.

"And that is where you stop. I hear it in your voice. You want Seth, but he is *mine*. I'll freaking kill you before you lay a hand on him." I growled out, my body shaking with restraint.

Xena gave me her power, as I struggled with controlling myself. Carter whimpered in fear, causing Alex to step in.

"Let her go Scarlett. She didn't mean anything by it." Alex said, putting his hand on my wrist.

I barely noticed it, my eyes stayed locked on Carters. No one is going to think they can touch what's mine. Seth growled now, pushing off of the Wrangler and shoving Alex.

"That's my mate!! We should get laid tonight!" Xena howled, eagerly watching.

"Don't get in the middle of something that doesn't involve you Alex." Seth snapped, standing beside me.

My eyes were on Alex now, but I never let Carter go.

Alex is testing boundaries. And this isn't going to end well for anyone involved if this continues.

"She's mine and you KNOW it. Scarlett doesn't need to be shoving her power around. Carter didn't mean anything by what she was saying and you know it. She is overreacting because she's stressed!" Alex snapped back, baring his fangs.

Seth growled, his eyes blazing red like fire.

CHAPTER
FORTY

"Do not speak about your Alpha like this!" Seth ordered, his body towering over Alex. "She has the authority to punish you to what she sees fit! Frankly, I have the same authority. Carter could obviously see our marks. She could see us being together. But she decided to test it!" He snapped, shoving him causing him to fall on his butt.

"Oh... Oh I really really like this!" Xena cheered on.

He will not disrespect my mate, his mate will also not disrespect us.

"Then Scarlett needs to show mercy on her! She is my mate and I won't let her hurt her!" Alex growled, although he stayed on the ground.

He couldn't win against Seth even if he tried. I tossed Carter on the ground next to him. This is where we put them in their place

"This is going to end well for us. And when I say that I mean we're going to get laid." Xena grinned as we watched Seth and Reign work.

"Ah you see that is where you are wrong Alex. I do what I

299

please, this is my pack. My territory. And I have the authority to do whatever I want and no one can tell me otherwise!" I growled, Seth stood behind me with my arms crossed.

I feel his support rush through my body, boosting me up even more..

"You don't have to act like this! When I knew you before you weren't like this!" Alex said, glaring at me now. "You were nicer than this!"

I should break his face for saying that.

"Hey we wouldn't have gotten to where we are now if we were nice all the time." Xena huffed. *"We're mean to everyone but our mate. Perfect."*

"I changed. I grew up. You should've grown up too!" I growled back, about to grab him.

Max ran up, his eyes were wide as he looked at all of us. He made me not move. I couldn't make him scared of me. He was already in a delicate place. I couldn't make it worse on him.

"Stop! Stop it! Stop it! Can't you see this is what he wants!" Max yelled at us all, his body shaking with fear. "He wants us to turn on each other. He wants us to not have each other to depend on! He wants to break us apart because we are weaker like that! Stop fighting and just see it from where I see it!"

I looked up at him, my eyes softened at him. "Maxxy... Sweetie... Don't be scared." I spoke softly, my body immediately relaxed.

Xena calmed down. Max had tears in his eyes as I walked over to him. Seth walked to Max and hugged him tightly, wrapping his arms around both me and Max.

Max is going to be okay. Everything will be fine once Pete is gone and things settle down in Ireland. I have to believe that.

"Maxxy... You are my little brother. You are my brother, no one will ever send you away. You are never going anywhere. I don't want you to worry about anything. Because I will protect you, nothing will happen to you..." Seth spoke softly, resting his head on Max's head.

Max cried into his chest, clutching onto both me and Seth. Nothing will ever happen to him again. I won't let anyone hurt him.

"You are our family Maxxy... I'm sorry you're so scared... I'm sorry you're still feeling the effects of your father... But I promise you. You are safe here, I will never let anything happen to you. Everything will be fine, I promise you. I won't stop until Pete is dead... Because you deserve to be safe... I love you Maxxy.

I'm sorry for scaring you... I didn't mean to scare you... I just wanted to make it known to Carter that Seth is mine. And if you believe I took it too far, I am sorry about that my sweetheart." I told him soothingly, rubbing his back gently.

Max sniffled, his blue eyes were red and puffy as he looked at us. The sadness written across his face makes my heart break.

It reminds me so much of Stormy and Grayson. I can't help but feel bad. He's like my little brother.

"I just don't want to lose anyone... Pete... Pete said all the time about how he was going to take everything and everyone away from us. He already took our pack. I don't want to lose the family that I made too... I just want us all to get along. Can we do that? We're brothers after all." Max said, turning his attention to Alex.

Alex grumbled as he stood up, a soft growl left him as he nodded. I want to really beat the crap out of him.

He needs to learn that just because of our relationship in the past. It doesn't mean that he can disrespect me or my mate. He needs to learn his place.

Seth reluctantly let go of Max and me as Alex walked up to the group. Seth clenched his fist and quickly swung, hitting Alex in the jaw. Seth didn't move to look at his hand, which makes me even more proud of him. My mate is stronger than he gives himself credit for.

Alex groaned, cupping his face as he closed his eyes from the pain.

"I deserved that." Alex grumbled, opened his eyes to look at us.

I couldn't help but smirk as I had an arm around Max. He was leaning into me with his arms crossed. Maybe I won't have to teach him a lesson.

"Yes. Yes you did. First, talking about eating my mate out. And second, thinking you could lay your hands on her without dying. You should be lucky I didn't break your neck for trying to force her to do something." Seth growled, crossing his arms as he was obviously not happy.

I couldn't help but giggle at the sight, a happy smile on my face. This is hotter than anything.

"Him protecting our reputation? Him not being afraid to lay someone out for us. I want to have that mans babies." Xena grinned, I felt her excitement and hornyness course through my veins.

It made my heart beat a little faster as I looked at Seth.

"And in further notes. I do hope that everyone now knows that Seth is mine and I'm just crazy enough to kill someone for even giving him a little bit of a look that I don't like." I stated proudly, which I was telling the truth.

He grinned at me, walking over to standing beside me now. Alex nodded in understanding, before drifting his gaze down to where Carter was still on the ground.

"Seth and I are equal Alphas. If you don't accept me, you can't accept him. We are one, and that is how we are going to rule our packs." I said, looking at Carter. "If you submit to both of us. You may stay in Scotland."

Submit and promise to never look at my mate again.

Alex helped her stand to her feet. She bowed her head in

submission, her gaze staying on her feet. Seth looked at Alex now, glaring ever so slightly. *He needs to get a handle on her before she pushes a wolf that doesn't have as much restraint as I do. And with another pack being mixed with ours? That could very easily happen. I want them both to be safe.*

"Speak with your mate about our customs and tell her that she needs to watch her tongue. The pack is filled with males and females that would do much worse to a wolf for doing less than what she did. We want everyone safe, but she needs to not push testy wolves buttons." Seth informed, motioning to his Jeep Wrangler. "You may go."

I don't think I've ever felt more whole than at this moment.

"Well besides us ya know mating." Xena snickered, thinking she was hilarious.

"Thanks guys... Scar... I'm sorry. I didn't mean what I did. I... I lost control and I'm sorry." Alex apologized, his eyes showed his sorrow. "You know I love you... You know I understand what you went through. I shouldn't have said the things I did out of anger. I didn't mean what I said, because I think you're amazing just the way you are. You're my best friend after all." He smiled innocently, locking eyes with me.

At least he knows he did something wrong.

I smiled, squeezing Max gently. "I think what Max said was right. Pete is boiling the water and is seeing how far he can push us until we snap. He knows we're stronger together and he knows with more and more wolves seeking shelter with us... Things are going to be more tense and more stressful.

*I'm sorry for hurting your mate, but she needed to be put in her place. I know you didn't mean anything you said... I know who you are Alex... I love you. I'm not upset." I smiled kindly, before looking at Seth.

My possessive sexy alpha.

"Him on the other hand is a different story."

Seth chuckled, smirking slightly. And I knew what he was thinking, that punching Alex in the face was helpful.

"He could've kept going. No one would've stopped him." Xena complained.

And it took everything in me not to laugh at what she said.

"I punched him in the face, I feel better. He was put in his place and everything is fine now between us. We're brothers after all. We always come back to each other." Seth said, nodding at him.

Alex smiled, walking to open the passenger door for Carter.

"I don't think I'm prepared for this." Alex whispered, his fear evident.

I laughed. Poor poor Alex, he's going to become a simp.

"You'll be fine. But don't be sad when she isn't as cool as me. Most she-wolves are more sensitive. I just like to kill people and call it a day." I teased, as Alex laughed.

He got into the drivers seat and closed the door.

"It's totally a joke." Xena grinned, showing the truth behind the words.

"How about you and Seth go watch a movie at our house?" I offered, looking at Max. "I will be home soon and then we can make cookies and watch another movie." Seth growled, shaking his head no.

"Do I typically not like when someone tells me I can't do something? Yes. But he can boss me around all he wants." Xena laughed at me. *"I enjoy myself a lot honestly."*

"Yeah right. As if I'm leaving you unprotected." Seth scoffed.

Max grinned at our little argument.

"I... If Seth wants to stay I will be okay to go home." Max offered, trying to be strong.

I turned my focus to him.

"I have some things I need to deal with. I can't just put it off because you want me to go home." I informed, standing my ground.

Seth grinned seductively at me. I'm going to go home with him, but I still like to push his buttons.

"I will throw you over my shoulder and carry you to the Bugatti if I have to." He said with a soft shrug.

Max took a few steps back, knowing things were going to escalate quickly. And he had the right mind to do so, because Seth can go real quick from zero to one hundred.

"You wouldn't dare." I said, although a small smile spread across my face.

Seth laughed, bending down and easily picking me up and throwing over his shoulder. I started laughing as he began walking back to the Bugatti. Max quickly went to get into his car to drive home.

"Wait wait I'll walk!! These shorts don't offer the most coverage." I giggled as I felt his hand plant itself on my butt.

No one gets to see what's his I guess.

"Yeah! You got that right!" Xena backed me up. *"Let him be possessive!"*

What a horny Alpha.

"I got you covered." Seth chuckled, only placing me down once we got to the passenger side of the Bugatti. "All the time. I don't want you hurt baby... Please let me be with you constantly... Pete has taken so much away from me already. I won't let him take you." He said, biting his bottom lip out of worry.

My heart broke at the worry on his face.

I nodded, feeling his fear through our bond. "I know baby... I will... I was just being playful back there. I didn't mean anything by it. Of course you can be near me constantly. I love you and if that helps keep you calm. Then that helps keep you calm. I just know this is going to be a long fight.

And when Max needs you with him... I will come too... But we should give him some attention to help him calm down. He needs to know that everything is going to be okay. I guess I lost sight of the fact that I didn't just save you. But I saved him as well..." I frowned, beating myself up over it.

He smiled at me, licking my cheek slowly. My whole body warmed up when he did that.

"I appreciate you caring enough to be upset. But like you said... He needs his own time to heal from his trauma... I think his friends are helping a lot with that." He informed, helping me into the Bugatti before getting in on the driver's side.

He quickly started the car and sped off .

CHAPTER
FORTY-ONE

After watching a movie together, I stretched as I stood up. The couch was comfortable. But I prefer sleeping in my bed. Seth had his shirt off, and his arms behind his head as he watched me.

"He sure does love to play." Xena grinned, and I knew what she was thinking.

"What are you doing?" He asked, as I walked to the couch where Max was sleeping.

I smiled softly as I looked down at him. I missed being able to take care of my siblings like this.

"I'm bringing Maxxy to bed." I told him bluntly, bending down and picking Max up quickly in my arms so he didn't wake up.

I slowly started walking towards his bedroom. Seth was quick to get off of the couch and follow after me.

Can I just say that I love that he's so attached to me.

He waited at Max's door, leaning against the doorframe as he watched me place him in bed. I knew he could tell that I was still tired. But I like being able to take care of people. Especially people who I feel are my family. I gently covered him with a deep blue comforter, Max looked peaceful in the middle of the large king sized bed.

I hope he loves it here. Because he deserves the peace and safety that I gave to my younger siblings.

"I love you sweet Maxxy... Sweet dreams." I whispered softly, before walking out of his bedroom.

Seth moved out of the way, shutting the door behind me. He picked me up, carrying me into our bedroom.

I may be the Alpha, but I sure do like being babied by this handsome man.

"I could've carried him to bed." Seth frowned, gently placing me down on the bed.

I groaned, laying back on the bed. I feel sore still, and I didn't even think that was possible for me. Especially since I'm used to sleeping horribly.

"Are we going to have this discussion again?" I sighed frustrated, closing my eyes.

We could just go to bed, I hope we could at least. But I knew he was worried, and he wanted to get his point across. For someone who hasn't been in touch with his Alpha side, he sure is stubborn. He growled, climbing on top of me. My eyes opened looking up into his.

His eyes were the most gorgeous brown... His face soft but hard and sharp. He was perfection in a physical form. And I'm blessed with the best. I don't think I could ever love someone more than I love him.

Here's to hoping that I make it out of this war to see our future together.

"Yes we are having this discussion again. We are going to continue to have this discussion until you realize what you're doing to yourself. You're exhausted. And I still don't have my full power that I should have so I can't give you much. The land runs on you... You give this territory power. You give our pack power.

I know you are so used to handling everything. But I'm here... I'm not going anywhere. I know you're scared... You are so used to being the Alpha. And I understand that, but please baby... Please I can't stand to watch you do this to yourself. I feel responsible, I want to help you with this." Seth told me, laying his body against mine.

He whimpered softly, nudging my nose with his.

I wanted to whimper to him... To tell him I'm sorry. But I'm not... If I had to die to protect him. To give him a chance at really living. I would. Because he's been through enough and I just want him happy.

Xena growled in the back of my mind. I knew she didn't like this plan. But she would go along with it. Because deep down she knows I'm right. Seth deserves a chance to live, even if that means I'm not in it.

His fear and worry broke my heart. And it took everything in me not to ask him to forgive me for hurting him when I didn't even mean to. Goddess, I'm so whipped for this male.

My eyes started to water as I looked up at him. "I need to handle this... I need to. This one thing I need to do by myself. It's my battle now... I can't let him take you away from me... I simply can't. I would rather die... You think before when I lost control that was bad? Imagine how bad it would get if Pete killed you actually.

I would burn the entire world to the ground if they took you away from me. I just need to protect you and then after this whole thing is done and over with, I will give you equal part of the responsibilities. I promised you when I brought you home that I would kill Pete. I would protect you and your brothers.

This is something I have to handle myself. I don't want to upset you. I just want you to be alive... I know that if anything happens to me that you will continue on with my pack and keep everything safe." I told him, my body tensing under his.

"I'm just going to say this now. You're stupid." Xena rolled her eyes at me.

And now I prepare for the anger I know is coming. Seth's whole body went rigid at my words.

I just wanted to protect him. How else could I show that to him? I've never been the most sensitive person.

"You did not just speak those words. You did NOT just tell me that I would continue on without you. Goddess! Scarlett! Don't you even see how much I love you? How much I need you in my life! You're the one thing that kept me from giving up all those years tortured and locked away! You are the only thing going in my life that I am happy about!

And then you hit me with THIS! You think I would just move on! There is NO life after you. You are my life! You are my world! And dang it woman if you die I will die too! I'll die right beside you and leave everything to be with you in the afterlife. You're not freaking leaving me. You're not freaking dying!" Seth growled, getting off of me as his eyes turned red.

I sat up quickly, watching as he paced the length of our bedroom.

I frowned as I didn't know the right words to calm him down. I wish I could take them back. They made sense to say at the time. I just didn't fully think it through I guess.

"You guess!?! Were you dropped on your head as a pup?" Xena growled.

No. I was just thrown against a wall numerous times.

"You drive me crazy. You're the world's most powerful wolf and yet you think that because I am here now... That you still have to handle everything by yourself! It won't make you weak, it won't make you pathetic. I know what you're thinking, it's the words that your father spoke to you all those years ago.

"If you don't handle everything then everyone will think you're weak and pathetic. Just like I know you always have been. You will be the ruin of this great pack that I built."

It's NOT true! He was a pathetic excuse for a wolf and if you didn't kill him I would've! Because he doesn't get to talk to you like this and I wish I could burn him alive for the trauma and self- sabotaging ways that he put on you. He was weak and pathetic because his mate left him and made him look like a fool to his pack.

You are completely different. You gave your pack a powerful couple leading it. You are going to give your pack heirs that will continue our line for generations. You are nothing like your father. Please stop putting this guilt on yourself! Stormy, Grayson, Max, and Alex. They are all adults, they can take care of themselves.

Now it's time for you to take care of you! You need to choose yourself. Because I promise you until my last breath, I will continue to put you first because there is no other option for me. There is nothing else for me. So please. Scarlett. Please." Seth told me, running a shaking hand through his hair.

His eyes were wild with fear.

My heart skipped a beat at his words. I knew he loved me... But I didn't think anyone could love me this much... That would get this upset at the thought of losing me. I didn't think I was blessed with this kind of love...

Xena whimpered, and I was happy she didn't say anything. Because she knew how hard it was for me to be loved when I was younger. Not just be loved... But accept that I actually was. I felt my bottom lip tremble and it took everything in me not to bawl out right here. Right now.

"Don't ever speak those words to me. Don't tell me that you are going to die. Because I won't let it happen. I need you. I'm always going to need you. Even if you decide that you don't want to run two packs. I would pick you through thick and thin. No matter what... Because you deserve someone like that." Seth told me, getting on his knees in front of me.

I was trembling as tears streamed down my face.

I was scared of losing him. I was scared of hurting him. And here I am screwing everything up even when I tried my best not to. I just want to protect him. To keep him and everyone safe. I don't know how to do this. How to be a good mate and I just want him to know that I don't want to lose him. He quickly got up on the bed and pulled me to him.

"I feel responsible for everyone... It was always my job to do everything for everyone. And if I didn't... I was told I was being a burden. I don't want to be a burden. I just want to be able to handle everything so no one else has to feel the stress I do." I cried into his chest as I held onto him tightly.

He gently rubbed my back, laying us back down on the bed.

After we make it out of this. I need to make it up to him, for hurting him. For screwing everything up.

"Shh... You're okay baby... You're okay... I promise everything will be okay my love." Seth reassured me, wrapping his arms tightly around me.

I curled into his body, my eyes were slammed shut. I didn't want to see his hurt or his worry. I could smell it strong enough and feel it.

Seth continued to rub my back, hoping that I would fall asleep and stay asleep. "I promise you I will get you the world. And I won't stop until you have everything you could ever want." He told me, rolling over so we were spooning now.

I don't remember anything after I pressed my body to his.

Darkness swallowed me, and I fell into a deep sleep.

CHAPTER

FORTY-TWO

I knew when I opened my eyes that it was a dream world. Different memories swirled around me, dancing together. If I didn't know that most of these memories were dark and torturous. I would've thought it was beautiful.

"You will never survive this dark world! You are not strong enough!" My father's voice rang out through my mind.

I refused to flinch, knowing it was a memory. My father was long dead.

"I'm the reason you're here Scar..." Xena said, walking towards me. "I needed you to believe me when I told you this. We are stronger when Seth is around. We can handle more. We can love more. We can be more. The things our father said to us... They're not true."

I winced at her truth. Deep down I knew it all along. That my father only said those things to me because he wanted me to think I was weak.

"I'm sorry Xena... I'm sorry..." I told her. "I was..."

I couldn't finish my statement, it seemed useless now.

"Scared. I know. And that's okay... But you can't push him away anymore. We are one now. He's our strength and can help us through so much more than he already has." *Xena promised.* "Lean on him. Give him power. Make him know he's strong and powerful just like us. You will know what to do."

I shook my head slightly. What is she even talking about?

"Have you seen something that I haven't?" *I asked, stepping closer to the powerful wolf in front of me.*

"You know I can't answer that. We can't go against the Moon Goddess' wishes." *Xena stated simply.* "But trust in the future. Trust in the destiny. You know what needs to be done."

Is she even trying to be helpful right now? Because she's leaving me with more questions than answers.

"Trust in what we've built. Everything will make sense moron. I swear you always forget about us sharing a mind. I hear everything you think." *Xena snickered at me.*

I laughed as I shook my head.

"If you really could know everything that I was thinking, you would know that I wouldn't like your mysterious questions." *I teased back, even through the confusion.*

We were the best of friends.

I trusted her with my life. And yeah I guess that's to be expected, but not all wolves are at our level. They were jealous of our connection.

I flinched as the world below me started to rumble. I knew what that meant. Someone was at the field...

"You need to go now. Go! Save him! Go to the field where our destiny started. I will be with you." *Xena promised, but before I could say anything else.*

I flinched awake, my eyes shot open as I felt the bed was empty beside me. I breathed in, smelling the scents in my room. I hate that someone else was in here. I hate that someone took him from me when I was sleeping. It was a wolf I had never met before. Which makes everything so much worse.

"And our mother." *Xena growled, showing her anger.*

I got off of the bed quickly, following the scent of my mate out of the house and into the woods.

I knew I should've hunted her down when I took over the pack. That it was going to bite me in the butt later down the road. How could I have been so stupid?

Worry coursed through my veins as I ran faster. But something else was there... Confidence? It was Seth's confidence in me. He knew that I was coming. That I was going to save him.

"It's time to show him why no one messes with us." Xena growled, I felt our power swirl around us in the air.

This is where we get to really have fun.

I felt Pete... My mother. And I felt their fear. Or at least Allison's fear. She was weak, far weaker than I remember her being as a child. At least I know that part of this battle will be quick.

As I got closer to the field, I started to hear voices. They were having a conversation? This family fights weird.

"You brought her here... Thinking she won't kill her mother without a second thought. She's hated her mother all of her life." Seth laughed, my body vibrated with his power.

He's tied against the tree... "You underestimate her. You underestimate her hatred for not only you but her blood mother. You are going to die a slow painful death and I think it's going to be quite a sight to see."

Seth was stalling, waiting for me to be able to get there. I forced my legs to push faster. I wish I could've just shifted, but I had to wait for the perfect opportunity. "If I didn't want you to watch your mate die. I would kill you right now." Pete growled out.

I saw the clearing up ahead causing me to slow down, only slightly.

"Can you feel her coming?" Pete asked, causing Allison to shake her head no.

The stars in the sky darkened as a deep purple shadow took control of the sky.

"Now's our time to shine." Xena grinned, and I let her take partial control. We are the perfect team.

"Oh, Pete... Can't you feel my power yourself? My power suffocates your land. My blood is killing you slowly. I feel your power slipping, I feel your power crumbling as the world around you bends to my will. My world is crushing yours." My voice boomed through the field.

My purple eyes glowed in random spots throughout the shadows.

It's so fun to play with my prey.

"Come fight me whore!" Pete yelled, he was spinning around slowly, trying to find where I was.

I laughed condescendingly. Like something like that would hurt my feelings.

"Such a childish insult for a childish male. You're scared, I know you are. I feel it dosing the air around you. Maybe I could just... Take the air out of your lungs." I threatened, walking out of the woods.

My eyes were a bright powerful purple as I stood with my head held high.

"But that would mean that I would need to sink to your level. And it will be so much fun to rip your throat out on this land. Maybe in the same exact spot that I killed my father. Wouldn't that be ironic?" I taunted, knowing that if Pete got angry it would be easier to fight him.

All older men like him were easier to fight when they were angry. My eyes landed on Allison, my eyes darkening. What a pathetic excuse for a female. Let alone a mother.

"Oh, it will be so much fun to kill the both of you." My voice was dark and deeper than usual.

I was letting every ounce of my power seep through. I appeared in front of Allison, grabbing her by the throat and getting in her face.

As much as I would like to make her death long and painful. I just don't have time for it right now. My mate is more important.

"You brought this upon yourself. *Mother.*" I hissed out the word, my fangs showing. "Leaving your four children in the hands of a monster. Leaving me to turn into who I am today."

Allison stared at me, her eyes wide with fear.

"Oh I do love when they're scared." Xena grinned menacingly.

"I can explain please!" Allison begged, but it was no use.

My claws grew, sinking into the flesh of her neck. I'm ending this once and for all.

"No words can change what I went through and what I have done to protect YOUR children! I am more their mother than you could EVER be!" I shouted, shaking with restraint as I slowly pulled out my mother's throat.

Allison gasped, grabbing onto my wrist to try and stop me. Blood was spilling quickly from the gashes that I left.

Allison's eyes turned light purple as she locked them on me. "It's... It's twins..." She said, closing her eyes and accepting her fate.

I growled, pulling and ripping out my mothers throat. Allison's blood sprayed onto my face as I let my mother's dead body drop to the ground.

"This seems kind of... Repetitive. Not to mention a really lame comeback to try and distract us." Xena teased, causing me to fight back a snort.

I hissed as I felt the pain that Seth was in. The chains were burning him as he fought against them. I was conflicted on what I needed to do. Go for Pete? Or go to my mate? Pete chuckled, his eyes glowing orange as I stalked towards him.

"What should you do first? Save your pathetic excuse for a mate from getting in more pain? Or come for me? Who knows what I have planned Scarlett? I have nothing else to lose. You've taken my pack, you've cursed my land, and you've taken my children. I have nothing, so I might as well take you down with me!" Pete said, his arms out as he kept stepping away from me.

I smiled evilly, my features were purely animalistic.

Xena stayed on the surface, we were sharing the control. He was trying to taunt me, and it wasn't going to work.

"Ah... Trying to taunt me? I have spent my entire life getting beaten and abused. It made me master the art of control. As for you... Peter Marie. You lose control at the drop of a hat. You are mad that me. A woman, who is also far younger than you. Has more power and respect by just being me. Than you. Who has tried for decades to scare the world into submitting to you.

And then this cocky powerful fourteen-year-old little girl walked into the Alpha meeting like she owned the place. I had more heads bowing to me and more people listening to me than you. And that killed you, that is the day you decided that you would come for me. And that is the day you signed your death wish." I laughed, licking my lips.

Pete growled, shifting into his wolf form.

Pete was a smaller brown wolf with orange eyes, he ran for me who easily shifted and dodged his attack. I towered over him, my massive body was purely black, besides the deep purple at my feet. Black and purple smoke swirled around me, my power radiated through the air... The darkness kept us secluded. No one would find us here

My purple eyes stood out against my dark fur, and the diamond in the middle of my forehead was glowing in the darkness.

Seth was fighting against the tree, his muscles straining as he tried to break the chains. "Scarlett! No! Let me do this!" He yelled, his eyes shining brighter.

The tree that held him started glowing, colors mixing together as they swirled around the tree. I only spared it a glance before focusing back on Pete. I couldn't stray from my task at hand.

Pete circled me, analyzing my steps as he tried to find a weak spot. I took this as a sign, I made a quick move. I snapped my jaw, sinking my fangs into his side and tearing out a piece of his flesh. He howled in pain as he sliced his claws through my leg. I growled, pushing him over before limping back into a defensive position.

Oh this is going to be fun.

The tree suddenly burst into flames, deep purple and red flames lapped up the sides of the tree. Xena stared for a moment, before she snapped out of it. He stepped free, his body immediately shifting into his wolf form.

His body was massive, snorting red smoke out of his nose. His fur was very similar to mine, but besides the purple it was red. Seth howled loudly, his eyes darkened to a blood red. Pete immediately whimpered seeing Seth in his true form.

"Not so bad Alpha." Xena watched Seth, and I couldn't help but stare at his form either.

He's... He's *gorgeous.*

I thought he was gorgeous in his human form, but there's something about this form...

'*Son...*' Pete started, but quickly realized that he wasn't going to get anywhere with him.

He ran for me again, but I dodged the obvious attack again. He's super obvious with his attacks. I clawed his side, but before Pete could react in any other way. Seth charged him, ramming him away from me.

"You act like you have a right to call me your son. The torture for over a decade really canceled that out for you. I draw the line at ME. You crossed it when you came for my brother, and you set fire to it when you went for my mate." Seth growled, fire burned the ground around his paws.

Pete was struggling to get up, his ribs were broken from the force that Seth took to ram into him.

I whimpered, limping to go and stand beside him. Pete stood up, determined to be defiant and stand up to his son. I felt Pete's poison seeping slowly into my blood stream. This isn't going to be good.

"You won't make it without me!" Pete hollered, his body was shrinking as he shifted into his human form.

Seth's shift was much faster as he stood taller than his father.

"You are wrong. I have already made it without you... I am here not because of you. But because of my mate that you set out to destroy. You brought this on yourself, we could've ruled peacefully side by side. But you decided that you wanted to destroy my life." Seth growled, placing his palm on his father's chest, his hand glowing red.

Pete growled with the pain that shot through his body.

"This is for Max... For Alex... For my mother. This is for Scarlett. My future. My children. This is for me and everything that you have taken from me. This is my power coursing through your body. And today is the day that I take it back. Today is the day that I can finally move past this." Seth spat out, Pete's body was paling as he stared in shock at his son.

Once Seth felt all of the power drain out of his father, he allowed Pete to fall to his knees. Seth was shaking with the power that coursed through his body.

"This is kind of fun to watch." Xena told me before we sat down, my eyes glowing as they stuck on Pete.

My vision started to blur as I tried to keep myself up right. If I had to die today... At least he would be able to keep living.

Before Pete could say another word, Seth grabbed his head and twisted. Hearing a deafening crack made him grin as he dropped his father's dead body to the ground. I wavered slightly before I fell on my side. My large body shrunk, and my fur disappeared, showing my human skin.

And no matter how hard I fought...

No matter how much I wanted to stay alive...

The darkness surrounded me once again...

FORTY-THREE

I felt like I was floating. My entire body suspended in the air, until I opened my eyes and saw a bright light in front of me. It seemed so welcoming... So comforting...

Maybe that's where my peace is...

Maybe Seth was there.

"No!" Xena yelled at me. *"No we're not dying! We're not done yet!"*

"Please baby... Please open those pretty brown eyes for me my love... I need you to wake up." Seth's voice filtered through my mind.

Wake up? Aren't I awake already? Am I dying? I don't know what's happening.

"Don't go into the light moron. I'm not ready to die yet! I haven't even got to meet Reign and run with him!" Xena shouted at me, causing me to groan.

My head was pounding. What's happening?

"Baby... Wake up!" Seth ordered, his power rolling through his command.

I gasped, my eyes opening, shining a powerful purple. I coughed as I looked at him. Am I alive? Am I actually alive?

"Oh thank the Goddess!" Seth said, holding me tightly to him.

I shivered slightly, my body felt cold. I held him back weakly as he stood up with me in his arms. "We're heading to the hospital."

"N-no..." I said, shivering slightly as I cuddled into him.

Oh can he just lay on top of me. He's so warm. He disappeared, before appearing with me in his arms. My stomach turned, oh I wish he warned me. We were standing in an empty hospital room in Scotland.

"You are not giving me no for an answer. You heard your mother, why did you continue to fight? You could've untied me and then I could've done it." Seth told me, gently laying me down on the bed.

He reached behind the bed and pushed a button to send a notice to the desk that someone was in the room and waiting.

I thought she was joking... Trying to get me distracted.

"I thought she was trying to mess with me. I heard your concerns but I couldn't snap out of it. Xena was in control, and she wanted blood. Pete's blood. We need to go to Ireland and make sure that the land is starting to heal." I started, groaning as I tried to sit up.

I want some clothes. Seth growled, gently pushing me to lay back down.

"Oh... *Someone's angry... I LIKE IT!*" Xena grinned in the back of my mind.

"I will handle that. Ireland is not the top priority. Scotland is not the top priority. You are the top priority. I should've figured out that you could be pregnant... Alpha's are more fertile than omegas... And are even more fertile during heat. So I should've put it together, but you weren't acting differently. Nothing changed..." Seth said, staring intently at me.

His eyes haven't gone back to brown yet. Oh he's more than angry...

He doesn't like being here. I don't blame him honestly. He could've taken care of me at home. I leaned back against the pillow on the bed. Preferably something that doesn't smell like a different male.

"Can you at least give me a shirt?" I asked, shivering slightly from the cold air.

Seth frowned, digging into the cabinets to find something for me.

"I'm sure the doctor will be here soon... I thought that your clothes would be here..." Seth started to mumble, before grinning as he found shorts and hoodies.

He growled, not liking the scent of different males on it. I couldn't help but laugh, knowing exactly what he was upset about. Hopefully he'll scent it so that I won't smell like someone else.

"I'm sure they just come in here and wash them every once and a while. I haven't been to the hospital in a while... I typically care for my wounds at home. It has been that way for a long while. I didn't feel safe enough to come to the hospital. Everyone would talk about their Alpha who got hurt and back then my reputation was weak and I couldn't risk it." I told him as he walked back over to me.

His muscles were tense, his veins bulging with his stress.

I don't know how to calm him down... Is he mad that I'm pregnant? Or that I could be pregnant?

"I really wish I could bite you." Xena growled at me.

Seems like I'm getting everyone mad at me.

Seth absentmindedly started to rub the clothes against his skin, marking them with his powerful scent. "I understand my love... I hope it is different now." He said, helping me get dressed.

He was gentle with his touches, not wanting to cause me any pain. I was shaking slightly, trying to help him.

I felt weak... Weaker than I should be. I didn't use that much power. Maybe it was the poison in my veins? But feeling his love rush through my veins. My body warmed as it rushed through my body. But with his love... I felt his worry. Maybe it was too soon for us to have kids...?

"I'm here now... We have a bond... We may have kids on the way. You will be the first Alpha in the entire world to have three packs under her control." Seth assured me, gently laying me back down on the bed.

He quickly slid on a pair of gray sweatpants. "I would fight and kill anyone for you. Why are you not drawing on my power?"

Okay good, I won't have to tell him to cover himself. I don't want to have to fight someone else now.

I closed my eyes, my skin was slowly coming back to its normal color. His power was slowly working it's way through me, healing me, strengthing me. It was a nice feeling.

"I am okay... I'm just tired is all. Going home to our bed sounds really nice. But someone is insisting that I get checked out." I smirked slightly, peeking my eyes open to tease him.

He smirked, sitting beside my legs and gently massaging them to relax me.

I wanted to moan. Oh that felt so good... I could just fall asleep right here.

"You can tease me all you want. But until I make sure you're okay. We're not going home. Yes there is a possibility that your mother was lying. But I think there is a possibility of your mother being right. So yes, you're staying here. And if the doctor doesn't get here soon, I'm going to go out find him and drag him here myself." Seth told me, licking his lips slowly as he eyed my body.

My cheeks heated up as he looked at me, I bit my bottom lip.

Even when things are just starting to heat up. He's always thinking about sex.

"I don't blame him." Xena growled.

And honestly, me either.

"I'm sure he's just getting his daughter settled with Alex... Everything will be fine." I promised, reaching down to hold his hand. He intertwined our fingers, rubbing his thumb over my hand gently.

I'm glad that he was finally calming down.

There was a soft knock on the door, before the doctor peeked his head in. "Alphas?" The doctor called out, before walking in.

Doctor Hunter closed the door behind him, striding into the room.

"It took you long enough." Seth huffed out, causing me to giggle.

He's the cutest.

"Seth!!" I laughed, smiling as I tried to stop laughing.

Doctor Hunter chuckled, shaking his head slightly as he brought an ultrasound machine closer to the bed.

Let's see if Seth even lets him examine me.

"I do know that I took a hot minute to get here... I didn't know that I was supposed to come here. Didn't quite think that I was going to be the Alphas personal doctor." He smirked slightly, turning his focus to Seth.

Seth growled, baring his fangs at the doctor. His eyes dark red, as he didn't take them off of the doctor. The doctor shifted uncomfortably. It took everything in me not to laugh. I knew he wouldn't like the doctor.

"Can you lift her shirt up please?" The doctor asked, keeping his gaze down.

I smiled, squeezing Seth's hand gently.

"Baby... He's not going to do anything to me... He just wants to make sure I'm okay..." I spoke to him soothingly. "So let's just lift my shirt up and then after he checks to make sure I'm okay. We can go home and cuddle and watch a movie okay?" I told him, knowing he was stressed and anxious.

I felt his worry and pain like it was my own. And I wanted to do everything to take that away from him.

Seth nodded slowly, helping lift my hoodie up to expose my flat stomach to the doctor.

"He's just anxious... Everything is just a bit overwhelming for the both of us." I explained, keeping my eyes on Seth to keep him calm.

Seth growled softly, watching the doctor's slow movements. So far so good...

"I understand... So Alpha Knight... I'm going to apply this gel to your stomach. It's going to be cold. And then I'm going to use this doppler and place it on your stomach. Nothing is going to hurt. All the doppler does is show me what's going on inside of your stomach." The doctor informed, telling Seth his actions before he did them.

Seth tensed, watching the doctor apply the gel.

I wonder if he could feel the gel.

"If you hurt her, I'm gonna kill you." He snapped, his body tense.

I smiled at Seth, gently rubbing my leg against him to keep him calm.

He is the only man I could ever want.

"I'm okay baby..." I assured, peeking over at the Doctor. "I appreciate you coming here so late."

"*Even though he really had no choice.*" Xena deadpanned.

She does have a valid point.

The doctor smiled, bringing the doppler to my stomach before turning his focus to the screen. "I'm just going to move the doppler around a little bit to see what's going on..." He told us , gently moving the wand around.

Seth inhaled sharply at the movements, rubbing his stomach absentmindedly.

"I feel that like it's on my stomach." Seth told me, smiling as he was slowly calming down.

I knew it!

Doctor Hunter chuckled, smiling as he turned his focus to us instead of the screen. "Congratulations Scarlett. You're pregnant."

To Be Continued in...

Ruthless Kingdom

ACKNOWLEDGMENTS

Wow... Wow. Just wow. I don't know where to begin with this. Can I just start by saying thank you to the Bookstagram and booktok community for being the best? I've truly found my people and where I belong.

I had the honor of meeting so many people through the book community. Allie, Gabbie, Blake, Jay, Nikki, Blaire & Tyler, Rebecca, Meghan. And I could keep going on and on. But let's get into it.

First things first, I gotta thank God. Because my faith is something I value and hold close to my heart. And I truly believe that this talent of writing comes from him.

Oran, my brother, my first best friend, thank you for being one of my biggest supporters. Thank you for never giving up on me, and for always being there for me. And listening to me no matter what. I love and appreciate you more than you know. You will always be my favorite person big brother

Nikki, my best friend, the first person who actually started talking to me from booktok and quickly became someone I can't live without. Thank you for always supporting, always listening, always being one of my favorite people. Always believing in me and hyping me up, and constantly listening to me talk about how excited I was about writing.

Allie, thank you for being in my life. Thank you for loving me and supporting me and being my biggest fan. Thank you for sitting down and reading my book in two days and needing more lol. But most importantly, thank you for being one of the best people in my life. I don't know where I would be without you. I love you.

Blake, my brother, you have no idea how thankful I am for you. I'm so happy that we got to meet, and were able to become fast friends, and quickly became family. You mean the world to me. Thank you for supporting me and listening to my endless babble about my stories. Thank you for being one of my biggest supporters, and for never giving up on me.

Gabbie, my bestie, my sister, thank you. For being one of my biggest supporters, my sounding board, the person I could ask the dumbest questions to and have no judgment. But more importantly, thank you for being you. I couldn't have made it here without you. Thank you for being one of the best friends a girl could ask for.

Jay, you came into my life at the best of times. And you blew away my mind. I didn't know I needed you at that point, but I just need you to always know that I love you more than words express. And I can't imagine my life without you. Thank you for supporting me, for hyping me up, for always checking in on me. Thank you for everything.

Blaire & Tyler, I have so many words I want to say. Thank you for being my friends and family. Thank you for listening to all of my nonsense when my ideas were just ideas and not in book form. Thank you for being amazing, and supporting me from so far away. I am so lucky to have you guys in my life and I never want you to forget that. I love you both so much.

Rebecca, another one of my bestest friends. Thank you for always listening to me. And supporting my sugar induced chaos. Thank you for loving me and being amazing and helping me throughout so much.

Meghan, I'm so lucky to have you in my life. Even when life is crazy, you still take a minute to come and check in on me. And that means more to me than you ever know. Thank you for everything, for letting me annoy you with all of my ideas. For reading my books and giving me amazing feedback.

Thank you to my readers, and anyone who has ever supported me on this writing journey. Even if I didn't say it above, or didn't acknowledge you directly above. I love and appreciate you all so much. I wouldn't be able to be here without any of you.

STALK ME ON MY SOCIALS AND BE MY FRIEND!

Facebook: Lauren Moon
Instagram: @Heartofanalpha or @Authorlaurenmoon
Tiktok: @Heartofanalpha
My Reader Group on Facebook: The Moon Pack

Or find my linktree in my bio on Instagram and everything will be linked there!